CRUSADE IN JEANS

CRUSADE IN JEANS
Thea Beckman

FRONT STREET
Asheville, North Carolina

First Front Street paperback edition, 2003

Library of Congress Cataloging-in-Publication Data
Beckman, Thea
[Kruistocht in spijkerbroek. English]
Crusade in jeans / Thea Beckman.
p. cm.
Translation of Kruistocht in spijkerbroek;
originally published: Amsterdam: Lemniscaat, 1975.
Summary: A young boy who volunteers
to travel through time to the Middle Ages
arrives during the Children's Crusade
and is caught in its momentum.

ISBN 1886910-26-X (pb)

1. Children's Crusade, 1212–Juvenile fiction.
[1. Children's Crusade, 1212–Fiction.
2. Time travel–Fiction.] I. Title.

PZ7.B38179Cr 2003   2002192870

Contents

LEAP IN TIME

"And this," said Dr. Simiak, "is the material-transmitter." Rudolf Hefting could not fail to be impressed by the enormous machine which covered one whole wall of the laboratory. He saw a high panel covered with dials, buttons, and levers. On each one, Dolf noticed strange figures and symbols. This extraordinary machine that made contact with the past made Dolf feel very small and insignificant. His father, Dr. Hefting, was a friend of the two men who had invented it and after months and months of persistent nagging, Dolf had finally been allowed, now that the Christmas holiday was here, to visit the laboratory. He had never expected the material-transmitter to be so huge.

"What is that?" he said, pointing at the central section. It resembled a telephone booth, but had thickly insulated walls and a transparent door. The door was not made of glass, however, but of a synthetic material that Dr. Simiak claimed was indestructible.

"That is where we put the animal cages or any other object we wish to transport," explained Dr. Frederics, who was Dr. Simiak's assistant.

"And do they come back in that, as well?"

"If everything goes according to plan."

"What do you mean?"

"Let me explain, Dolf," said Dr. Simiak. "If, for example, we send an animal in a cage back into the past, we have to wait three hours before we can retrieve it, because the transmitter expends so much energy that it overheats and we have to wait for it to cool. During that time the cage must remain on exactly the same spot at which it is placed in the past. This is essential because the machine's coordinates have been set for that precise point. If someone should remove the cage or if it lands on an unstable piece of ground and falls over, then, when we try to get it back, all we will get is a heap of sand and earth. In other words, the animal will be lost."

"Why do you experiment only with animals, when they can't tell you what they have seen in the past?" Dolf asked.

"Because before we can consider sending people back to the past, we must be sure that there is absolutely no risk to them. If a person were to land in a marsh or a lake, for instance, he would not be able to contact us and would be lost."

"Weight is a factor, too," interrupted Dr. Frederics. "When we have used a heavy animal for the experiment, such as a chimpanzee or an ape, the energy expended melted all the fuses. It takes months to make repairs."

"That's incredible. Is the machine in working order now?"

"Yes, and we have planned an experiment for the new year in which we will be able transport apes. These apes have been trained to collect objects that are in reaching distance of the cage."

Dolf nodded and looked at the booth, trying to imagine what it would feel like to be inside, waiting to be transported to the distant past.

Suddenly he said, almost involuntarily:

"I would go."

The two scientists were dumbfounded. In front of them stood a boy who was quite tall for one not yet fifteen years old, a schoolboy with a passion for history, but who was still hardly more than a child. And he was saying … But, of course, he wasn't serious. Obviously he was thinking of some sort of science-fiction adventure.

"I weigh less than an ape," said Dolf.

"Of course you do but ..."

"I have eyes and a mouth," Dolf interrupted. "And when I returned I would tell you what I have seen," Dolf went on quietly, though he felt anything but calm. His heart was pounding furiously.

"No, no, it's utter nonsense," murmured Dr. Frederics.

"Much too dangerous," Dr. Simiak said, but his voice sounded thick and uncertain. The more the scientists insisted that it was impossible, the more Dolf was determined to go.

"I would be the ideal guinea pig. I am the right weight and I have a perfectly good pair of eyes," he said. "I could always take a weapon with me. Of course, I understand that it is dangerous, but I am quite capable of getting out of tight spots, and anyway it would be for only a few hours, just enough to ... At home, you know, I have a book in which a tournament is described. It was organized by the Duke of Dampierre on June 14, 1212, at Montgivray in central France. Why don't you send me there? That would be great. What can those apes tell you? I suppose you can examine them and extract particles of dust from their fur but what use is that? I can provide you with undeniable scientific evidence."

He noticed the two men hesitating.

"... and I'm not scared," he added quickly.

"My dear boy, you don't seem to realize," said Dr. Simiak gravely, "that even if we gave you permission, which of course we would not, we could make only one attempt to bring you back. If that failed and you were not in the right place at the right time, you would be left to wander in the Middle Ages for the rest of your life."

"But I would be in the right place at the right time." Dolf said firmly.

"You are treating it all far too lightly," said Dr. Frederics, but there was an excited gleam in his eyes.

"Surely the computer could accurately fix a point of arrival," said Dolf. "I could take something with which to mark the spot, so that I would have no trouble in finding it again a few hours later. I can also take a knife, in case I have to defend myself and ..."

"Now stop this, my boy," interrupted Dr. Simiak with a trembling voice. "The whole thing is much too risky. Too many things could go wrong and we cannot take that responsibility."

"Well, someone's got to be the first and why not me?" Dolf answered. He did not want to think or hesitate further. He wanted to go as quickly as possible.

The two physicists continued to explain why it was out of the question, but he was not even listening. He was gazing at the "telephone booth," the gateway to the past. Outside the laboratory winter reigned cold and gray, but inside it was warm. Dolf stood there, holding his jacket. On an impulse he put it on.

"Let me go!" he said. "Please!"

Dolf glanced at the chronometer suspended above the material-transmitter. It was a quarter to one. He looked at his new watch, a Christmas present, and synchronized it with the chronometer.

"We must agree on the exact time at which I am to be at the place from which you will transport me back," he said.

Then the incredible happened. Whether they surrendered to his persistent arguing or to the temptation that their invention could now be put to a real test, Dolf did not know, but both men began to nod simultaneously.

Dr. Frederics hurried to the computer and began feeding it information.

"Now what was it? June 14, 1212? Montgivray in France? Let me get a map to find out exactly where that is." He continued to mumble while working with the computer.

Dr. Simiak, too, had gone into action. He went away and came back a moment later with two broad-tipped felt pens, one black and one bright yellow. He also gave Dolf a long, sharp breadknife, which the boy tucked under his belt, and some matches he put in his pocket.

"To allow for the least possible risk," Dr. Simiak said, "let's set your time of return at four complete hours from now." He noted the time; it was five to one.

"It will take a few minutes to adjust the transmitter, so we will transport you at one o'clock precisely. Don't forget that, at five o'clock to the very second, we will bring you back. Have you got that?"

"I will be there," said Dolf, already walking toward the booth.

Dr. Frederics reappeared, holding the results of the computer's calculations. As Dolf opened the door of the booth Dr. Frederics suddenly grabbed his arm.

"Just a minute," he cried to Dolf, "are you sure you want to go through with this? Remember that we can make only one attempt to bring you back."

"I am sure," said Dolf, and he stepped into the booth.

"For your own protection, show yourself to as few people as possible, because you are wearing the wrong clothes."

Dolf nodded, hardly paying attention.

With the door still open Dr. Simiak said hoarsely:

"All right then. Place your feet exactly in the middle of that metal square. That's right. On no account touch the walls. Just close your eyes and keep still. Don't get impatient. It'll take us a good three minutes to build up sufficient energy to … don't touch anything, my boy, I …"

Dolf shut his eyes and heard the door being closed. After that he heard no sounds.

He stood stock still, like a statue. Count, he thought. I must count up to sixty slowly, three times.

Deliberately, he began to count, just to stop himself from thinking. Not for a second must he change his mind. He must not get scared. He must not panic.

"Thirty-one, thirty-two ..."

Was he on the second or the third minute? What were they up to all this time? "Forty-five, forty-six ..."

With his eyes shut, he tried to make numbers out of the whirling spots he could see before his eyes. "Fifty-eight, fifty-nine ..." And suddenly the world seemed to come to an end. Dolf reeled from the impact of a heavy force, which sent pain stabbing through his whole body. He felt as if he were in a mist of ever changing shades of blue, through which he gradually became aware of familiar sounds: the wind in the trees, the singing of birds. Still, he dared not move or open his eyes. He could feel the warmth of sunshine on his hand and the whirling mist cleared from inside his head. He opened his eyes ...

He was there. But where?

Stranded

Dolf Hefting was standing by a deeply rutted road. On either side were steep banks covered with trees, ferns and wildflowers. To his left the road ran down to a bend; to his right, it climbed up and disappeared around another bend. Looking down at his feet he discovered he was standing on a flat stone. This gave him the courage to think, even though he hardly dared to move.

At the very least he knew he had been transported to a different place. Whether to a different age also, he had yet to discover. His watch read two minutes past one—it was still working. He looked down at the stone. Of all the possibilities, the very best had occurred. He had a clear reference point which he could easily mark. From his coat pocket he took the felt pens and around his feet he carefully drew two circles, one yellow, one black. Relieved, he put away the pens and stepped down from the stone.

"Now I must note which way I go," he thought sensibly, "or I won't be able to find this stone again in time. That tall birch tree over there will be a good landmark."

It was very hot and he was stifling inside his coat. But he dared not take it off, even though underneath he was wearing a sweater. In addition, he had on jeans, wool socks and heavy winter shoes. All in all, it was quite the wrong clothing for June weather. The sun beat down on his head. The dusty, unpaved road shimmered in the bright light.

It seems to be a hilly region, he thought. Let's see where this road leads.

He walked a little way down the road, his feet kicking up the dust, and rounding the bend he gazed out over a valley. In the distance was a town.

"That must be Montgivray," he said out loud. "It's worked! It's worked perfectly." Although the town was half-hidden in the haze, he could see that it was not modern. He could vaguely distinguish turrets and ramparts. Far below him, a covered wagon trundled along the road toward the gates, and he could see people working in the fields in the valley.

I'm back in the Middle Ages. This is thirteenth century France, he told himself, though even now he could scarcely believe it. He was about to continue his descent when he heard, far behind him, the sound of hoofbeats, cries, and a general commotion. Startled, he looked back, but the road was hidden from view.

There were more cries and the clashing of weapon on weapon. Dolf thought that perhaps they were two knights, old enemies, meeting on their way to the tournament and starting a fight.

I must see that, he said to himself, but I must also be sure that they don't see me.

He ran back, ready to dive into the bushes at any moment. A little way past the stone he had marked, he rounded the bend and, in the cloud of dust before him, was a sight so surprising that he forgot to hide.

There was a fight indeed! Two men on horseback had attacked a third man, on foot, who was wielding a great cudgel and shouting. A mule was standing in the bushes, braying. The two mounted ruffians were wearing brown cloaks, leather jerkins and leather helmets. They were definitely not knights. Their clumsy, ill-kept horses wore no armor and their swords were blunt and rusty. As Dolf arrived, the man on foot landed a blow of such strength on the arm of one of his assailants, that the sword flew from his grip, but it was still an unequal fight. Dolf could see the man would soon be overpowered.

"Robbers," he muttered.

Furiously, Dolf wrenched out his breadknife and leaped forward. Right before him was a leg, spurring on the horse. He stabbed, and a shriek from above made clear that his thrust had reached its mark.

At that moment, there was a scream as the other robber was dragged from his horse by the man on foot. Dolf's opponent, his leg bleeding profusely, turned his horse and rode it straight at him. Dolf jumped aside, receiving a blow on his shoulder. The robber did not rein in for another attack, but galloped away. In an instant he was out of sight, leaving his companion groaning in the road. There was a thud, then another. The groans ceased. The fight was over.

Gasping for breath, Dolf collapsed onto the dry grass by the side of the road, his left shoulder burning with pain. He stared at the bloodstained knife in his hand. He was bleeding heavily, I've wounded a human being, he suddenly realized.

The man he had aided was standing in front of him. He, too, was panting and wiping the sweat from his face. He spoke, but Dolf was too shaken to pay attention. He could have wept with the shame of his deed.

The man recovered his breath and went to get his mule. He tied the animal to a tree and walked over to the motionless robber, still lying in the road. Angrily he kicked the body.

Dolf stiffened. The robber was dead; killed by the man's mighty cudgel. He shivered.

The man beckoned toward him. Dolf rose stiffly, clutching his left arm.

The man grabbed the dead robber under the shoulders and indicated to Dolf to take his legs. Together they dragged him off the road. Then they looked at each other and the man grinned. Dolf realized that there was no need to be afraid. He had saved the man's life! The man spoke and Dolf thought he heard a word that sounded like "Thanks."

The man untied the mule and gestured to Dolf to follow. The boy was only too pleased to accompany him. It seemed to him that one risked one's life to be found on the road alone.

Instead of heading for the town, a little way down the road, they turned up a track leading toward an open, grass-covered space on the hillside. From there they had a broad view over the valley and the distant town. All around them the birds were singing cheerfully, while high above hawks circled in the blue. The air was warm and scented. Dolf felt as if he were on a summer vacation. From his pack the man took out bread and cold meat and offered some to Dolf.

The bread tasted exceptionally good and Dolf was surprised by his first taste of the meat. He didn't know whether it was lamb or pork, but it tasted ... it tasted ... wild! He could think of no other word for it. In any case he was famished. His companion concentrated on his own food. With strong, white teeth he bit into the bread and tore chunks from the meat. Next, he took a deep drink from his leather flask, then handed it to Dolf. To the boy the liquid seemed a little sour, but sparkling, and at once it quenched his thirst.

His shoulder still hurt, but less than before. He was now feeling so comfortable that he at last had the courage to take off his coat. The man stared at his sweater and jeans in amazement. When Dolf looked back at his friend he realized that he was a young person. He had long dark hair, beautiful brown eyes and his skin was tanned. He was dressed in a green cloak with a leather belt around his waist, from which hung a sheath containing a short dagger. In addition, he wore brown boots and beside him lay a green hat—a kind of skullcap.

They had finished their meal and the young man now

looked Dolf straight in the eye and pointed at his own chest.

"Leonardo," he introduced himself. "Leonardo Fibonacci
—da Pisa."

"Pisa?" Dolf stammered in surprise. He thought that he
must have misunderstood, but the man nodded. Dolf sensed
that he should now introduce himself. It seemed that one's
birthplace should also be included. Pointing at himself, he
said:

"Rudolf Hefting—from Amsterdam." At that moment
he realized that he was probably going to have language
problems. He knew no French, let alone medieval French,
and he was not exactly fluent in Latin either.

Leonardo began speaking very quickly. Dolf's ears
buzzed, but he soon realized that this was no medieval
French—nor Italian. It sounded a little like Dutch or
German, but it was still quite unfamiliar.

"Slowly," he exclaimed. "If you speak so fast I can't
follow."

The man understood and began his story all over again,
very slowly and emphatically and supported by many
gestures. Dolf listened attentively. Here and there he recognized words; it was old German. Something like old Dutch,
he thought, and it's not so difficult to follow if he speaks
slowly.

Indeed he managed to understand some of what
Leonardo was saying. He learned that the young man had
been a student in Paris for two years and was now on his
way to finish his studies at Bologna. He had been travelling
for many weeks and until now he had met with few difficulties. Then, less than an hour ago, he had been suddenly
waylaid by two robbers, who had expected such a lonely
traveller to be an easy victim. But they had not reckoned
with Leonardo's fearsome cudgel, his swift movements or
the timely help from the stranger.

There were many more words but that was as much as

Dolf could gather. Naturally the student now expected him to tell something of himself. Trying to copy Leonardo's pronunciation, Dolf explained that he was on his way to the grand tournament being organized by Count Jean de Dampierre at Montgivray. Dolf pointed at the town in the distance.

"Dampierre? Montgivray?" Leonardo asked with surprise. Dolf nodded and again he pointed toward the town which was shimmering in the heat.

"There, Montgivray."

Leonardo shook his head, seemingly in disagreement. "That's not Montgivray. That's Spiers," he said.

"Spiers?" Dolf said, pointing to the north in consternation. "Then ... where ... Montgivray?"

Again Leonardo shook his head with certainty. He, too, pointed north: "Worms is in that direction."

Dolf gaped. That was impossible. Worms was a town in Germany, on the Rhine. And Spiers, over there, was that also ...? Shocked, he gazed at the town, shielding his eyes from the sun. The town was still partially obscured by the haze and its features were difficult to discern, but gradually Dolf thought he could see a church spire towering above all else. After a while he seemed to recognize its shape. Three years ago, on his way to Switzerland with his parents, they had passed through Speyer. He remembered a busy industrial town, a beautiful bridge spanning the Rhine, broad avenues and, most of all, the impressive cathedral, part of which dated back to the twelfth century. Was that the same church? And were Speyer and Spiers the same place? But if so, he was not in France, he was in Germany. No, that could not be.

Beyond the town he noticed a wide river, a silver ribbon glistening in the sun. He pointed at it.

"Is that the Rhine?"

Leonardo nodded.

Oh no, Dolf thought, it is the wrong place after all. He jerked round and faced the student.

"What year is this?"

"1212."

Well, at least that much was right.

"What's the date?"

Leonardo looked perplexed.

"What day of the month is it?"

"Ah," said Leonardo, suddenly understanding, "St. John." This meant nothing to Dolf, but he dared not pursue the point. Leonardo's curiosity might turn into suspicion.

This is getting a bit difficult, Dolf thought worriedly. He had not expected to have to speak to someone in this era. He heaved a sigh and tried to recall some of the things that he knew about the Middle Ages. He knew that everybody was a Roman Catholic and the German emperors struggled for power with the Pope. Awe-inspiring cathedrals were built, like the one below in Spiers. Roads were unsafe, connections difficult. Though the roads and seas were hazardous, there were many travellers. There were crusades, tournaments and local feuds between rival princes. Science was hardly born and people were very superstitious. They carried magical charms to protect them from evil, crossed themselves at the least sign of trouble and when times were bad blamed the Devil.

"Where do you come from?" Leonardo asked.

Rudolf had said when he had introduced himself but he repeated, "From Amsterdam."

Leonardo shrugged his shoulders.

"It's in Holland," Dolf added.

"Oh ... you're from Holland, are you?"

"Yes."

"Then how come you hardly understand me? After all, you speak German there too, don't you? Or do you speak only a dialect?"

Speaking slowly, he said to Leonardo:

"My friend, please trust me. I'm an ordinary boy, a student like you—and I'm lost."

"Ah, so you know Latin?"

"Not very well."

"Then what do you know? Mathematics?"

"Yes," said Dolf eagerly. He was not very fond of arithmetic, but he suspected that in this, at least, he would be able to hold his own against this student from the Middle Ages.

He glanced at his watch. An hour and a half had already passed. Since he had come to the wrong place, he couldn't very well attend the tournament, but it would be worthwhile to take a closer look at the town in the valley.

However, Leonardo was pulling him toward a sandy he patch had found. With a dead twig he drew a triangle, a parallelogram. Dolf laughed, took the twig and drew a truncated cone, a square and a pyramid. Then they warmly shook hands. Two young students had met each other.

For the first time in his life, Dolf regretted that he did not know more than a few rudiments of mathematics. For fun he wrote down Pythagoras's theorem $a^2+b^2=c^2$. For a moment Leonardo seemed puzzled. Questioningly, he pointed at the symbols. Of course, he must use Roman numerals, Dolf thought in alarm. Quickly he erased the signs and wrote down the Roman numerals from I to X. Underneath, he put the Arabic numerals 1, 2, 3, up to 10. Leonardo at once became enthusiastic.

"Those are Eastern figures," he exclaimed.

Dolf nodded. "Yes, we always use those. It is easier than using Roman figures."

Had Leonardo understood? At least he knew what Dolf was talking about.

"I have heard of them, but do not understand them. Please show me."

They moved over to a larger expanse of sand, and Dolf began. For some time he taught primary school mathematics to this travelling student from the Middle Ages. Dolf repeatedly found difficulty with the unfamiliar language, but Leonardo had a quick mind. The use of the zero, in particular, made him very excited.

Time was slipping away.

"Where did you learn that?" the Italian asked.

"At school in Holland."

"But that's impossible," scoffed Leonardo. "The only people living in Holland are barbarians, stupid knights and even more stupid priests who barely know any Latin. There isn't even a university."

Dolf was feeling troubled again. Stealthily, he glanced at his watch. Heavens! Half-past four! He had completely forgotten the time. There was no possibility now of his visiting that medieval town. He had wasted his four hours time-travel in chatting, doing sums and even fighting. He had nothing to show Dr. Simiak from the Middle Ages. It would not be of much value to tell him about the fascinating Leonardo.

He got up, dusted the sand from his trousers and picked up his coat.

"I must be going," he said reluctantly.

Leonardo had also stood up. "Why? Where do you have to go? Couldn't we stay together?" he suggested. Dolf shook his head sadly. He thrust his hands into his pockets, and his fingers closed round the felt pens. He no longer had any need for them, and Leonardo would be pleased to receive them—or so he hoped.

"Here," he said, offering the student the two pens, "these are for writing. Please accept them as a parting gift and a sign of friendship."

Had the young man understood? He looked in wonder at Dolf and then at the two sticks in his hand, which he fingered gingerly. Dolf searched around, picked up a stone, and made a stroke on it with the black felt pen.

Leonardo was beaming and nodding excitedly. Then, from around his neck he took a thin chain from which hung a pendant; it was an enameled image of the Virgin Mary. He placed it in Dolf's hand, at the same time accepting the felt pens.

Dolf was so delighted with this exchange of gifts (just imagine, a thirteenth century pendant! Dr. Simiak would indeed be pleased!) that he raised the pendant to his lips. Leonardo regarded him with a look of satisfaction. Then they happily shook hands in farewell.

Dolf hung the cord around his neck, put on his coat, gave a brief wave and raced up the hill. If he had remembered correctly, the dusty road should be right behind it. It was a quarter to five. He had plenty of time to reach the marked stone and wait to be flashed back to the twentieth century.

The sight which greeted him when he reached the top of the hill made him stiffen with fear.

Only now did he really think about the noise that had been in the background for some time. It was the sweet sound of children's voices singing to the rhythm of many trampling feet.

Stunned, he gazed down on countless small heads. A procession of marching, singing children was filing past— hundreds of children; no, thousands. Their number was immeasurable.

They filled the road from bank to bank. The column stretched away to his right as far as the bend. Could it be a procession for St. John's day? He must get back to the stone immediately! It had been clearly visible on the empty road, but now it was lost somewhere behind the surging throng and the clouds of dust.

And they were no sluggards, these children. They marched on and on, down the hill, toward Spiers. Could that town be large enough to house so many?

There were many questions, but no time for answers. Dolf knew he must find that stone, and quickly. Nervously, he went a little farther down the hill. Away to his right he spied the young birch tree he had noted as a landmark. The stone was directly opposite it. He moved off in its direction. Suddenly he was feeling frantic and his heart was thumping. If only the children would step aside for a moment. If only they would make way …

But the road was too crowded. The children tried to step back for the tall boy trying to elbow his way against them, but they were pressed forward by those coming behind.

Small hands clasped hold of his arms and back. Thin bodies bumped against him. A shriek of pain told him he had trodden on a bare foot.

The stone! Where was the stone? He looked around desperately and spied Leonardo standing on the hilltop. He, too, was gazing down on the stream of children in amazement. The student beckoned to him, but Dolf didn't respond. He was intent only on his struggle to reach the stone. He was almost there.

Someone pushed him. Several girls clung to his arms to prevent themselves from falling. Suddenly, a boy, in gray rags, appeared above the heads of the crowd, gesticulating wildly. He was shouting but Dolf could not hear over the din what he was saying. In horror, Dolf realized that the boy must be standing on the marked stone! The children nearby were pointing and laughing at the gray-clad fellow. Some shouted a few words of encouragement. Dolf, buffeted to and fro, had to brace himself to avoid being swept away.

"Let me through!" he shouted above the ocean of heads. "Hey you, get off! I've got to stand there."

The boy on the stone was capering and making funny faces. The flowing tide of children was applauding him and some, bracing themselves, had stopped, forming a barrier between the boy and Dolf. In sheer panic, Dolf hit out in all directions and a number of children moved back, yelling. Reaching the stone, Dolf looked up and found it empty. Where the circles had been there was now just a hint of an indentation. With a leap Dolf was on the stone. He stood rigidly still, his heart almost bursting from his breast and his throat tight with fear. Fearfully, he began counting, "One, two, three ..." He closed his eyes, trying not to think about what had happened to the boy who had been on the stone a moment before.

"... twenty-three, twenty-four (he must have jumped off), twenty-eight, twenty-nine (the children were shouting because I was pushing, not because ...), thirty-five, thirty-six (in a minute there will be a bang and I'll be standing in Dr. Simiak's laboratory again), forty-eight, forty-nine (I'm sure he jumped. I'm not too late)."

He dared not look at his watch. He dared not move. Least of all he dared not admit what his eyes had seen—in the middle of his dance, the boy from the thirteenth century had disappeared.

But, no matter how hard Dolf tried to convince himself otherwise, he knew in his heart that the boy had been transported. For him, Dolf Hefting, it was too late.

At that moment, Dr. Frederic's warning voice came back to him: "And if it fails—I mean, if you are not there in time—you will be left to wander in the Middle Ages for the rest of your life."

Summoning up his courage, Dolf took a deep breath, opened his eyes and looked at his watch: six minutes past five. Still he stood on the stone, hoping against hope. The minutes ticked slowly away and nothing happened. "I'm stranded," he said to himself. "I have missed my chance, my only chance!" Gradually the shock of fear and disappointment subsided somewhat and he tried to think. He looked at the slight indentation on which he was standing. He realized how that had happened. Dr. Simiak, not daring to risk anything, must have charged the material-transmitter to its extreme limit. The machine would be out of action for several months ...

Utterly exhausted and in complete despair, Dolf collapsed on the stone and with unseeing eyes stared at the children still filing past. They were moving more slowly now and with large gaps in their ranks. These stragglers, mainly girls or very small children with thin, dirty faces and dressed in rags were exhausted also; unable to sing, joke, or laugh they shuffled past. As Dolf watched still more came, dragging themselves along without even the energy to speak. In front of him a boy stumbled and fell. He could have been no more than six years old. Another child, only a little taller, helped him to his feet and dragged him along. Just then, an older boy came striding along vigorously. He was sumptuously dressed and wore soft leather boots. A dagger hung from his silver-studded belt. He looked really fine. On either side he pulled a small, exhausted child, all the while talking encouragingly to them.

Where did all these children come from? Where were they going? What could this seemingly endless procession mean? A little girl fell to the ground in front of him. She lay there motionless; there were no helping hands this time. Trudge, trudge, trudge, more bare feet dragged past her. Dolf could bear it no longer. He jumped up, ran forward and stooped over the girl. Lifting her to her feet, he looked at her face with horror. Her tiny, tight-shut eyes were sunk deep in the sockets. Her cheeks were hollow. She weighed nothing at all and looked barely alive.

Dolf looked helplessly at the unconscious child in his arms. Then he saw Leonardo walking toward him, followed by his faithful mule.

"She is dying," Dolf called to him anxiously.

Leonardo took the paper-thin wrist, but let it fall again. "She is dead," he said sadly.

Slowly, Dolf let the child's body slip from his arms. The tears streamed down his cheeks.

"Why? What is happening here? Where are they all going to, these children?"

Leonardo made no reply. He dragged the dead child to one side and put her under the bushes. He folded the hands on the chest, made the sign of the cross over the tiny body, muttered a prayer and began to cover the body with stones. Dolf knelt down beside him to help. Behind him he could still hear the tramp of yet more children ... Would the procession never end?

Leonardo stood up. "It is getting late. We had better go to the town, though I fear that, tonight, they will be keeping their gates locked."

Dolf was becoming accustomed to the language and beginning to understand rather well. But his questions had not been answered.

"Who are they ... these children?" he persisted. He shook his head sadly.

"I have heard about them. It is the crusade of the children."

"What?"

"They are on their way to the Holy Land, to liberate Jerusalem from the Saracens."

Dolf's mouth fell open. "Those ... those toddlers?"

Leonardo nodded.

"They are going to fight the Turks?" Dolf asked in amazement.

Leonardo stared forlornly at the pile of stones.

"But how on earth are they going to do that?" For the moment Dolf had completely forgotten his own misery and despair. "Some of them were no more than six or seven ... What kind of crusade is that? Surely, they can't be ..."

Whether Leonardo had understood or not, Dolf did not know, but eventually he got something of an answer.

"It is a children's crusade. There was once something like it in France, but there were not so many then."

"I don't understand," Dolf stammered.

"Neither do I. When I first heard I also refused to believe it, but now I have seen it with my own eyes.

"No," cried Dolf. "It can't be true; it is a nightmare. Soon I will wake up. A children's crusade! It is just too ridiculous. It's unthinkable. Crusades are for men; for knights on horseback, in coats of armor. Not for children!"

Leonardo was silent. He grasped the mule by its reins and started walking. Dolf, suddenly terrified at the thought of being all on his own in this incomprehensible world, followed. They overtook a small boy, struggling along on bare and bloodied feet. Leonardo said nothing, but gently raising the boy, he sat him on the mule. A moment later, he rescued a sobbing girl from the roadside and placed her behind the boy. Dolf did not speak but his heart felt warm and full, as if the hot tears which he was restraining were collecting in his chest. Dolf glanced at the grim, set face of his companion, but quickly looked away. On the far side of the road he thought he had caught a glimpse of yet another dead child, staring up with broken eyes. He hardly dared open his eyes again.

Silently they wound their way down to Spiers, where the bells were tolling, and found the gates closed.

The Thunderstorm

The clanging of bells sent the people of Spiers scurrying into the streets. They ran to the ramparts, anxiously inquiring what danger approached. The answer was not long in coming. Those who had vantage points on the wails gazed out at the children streaming down the road toward the town … There was the danger.

"It's the children! The children bound for Jerusalem!" they cried to the others. "Thousands of them! Looters and thieves all of them."

Some of the womenfolk insisted that the gates be opened and the children allowed into the town. But the aldermen refused, saying that few towns in Germany had let the children in. There were too many of them. Most of the little ones would be starving, and if they came into the streets they would grab everything within their reach. After all, they are convinced that God will forgive them their sins because they are going to free Jerusalem. It would be better, the aldermen pointed out, for the townspeople to keep their own children indoors. It was a well-known fact that Nicolas's army of children had a great appeal to all the young. Even the children of knights and noblemen had escaped from their castles to join the children's crusade. Nevertheless, said the aldermen, the vast majority were nothing but vagabonds and orphans who had the gall to rob honest citizens. Had not young Nicolas, their leader, been a serf himself? He was nothing but a stupid, illiterate shepherd, who claimed to have seen visions and have heard the voices of angels.

"Oh yes," said one alderman mockingly. "Visions of wealth and the call of gold, that is all he's ever seen."

"That's blasphemy," a man's voice called out from the crowd. "Nicolas is a holy boy and the chosen one of God."

Obviously, opinion in the town was sharply divided, but since the majority were concerned for their own possessions, they insisted that the gates remained locked—and they did.

A few of the more compassionate townsfolk climbed onto the ramparts and watched the children marching past. They passed down loaves of bread to the begging children, who, with terrifying shrieks, threw themselves toward the food, clawing, fighting and clambering over each other. In the frantic struggle much of the bread was trodden into the dirt. The smallest and weakest got none.

Some while later, the citizens of Spiers saw the children set up an enormous camp on the riverbank, not far from the town. There the exhausted children could quench their thirst and catch some fish. Hundreds of them scrambled down into the river.

In the town square, in front of the cathedral, an outraged priest was giving an impassioned sermon.

"Woe to us, citizens of Spiers. God will punish us for this heartlessness," he cried. "Those children out there are the bearers of His will and we have cruelly locked them out. It is our deeds that force them to steal and plunder. If they drag from the sties pigs which do not belong to them, it is we who are responsible. We, the merciless citizens of Spiers, have burdened these children with the most terrible of sins, therefore, we have insulted God!

"It is written that we shall feed the hungry, refresh the thirsty and clothe the naked. But what have we done? We have locked the gates and ignored God's holy command. Woe to you all, you impious people! God will be avenged ..."

Still, the fear that so many greedy and grasping hands

might exhaust their provisions, overcame the townspeople's sense of pity and the gates remained shut fast. Curfew was sounded, the house fires extinguished and the people of Spiers took themselves to bed.

It was around seven o'clock when Leonardo and Dolf reached the town and were unable to enter.

"It seems that they are refusing entry to everyone; even peaceful travellers who are in no way concerned with this absurd children's army," said the student dejectedly.

"With these two on the mule, no one is going to believe that we have nothing to do with the crusade," Dolf laughed, indicating the two toddlers who were sleepily nodding. "We might as well find somewhere to camp for the night."

Leonardo stared at his new-found friend in amazement.

"You just want to sleep somewhere along the roadside?" he asked in disbelief.

"Why not? It is a warm night."

Leonardo shook his head emphatically. "Friend, our throats would be slit before we could close our eyes. I think you must be getting confused again, Rudolf. I can not imagine how you have come so far from Holland and have remained alive. You are so careless."

"What do you suggest then?" Dolf asked helplessly.

Leonardo pointed to the riverbank. "We will deliver these two little ones over there and spend the night in the camp. Right in the middle we should be relatively safe."

"I don't want to sleep among the children," Dolf said anxiously. "I can't bear to see their misery."

Seemingly, Leonardo had not understood properly.

"Their large number provides us with a protection that we would not have if we were camping alone," he said.

Reluctantly, he agreed. Under a steel-gray sky they set off toward the children's camp. Dolf was thirsty but when they reached the river and he saw all the children walking along the bank, cooling their feet in the water, washing in it and drinking, he was horrified.

"They're drinking the river water!" he exclaimed.

"Of course they are," replied the student tersely. He, too, strolled toward the water, leading his mule. At once the animal lowered its head and lapped thirstily. The student knelt down, filled his flask, soused his face and drank at length.

Dolf decided he could use a bath, too, and took off his clothes until he was wearing only his underpants. Placing his clothes under a bush, he walked to the water's edge. Around him the naked children were playing, laughing and splashing each other. Their thin, white bodies glistened under the darkening sky. Then Dolf saw, to his great surprise, that the water was clean! With the water already up to his hips, he could still see his feet. He drank a little and found that it tasted wonderfully pure. Suddenly, a desperate cry for help drew his attention to a boy who had ventured too far out and was being borne away on the current. Clearly he could not swim and would be unable to reach the bank. Dolf hesitated no more than a second, then he dived forward and struck out for the child. He grabbed the boy by his long hair, taking care to stay out of reach of the grasping hands, and struggled back to the bank. He lifted the little boy onto the grass and immediately dived back into the river, in answer to the screams of yet another child out of its depth. A boy was suddenly swimming by his side and in next to no time had saved the drowning child. Dolf trod water, nodded to him and started back. But before he had reached the bank, he heard still more cries. Was there no one to look after the careless ones?

After a while Dolf lost count of how many children he rescued. Perhaps six and he had by no means been the only lifesaver.

Finally the children went away to dry themselves by the

campfires and to grill fish and pieces of stolen pig's meat. They ground stolen grain and baked hot, but very hard cakes. Gradually the children relaxed. Many, completely exhausted, fell asleep in the middle of their meal. The pieces of cake which they still clasped in their small fists were taken from them by others. Some were fighting for the most comfortable places to sleep ... The strongest acquired the most food and the softest "beds." Dolf discovered Leonardo seated by a fire where he was feeding his two wards and several other toddlers with bread and meat. Neither he nor Dolf ate anything.

Dolf had a lot of questions to ask, but he was worn out. Like Leonardo, he lay down in the light of the fire. The mule lay between them and in one hand the student clasped the reins.

"These little savages are quite capable of stealing and slaughtering it while we are asleep," he mumbled, by way of explanation. When the curfew was sounded in Spiers, the children reacted by throwing sand onto the fires so that they would burn lower. Soon everyone was sleeping soundly. Dolf stuffed his coat under his head and tried to sleep also.

Many thoughts and the strange surroundings kept him awake. Dolf realized with a painful shock that just twelve hours ago he had still been living in the twentieth century, a boy who had been allowed to visit the laboratory because he was lucky enough to have a father who was an old friend of Dr. Simiak. This morning he had felt the winter cold upon his face. And no more than nine hours earlier that he stood by the time machine pleading with the two scientists.

Now he was lying here, on the cold, hard bank of the Rhine, the grass tickling his neck, his shoulder still aching, his stomach contracted with hunger and surrounded by thousands of children, all dreaming of Jerusalem. He thought of his mother. He knew that she would be very upset.

Suddenly, he remembered the boy who had been transported to the twentieth century in his place. At least I am not the only one who has been stranded in the wrong time, he thought. He must be feeling just as strange and uprooted there as I am here. Oddly enough he derived some comfort from this thought and he fell asleep trying to imagine the boy's reactions to the alien twentieth century.

In the dead of night a raging thunderstorm broke. A loud clap of thunder brought many of the children leaping to their feet. In the brilliant lightning flashes, which came one after the other, the river seemed to be on fire. Dolf, too, had been startled from his sleep and sat up. A moment later sheets of rain poured down on him. The last of the fires sizzled out. Children screamed. Frightened prayers were murmured. A few halting voices began a song but it was drowned in the roar of the thunderclaps, the pounding rain and the howling wind. Dolf grabbed his coat but was soaked to the skin before he could get it on. He heard Leonardo trying to calm his terrified mule. The children huddled together, clinging to each other, their faces uplifted to the furious sky. The storm, it appeared, could not cross the river and continued to vent its anger directly overhead, with a force that seemed to herald the end of the world. A little girl about ten years old crouched, shivering, next to Dolf. She had on only a ragged dress. Dolf took his coat off and draped it on her thin shoulders. The child tried to creep under the protection of his arms.

The children's camp was not the only prey of the thunderstorm. In the town of Spiers lightning had struck one of the smaller churches and its spire and wooden timbers were soon ablaze. Despite the pouring rain the flames were fanned by the strong wind and large chunks of burning wood were hurled through the air to land upon the thatched or wooden rooftops of the houses. A disaster was imminent. Everywhere people ran from their houses carrying two pails. They formed a long line which stretched back to the harbor and passed the wooden pails back and forth.

From their camp by the river the children stared across at the town and saw the flames. Leonardo and Dolf stood together.

"The whole town will go up in flames in a minute," Dolf said. But the student shook his head.

"Not in this weather ..."

And, indeed, most of the houses were now so drenched that the flying sparks died the moment they landed. Bucket upon bucket of water was thrown onto the church which, with the surrounding houses, had become an ocean of fire. Sizzling, the water evaporated instantly and clouds of steam rose up to merge with the smoke and form a threatening blanket over the town. This fearsome drama was made to seem even more like hell on earth by the intermittent flashes of lightning and the dancing of hastily lit torches carried through the streets and on to the ramparts by the panic-stricken townsfolk. In the camp the children had fallen silent. Absorbed in the awesome scene of the burning town, they had forgotten their own fear. Perhaps also they felt they were being avenged. They gazed speechless as a spurt of flame leaped into the sky and disappeared, only to be followed by another flash. Above the storm's racket could be heard the clanging of bells. This signal of distress and emergency rang out over the surrounding fields and forests.

At last the storm's fury lessened. The rain slackened, the clouds began to break up and a few stars peered through. For a moment, a half moon, low over the river, cast its beam over the camp then disappeared. Dolf sensed that this wink from the moon had reassured the children. The girl in his arms stirred and mumbled something. She was no longer scared but felt safe, warm and secure. I never had a sister, Dolf thought hazily, but at once forgot it. He was wondering whether he should offer his help to the town, but his legs in the saturated jeans felt like lead. In any case, what obligation did he have to the population of Spiers?

Beside him, Leonardo said: "I'm glad they didn't admit us last night."

Dolf thought the same. What was ablaze in there? An inn, the town hall, a storehouse? He did not know and he did not care. Out here in the countryside, under the open sky, he was safe. He was cold and wet through, but the children's camp had been spared. All about him, prayers were being said. In the growing light of early dawn, he saw Leonardo cross himself and somewhere deep inside him he felt an urge to do the same, to express his gratitude. This feeling surprised him, for religion had never been a part of the Hefting family's life.

A watery sun greeted the day and gradually grew stronger. The fire in the town seemed to have been vanquished. Columns of smoke from the smoldering ashes still towered above the town, but the greatest danger had been averted and the weary population were extinguishing the last glowing embers.

The priest of the day before, once again held forth on the cathedral square:

"Citizens of Spiers! Did I not tell you to beware the wrath of Heaven if you denied succor to the holy children? You have ignored that warning to your own cost. God, Who, in His great mercy will forgive so much, could not permit the cruelty you showed to His children to pass unavenged. He sent His wrathful fire to destroy your sinful town. You say, 'Ah, but it hasn't been destroyed' and why do you think that might be?

"It was the children, citizens! It was these children outside there in the field, those children who have been called upon by God to liberate the Holy Land from the heathens, it was those pious children! They have taken pity on you, people of Spiers. They have prayed to God to forgive you and God has been merciful. He has removed His fire and sent His life-saving rain. You owe your town's survival to the prayers of those children. The selfsame ones to whom you refused food and shelter!

"Citizens, repent! You must do penance for your sins and reveal to God that you are not entirely the servants of Satan. Repent and show your gratitude. Take now your offerings to the children, for without them all that is yours would have been lost."

Shame-faced and with bowed heads, his congregation crept away to their houses.

The children's camp was bustling with activity. They were busy drying their clothes and collecting together their few possessions which had been scattered by the storm. Some of them straightened their hair with handmade wooden combs and brushes. They washed the dirt from their faces and filled their empty stomachs with water from the Rhine. Scurrying around the field doing these small chores, they seemed almost cheerful. Indeed, they were glad to have survived the night. Moreover, they were happy with the prospect that every step brought them nearer to the gleaming White City of their dreams, Jerusalem. Their coming would send the Saracens screaming from the gates, to be scorched by God's red-hot breath. An empty White City—the richest, most beautiful and most sacred in the world—would welcome them. There they would be happy for ever more. It had been promised to them ...

"I'm hungry," Dolf said to Leonardo, who was wiping the dirt from his mule with a handful of grass.

"I think," Leonardo replied quietly, with a wide sweep of his arm, embracing the entire camp, "that they are too."

Ashamed of himself, Dolf was silent. The girl who had

sought his protection during the night was looking up at him with wide, expectant eyes. She followed him like a shadow. Dolf had undressed to dry his clothes in the sun and the girl, too, removed her damp dress. Underneath, she wore nothing but a torn vest. She scratched herself, said something he did not understand and walked away toward the river.

He was suddenly anxious for her safety and went after her. She might venture too far and get out of her depth. His concern was unnecessary, though, because the girl merely knelt down by a shallow creek, removed her vest, meticulously rinsed her clothes and waded no farther than up to her waist in the clean water. Then she thoroughly bathed herself and washed her hair. At school Dolf had learned that in the Middle Ages people were dirty, knew nothing about hygiene and, therefore, were afflicted by the most dreadful diseases. He could tell he had more to learn.

When she had scrambled back onto the bank she put on the still wet vest. Smiling, she looked up, pleased that the boy had followed her. It was only now that he really saw her face, framed by dripping, auburn hair. She was a sweet girl and he held out his hand to pull her up. He gazed straight into her large, gray eyes, which were made to seem even wider by the tiny, thin face. He noticed the high line of her forehead and the soft roundness of her chin and felt strangely moved. Who was she? How did she come to be involved in this children's crusade?

He picked up her wet dress, wrung it out and spread it on the grass. The girl calmly sat down beside him.

"What is your name?" he asked, hoping she understood him.

"Maria." Her voice was soft and clear.

"Where do you come from?"

She looked at him blankly. She had understood the word "name," but "where do you come from" left her puzzled.

Dolf tried again this time she nodded, smiling brightly.

"From Cologne."

A city-dweller! She had no doubt grown up in the shadow of high walls, and the noise of the construction work on the cathedral. He just happened to know that in 1212 the Cologne cathedral, which would later become so famous, was still unfinished.

Dolf did not pursue his questions further. What inspired her, what had brought her on this foolhardy adventure, his twentieth century mind would probably never be able to understand.

"Come on," he said, standing up. But she refused to move and tugged at him to sit down again.

"What is it?" he asked.

"Your name."

Of course, he could not go round asking questions without being open to questioning himself. With a sigh, he knelt down and pointed to his chest:

"Rudolf Hefting from Amsterdam," he said.

The girl paled and fear and wonder were in her gray eyes.

Rudolf ... She drew away from him, her lips trembling.

"Don't be afraid," Dolf said hastily.

"A nobleman ..." she whispered shyly.

Suddenly he understood. She must think that he was the son of a knight or perhaps a run-away page boy. It seemed that the name Rudolf suggested to her one of noble birth. He shook his head vehemently.

"My father is a scientist, a ... a clerk."

Would she understand that? Apparently, she did.

"Can you read as well?" she asked in awe, "and write?"

He nodded.

"Where is Amsterdam?"

"Far away, in Holland."

It seemed that she knew where that was. She raised her hand and stroked his hair.

"Did your father let you go? Or did you run away?"

"My father does not know where I am," he said.

Maria seemed satisfied with his reply. She looked at him admiringly, stood up and pulled him off toward the camp.

Leonardo had finished tending to his mule and Maria put on her dress which was almost dry.

"Shall we be off?" asked the student.

"Where to?" Dolf, who was also getting dressed, wanted to know.

"Well, to Bologna, of course!"

For the moment, Dolf was lost for an answer. But before he could recover himself, Maria had excitedly grasped his arm, pointing toward the town. All three stood staring in disbelief.

The gates had been thrown wide open and a host of men, women and children poured forth, laden with baskets, dishes and parcels. They marched speedily toward the camp, where the children stood silently awaiting them. Then Dolf noticed one boy emerge from among them. He was dressed in a long, white cloak and sturdy boots. Two monks, in somber habits, followed him. Dolf wanted to ask who these people were but put off his questions. This impressive trio moved forward to meet the approaching procession. For a moment, they appeared to exchange words with those at the head. Then, the boy in white gestured expansively, as though he was blessing the heavily burdened people. Accepting a large loaf, he stepped to one side and turned to face the astonished children. His high-pitched voice rang out clearly:

"Children, here is a gift from God. Thank Him for His mercy."

Every single child sank to the ground and offered thanksgiving prayers to Heaven.

"Well, well, they've decided to bring us some food," observed Leonardo.

The citizens spread out through the camp, distributing the food in generous measure. There was enough for all, even the little ones.

Maria eagerly clasped a still warm pie and bit into it with such relish that it was a pleasure to watch. Dolf and Leonardo shared a roasted cock and Dolf felt he had never tasted anything so delicious.

Why should the people of Spiers, who had themselves, after all, suffered so much during the night, suddenly have such a change of heart? Their charity now was in sharp contrast to their heartlessness of the previous evening and Dolf could not understand it.

Leonardo pointed toward the burnt out church spire:

"They have had a fright," he said cynically and thrust a loaf, which they had also been given, into his knapsack.

The children were now in high spirits.

They began to leave the field in groups and passed by the town walls to follow the old military road, which went away south along the river. Dolf followed them with his gaze.

"Now what am I going to do?" he thought despairingly.

Perhaps it would be most sensible to remain in the vicinity of Spiers, near the stone. That was the only possibility he had of returning to his own century. But how would Dr. Simiak know that he was waiting here for the transmitter to be repaired? That might not be for another two months. Could he keep himself alive for so long?

The children were filing past him, singing happily. The grass rustled under their bare feet. Leonardo had discovered a girl with a swollen ankle who could hardly walk and set her on the back of his mule.

"I think," Leonardo said with an air of indifference, "that I will journey with the children for the time being. They are going my way and although it will be much slower, it will also be much safer."

Dolf barely noticed that his friend was speaking, for, at this moment, he realized that he must make a decision on which his whole future depended. He had allowed himself to be transported to the Middle Ages in the romantic hope that he might attend a tournament. A miscalculation had pitched him into the middle of the children's crusade, which to him seemed no less than insane, but which he also found deeply moving. He looked at the injured child on Leonardo's mule and the innumerable bare feet passing by. He suddenly knew the answer. He could not desert these children. He was stronger, more knowledgeable and more versatile than any of them. Maria already depended on him. Among the fanatical little pilgrims, at least a thousand were suffering severely. He recalled the children he had rescued from the river. He wondered about Leonardo. Surely he too was joining them because he felt the children needed help.

"I will go with you," Dolf said to Leonardo.

There, he had made his decision. With these five words he had relinquished all ties to the stone near Spiers and declared himself a medieval person. There could be no return.

"Good," Leonardo said with pleasure.

Maria slipped her small hand into Dolf's and they set off—for Jerusalem.

The King of Jerusalem

Slowly, the huge army of children made its way along the bank of the Rhine, following the old military road in the direction of Basle. Leonardo, Maria and Dolf walked among the rear-guard. Dolf suspected that Leonardo lagged intentionally, so that he could pick up children who collapsed and give them a ride on his mule for a few hours. He had unburdened the animal and he and Dolf carried their possessions on their backs. For much of the time, this faithful creature was plodding along bearing three or four small children. Two of them were seriously ill. They did not sing, refused to eat the bread Dolf offered them and stared ahead with feverish eyes.

For the time being Dolf had ceased to ask questions. The rhythmic, laborious tramping over the rough, hot road and the monotonous chanting all around made him feel heavy and drowsy. The heat was less humid than the day before, but he was still perspiring profusely in his winter clothes. He tied his coat to his back. After an hour, he had also taken off his sweater, but his pale skin was in danger of being scorched by the hot July sun and he was forced to put it on again, though it was much too warm. His injured shoulder, however, was feeling better and his feet, in the sturdy boots, were untroubled by the badly rutted road. He was amazed to see others tramping on over the sharp-edged stones in their bare feet.

So far Maria was the only one in the procession Dolf knew. Sometimes he caught a glimpse of the finely dressed boy whom he had noticed the day before. He was constantly hurrying back and forth through the rows of children and occasionally his high-pitched voice rang out above the singing. He seemed rather bossy to Dolf.

In the distance, church bells could be heard, and the children reacted almost as one. As if instructed by a secret sign, they knelt down, and started praying, some on the ground where they stood, others spreading out over the grass along the road. Maria did likewise and even Leonardo. Dolf followed their example, because he did not wish to be conspicuous. According to his watch it was twenty past twelve. The bells apparently were tolling mid-day and the start of an afternoon rest. Maria was kneeling directly in front of him and he could see the soles of her feet. The skin on them was hard and rough, a toughened crust of dirt and blood. He could not imagine how she managed to walk, but perhaps she had gone barefoot all her life.

After the prayers, the children settled themselves on the grass and ate the rest of their food. Those who had none left sat quietly conserving their energy for the hours ahead. Just then, Dolf saw one of the monks he had seen accept the food from the people of Spiers. He walked past them now, in his dark habit and sandals, peering searchingly, with a stern expression, over their ranks.

Dolf thought he looked like a general reviewing his troops and guessed he must be one of the leaders. But where was he yesterday, when that child dropped dead in the road?

Dolf's curiosity was again aroused. His strongest desire was to unravel the mystery behind the children's crusade. As soon as they were on their way again, he began to ask Maria more questions.

"When did you leave Cologne?"

He had to repeat the question three times before she understood it. She was giggling.

"You've got such a funny way of talking," she said.

"Yes, but remember I come from far away."

"Yes, I suppose that's why."

The Cologne dialect spoken by Maria was even more like Dutch than the solemn, medieval German of Leonardo, but she pronounced her words with a kind of croak to which Dolf had yet to get accustomed.

"When did you leave Cologne?"

"Ten days before Whitsuntide."

"What made you come?"

"Nicolas brought us the call. He was speaking in the new church. Oh, it was so beautiful, we just had to follow him."

"Nicolas?" He had heard the name mentioned before. Maria pointed ahead over the tide of children. Nicolas has heard the angels of God, she told him enthusiastically. "They told him of God's will."

"And they told him to organize an army of children?" Dolf inquired, disbelievingly.

Maria nodded. "It was a miracle," she exclaimed. "A miracle! I saw it!"

"What, the angels speaking to Nicolas?"

"No, afterwards, when Nicolas spoke in the church square in Cologne."

"Then what happened?"

"We all took up the cross and followed him. There were lots of us, some from the town and some from the country. It was so beautiful."

"And now it is not so beautiful?" Dolf asked. She looked up at him, perplexed.

"Do you still find it beautiful?" he repeated. "Aren't you disappointed? Aren't you sorry you left home?"

She seemed only to have understood the last question.

"I haven't got a home."

"Not in Cologne?"

"No. You see, I am an orphan."

"You haven't a father, or any relatives?"

Maria shook her head.

"What about your mother?"

"She is dead." She was indeed an orphan, belonging to no one.

What did the angels say to Nicolas? he inquired. "God wanted Nicolas to gather together as many children as he could, though we all had to be virgins. Then God would guide us to the Holy Land. First he will lead us over the mountains and then down to the sea. When we reach there, Nicolas will stretch out his hands and the ocean will divide. That's how we will be able to walk to the Holy Land, and we won't drown or get wet. Nicolas will lead us to Jerusalem and ..."

"But the Turks are in Jerusalem!"

"God has sent us. He will protect us. He will strike the Saracens blind and send lightning to burn them. Then, He will make the earth swallow them up because they are devils and children of Satan. We are all going to be allowed to live in the beautiful White City and we'll never ever be cold or hungry again. And we'll always be happy and we'll plant flowers on the Lord Jesus's grave and we'll look after the holy places and we'll make the pilgrims welcome and feed them and ..."

She went on, but Dolf was no longer listening. It was clear to him that she was simply repeating what she had been told over and over again. Dolf shuddered. How could these children believe such blatant nonsense? From where had Nicolas got this crazy idea? Was he a madman?

"Who are those monks?" he asked angrily.

"Dom Anselmus and Dom Augustus, who came to Cologne with Nicolas. They said that Nicolas was the messenger of God. They told us that one spring morning while he had been tending the sheep, Nicolas had seen a big, shining cross, high in the sky and angels voices had come from it. It must be true because they told us."

Dolf remembered the burning eyes of the monk who had "inspected his troops" at lunchtime. He asked Maria which one he was.

"That was Dom Anselmus, but we like Dom Augustus best."

"Do the monks try to take care of you?"

"I'm sorry, I don't understand."

"Who is watching over so many thousands of children?" Dolf persisted.

"But God is!" exclaimed Maria, who had finally grasped what he meant.

"What, all the time?" Dolf asked with a smile.

"Rudolf of Amsterdam, you are a stupid boy," Maria said with impatience. "Didn't you see this morning how the people of Spiers brought us food? God ordered them to."

"Maria, do you believe that the sea will part for you?"

"Oh yes, Dom Anselmus told us that the sea parted for Moses too. It always parts for a holy man."

It's becoming more ridiculous all the time, thought Dolf. But then, I'm in the Middle Ages. People not only know the story of Moses dividing the waters of the Red Sea, the escape of the children of Israel and the drowning of the pursuing Egyptians, but they also implicitly believe it, I expect. In which case, they probably believe that such a miracle can be repeated. So, here they are, all these children following Nicolas in the hope of seeing an entire ocean divide for them to walk over the seabed to the Holy Land. They probably think it will be a half-hour stroll! And it is the prospect of seeing this miracle, which will keep them going over thousands of miles. Am I the only one who knows it can't be done?

Maria was tugging at his sleeve.

"Are you cross with me?" she asked. She had been frightened by the angry expression which had set on his face. Reassuringly, he put his arm around her thin shoulders.

"No, not with you, dear Maria."

"Who are you angry with, then?"

He didn't know the answer.

"Wouldn't it be better to leave crusades to Godfrey of Bouillon?" he asked tersely.

"But Godfrey of Bouillon has been in Heaven for ages!" Maria exclaimed.

Dolf recalled a few dates: first crusade 1096.

"You are right, Maria. I'm a little confused with my dates. I really meant Richard the Lionheart."

"He is dead too—or so I've heard it said," said Maria sadly.

"But there are others like him—fearless knights in coats of armor, mounted on mighty chargers; and there are bowmen too. They're the ones who should be liberating the Holy Land. It's not a job for defenseless children."

Maria looked up at him reproachfully.

"Rudolf, you are the son of a nobleman. How can you talk like that?"

"My father is a clerk and nothing more," he said and became silent as Maria helped up a child who had fallen. The day was drawing to its close and many children were lagging behind.

Dolf wondered how many children were going to die each day on this journey and what he could do to help them. He could hardly carry them all. For an instant he caught another glimpse of the ever-active boy in the fine clothes. He was running along with a small child on his back. Dolf thought the boy must be strong. Leonardo's mule had all but collapsed under the weight of the sick and the injured. Leonardo himself was supporting a child on each arm. There were four children in Dolf's care. Around him, he noticed that many children were supporting each other and he realized that they were not quite so oblivious of their mutual suffering as he had at first thought. The long, hot day was taking its toll.

The rear guard was now progressing so slowly that they were in danger of losing contact with the main body. Dolf's legs were feeling weary and he was very thirsty. His watch informed him that it was half-past four. Twenty-four hours ago he had still had some hope of returning home. But he had missed his chance. His life was now in 1212 and in the hot summer afternoon he was trudging along a stony road toward the sea. He simply wanted to forget the past; or was it the future? Whatever it was he had to forget it and concentrate on survival.

Perhaps I could stay in Bologna with Leonardo, he thought. To him I'm a bright mathematician and I know the secret of Arabian numerals. Maybe I could become an accountant; they must have a need for them in this century too. Somehow, I must learn to live in the Middle Ages. Then in my old age I will be able to record my adventures as a traveller lost in time, for future generations.

At long last they reached a field where they could camp for the night. Those who were not utterly exhausted, tramped off to search for wood. Others, who went down to the river to catch fish, as usual, returned disappointed. The ground was too marshy and a wide field of reeds barred their way to the river's edge—there would be no fish tonight.

They quenched their thirst with water from a tiny brook which slowly trickled its way through the field to the river. Although, throughout the day, the sun had been burning fiercely, the field too was soggy. This place had probably been drenched by the thunderstorm of the previous night. Dolf gazed around and was not impressed by the suitability of their chosen campsite. Another storm and they would be up to their ankles in mud.

Leonardo noticed his concern and seemed to guess his mind. "You need not worry, Rudolf. There will be no storm tonight. The air is clear, which will mean a cold but dry night."

Dolf knew nothing about weather. At home, if he was going camping with friends, he would look in the paper or watch the television to know what to expect. But he trusted Leonardo and, his mind at rest, he went off to find wood.

That also proved hard to come by. The little that the children had found was either too damp or too green. Dolf gathered as much fuel as he could find. Some were extremely adept in the building and lighting of camp fires, as if they had had years of experience. But others had little know-how and they struggled long to get a blaze. Though the night would be cool, it would not trouble Leonardo or himself. But what of the thinly clad Maria or the two sick children who had shivered all day on the back of the mule? Dolf suspected that they had caught a cold during the thunderstorm. If they were not kept warm they would get pneumonia and that would be more than he could handle.

As soon as the fire was ablaze, Leonardo took from his knapsack the last of the food—a bag of peas, some herbs and a lump of bread. Dolf offered to look for a pot so that they could make a soup.

He wandered around the huge camp and saw that many children were already asleep, while others were busy grilling strange-looking food. But he saw a lot more besides—children shivering with fever (how many more had taken a chill during the night?); children with untended, bleeding feet; children with injured knees, covered with blood, scabs and flies; children with head wounds, boils, nosebleeds, inflamed eyes and swollen ankles. There seemed to be nobody to care for them.

It was true to say, however, that the majority were healthy and cheerful. They teased each other, sang songs and played games. Beside two of the fires a few were playing instruments that looked like flutes. Far away, bells were tolling. There was neither village nor house in the immediate neighborhood.

Eventually, Dolf came across four boys sitting silently around a smoking fire. On the ground beside them was an iron pan. He asked if he could borrow it.

"—since you have finished eating anyway."

But it turned out that the boys had not eaten.

"Bertho gave away the last of our bread this afternoon," said one timidly. They were distrustful of Dolf's odd clothes.

"Come and join us. We are going to make some soup," Dolf offered. He thought he recognized one of the boys as the fast swimmer of the night before. After some whispering among themselves, they stood up and followed Dolf back to Leonardo. Maria went to fetch water for the soup.

"Look," said Leonardo, not in the least concerned that there were four more hungry stomachs to feed. He held out his hand in which lay two spotted eggs.

"Where did you find them?"

"In the reeds. There are a number of nests over there, but there are few eggs left which are whole."

Nevertheless the four boys ran off to see what they could find. Half an hour later they returned with six more eggs and a very young duck, hardly more than a duckling.

When it was cooked, the soup was more like a strange stew, thick on account of the eggs and the peas and tasty thanks to the herbs. All in all it was considerably better than Dolf had expected. Leonardo produced a wooden spoon with which Maria poured some of the mixture into the mouths of the sick children. They looked up at her like grateful little puppies. Then Maria, Dolf, Leonardo, and the boys sipped the rest from the pan in turn. Each share was very small, but it warmed them.

"Good," Dolf said with satisfaction, when, after a few minutes, they were happily seated around together. Now he took a closer look at the boys.

They introduced themselves. The tallest (Dolf estimated his age at about fourteen) was called Frank and was the son of a tanner from Cologne. It was not too clear why he had joined the children's army. The swimmer's name was Peter. He was short, thick-set, with a solid pair of fists, and said that he thought he was twelve. He had lived by the side of a lake on the estate of the archbishop of Cologne, east of the city. The third was smaller and called himself Hans. His father was a woodsman and his knowledge of woods and animals was unlimited. The last was Bertho, another tall and strongly built boy, who refused to talk about his former life.

"I'm now a crusader and that is all that matters," he said stubbornly. Still, Dolf liked him.

As had become his fashion, Dolf introduced himself as Rudolf Hefting of Amsterdam, a name which visibly impressed the others. He gestured with his arms:

"This is not a good place for a camp."

Hans immediately agreed:

"It would have been better to have gone on a little farther." He pointed to the south. "Over there the bank seems higher and there is a forest."

"Who decides on the night's resting place?" asked Dolf.

"Nicolas," said Frank unhesitatingly. "He's the leader though he usually follows the advice of Dom Anselmus."

"The monk?"

The boys nodded. Dolf stood up.

"Well, I think it's high time that I had a word with this Nicolas fellow," he said.

Bertho's mouth fell open in amazement.

"Can one of you take me to him?" asked Dolf.

"You can't just ..." Bertho began haltingly.

"Of course he can," Maria broke in sharply. "Rudolf is of noble blood."

It seemed that she had firmly fixed that idea in her head. Frank too got up.

"Come along," he said softly. "His tent is over there, behind that grove."

"His what?" Dolf felt sure he had misunderstood.

"His tent, and the hooded wagon."

"Well, I've just got to see that."

Together they threaded their way through the camp. Most of the children were now asleep. Some of the fires were still smoldering, others had sputtered out. Almost all day long Dolf had heard the chiming of church bells, but he had more confidence in his watch which was waterproof, shock-proof, accurate and self-winding and which now confirmed that it was nearly eight-thirty. As always at the end of a hot day, mists were rising from the river and the fields, clinging damply to the sleeping children and shrouding the view.

"That's a fine bracelet," said Frank who had noticed Dolf looking at his watch.

"Yes, it was a present from my father."

"Is it silver?"

"Stainless steel."

"Damascus steel?"

"Something like that."

"Is your father rich?"

"Fairly," said Dolf feeling a little uncomfortable. Compared with people in the Middle Ages his father was rich beyond imagination. In the twentieth century he was a scientist of average income.

"Why did you run away from home?" Frank asked.

"Just for the adventure."

Frank nodded understandingly.

After some while, the rough field began to slope upward and the ground was drier. They passed along a thicket and came upon a group of people sitting around a roaring fire. Though dusk had fallen, Dolf saw on the farther side of the fire, an old, round tent. He also noticed two oxen, peacefully chewing near the bushes. A little farther off was a white covered wagon, guarded by about twenty boys, armed with cudgels. Nicolas, apparently, took no risks.

The group around the fire was enjoying a meal, the smell of which made Dolf's and Frank's mouths water. The little soup they had eaten had barely satisfied their hunger. On a spit over the fire Dolf recognized fowls being roasted and it seemed that several had already been consumed.

The group consisted of the boy in white, the two monks and eight children, whose fine clothes, polite manners and delicate hands indicated that they were of noble birth. Among them, Dolf noticed the energetic boy he had seen before.

They looked in amazement as the newcomers strode into their midst.

"I am Rudolf Hefting of Amsterdam," Dolf spoke deliberately and clearly. As before, the name impressed them. One of the monks, who was Dom Anselmus, raised his hand involuntarily. The second monk, Dom Augustus, who was much younger, fat and friendly-looking, nodded to him. Nicolas made as if to get up, but then thought better of it. The other children looked on with interest, their meal for the moment forgotten.

"… and I am hungry," Dolf continued calmly, pointing at the spit. At once, the boy with all the energy handed him a piece of meat and made room for him in the circle.

"Sit down, Rudolf of Amsterdam, you are welcome."

Clearly, this elite group regarded him as one of their own kind, though they must have been puzzled by his clothes. Dolf beckoned Frank to sit down too, a gesture which was greeted by an exchange of disapproving glances from the others.

"Who are you?" Dom Anselmus inquired sharply. Frank introduced himself. Dolf quickly put his arm around Frank's shoulder.

"He is my friend," he said. There was an embarrassed silence. Nevertheless, the same boy as before pushed a piece of meat in Frank's direction. Dolf thought he might like this boy after all.

As he ate, Dolf looked around at his companions. The children returned his stare. One was a beautiful girl, in a long, finely woven linen dress. She was adorned with ornaments and, on a silver chain, wore a cross which glittered with jewels. The boy sitting next to her was wearing a dark red cloak, yellow breeches and a belt inlaid with silver from which hung a wonderful dagger, the handle of which was encrusted with precious stones. The other children were no less grandly dressed and the boy in white was, of course, Nicolas.

Dolf began to speak, lowering his voice so that his strange accent would not be too noticeable.

"I joined the children's crusade yesterday. I wish to come with you to the Holy Land to deliver the White City," he said to convince them of his loyalty. The monks nodded approvingly and Dom Anselmus, in particular, looked at him with satisfaction. "I come from Holland where people talk and dress differently," Dolf continued, attempting to explain all that was strange about him (which, of course, was much more than they realized!). They accepted the information without question.

"But what I have seen of this children's army, I don't like very much," said Dolf, coming to the point. "I have been deeply upset by what I have seen. I'm concerned for the welfare of these children. There seems to be no one to look after them. I have seen the injured receive no assistance; I've seen some collapse with exhaustion in their own footsteps and others drown. Father," he turned abruptly to face Dom Anselmus, "this crusade is badly organized and could be improved a great deal."

The swarthy monk scowled but remained silent. Dom Augustus, however, began to take a closer interest. Nicolas raised his hand.

"God protects us. God is watching over us," he said mechanically.

"But surely God won't be angry if we help Him with the task." The words were out of his mouth before he could stop them and a wave of dismay passed around the circle.

"Rudolf of Amsterdam, have you come to preach to us?" Dom Anselmus said menacingly.

"Yes. When I said I was hungry, I was immediately given food. I am grateful for that, but out there are eight, maybe ten thousand more who are also hungry. What is being done for them?"

"God will feed them," Nicolas spoke again, a fraction too quickly.

Dolf turned toward the shepherd boy.

"Nicolas, listen to me," he spoke deliberately and in earnest. "God commanded you to lead these children to the Holy Land. He put them in your care. It is your difficult task to bring them all safely and in good health to the gates of Jerusalem. The journey is long and the dangers are many. But with better organization and a measure of common sense, much of the suffering could be avoided. It cannot be God's will that most of His children die on the way. God has entrusted you to be their leader, but that means taking care of your flock."

"Rudolf of Amsterdam is right," the magnificently dressed boy beside him suddenly said. "When my father went to war, he always made certain that his soldiers had enough to eat along the way."

"Be quiet, Carolus," snapped Dom Anselmus, but Carolus refused to be silenced.

"How can you know, when you are always riding at the front?" He raised his voice. "The chaos at the rear is terrible. I have complained about that before and I am glad that Rudolf of Amsterdam now supports me."

Well, at least someone is on my side, thought Dolf gratefully. "Rudolf of Amsterdam is not right," the cold voice of Dom Anselmus broke in. "This is no ordinary crusade. It is not our intention to shed blood or to take Jerusalem with the sword. The Saracens will flee before our innocence."

"I know that," Dolf replied calmly, "but neither should it be our intention to die of hunger, cold and misery. All these children," and he pointed out into the dark, "all these children expect to see Jerusalem, but the way things are going, barely one tenth will survive until the end. And why? Because their leaders have no concern for them, while they themselves lack nothing." He pointed accusingly at the remains of the meal, the tent and the wagon.

"You don't walk, you ride. You are not hungry and you don't catch cold in the pouring rain or the howling wind. You select the site for the night's camp, but you never ask yourselves whether it is suitable for thousands of children who have no cover ..."

"The oxen were tired," the over-decorated girl said lamely. Nicolas tried to defend himself: "It is a wide plain with room for everyone ..."

"... and it is marshy and unprotected. Last night many people caught a cold. Tomorrow they will be ill. What will be done for them? Who is going to look after them, supply them with hot drinks and keep their fires burning?" Dolf was getting overwrought.

"Now listen, Nicolas. God will heap many obstacles in the way of this army, though not with the intention of destroying us. As the leaders it is our duty to insure that all the children survive to stand before the gates of Jerusalem. God commanded not just you, but all of us to go to the White City. That is God's will and, therefore, we must carry it out to the best of our ability. But at the moment, we are failing God's trust. No doubt He wishes us to suffer, but He also demands that we help each other to perform the task that He has given us. That is why we must organize ourselves better. That is why all of us must do what we can—for the honor of God."

"Amen," said the boy beside him.

Dolf's outburst made him feel a little ashamed, but it was obvious that his speech had made a deep impression on the others. The boy beside him applauded, crossed himself and embraced Dolf.

"You are a worthy son of your noble father, Rudolf," he said delightedly.

The two monks remained seated. Anselmus's hostile eyes followed Dolf's every movement, but a wide, warm grin spread over the round face of Augustus.

"Rudolf of Amsterdam, I think you will be a valuable recruit to us," he said in a friendly manner. "May I hear some of your proposals?"

Dolf was ready for this question. Throughout the day he had been thinking of how things might be improved.

"In the first place, we must divide the children into groups and give each one a task. There are so many, it should not prove too difficult." He began to tick them off on his fingers. "One, there must be a group to keep order. This will have to include the elder children, who must equip themselves with some sort of weapon, like a club. They will be responsible for the children's safety, preventing internal fights and protecting them from outside attack. Then, there should be a large group of hunters, who will have the task of providing the day's supply of fresh meat. I have noticed that this area is very rich in game ..."

"Just a minute," interrupted Nicolas angrily, "we can't do that. It would be poaching."

Dolf pointed at the spit.

"Well, where did you acquire your wild ducks for this evening?"

"Carolus shot them," Nicolas explained.

The boy at Dolf's side nodded enthusiastically, pointing

toward the tent. A hand-made bow stood by the entrance and there was a quiver alongside.

"I can hit a bird in flight," he said proudly, "and I don't need a falcon."

"And isn't that poaching?"

"Sometimes ..." Nicolas shrugged his shoulders.

"Nicolas, do you mean to tell me that the game in the lands through which we pass is protected?" Dolf asked.

"Protected?" Language problems were looming again. "The animals belong to the lords of the region. Only they have the right to hunt it. Surely you don't expect religious children to steal pheasant and deer from a noble lord?"

"Well, as far as I am concerned, they can," grunted Dolf. He turned to the young marksman. "What do you say, Carolus?"

The boy was already beaming brightly.

"I'll form the group of hunters," he cried. "I can teach them to make a bow and arrows. We'll show you some real shooting. And we'll hunt even though it is forbidden, because Rudolf of Amsterdam is right, the children must have food."

"It's a fine nobleman who poaches," shouted one of the others.

"It is not poaching," Carolus shouted back. "It is executing God's will."

The group was somewhat perplexed by this statement, but it effectively silenced the protests.

"In any case, since I am the king, I have the divine right to form a hunting group, isn't that so, Rudolf?"

Dolf did not have the least idea of what the boy meant, but he nodded in agreement, because he had taken a great liking to Carolus. And he knew that somehow the children's army must be supplied with food. Hunger has a way of disregarding the existence of laws.

"We will also need a group to fish," he said. "Some of

the children I have seen are good swimmers and others have nets, but only the swimmers should be members of the fishing group, because it is a dangerous job." He looked at Frank. "Do you think that Peter could organize that?"

"Oh yes," said Frank with conviction. "He is almost a fish himself and he has friends among the children."

"Good! Carolus can train the hunters and Peter, the fishermen. Who could take charge of those who will keep order?"

"I can do that," said a strong-looking lad. "Those boys over there by the wagon are under my command. I think that Rudolf is right. The whole camp should be guarded, because sometimes children have been kidnapped during the night."

Dolf shuddered. The boy who had spoken was called Fredo and he seemed pleased with the prospect of forming his own private army.

"We will also need a team of nurses to take care of the injured and any who fall ill along the way. And this means that during the day the march will have to be organized differently. In the front ranks we should station guards to keep off troublemakers. The smallest and weakest must come directly behind them with a few of the bigger children to help them along. We can use the wagon for transporting any who are no longer capable of walking. At any large town we should try to leave the sick and wounded. Following the little ones there ought to be an energetic group to attend to those who lag behind. Finally, there must be another group of guards to protect the rear from attack. In that way no one will get left behind unnoticed to suffer some terrible fate. What do you think, Fredo?"

"I think it's a very good plan," the boy replied.

"Does it mean that I'll have to walk?" asked the decorated girl with concern.

Dolf glanced at her shoes, which were in fact little more

than silver-colored slippers. She would not get very far wearing those, he thought.

"Who are you?" he asked.

"Hilda of Marburg."

The name meant nothing to him, though it sounded rather grand.

"If you're prepared to look after the sick, you can ride in the wagon." Hilda nodded in relief.

Carolus turned to Dolf.

"I haven't been riding much, you know, because I didn't think it fair," he said. "Furthermore, it is a king's responsibility to look after his people. I can walk perfectly well."

Dolf gave him a friendly smile; he had grown to like Carolus. When they became better acquainted he would find out why he called himself a king.

"You talk as one who is used to giving orders, Rudolf of Amsterdam." It was the voice of Dom Augustus. "How large is your father's estate? Are you the eldest son?"

Dolf straightened his back. At the age of fourteen, he was almost as tall as the average adult in the Middle Ages. These people probably thought he was about eighteen and were intimidated by his size and assurance. His behavior would not have been unusual in the twentieth century, but in this era no one but a nobleman would dare to speak in a similar manner. Dolf decided to exploit to the full the impression he had created.

"Forgive me," he said, "but I would rather not speak of it. I cannot recall my past without considerable pain."

The circle of children nodded sympathetically. They too preferred to think of Jerusalem, the center of the world, where it was perpetual summer and flowers blossomed all the year round.

Now that he had successfully silenced the questions about his origins, Dolf continued to unfold his plans.

"The camps must be organized along different lines also.

We will need groups for gathering wood, cooking and sentry duties. We must collect together as many large cooking pots and eating bowls as possible. Any food that we find or are given during the day will be kept until the evening. Then the cooking teams will prepare food for the whole army over large fires. During the night, the strongest and tallest must be organized into groups to keep watch."

Carolus and Fredo were nodding in agreement, but Dom Anselmus protested.

"That's all going to take far too long. We will hardly advance at all and we must cross the mountains before the autumn sets in."

To this Dolf replied:

"It will take a few days to get it organized, but once everyone understands the duties, you'll see us moving faster than ever." He glanced at the other monk, who seemed to be in agreement. At that moment Carolus shouted:

"Rudolf of Amsterdam is the embodiment of wisdom itself. It is essential for an army to have a good organization. Rudolf, you have my full support." Clearly Carolus's words carried considerable authority, for none of the others dared to argue with him. Dolf noticed that Nicolas was dejectedly shaking his head and pressed his cause further.

"All the children out there," he said pointing in the direction of the sleeping camp, "come from somewhere and have some kind of special knowledge. For instance, in my part of the camp there is a boy who was brought up in the forests and he knows just about all there is to know about tracking. He and others like him would be of great use to Carolus and his hunters."

"What's his name?" asked Carolus excitedly.

"Hans. I'll send him to you tomorrow. I'm sure you'll like him. Now, if we want our groups to be able to provide food for everyone and to be able to give us complete protection, then we must let the children choose what they want to do as much as possible. Every one of them must surely have some little skill that will benefit all."

These words were greeted with amazement. In the Middle Ages everyone knew his place and stuck to it. One was born into a position and for the most part died in it. Of course it was possible to pursue a career, even in the thirteenth century. Society was not completely inflexible and those who were clever enough could succeed in improving their position.

But to let every child choose his or her own task and, moreover, "for the benefit of all," that was something so novel to this elite group around the fire that they all shook their heads in disbelief.

Dolf himself knew what he was saying, but realizing that it must seem strange to the others, he quickly changed the subject.

"I heard Dom Anselmus say something about mountains. Which route are we taking to the Holy Land?" He was well acquainted with the map of Europe and was wondering how these people knew the way.

It was the friendly Dom Augustus who answered him.

"We will come to the sea at Genoa."

"Genoa?" Dolf asked. "I don't understand. Why should we go to Genoa?"

"God ordered Nicolas to take the army there," replied the glowering Dom Anselmus curtly.

"It seems crazy to me," thought Dolf. Then a thought struck him that chilled his blood.

"But that means that we must cross the Alps!"

The monks nodded. What would the Alps look like in the thirteenth century, Dolf wondered. Would there be any roads?

Yes, of course. The Romans had crossed them a thousand years earlier and Hannibal, also, with his elephants. But the idea of taking so many children across Europe's highest mountain range ... Dolf could hardly imagine it. He could foresee a gruesome end to the children's crusade. He knew the Alps well. How many times had he been to Switzerland, Austria or Italy with his parents? But that was in a comfortable car along paved roads, lined with hotels, restaurants and camping sites. There were patrols of police and break-down services, so there was little danger for the tourist. This time, he realized only too well, it would be quite different.

"So, across the Alps to Genoa," he said aloud, "and then where?" He knew what the answer would be, but he wanted to hear it from the mouth of an adult and hear it he did.

"God will work a miracle," said Dom Anselmus. "The sea will part and we will be able to reach the Holy Land on foot."

Did the monk himself really believe it? Dolf wondered.

A little while before, he had noticed an obscure figure, standing just outside the circle of light, who seemed to be listening intently to the conversation. He thought he recognized it to be Leonardo, with his cudgel. What was he doing here?

"Well then, if we must cross the Alps, I suggest that we take the Brenner Pass. It is the lowest of the Alpine passes.

"We are planning to travel along the old military road over Mount Cenis," Dom Anselmus said reluctantly. "That is the shortest route and I know it, for I once made a pilgrimage to Rome."

"I also know that way," cried Dolf in horror, "and it is terrible! It's almost as bad as the Great St. Bernard."

There was a shocked silence. Dolf blushed.

"I have travelled a great deal," he said softly.

His mother had never liked flying. She used to say that it was such a shame to miss so much beautiful countryside while travelling. So the Heftings had always taken their car on holidays and they had driven over all the passes in the Alps. Dolf's father viewed it as a sport and even refused to go through the tunnels. That way one saw so much more and, like all inhabitants of flat countries, Dolf loved mountains and wild countryside. He had always enjoyed those journeys immensely, but now …

"Why don't we change direction at Strasbourg," he suggested, "then we can pass through the Black Forest, Bavaria and over the Karwendel Mountains to Innsbruck. The Brenner Pass begins right on the other side. We would then be heading straight for Bolzano. I admit that it is rather a long way around, but it is the only hope of getting thousands of children across the mountains alive."

"No," said Anselmus. He was beginning to lose his patience. "It is senseless to go by such a roundabout way. Moreover, the Karwendel Mountains are full of robbers."

"No doubt that applies to all the mountains," replied Dolf innocently.

"Have you been there?" asked Carolus with great excitement.

"Yes, I have crossed all the passes."

Naturally they did not believe that.

Dom Augustus said quietly:

"There is a famous abbey on Mount Cenis, where travellers can get food and shelter."

"Eight thousand at once?" asked Dolf. "Or rather, four thousand, for we are sure to have lost at least half our number before we get there."

Unexpectedly the figure that Dolf had noticed in the background earlier stepped forward into the light of the fire. It was indeed Leonardo. Leaning on his cudgel, he said in a quiet voice:

"Forgive me for eavesdropping on the meeting of such an illustrious company. I am Leonardo Fibonacci da Pisa, a travelling student on his way to Bologna. Out of pity I have joined the children's crusade for a short while. I, too, am acquainted with the Alps and some of the passes. I can assure you that Rudolf of Amsterdam is right. Mount Cenis is an impossible route. Thousands of the children would die. Nothing, not even the tiniest, hardiest shrub, grows at that height and the cold is unbearable. The children would starve or freeze to death during the nights … The Brenner is not as high, nor so inhospitable."

"In the Karwendel we will be destroyed by the bears," Anselmus said gloomily.

"Bears!" Dolf cried in alarm and at once wanted to bite off his tongue with annoyance for this slip. Nicolas reacted immediately.

"It seems your knowledge of the mountains is not as great as you would have us believe."

For an instant Dolf lost his composure. But not Leonardo.

"And are there no bears or wolves on the bare slopes of Mount Cenis?" he asked abruptly.

The monks had to admit that there were.

Dolf had not counted on bears and wolves. He could not believe they would come through alive.

Leonardo remained calmly resting his weight on the cudgel and gazing around at the circle. He was slim and a little taller than Dolf, and he radiated authority. Dolf admired him and no more so than when, tapping his club gently on the ground, he said:

"At least, with my friend here, I need fear no bear."

Little Carolus, who was almost exploding with excitement, cried aloud:

"How can we ignore the advice of two such hardened travellers?"

"Oh, keep quiet," said a boy in a blue cloak. "I'm scared of bears and wolves."

Meanwhile Dolf had recovered his self-assurance.

"We are all scared," he said, "but if we take the proper precautions and have groups of brave hunters and sentries, we should be able to keep the wild animals at a distance."

The debate continued late into the night. Eventually it was decided to abandon the journey across the infamous Mount Cenis and to take the road proposed by Leonardo and Dolf. Hilda had fallen asleep against Carolus's shoulder. She was not much older than twelve and very beautiful, with her long, blond braids. Carolus had put an arm around her and looked down lovingly on the little, golden head.

"Is Hilda your sister?" Dolf inquired.

"Hilda of Marburg is the daughter of Count Ludwig," Carolus whispered. "She was brought up in the palace of her uncle, the Archbishop of Cologne; though she lived in the nunnery, of course. The Archbishop ordered her to travel with us. She will be the queen of Jerusalem. And I ... said Carolus, as if in a dream, "I will be crowned king of Jerusalem. I will live in the white palace with Hilda, my bride, and we shall be happy forever."

The fantasies and dreams of a child, mused Dolf. What could he say. He could think of nothing better than to bow slightly to the little king. Carolus graciously accepted this show of respect.

"Rudolf of Amsterdam," he said without rising, so as not to wake the girl, "I hereby appoint you to be my first page."

With his free hand, he lightly touched Dolf's shoulder.

"That gives you the right to sleep in the tent," he added conspiratorially.

"Thank you, Carolus, but I prefer to sleep by my campfire. You see, I too have young boys and girls to protect."

Carolus nodded understandingly. Dolf stood up.

Along with Leonardo and Frank, who was half asleep, Dolf returned to his campfire. Peter was still awake and patiently watching over the others. Frank briefly related the main details of the debate. As Dolf lay down to sleep on the hard ground beside Leonardo he asked in a hushed voice:

"Where did you suddenly appear from? Did you follow us?"

"Oh," Leonardo mumbled, "just call it a precaution. When I saw you go off with Frank, the look on your face was so determined, I thought your tongue might lead you into trouble and I thought it better for me to be around. By the way, what did you make of those two monks?"

"Stupid," said Dolf unthinkingly.

"Oh no, Rudolf. Certainly Anselmus is not stupid ... but he is a fraud."

"What!" cried Dolf in a shrill voice.

"Ssssh, not so loud. Yes, I mean it. I noticed them yesterday. Something is wrong somewhere. What do they want of this children's crusade?"

"To take Jerusalem."

"So they say," muttered Leonardo.

Dolf was feeling relieved that he was not the only one with doubts.

"What makes you think that they are not genuine?"

"I was surprised that they permitted you to go as far as you did," Leonardo said vaguely. "I was surprised that they did not at once accuse you of being a heretic."

"But I thought my speech was extremely devout," protested Dolf innocently.

Leonardo shook with laughter.

"Rudolf, my friend. I have never heard such unusual things as you uttered this evening. You are a very clever person and I don't know how you have acquired your knowledge and experience at your age, but you are a heretic and, if I were you I would be more wary in the future."

Dolf sighed. It was true. No matter how hard he tried,

he could make neither head nor tail of thirteenth century religious ideas.

"I tried to say only what they themselves proclaim," he said apologetically. Leonardo sat up and looked down at him earnestly.

"And did you really believe what you were saying over there?"

The boy felt the color rise to his cheeks. Fortunately, the fire had burned down low, so that the Italian would not notice.

"You believe about as much of that as I do, Rudolf. I have travelled a fair amount and seen much of the world. Nicolas seems to be honest enough for me, but he is being misled by those two characters with their stolen habits and pious faces. They are no priests. I could tell that from the fact that they raised no objection to what you were saying. Something had to be wrong. Not even the most stupid priest would have let you continue. But those two? They listened with the utmost interest. It looks to me as though they have something to gain by getting as many healthy children as possible to Genoa. Now why could that be? Have you asked yourself that?"

"Yes," said Dolf quickly.

"Good, then you know what we must be on the lookout for and why you must be more careful."

Leonardo turned over to go to sleep, but Dolf gave him a gentle shake.

"Do you believe that the sea will divide for us, my friend?"

"Eh, what's that?"

"Do you believe in miracles?"

"Sometimes," said Leonardo, sitting up again. "You are a miracle. Just when I was in danger of losing my life to those two robbers, you appeared from nowhere to rescue me, bringing with you an extraordinary knowledge of

Arabic numerals. Then, we both suddenly discover ourselves in the middle of a children's crusade, and another miracle happens. The stranger who saved me on St. John's day stands forward as a counselor with more sense and travelling experience than all the other so-called leaders together. Now you ask me if I believe in miracles. My friend, I am experiencing nothing else."

They grinned at each other.

"Good night."

Five minutes later the two of them were sound asleep.

Skirmish with a Boar

Following the evening in the marshy field, the children's army progressed in a more orderly fashion. Each morning, after prayers and a sermon from Dom Anselmus, in which he reminded the children of their objective, Dolf, Leonardo, Frank, Peter, Fredo and Carolus began to organize the groups. At first it was all a little chaotic but gradually it sorted itself out. The sickest, who now had continuous care, rested on straw in the wagon. Hilda, the aspiring little queen of Jerusalem, was in charge of the nursing and not simply because she wished to ride. In the convent where she had grown up, she had been taught to care for sick people and she was pleased to have an opportunity to practice what she had learned. She herself selected the girls she wished to help her and instructed them in the making of herb tea and the preparation of food that would strengthen the patients. There were no bandages, but these the children made themselves. Dolf was amazed by the curious method they employed.

Some of the girls collected strong grasses which they braided into wide strips. These were rolled up and stored away. Bleeding wounds were covered with fresh grass which had first been chewed by healthy people, then mixed with saliva; this staunched the blood and prevented infection. Finally, a bandage was tied over all. Much to Dolf's surprise there were few cases of blood poisoning. It seemed that the saliva of a healthy person resisted infection. Dolf soon realized that Hilda of Marburg was quite capable of looking after the patients. Giving orders and making decisions came naturally to her.

Maria, who had had little or no education at all, had no special skill, but she still tried to make herself useful. She made friends with a girl called Frieda, the daughter of a serf who had been raised in the country and knew a great deal about berries, herbs and edible roots. They formed a group which looked after the supply of nutritional plants, gathering blackberries and searching for herbs. Hilda appreciated their help, for they supplied her with herbs for the sick, which she used to combat attacks of fever.

Nicolas too escaped having to walk, for someone had to drive the wagon. But when the two monks tried to climb up, Dolf protested.

"How can you refuse to share the trials of the children?" he cried out loud, so that all those nearby could hear. Since they did not want to lose their position of authority with the children, the men had no alternative but to walk like the rest. Dom Anselmus cast a glance full of hatred in Dolf's direction, but the boy was unperturbed.

Fredo, who was the son of a knight at arms, knew exactly how to organize the group of sentries. Dolf thought of them as the orderlies. A start was made with the manufacture of bows, arrows and cudgels. Carolus gave instruction in shooting and Leonardo told them how to use the club. These were the children who patrolled the camp at night. They were relieved from their duties every two hours. During the day they could be seen at many different points along the length of the procession, protecting the front and the rear and keeping wild animals at a distance. The wild animals were sometimes human ... Angry farmers who feared their crops might be trampled or their barns plundered; impoverished noblemen, who tried to lure the children into their clutches, in order to sell them or make them work as laborers; other unpleasant characters who mingled with the procession. All of these and more were chased off by the orderlies.

Although Dolf had never really intended it, with Leonardo's help he had become the effective leader of the children's crusade. He had brought from the twentieth century something completely unknown to these children— a sense of responsibility, a social awareness. In his own age, it was something he had learned almost from the day he had been born. To him all children were equal. He made no distinction between serf and noble, between the free and the enslaved, between the citizen and the outcast. He judged every child by his or her merits and if one turned out to be particularly adept at a certain task, then that was what he was given to do. Thus Peter, who had never been anything but the poorest of serfs, became the unrivaled leader of the fishing group.

He instructed others how to make fishing nets, how to detect dangerous currents in the rivers and how to detect shoals of fish. All those in his group could swim and since they contributed a large proportion of the total food supply, they were treated with respect.

Carolus, the master hunter, chose Hans and Bertho as his principal assistants and he trained his band with great enthusiasm. Well aware that what they were doing might be interpreted as poaching—in the Middle Ages a crime punishable by death—they avoided encounters with others on their hunts as much as possible. They were not always successful. Sometimes they came across an irate forester, a bad-tempered farmer or a furious nobleman. Then, they either ran for their lives or left Carolus to use all his fluency and knowledge of court etiquette to explain to the angered gentlemen that God had given the children the right to feed off whatever they might find on the land. The hunters soon became very skilled in their task and, since they moved on each day and never poached on the same domain twice, they successfully escaped vengeful pursuit.

Dolf, who was increasingly concerned about the wild

mountainous area which they would soon reach, stared in deep thought at the bare, bleeding and blistered feet trudging past. He mentioned it to Frank, the tanner's son who understood at once what was expected of him. Each night the skins were stripped from the day's hunting bag. The soft hides of rabbits, beavers, hares and deer were gathered. In the evening, hundreds of children set to work scraping the skins clean and soaking them. Later they were cut to size and sewn together. It was a difficult job, since the children's army possessed few implements, but they were extremely inventive. Some of the children spent all their time making strong, thin thread from tough plant fibers. Bark from trees, strengthened with leather, was also used. Soon, there were stout shoes for all the badly injured feet.

Apart from the food provided by the fishermen and the hunters, the children also received supplies from the inhabitants of the villages and towns through which they passed.

Despite the poor communications, news travelled surprisingly fast in the Middle Ages. The fate of Spiers was known in places as much as eighty miles away. Everyone had heard how the townspeople had at first been so selfish toward the children and how God had sent fire from Heaven to punish them.

Everywhere, heed had been taken of these events. As soon as the massive column of children appeared, townsfolk and merchants came hurrying with food, to buy themselves protection from the vengeance of Heaven ... Fredo's orderlies insured that all was stored safely away until the evening. Only at the noon break were the children permitted to eat some bread. To privately hoard food for oneself was labeled a "sin."

"Because," Dolf explained, "we all have to cover the same distance and we all have the same objective. Therefore we are all equal. Anyone appropriating more than is his due is committing a sin against the sacred children's army and has no right ever to see Jerusalem." That they could understand.

And thus the march continued along the Rhine to Strasburg. Naturally some days were more difficult than others. Sometimes the sun was hidden by brooding storm clouds and an icy wind swept over the hills, whipping up the waters of the Rhine and making fishing a hazardous occupation. On such days the children most poorly dressed suffered with the cold and wet and the number of patients increased alarmingly. When feet were slopping through the mud and there would be no chance to dry one's clothes for two days, when the cooking fires had to be built with soggy wood, even the children could see little sense in their suffering. It was at times like these that Carolus proved to be the greatest inspiration, with his deerskin boots, magnificent cloak and silver belt. He seemed almost charged with electricity. Through the length of the procession he seemed to appear everywhere at once, like a young dog covering twice the distance of everyone else. He took charge of sobbing, shivering children, sore feet and little bodies doubled up with spasms of coughing. For a young girl who had turned blue with misery, he lent his cloak. At another time, with agile fingers, he wove a kind flat umbrella from twigs and long grass, under which four children could find some protection from the lashing rain.

Some of the children had watched him while he did this and then copied his method. Dolf could not help laughing at the sight of numerous boys and girls, grouped in fours, holding up their makeshift raincovers and singing happily as they splashed their way through the puddles.

One cold but dry day, when the little king was out hunting with his band, he discovered three sheep which had strayed from a flock. He prevented his followers from killing them and led them in triumph back to the camp.

"They will provide us with wool," he said to Nicolas.

"We will shear them and spin the wool from which clothes can be made."

"And we can eat their meat," nodded Nicolas without thinking.

"No," said Carolus emphatically. "We will take them along with us. Sheep can walk perfectly well."

"I demand that they be slaughtered," Nicolas retorted, quite looking forward to a joint of roast mutton.

The hunting that day had been none too successful and they were passing through a sparsely inhabited region. Carolus summoned Dolf. Officially Nicolas was the leader, but the little king had more faith in Rudolf of Amsterdam.

When Dolf heard about the matter, he was resolute.

"Of course the animals must stay alive," he said in a loud voice for all to hear. "They will only be slaughtered if we are in danger of starving."

Nicolas was not a stupid boy, but he was inexperienced, for he had never known anything but praying and herding sheep. He was a little frightened of the tall stranger from the north, for he knew that in a short time Rudolf of Amsterdam had made many friends who seemed prepared to give their lives for him. He had seen how, within the space of a few weeks, a disordered rabble of children had been transformed into a well-organized army, but he could not understand it. From where did this stranger derive his authority? And what did he mean when he said: "All for one and one for all"?

To Nicolas's superstitious mind Rudolf was someone to be reckoned with and seldom contradicted. Therefore, for the time being, the sheep were spared and that very evening Nicolas himself sheared them. He was an expert and the wool came off in perfect condition. After it had been washed and well brushed out, it was divided among those who knew how to spin. Dolf was fascinated as each girl or boy wound a few handfuls of wool around a small stick which they held under the left arm. Carefully they plucked the fibers loose, one by one, and rolled them between their fingers until they had formed a coarse thread, which Dolf found surprisingly strong. A different person would catch the thread as it was completed, winding it around another stick, so that gradually a ball was formed.

"I didn't know one could spin wool like that," thought Dolf. "I thought one needed a spinning wheel."

It did not at first occur to him that, in 1212, such a machine had yet to be invented.

With this spinning method the work could be done while they were walking. Nicolas and the two monks were forever urging the procession to greater speed. With every delay they fretted. And yet, since there were now fewer who lagged behind, and since the sick were now carried in the wagon and little time was lost in poaching, begging or otherwise finding food, their progress was by no means slow. All the hunters were athletic types who could easily catch up with the main body when they stopped for the night's camp. Dolf had made a new regulation whereby the day's march ended at four o'clock. The monks were not pleased with this and Anselmus, in particular, wanted to continue until just before sunset. Once again Dolf had his way, mainly because by the end of the afternoon most of the children were feeling weary and wanted only to complete their simple duties, have some food and go to sleep. By stopping early there was adequate time for the fishing group to go down to the river, for the orderlies to set up the tent and tend the oxen and for wood to be gathered.

By the time the fires were burning the first fish had been brought up from the river and the hunters were returning with fresh meat. On most occasions the evening meal was over before seven o'clock and they took advantage of the last hours of daylight for weaving, preparing skins, washing and repairing clothes and making weapons. Dolf encouraged them to bathe, but always under the watchful eyes of one of the best swimmers. No more children drowned.

Soon they arrived in Strasburg, where they were warmly welcomed. They received help and food and were permitted to leave behind those who were most seriously ill. They crossed the Rhine by a large wooden bridge. They now intended travelling in an easterly direction, first through the Kinzig valley, then through the Danube valley and thereby come to Constance. For the last time Dom Anselmus tried to persuade Dolf to take the shorter road across Mount Cenis, rather than the longer way through Bavaria. But Dolf refused to listen.

"If we want to get to Genoa quickly and safely, then we must take a path that is suitable for thousands of children and not one which will lead them to their destruction," he said firmly.

At the same time he was wondering why Anselmus was in such a hurry. It was still warm enough to cross the mountain barriers. But he did not ask or say anything. He was mindful of Leonardo's warning.

Unlike Anselmus, Dom Augustus was always cheerful and knew how to raise the children's spirits on wet and difficult days. The very small ones trusted him with the blind faith of innocence, while the sharp eyes and stern voice of Anselmus frightened them.

Maybe Dom Augustus is a scoundrel, thought Dolf, but at least he is a friendly one.

They had now entered the Black Forest. The heavily wooded mountains rose high all around them, bisected by a narrow, clear, trout-laden river. Dolf continued to marvel at the unspoiled nature of the countryside—the cold, but delicious water, the numerous beaver dams and the forests abounding with game. The animals were not in the least timid and were an easy prey to the little hunters, who moved stealthily, yet speedily through the thick undergrowth. Dolf never accompanied Carolus, Hans and Bertho on their hunting trips, for, although he understood that poaching was necessary, he could not bear to watch the slaying of a young doe or to see little rabbits being clubbed down. In the twentieth century hunting had almost been outlawed and his disapproval was etched deep in his conscience.

The Black Forest, with its many wild animals, was fraught with dangers for the children. Since Dolf always stayed in the camp, he was unaware of the dangers faced by the children when they went out on their different tasks. Nor did he know that Carolus, ever-conscious of his noble birth and royal future, took risks which were sure to end in disaster sooner or later. The woods teemed with wild boars. These animals moved through the forest in large herds, the females and the young surrounded by a protective wall of strong males with fearsome tusks. The hunters did not hesitate to attack such herds. Sometimes they paid for it with serious injuries. One evening Bertho was carried into the camp with his thigh torn open. Hilda was white with shock, but she wasted not a moment and sent someone to find Dolf.

"I need help. That wound must be sewn together."

Bertho was laid on a bed made of branches of fir and four strong boys gripped him firmly. Unflinchingly, Hilda put a clean needle into the flesh and sewed the edges of the wound together with strong fiber. Bertho was grimacing with pain, but he did not utter a sound. Beside him Carolus stood crying.

"He saved my life," he said between sobs. "The boar attacked me and Bertho jumped in front of it. He caught the animal on his spear, but it snapped."

"Do not blame yourself," Dolf consoled him. "The wound looks worse than it really is. Believe me, all that blood looks terrible but it has cleaned the wound. Bertho will quickly recover."

Nevertheless, after this incident, he forbade the hunting of boars.

The road along the river was little more than a rough path, and at times it was so narrow the wagon got stuck so that they had to ease it around projecting rocks or over boulders, taking special care that it would not overturn and topple into the river. Sometimes it meant hours of hard work and all the patients had to be taken out. Dolf earnestly longed for the day when the last of the mountains would be behind them.

THE MIRACLE OF THE BREAD

When, at last, they reached the town of Rottweil on the river Neckar, the town gates were locked fast. Word of the happenings at Spiers had apparently not reached this far or, if it had, the townspeople had been unwilling to believe it. The evening was gray and drizzly and the children were looking forward to some food and shelter. They decided to set up their camp on a slight incline not far from the city. A small delegation, including Nicolas, Dom Anselmus and Peter, was admitted to negotiate with the town council for food. Dolf had been occupied elsewhere in the camp and Nicolas and Dom Anselmus had left before he could intervene.

Nicolas was so tactless that the meeting was doomed to failure from the start. His manner toward the aldermen and the Canon was very haughty and, encouraged by Dom Anselmus, he proclaimed his sacred mission. It was true that his task would have been a little easier had not Dom Anselmus demanded in a threatening fashion that the children be fed in the field outside the town. Earlier in the day he had promised the children an evening of plenty. Finding himself now faced with an attitude of rejection, he grew flustered and careless.

"God punishes all those who refuse the children food and assistance," he exclaimed. The Canon, however, after subjecting him to careful scrutiny, shrugged his shoulders.

"We do not intend being fooled by impostors. You could well have started the fire in Spiers yourselves. If you have any children who are seriously ill, you may bring them to the town and we will tend to them. But, if you think that the town of Rottweil is sufficiently rich to feed thousands of children, then you are wrong. The harvest is still in the fields. If any of your children attempt to steal cattle or grain, we will order our bowmen to shoot at them. That is a warning, do not forget it!"

Rottweil was a thickly walled town, built on a hill and overlooking the entire valley. Nicolas and Anselmus realized that poaching was quite out of the question. Through the window in the high tower where the negotiation was being held, they could see the fields and meadows—there were guards everywhere. The region was fertile, but much troubled by robbers lurking in the hills, who could only be kept at a distance by a display of force.

"Do you not fear the wrath of God?" Anselmus made one last effort, but his words were in vain.

"No," the city fathers replied. They had surveyed the sky long before and had realized that there was no danger of a destructive thunderstorm that night. They wished to have as few dealings with the children's army as possible and, in any case, tomorrow they would be gone.

Peter, who had sat silent and attentive, suddenly interrupted. With a great show of respect he informed them that there were four children with a high fever.

"I will have the doctor visit them," the Canon promised.

Timidly, but obstinately, Peter pointed out that the Canon had promised to take the seriously ill into the town. There were too many witnesses for this to be denied.

"All right, have them brought here."

Peter, who betrayed nothing of his feelings, bowed reverently. Then the delegation departed with empty hands. After hearing Peter's report, Dolf was thankful for the promise that the sick would be accepted into the town. The four children to whom Peter had referred were indeed seriously ill and Dolf feared for their lives. Their bodies were simply burning with fever and their stomachs refused to retain even herb tea. Exactly what disease it was, Dolf did not know, but he didn't think they would recover.

Bertho and some of the other wounded refused to leave the camp, because their injuries were healing fast and they had started to walk again. Dolf asked Frank to hitch the oxen to the wagon and drive the four patients into town. But, at the last moment, he too jumped up alongside Frank.

"You take the wagon back to camp," said Dolf after they had delivered the children. "I want to look around the town."

"Why?" Frank asked surprised. "Rottweil is much smaller and not nearly so magnificent as Cologne."

"I don't doubt you, but I am here now and not in Cologne." Dolf laughed.

By now Dolf was speaking the language fluently for he spoke nothing else all day. Confidently he began his tour of sightseeing in medieval Rottweil. The town was much like he had imagined: narrow, winding streets, sometimes connected by arcades. In certain areas of the town artisans plied their crafts in the open street under awnings. It was seven o'clock and most of the townsfolk were having their evening meal. Nevertheless, the streets were crowded and full of activity, or at least that was the impression, since it needed only four passersby to block the narrow lanes.

Dolf was the object of many stares, not only because of his clothes but also because his face seemed out of place. Beggars tugged at his sleeve, asking for alms. They were in a pitiful state, often blind, some without legs ... Dolf shivered and walked quickly on his way. He had nothing he could give them.

Wandering around, he happened upon a street of jewelers and swordsmiths. He gazed fascinated at the displays. The stainless steel breadknife dangling from his belt had been invaluable for the past two weeks. But it could not compare to the beauty of the ornamented silver daggers in their leather sheaths. He inquired of the smith what the price might be for one and was told twenty pieces of silver.

Dolf sighed. He didn't have a cent, but . .

He suddenly remembered the Dutch money in his purse in his trousers. For a fortnight he had forgotten its existence and, curious about how Dutch guilders would be received in thirteenth century Rottweil, he pulled out the wallet, removed two guilders and showed them to the smith. The latter was not impressed. Two silver coins? He wanted at least twenty for the dagger. The man had, however, noticed something strange about them.

"What kind of money is that?"

"It's from Holland."

"I have never seen those before, but if you want to change them you should go to the next street. There you will find a moneylender who might make an exchange with you."

Dolf followed the directions and shortly afterward was standing in the dark room of the moneylender. The beginnings of a crazy plan were forming in his mind. He did not want to buy the dagger, but ...

"I wish to exchange this money for the currency in use here," said Dolf and he placed on the table a handful of guilders. Intrigued, the man pored over them.

"What kind of money is this? I have never seen its like before."

"It comes from Holland."

"But surely you are not trying to tell me it is silver?" the man asked with a voice full of suspicion.

"No indeed," replied Dolf. "But the alchemists in Holland have discovered this metal which is harder and more valuable than silver, more valuable even than gold. Count William has three alchemists at his court who make the white metal for him. The Count has ordered the metal to be used for the minting of coins which cannot melt, bend or be cut into pieces. In the north these coins are very much in demand. The Danes, in particular, have been sailing into Dutch harbors in their hundreds, their boats laden with skins and precious stones, which they barter for the coins."

Would the man believe him? He was studying the guilders intently, especially the portrait of Queen Juliana of Holland.

"Who does that image represent?"

"That is Saint Juliana, our patroness," said Dolf.

The strange, hard, unblemished coins lay glittering in the light of the lamp.

"I will give you ten denarii for them," he said uncertainly after biting on one. They were so hard that not even the sharpest knife could mark them. The man was astonished. How could poverty-stricken Holland produce such wonderful coins?

"Then that will be fifty denarii for the five," Dolf said calmly, deliberately misinterpreting the man.

"You're mad!"

Dolf drew himself up to his full height, rested his hand on the breadknife and said sternly:

"Do not forget that you are talking to Rudolf Hefting of Amsterdam!"

"No, my lord," the old man cowered. "Please forgive me … I am only a poor man and few trade caravans pass through Rottweil."

"Tell me," Dolf said, giving his voice a stern edge, "how many loaves can I buy for one denarius in Rottweil?"

"At least fifty, sir."

"Do you know anyone who would still bake them tonight?"

"Perhaps Gardulf will …" The man hesitated.

"Then I will offer Gardulf my coins."

Quickly the man covered the coins with his hands.

"But sir, what does Gardulf know about money? He is only a stupid baker."

"I am not concerned with that. I need loaves, a great many of them. Outside there are more than eight thousand hungry children, lying by their campfires."

"You want to buy food for those children?" the money-lender asked in amazement. "But why?"

"Because my heart is softer than those of the people of Rottweil." Dolf shook the remaining contents of his purse over the table—five, ten and twenty-five-cent pieces. The bronze coins, in particular, interested the man.

Eventually, Dolf got twenty denarii. He had nothing in which to carry all the heavy silver coins, so he exchanged his purse for a leather bag. The purse was still fairly new and the moneylender seemed delighted with it. Dolf set off to see Gardulf, the baker.

The ovens had long been extinguished and Gardulf was sitting down to his evening meal. Dolf burst through the door, uttered some blessing he had just thought up, mentioned his impressive name and ordered eight hundred of the largest loaves the baker could produce. The baker must start immediately and he, Rudolf of Amsterdam, was prepared to pay twenty silver denarii.

"But that is not nearly enough," protested the baker, "and how can I bake so many loaves in one night? The curfew will be sounded soon and then all fires must be extinguished. Moreover, I only have two apprentices and they are already in bed. Have pity on me, sir."

Gardulf was a man with red hair, green eyes and a pallid skin. His four small children, who were sitting around the table yawning, had the same hair and dreamy green eyes. Dolf thought they were charming.

"I must have the bread, dear baker," he persisted. "There are hungry children waiting outside and, if they are not fed soon, they will call down the vengeance of God upon the town."

"But sir, no one believes that story. I've heard about the monk and his account of what happened at Spiers, but I have also heard that he is an impostor."

"Stop," said Dolf holding up his hand. "Baker Gardulf, you may be right, but surely children cannot be left to starve just because a scoundrel has been telling a ridiculous story. Look!" He shook the silver pieces from his pouch right under the noses of the astonished red-haired children.

"In one night you can earn all these."

The man stared greedily at the silver coins.

"But my men will fall asleep while working. They have been working all day and the guildmaster forbids ..."

"My good man, I know all about that," said Dolf quickly (though of course he did not). "Wake them up anyway and I will help you. Just tell me what to do."

Once again the baker looked longingly at the money.

"Where will I find wood?" he muttered. "I'll need a cart-load of it."

"Within the hour you will have your wood. I'll see to that." Dolf regretted that he had already dispatched the wagon back to the camp.

"Listen Gardulf, I will leave these two silver coins with you, as a token of my good faith. I must go away to arrange the collection of the wood before curfew. You might as well start the dough. I'll be back soon."

He thrust his remaining money back into the pouch and raced off, leaving behind him the stunned baker and his family.

The sentry at the western gate agreed to let the wagonload of wood into the town, even if it arrived after curfew. Then Dolf made his way to the camp as fast as he could and called his friends together.

"Get as many to help as you can. We need a cartload of

dry fuel, because tonight Gardulf the baker will bake bread for us." The announcement was greeted with cries of joy and Carolus ran off, followed by Frank, Leonardo and Fredo.

"Gather wood!" Fredo's commanding voice resounded around the camp. "Wood for bread!" That shout alone set at least a hundred boys into action. Only Peter remained standing by Dolf.

"What's the matter, Peter? Aren't you going to help?"

"But how are we going to get the wood to the town?"

"In the wagon, of course."

"But that's impossible. There are five patients in it."

"But we took the patients to town this ... what? Five more?"

Peter nodded dejectedly.

"All little ones—and they have got the same thing as the other four—pain in the throat, inflamed faces, fever."

It must be an epidemic, Dolf thought. Four during the day, five now, how many tomorrow? And what disease is it? It must be some kind of virus ... Hopefully, he turned to Peter's inscrutable face.

"Have you seen this sickness before? Is it common?"

Peter nodded.

"The little ones die from it."

"Only the little ones?"

"Usually."

So it was an illness of childhood and probably one of the scourges which twentieth century drugs had long been able to cure. How could he do anything about it? He remembered then that all suspected cases should be isolated in a separate camp and then perhaps it would cease to spread.

The news of this disaster had greatly shocked him. He did not wait to ask any more but ran to the cart where Hilda and Frieda were in the process of cleaning up one of the patient's vomit.

This was the wagon he needed to transport eight

hundred loaves to the camp the following day, but now it was infected. Dolf felt faint and leaned against a wheel until the feeling passed. The responsibility was becoming simply too great for him. He knew too much, understood too quickly and felt too much pity for these simple-minded children. He began sobbing.

"My son, are you not feeling well?" The voice which spoke came from just behind him and sounded friendly. Looking up, Dolf saw a Benedictine monk, but it was neither Anselmus nor Augustus.

"We are being threatened by an epidemic," Dolf whispered miserably. "Can you help us, father?"

"What is threatening us?"

"A dangerous, contagious disease which can cause the death of a small child."

"Take me to those who are afflicted, my son."

"It's this way."

Together they climbed up into the wagon. Hilda looked up startled.

"What is it?"

The children were lying on beds of rough straw. They were delirious and their heads were swollen red. Heat seemed to radiate from their little bodies. The monk looked at them, nodded and said sadly:

"Yes, this is serious. It's the Scarlet Death."

"The—the plague?" stammered Dolf. In silence he offered up a prayer. The priest crossed himself and looked Dolf in the face. A wealth of goodness was reflected in the man's eyes.

"No, my son, it is not the plague. It's Scarlet Death. That is why the children are bright red."

Dolf nodded. He had been puzzled by this strange symptom and assumed it was a consequence of the fever.

"Will they die?"

"That rests in the hands of God. Maybe the strongest will

live and perhaps also those who receive proper attention."

"I have been doing my best," said Hilda quietly. Her jewels now hung from her neck like a bunch of straw. She looked exhausted. How many hours, Dolf wondered, had she been working today tending to these vomiting and delirious children?

"Hilda, you and Frieda must stay in the wagon and keep out of the way of others. I will set guards outside to prevent anyone approaching. This disease is contagious."

"But won't we catch it too?" asked Frieda worriedly.

"No, I don't think so," the monk said. "Scarlet Death usually attacks only the little children, rarely the larger ones."

"I must get things organized at once," said Dolf and he jumped down from the wagon. Already boys were returning with firewood.

"Father, please tell them that they are not allowed in here," Dolf asked.

"Where do they have to take the wood?"

"To the town, to Gardulf the baker. Tonight he is going to bake bread for us. The guard on the western gate has agreed to let us enter with the fuel."

"I will see to it."

The monk went to meet the boys. Dolf watched as he collected the boys around him and led them off in the direction of the town. With relief, he then turned back to Hilda.

"I will have the wagon moved. You wait here and don't admit anyone."

He hurried off to tell Leonardo the news. Then Fredo joined them and soon things were moving fast. The covered wagon was pushed out of the camp and placed behind a thicket. At a safe distance, boys with cudgels were stationed. While this was happening, Leonardo and Peter made a tour of the camp inspecting the sleeping children. Wherever they saw a scarlet face or heard a complaint about a sore throat, which appeared to be the first symptom, they placed the child by a separate fire, which was also strictly guarded.

Once all the suspected cases had been isolated, Leonardo ordered them to be given strong herb tea. In the space of half an hour he delivered six patients to the wagon, all of them bearing clear signs of infection.

"We will have to keep a close eye on the group by the separate fire," he said to Dolf.

"I must leave that to you," the boy answered. "I have to go to the town, for I promised the baker I would help him with the bread."

"I hope he hasn't got any young children," said Leonardo sensibly.

Dolf suddenly realized that he would be a danger to those four blushing faces with their freckles, red hair and green eyes.

"I'll disinfect myself first," he said and ran down to the river. He took everything out of his pockets, undressed and dived into the icy black water. It bit into his shoulders, face and arms, but he came out greatly refreshed. Then he dragged his clothes through the water several times, wrung them as dry as possible and got dressed again. He quickly put everything back into his pockets and started running. He arrived at the western gate steaming and out of breath. At first, the guard would not let him in.

"What happened to the wagon you mentioned?" he asked accusingly. "There was no wagon at all, just fifty young boys carrying bushels of wood."

"Did you let them through?" asked Dolf anxiously.

"Yes, but only on condition that they returned as soon as they had delivered the wood. And so they did. There was a monk with them, otherwise I definitely would not have let them pass."

"You are a good man," said Dolf. "I wish I had something to give you, but ... just a minute."

He had just discovered a curious object in his pocket—
he had come across a plastic doll, about the size of his
thumb. He could not remember how he had acquired
anything so useless, but he now extracted it from his pocket
and, with a flourish, handed it to the amazed watchman.

"Take good care of it," he said solemnly. "It is an image
of ... of Saint John and it has great protective power."

The guard let him pass.

It was much more difficult finding his way back to the
baker's house in the silent and dark town than he had
expected. But just when he thought that he was completely
lost, he discovered that he was standing right in front of
Gardulf's bakery. A thin beam of light escaped from a crack
in the shutters. Dolf rapped on the door.

"Ah, there you are at last. You certainly took your time,"
grumbled the baker who opened the door himself.

"I'm sorry. There were a few problems in the camp,"
Dolf said, forgetting to behave like a young nobleman.

"What happened to your clothes?"

"I fell in the river."

Shaking his head as if in disbelief Gardulf showed him
into the bakery. To his great joy he saw that Frank was
there as well, busy kneading the dough. The apprentices
were also hard at work.

"I thought I would stay and lend a hand," Frank said
simply. Dolf could have hugged him. He tore off his wet
jersey which the baker hung up to dry, and set himself to
the work.

Kneading dough is heavy work. Gardulf with his
muscular arms could do more in an hour than the two boys
together, but he did not complain. He realized that they
were unused to the work and also that they were so tired
that they could hardly stand.

As the night went on, tray after tray of golden brown

loaves emerged from the oven. The apprentices piled them up outside the door, for the bakery was too small to hold them. Dolf watched the heap grow with just one thought going round and round in his head: "The children must eat, or else they will get ill. The children must eat!"

Frank had turned white with exhaustion. Dolf felt little better. As the men carried the final loaves from the oven, the baker said:

"Have you got the money?"

Silently Dolf handed him the pouch and watched as the man's eyes lit up. Perhaps he had paid too much after all, but he did not care, for there was now a breakfast for the children's army.

"No doubt you will be bringing a cart for the bread, won't you?" asked Gardulf. Just then his wife appeared with cakes and hot milk. The boys were really too tired to eat, they longed only for rest, but they forced themselves to drink the milk and eat the cakes, which tasted quite good.

"A cart?" stammered Dolf suddenly realizing what the baker had asked. "No ... it's become useless. Frank ..."

"I understand," said Frank with a yawn. "I'll go to the camp and send carriers."

An hour later, about a hundred boys came marching into the town to collect the bread. Proud that they had been able to overcome their difficulty without the aid of the Rottweil people, they held their heads high as they strode through the streets. The early passersby stopped and stared at them in wonder. Soon the rumors were running rampant through the town. During the night, an angel had descended from Heaven and baked hundreds of loaves for the children.

Dolf himself did not go with the boys, for he had yet another errand. On legs which were in danger of collapsing he ran to the hospital and told the lay-brother that the four patients they had brought in the previous day were suffering from the Scarlet Death. A look of deep concern grew on the man's face. One of the children had died during the night; of the other three, two seemed to have improved a little, while the third was unlikely to survive until the evening.

"The only hope is careful nursing," said Dolf. "And please keep them isolated from all others, especially the parents of small children."

"Why did you bring the disease into our town, my boy?" asked the lay-brother sadly.

"We did not know then what they were suffering from. We have many more patients in the camp now, but we will not burden you with them."

The lay-brother shook his head sorrowfully.

"But how can that be?" he asked. "Are the children not under divine protection?"

Dolf was too exhausted to argue about that. Almost automatically he said: "We have our trials, too," and with that he left, stumbling rather than walking.

Once outside the town gate, he found Leonardo waiting for him with his mule. The student caught him and set him on the animal's back, where he at once fell asleep.

The Scarlet Death

Dolf awoke feeling a tug at his sleeve. It was a few seconds before he realized where he was. The sun was high in the sky and everything about him seemed surprisingly quiet. Leonardo was leaning over him.

"We are going."

The camp was almost deserted. In the distance, some way past Rottweil, he could hear the singing of the children already on their way. Only the wagon still remained, together with the rear guard. Waiting on the edge of the camp were ten mounted soldiers dressed in coats of mail.

"But we can't travel!" cried Dolf, suddenly recalling the situation.

"We've got to," said Leonardo dejectedly, pointing at the soldiers. "I have let you sleep as long as possible. A message came from the town council to say that we must be out of the region by noon."

Dolf stood up stiffly. His whole body was aching, but he took off his sweater and let the warm rays of the sun soothe him.

Without further comment he gathered his possessions together. Maria slipped her hand into his and led him forward. Leonardo, Frank and Peter followed, while Fredo drove the oxen pulling the wagon. The orderlies fell into line behind them.

Dolf stole an apprehensive glance at the cart.

"How many are there now?" he asked fearfully.

"They say that there are twenty-four, all little ones," replied Maria softly.

Dolf mumbled the figure to himself, trying to grasp what it really meant. Twenty-four dangerously ill children in a trundling wagon—did the people of Rottweil have no heart at all?

But then he realized that they were only trying to protect their own little children.

Though he felt outraged, he did not really blame the inhabitants of Rottweil for wishing to be rid of the infectious army of children. He glanced around again and noticed that the ten soldiers were following.

After a long, hot day without rest they arrived by the side of a lake, which Dolf realized must be the lake of Constance. They made their camp on a low hill near the shore and then the battle against the Scarlet Death began in earnest.

First of all, Dolf divided all the children into groups. These groups were led one at a time down to the lake and, under the watchful supervision of the best swimmers, were told to wash themselves thoroughly and clean their clothes.

As far as it was possible, Dolf divided up the smallest and allotted each one to a group of elder children. So far they had discovered only one suspected case among the children over eight years old. It really did seem that the older ones were immune. By spreading the young ones through the camp, Dolf hoped that the minimized contact between the younger children would halt the disease. Whether or not the herb tea they were continually forced to drink strengthened their resistance Dolf did not know, but he hoped so.

One corner of the enormous camp was cordoned off as a hospital. By now more than eighty patients lay there side by side, delirious and seriously ill. They were covered with anything the nurses, both boys and girls, could find. Carolus, the extraordinary little king of Jerusalem, had devised a way of weaving blankets from grass and straw. When a child died his blanket and bed were immediately burned. The bowls from which the children were spoon-fed, were diligently scrubbed clean with boiling water and sand after every meal. There was no shortage of water and more than a hundred boys and girls were employed all day collecting and carrying wood, while others spent their time weaving blankets and rugs. Fishing went on continuously as did the gathering of other supplies by the hunters.

At the height of the epidemic, three days after their arrival at the lake, thirty children died on one day and forty-two new cases were discovered. Dolf had ordered a deep hollow to be dug a few miles away to serve as a mass grave. Around this pit huge fires were kept burning twenty-four hours a day to ward off wild animals and anxious peasants from the neighborhood.

On the fourth day eighteen died, one of them a boy of about fourteen years, and there were twelve new cases.

The wagon was used only for transporting the dead to the grave. The grave diggers were volunteers and Peter had offered to act as their coordinator. The fishing group could manage quite well without him. For some reason he seemed fascinated by the disease. He would wander around near the hospital helping to draw the bodies away and burn the beds. After a while he no longer entered the healthy part of the camp.

On the fifth day there were six dead and seven new cases; on the sixth, one new case and seven dead; on the seventh there were no new cases but fifteen died.

Death was a constant companion to people in the Middle Ages. It was feared but also welcomed, for it meant the passing from an earthly to a spiritual existence. Those who had lived a not too sinful life died calmly, for they knew they were about to enter Heaven. Any child who died was believed to be transported at once to the kingdom of God, because God loved purity and children were pure by definition.

The children seemed so calm and cheerful, even though

death was all around them. Those who were healthy were playing, laughing and generally having fun. This delay by the lake had turned out to be a blessing in one respect, for it provided a kind of much needed holiday for many of the children.

Even when they reported a new case of the fever, it was with an air of indifference. Perhaps one of the older children, with a sobbing youngster clasping his hand, would approach Hilda and say. "Veronica has a sore throat and does not want to eat anything," or "Little Samuel keeps crying for his mother. I think he must have a fever ... " and, then, would turn around and walk away, leaving Hilda to take over. Whenever a child fell ill it had to be taken to the sick-camp; but for the rest, life went on as usual.

Hilda had proved to be an indestructible pillar of strength. She was indeed like a queen as she strode past the beds. She did not miss a detail; here a child had dirtied itself and needed cleaning; over there, one had vomited; yet another had fallen from its bed in a delirious dream or had kicked off the blanket; now there was one calling for a priest...

Nicolas, on the other hand, instead of helping preferred to pray and ask God to remove the terrible disease. Dom Anselmus and Dom Augustus spent their time comforting the dying children and organizing the funerals.

After eight days or so, Dolf felt that victory over the Scarlet Death was in sight. There had been no new cases for two days. There were still seventy-eight patients in the sick-camp, but most of these were recovering. Dolf heaved an immense sigh of relief. In a week, or maybe two, they would be able to continue their journey.

That same afternoon he was invited to visit Nicolas at his tent. Tired as he was he decided to go because he was curious to know why the shepherd boy might want to see him. Perhaps he was going to thank Dolf for averting disaster.

Dolf had little respect for Nicolas, though he mentioned it to no one—not even Leonardo. To the children, Nicolas was a saint. His magnificent white apparel, his clear voice which had conversed with the angels and his pious eyes which had seen visions, encouraged the children to view him as a person worthy of worship.

Dolf, they regarded more as a powerful master—stern but righteous and one whose orders and requests could be executed unquestioningly, for they were so sensible. They also trusted him because he had made the journey easier.

In the tent, Dolf was received by Nicolas and the two monks. "Sit down," said Nicolas affably. Dolf dropped to the floor and waited for Nicolas to make the first move.

"There are few patients left," Anselmus began. He was not asking, but stating a fact.

"Thank goodness," Dolf replied. "And the majority of those are recovering. I think that in a week's time we will be able to move on."Tomorrow," Anselmus said brusquely.

"What!"

"The delay has lasted far too long already."

Dolf's eyes blazed with anger.

"And what do you intend to do with the children staying in the sick-camp? Were you thinking of leaving them behind?"

"Certainly not. Some of them will die tonight and those who are too ill or too weak to walk tomorrow can travel in the wagon.

"That is out of the question," Dolf retorted. "Until now we have been able to leave most of our patients in towns, but they were ordinary patients with pains in their stomachs or heavy colds. These children cannot possibly be left in someone else's care. As you know, they must be isolated from all healthy children. Surely you are not so stupid that you can't see that?"

Anselmus went white with rage.

"We must go on," said Nicolas. "Last night an angel appeared to me. God is angry that we have been dawdling so long. Jerusalem awaits us."

"Jerusalem is four thousand years old and can easily wait a few weeks more," Dolf blurted back at him. Nicolas stared at him in horror. Dolf was struggling to keep himself in check.

"We cannot waste time finding shelter for the sick. We must take them with us," said Anselmus as if that were the last word in the matter.

That was too much for Dolf. His voice crackling with fury, he exploded:

"You know, I wish you would get sick, so that you would know what it is like to lie for days on end in a rickety, jerking cart, your bones aching and your head throbbing!"

"Those are sinful words, Rudolf of Amsterdam," thundered the monk.

"But not half as sinful as your hurry, Dom Anselmus. We cannot leave yet; in a week maybe but certainly not tomorrow. Your suggestion is a crime."

"Who are you to think that you can make the decisions here?"

"Who I am is my business," Dolf answered back. "But one thing I do know is that you are intent on getting as many children as possible to Genoa as quickly as possible. But why is a complete mystery to me, for once there they will get the biggest disappointment of their lives."

Dolf could not have spoken more plainly. Anselmus was quivering with anger. Nicolas mumbled:

"In Genoa, God will perform a miracle."

"What kind of miracle?" asked Dolf, raising his voice. "Oh yes, I know, the sea will divide. Do you really believe that?"

"God promised me," Nicolas protested.

Dolf replied with a short, sarcastic laugh.

"If the miracle does not occur, you will be torn to pieces by the children," he growled. Nicolas paled and started trembling.

"Rudolf of Amsterdam, your words are like daggers in our hearts," said Anselmus, changing his tone. "Why do you work so hard on behalf of the children if you have no faith in Nicolas's mission?"

"Because I can't stop them, that's why!" screamed Dolf, losing all control of himself. "You ... you have beguiled these children with a fairy story, more beautiful than any they have ever heard before. But, Dom Anselmus, I tell you, that if this thing does not work in Genoa and the children are left wandering and weeping along the beach, you will have something to reckon with. That much I solemnly promise you!"

With those words he stood up and stormed out of the tent, almost bumping into Leonardo.

"I suppose you thought I needed protection again, did you?" Dolf snarled at him, his temper still quite out of control. Unperturbed, Leonardo smiled.

"I hear that we're leaving tomorrow."

"Over my dead body!" Dolf yelled over his shoulder as he ran off toward the sick-camp. He had noticed a column of smoke rising from Peter's fire and that the oxen were being hitched up to the wagon.

"How many?" he asked curtly, as he came up to Peter.

The young fisherman poked the flames and replied reluctantly: "Three."

That leaves another fifteen serious cases, thought Dolf. He had by now become so hardened to the sight of death that three more had little effect on him. Moreover, the future looked grim. In a few days it would not be just three but thirty ... or three hundred.

He had come to know Anselmus well enough to realize that, this time, Nicolas and the monks would go ahead with their plan to move off early next morning. Why was there such a hurry? Preoccupied with his thoughts he gazed at Peter. His anger was gradually subsiding, only to be replaced by fear, worry and a deep sadness.

"Peter, are you looking forward to reaching Jerusalem?" he asked suddenly.

"We are all looking forward to that."

That was typical of Peter, he always gave an evasive answer. Nevertheless, Dolf was very fond of him. Not only was he a natural leader, he was also intelligent. In just a few weeks he had developed into a young person with a clever and alert mind—and he had discovered freedom.

"Why did you run away from home, Peter?"

The boy raised his head.

"Wouldn't you do the same, Rudolf of Amsterdam, if you got more whippings than food and when you know that in Jerusalem the sun always shines and no one has to work?"

"But didn't you have any brothers and sisters who wanted to come also?"

Peter bit on his lip.

"I was the eldest. I had six brothers and sisters but a few years ago three of them died with the Scarlet Death. I too was ill, but survived."

That explained why he had recognized the disease in the first instance. Perhaps it also explained his fascination for the sick-camp.

A thought suddenly occurred to Dolf.

"Peter! Did you know that those four children had the disease when you begged the citizens of Rottweil to take them in?"

"Of course I knew. I'd seen them, hadn't I?"

"And yet you still ... Peter, how could you do such a thing? Why didn't you tell me right away?"

Again Peter stared distantly into the fire, pushing some straw closer to it.

"They were mean, those people of Rottweil, they could not even give us a bowl of porridge."

Dolf felt as if the earth was splitting open under his feet.

"There we were in that high room of the town hall," Peter continued in the same soft, expressionless voice. "They received us there for a purpose, you know. It was so that we could look out over their cornfields, their meadows and rich herds of cattle. And it was obvious that there were even more fertile lands behind the hills. Oh yes, they were rich those Rottweil people. They have a fine town and many of the houses are built of stone. They have quarries in the mountains, they get gold from the Danube, silver from the hills, iron from the mines in the north ... And yet they told Nicolas that they would guard their fields and herds and any child seen trespassing would be shot without mercy. And, Rudolf of Amsterdam, I had to sit and listen to that."

"Yes," whispered Dolf. The color had drained from his face. "Then," Peter continued in the same tone, "Dom Anselmus threatened the aldermen with the wrath of God. He told them the fate of Spiers, but they just laughed at him. I knew why they were laughing. There was no need for them to fear a thunderstorm that night."

"You thought of the patients," Dolf said, horrified. "And you had them taken into a healthy town, with many little children."

"It was the will of God," Peter mumbled. "I heard His voice whispering in my ear."

"Oh Peter ..."

The young fisherman said nothing. He was throwing handfuls of sand onto the heap of ashes which had been the funeral-fire of three little souls. Dolf stood and watched him sorrowfully. How much hatred could a child harbor. What dark recesses were hidden in the pious souls of these people of the Middle Ages? How easily they renounced responsibility for their deeds! It was God who ruled the world, not them. They unhesitatingly declared God or the Devil to be responsible for their deepest emotions, their desires for revenge or their illusions.

Dolf tried to understand, but he found it difficult.

Trembling, he gazed at the friend who every day risked his life to provide the children with sufficient food. It was he who had saved countless children from drowning. Tirelessly he had driven his body with the one aim of making the journey as bearable as possible.

Dolf sighed and turned away. In the sick-camp he made a tour of the beds but he said nothing to Hilda or to the monk kneeling beside a dying child. Tomorrow, they would move on.

Tomorrow he would see all his efforts of the past week rendered quite useless by Anselmus's absurd desire for speed. How could one talk any sense into a man like that?

The kneeling monk stood up and then stooped over the straw bed. He folded the hands of the dead child around a crucifix made of twigs. Gently he closed the lids over the staring eyes and turned around.

He suddenly felt the eyes of the Benedictine watching him. He turned to face the man and was greeted by a look of extreme benevolence from a pair of clear, blue eyes.

"Y-ou!" stammered Dolf, remembering the monk who had comforted him on the night the disease had first been recognized.

"Yes, my son.

"How did you get here?"

"Walking, like the rest of you."

"From Rottweil?"

The monk looked at him with a kindly expression.

"No, my son. I have been a companion of yours for the past two weeks."

Dolf's mouth fell open.

"But how come I haven't seen you?"

"Maybe I'm the sort that does not get noticed," the monk said with a grin.

"Who are you?"

"Dom Thaddeus. I am from the Haslach monastery."

"Where is that?"

"East of Strasburg. You passed by the monastery."

Dolf recalled that they had seen several abbeys in the tall mountains of the Black Forest. This monk must have come down from one of them, but Dolf had not even noticed, except for that one moment, outside the walls of Rottweil, when this strange man simply appeared by his side and lifted some of the burden from his shoulders.

Exhausted as he was from overwork and worry, Dolf gave way to a strong desire to share his troubles with this kindly man. Perhaps also he would find an ally in his conflict with Anselmus and Nicolas.

"Dom Thaddeus, could you spare me a little of your time?"

"Of course, my son."

They walked to the edge of the sick-camp and seated themselves on a large rock.

"What is it that troubles you?"

Dolf pointed to the four rows of straw beds.

"Father, I know what causes this horrible disease. Tiny animals, sent by Satan and so small that you cannot see them, have jumped onto these children. There are a great many of them, because Satan is so powerful."

Dolf tried hard to express himself after the fashion of the times.

"Dom Thaddeus, these animals are very dangerous. They penetrate the throats of unsuspecting little children and creep further into the blood, where they destroy the child's health. You can't catch them and kill them, because they are too small. The only way to fight them is to make certain that they do not reach the children in the first place.

They can be killed with large quantities of clean water, fire and smoke. If they attack a child one of two things will happen. If the child is strong and healthy his body can resist the attack. If he is not, the child will fall ill. An attack on a healthy child will fail because these devilish hordes will drown in his pure blood and he will recover. Unfortunately it is the very small children, many of whom are already weak from hunger, fatigue and other diseases, who have the least power to resist and they will die. Do you understand this, Dom Thaddeus?"

The monk nodded silently. Dolf took a deep breath and continued:

"As soon as one of the victims has died these satanic animals try to jump onto another child. That is why all those affected had to be isolated from the rest and also why the beds in which they die have to be immediately burned, because they too are infected with the little devils. I have ordered all those who are unaffected to bathe frequently, eat well and drink strong herb tea, so that they would build up their strength and be able to resist an attack.

"It is a battle, Dom Thaddeus, a long and bitter one, because the Devil does not, as you know, surrender quickly. And we had almost won, for there have been no new cases over the past two days and most of the patients are recovering."

"Yes, God has destroyed these devilish hordes," Dom Thaddeus agreed. Dolf tried to control his temper.

"Indeed father, we must thank God for that. He has given us warm sunshine and mild nights, because He took pity on the sick children lying in the open fields. He has also blessed us with the ability to realize that all the infected children had to be isolated. But these agents of the Devil have not yet been completely defeated.

"That is why Satan has whispered falsely in the ears of Nicolas and the other monks that they should continue the journey again. But if that happens, there will be a disaster because the sick and the healthy will mingle together again and the animals will be able to jump from one to the other … Do you see? It must be prevented."

"My son, God is infinitely more powerful than the Devil. If it is His wish that we do not depart, then He will prevent us."

I'm getting nowhere fast, thought Dolf desperately. "Do you not believe that those animals are Satan's agents?"

"I believe you because I have seen that your measures are successful. I am glad that God has given you the medical knowledge and good sense to fight this evil. But, my son, why can you not have a little more faith in His good leadership? The Almighty in Heaven will protect us."

"Yes," Dolf responded, "but only if we show ourselves worthy of that protection."

Shocked, the monk stared at the boy. Dolf continued timidly:

"The love of God is immense, but is it not so that He has no patience with foolish people? Anyone stupid enough to jump into deep water when he cannot swim will drown. God will not rescue him from his own foolishness."

"You come from the north, don't you? Did they tell you all that over there?" the monk asked suspiciously.

"Yes, father, and I know it is true. Leaving tomorrow would be unforgivable foolishness."

Dom Thaddeus shook his head in bewilderment.

"You are a strange boy, Rudolf," he murmured.

"Yes, I know, but that is not important. I simply don't want the children to meet with disaster. I do not want to see any more of them die than I have to. I want them all to reach Jerusalem safely.

"That is why I must fight, not just against these devils which bring disease, but also against the foolishness of Dom Anselmus. And I'm asking for your help."

Dom Thaddeus placed his hand on the boy's shoulder. "If everything you have told me is true, my son, God will prevent our departure. You must have faith."

Just then there came a call from Hilda and Dom Thaddeus got up and left. Dolf watched him go with great disappointment.

He is a good man, but I can't see that he will be much help, he muttered to himself.

It was time for supper. The last children were returning from their daily bath, chattering and laughing. The smell of cooking drifted over the camp and reached Dolf's nose. He suddenly felt very hungry. Wearily, he got to his feet and strolled over to his own section, where Maria was busy giving out the rations. Leonardo was nowhere to be seen.

They had all finished eating when the student at last appeared, sat down and hungrily began to eat his own portion.

"Where have you been?" asked Dolf.

"Oh, I thought today I should spend some time waiting upon our young lords and masters in their tent," Leonardo replied airily.

"What! They have got far too many helpers already."

"Yes, but they are all busy preparing for tomorrow's departure."

Dolf was suddenly overwhelmed by the weight of his worries. To the consternation of Maria and the others, he burst into tears. He did not see the student's knowing wink at Maria. Angrily he lay down with his back to the fire and closed his eyes. "I don't care what they do. If they are not going to listen to common sense, then that's their business, but it will be their downfall. I have done what I can."

THE HERETIC

They didn't leave the following morning after all. Around daybreak a large commotion broke out in the leaders' tent, where Anselmus and Augustus were found on the ground writhing with pain. Dom Thaddeus was called, but he could do nothing but pray for them.

"Call Rudolf of Amsterdam, he knows a lot about diseases," he told the others.

Barely awake, Dolf staggered to the tent and looked down in astonishment at the two monks, who were fighting for breath. Their faces were green and their mouths were twisted with pain. What was the matter with them? It certainly was not the fever.

Of the two, Anselmus seemed to be in a worse condition. He groaned that his stomach was in knots and fiery knives were piercing his intestines. Beads of perspiration stood out on his forehead and it was obvious that the man had never felt such agony in all his forty years. Dolf found himself almost pitying this man he hated. Nicolas stood looking on helplessly; Carolus was kneeling down by the sick monks.

"What is the matter with them?" he asked, looking up at Dolf.

"I don't know. Perhaps something they ate has upset them."

"But that can't be possible. We all had the same yesterday—boiled fish, grilled partridge and a bowl of herb tea. If it were the food, we'd all be sick."

He placed his hand over Anselmus's damp forehead and said consolingly:

"Don't be afraid, father. We won't leave you. Nor will you be expected to make the long march today on foot. We will carry you and Dom Augustus in the wagon with the other patients."

"We must postpone our departure," cried Nicolas.

"Why?" asked Dolf coolly. "We have many more patients who are seriously ill, but you didn't want to delay because of them. You made that decision yesterday, didn't you?"

Dumbstruck, Nicolas stared at him.

"But Rudolf ... look, they're in a very serious condition. They will not survive a journey," he shouted desperately.

"Neither will most of the other patients," said Dolf in an off-hand manner. He was enjoying the situation immensely.

"No, no," screamed Nicolas. "I don't want to go on, not now."

"All right, you are the one who makes the decisions," said Rudolf, as if reluctantly, but secretly his heart leaped for joy. "We will have them moved to the sick-camp."

Augustus found just enough breath to gasp a protest.

"No, leave us in the tent," he pleaded. "Stomachache is not contagious."

This remark made Dolf recall another word—cholera. Could this be the first symptoms of that disease? Dom Thaddeus came to his aid.

"Maybe it is contagious," he said. "I think, it would be safer for all of us if they were isolated from everybody else."

"And who will nurse them?" inquired Carolus indignantly.

"I will," said Dolf with determination.

Two new beds were laid out for the stricken monks, at a safe distance from the sick-camp. There they lay, doubled over with pain, while Dolf tended them all day long. The cramps not only caused them agony, but also diarrhea and Dolf had to wash their soiled habits himself, in a nearby pool. He fought off his disgust and refused to think any more about cholera, though in fact he could not help thinking that he should burn their clothes.

But later in the afternoon, when Leonardo came to see him, Dolf learned that there was no need for concern.

"You'd better keep away from here," Dolf called out as he approached. "We still don't know what it is."

The student grinned nonchalantly, came up and bent over to look at the sick men.

"Hm, quite serious, isn't it?" he murmured, with no attempt to conceal his satisfaction.

Dolf, missing the look in Leonardo's eye, pulled him to one side anxiously.

"You don't think it could be cholera, do you Leonardo?"

The Italian glanced at him derisively.

"Aren't you satisfied with the epidemic you have already got, Rudolf of Amsterdam? Don't mention that word again, because you are tempting fate. And do not trouble yourself over much. It isn't cholera, nor is it even a disease. Within a week the two of them will be fully recovered, I assure you."

"But how can you be so ..."

Leonardo shrugged his shoulders. "Oh, I just happen to know."

"You wretch," Dolf whispered, stifling the joy in his voice. "You put something into their food yesterday, didn't you? Some mixture or other, which was just enough to make them ill for a few days. Leonardo, I cannot say that I agree with your morals, but I will be grateful to you for the rest of my life."

"Just as you wish." The student grinned back.

In the sick-camp there were now seventy patients quickly recovering from the Scarlet Fever. For the rest there was little hope and they soon died. No new cases developed and Dolf knew that the battle had been won. He ordered the grave to be filled in and then covered with stones. Large fires were built and kept burning for twenty-four hours on the hill. A few days later the children erected a wooden cross on the pile of stones. It was a ceremony in which the many thousands of healthy children, as well as Nicolas and the three monks, participated. The shepherd boy addressed the gathering:

"Children, God has been merciful. He has vanquished the Scarlet Death which came among us. Moreover, He has saved the lives of the two holy guardians which He sent to guide me in leading this crusade. For all of this, we must thank Him, children. Tomorrow we will be able to continue our journey and soon we will reach the high mountains. Once we are across, we will come down to the sea, where God will perform His miracle. Let us pray."

Almost two weeks had passed. Even now Dolf separated all those children who had just recovered from the others and insured that they received extra rations so that they would quickly regain their strength. Still, he realized, his worries were barely over. Indeed, would they ever be during this journey? Hardly had one crisis been overcome, when another appeared. In this case, Nicolas was resolutely refusing to part with the wagon.

"We cannot do without it," he protested, when Dolf suggested that it should be pushed into the lake or burned.

"It must be destroyed," insisted Dolf. "It is contaminated. It has carried the patients and the dead bodies and it is now a great danger to us all."

"That is nonsense," said Nicolas. "That wagon was given to me by the Archbishop of Cologne. You are burdening your soul with a grave sin, if you say that it is a source of danger."

Anselmus and Augustus sided with Nicolas and Dolf's anger began to rise.

"What do you know about it?" he snapped.

"Why do you always behave as if you are our master, Rudolf of Amsterdam?" cried Nicolas. "Who are you anyway? You are forever disagreeing with us and ordering us about. Who gave you the right?"

"No one," Dolf shouted back. "But if that wagon is not destroyed, several hundred will die within the week. Is that what you want?"

Dom Thaddeus rested his hand on the boy's shoulder to console him.

"You must trust in God, my child. He is watching over us."

"Oh, you don't understand," said Dolf, stamping his feet with frustration. "You just don't want to understand anything. That cart is poison. It is no longer a gift from the Archbishop, but a vehicle of the Devil. If you insist on turning this crusade into catastrophe, then go ahead. But don't blame me when everything begins to go wrong ..." Once again he stormed from the tent in fury.

That very night the wagon went up in flames ... just like that. All that was left was a smoldering heap of ashes, charred wheels and twisted axles. The sentry said he saw no one suspicious near the wagon.

"Are you sure you saw no one?" Anselmus interrogated them with doubt in his voice. "Are you certain that Rudolf of Amsterdam was nowhere nearby? Or Leonardo, the merchant's son?"

"No one," the boys replied. "Dom Thaddeus blessed the wagon just after evening prayers, but apart from him no one came near."

Fredo glowered indignantly.

"Are you suggesting that my boys are lying?" he asked with a sharp edge to his voice.

With that, Dom Anselmus had to admit that the fire had been yet another trial inflicted on them by a higher power. A credulous fear was creeping into his heart. Whenever he opposed the wishes of Rudolf of Amsterdam, something went wrong ...

When Dolf heard the news he hid his great relief. He thought privately that Dom Thaddeus should be given the credit.

For many days they travelled along the north bank of the lake and through the hills, which gradually became steeper as they grew into mountains. To their right, they could see the massive mountain walls towering up to the sky, since, for the time being, they were not attempting to cross them, but were travelling east through the wide river valleys and the huge forests. The region was thinly populated, for the winters were cold and severe. Even now, in the middle of summer, the weather was unpredictable. Bright, sunny days were immediately followed by driving rain, freezing nights and icy fog. Dolf could not keep his eyes from the mountain barrier that blocked their escape to the south. One day soon they would be forced to attempt the crossing. How could one possibly hope to take eight thousand children across a mountain range many miles wide and ridden with ferocious animals? All that they had so far suffered would pale beside the horrors that awaited them in the mountains.

With these thoughts in mind and without consulting anyone else, Dolf ordered a few days of preparation before they entered the narrow valley leading to the Karwendel. Once again Anselmus protested most loudly at the delay.

"We have got to stock up," Dolf told him tersely. "Don't you want the children to get through the Alpine pass to Lombardy safely?"

When Nicolas, who always sided with Anselmus, once again voiced the opinion that God would protect them, Dolf snapped:

"Shut up, you fool. You have never seen anything but meadows and herds of sheep. I know the mountains and what we can expect."

With the aid of Leonardo and all his friends he set to work at once. They were encamped in a broad field, close by a small crystal-clear lake. Dolf dispatched Peter and scores of other fishermen with their home-made nets to the water's edge, with orders to fish the lake until it was empty.

Meanwhile the camp was transformed into a smoke house. As the fires were fed with damp wood full of resin, black clouds of smoke wafted over the heads of the children. As soon as the fish were brought up to the camp, they were cleaned, strung onto long poles and then smoked. They also dried or smoked the meat brought back by the hunting parties, cutting it first into long strips. From the gristle, bones and fatty remains they made a thick, greasy soup. For three days this was all they had to eat. The rest of the food was stored.

To the annoyance of a few of the neighboring farmers they also indulged in a little looting. But for the most part this was unnecessary, for it was going to be a good harvest and they preferred to negotiate for charity. Dom Thaddeus, always accompanied by fifty orderlies, visited the peasants in their farms and the knights in their castles. News of the vast army of children on its way to Jerusalem and the miracles which had occurred during their journey, had reached this place too. Hence, more out of fear than pity, the people were prepared to part with a small proportion of their harvest.

Sacks of millet, rye and barley poured into the camp. With crude implements the children ground the grain and baked it into hard, dry cakes. Their provisions were rapidly increasing and Dolf hoped that they would remain in an edible condition until they were across the mountains.

Meanwhile, minor dramas were occurring among the children daily. One of them concerned little Simon. Dolf found him crying his heart out and surrounded by a group of little girls who were trying to cheer him up.

Dolf guessed that Simon was about seven years old, for he was lacking a few of his front teeth. In Dolf's own century he would be a small, happy boy in elementary school. But here he was a crusader, subject to all the dangers of the open road, heading for Genoa. Pleadingly, the girls looked to Rudolf of Amsterdam for help.

"What's the matter?" asked Dolf, kneeling beside the miserable boy. It was difficult to make any sense out of the story, but eventually Dolf managed to extract from among the many sobs and sniffles that some of the elder boys had teasingly told him that when they crossed the mountains he would be eaten by enormous bears.

"Which boys?" asked Dolf angrily. "I will have them punished."

Simon's sobs subsided and he looked up at Dolf. He really was a pitiable sight with his tear-stained face and tousled hair.

"But what about the bears?" he protested with the relentless logic of a child. He fully approved that the boys would be punished, but he did not see how that would stop the bears from making a meal out of him. Taken aback, Dolf tried to think. It would not help to deny the existence of wild animals, nor was a vague promise of protection and security likely to appease him. Moreover, Dolf sensed that the boy's fears were to some extent shared by the girls.

Not quite sure what to say, he was looking around for help when he spied Leonardo.

"Come over here a minute," he called.

"What's the trouble?" asked Leonardo, leaning on his cudgel and gazing down on the children. "Is something wrong?"

"Leonardo, would you mind repeating to these children what you said in Nicolas's tent. You know, the evening we decided to take the Brenner route."

"What did I say then?"

"About the bears. Do you remember?"

"Oh that," laughed Leonardo. For a moment he stroked his mighty club and then, tapping it lightly on the ground and lowering his voice to a whisper, he said:

"My friend here is rather fond of seeing off bears."

The children were greatly impressed by this statement. They looked at the cudgel and then up at Leonardo who, in their eyes, seemed strong, tall and very powerful. They observed his relaxed manner and calm look in his eyes and, as one, they heaved a sigh of relief.

"… and if we do meet a bear," Leonardo continued with the air of a conspirator, giving his voice a dramatic tone, "then I will give him such a blow on his head that he will be dead before he hits the ground. I will remove his beautiful skin, head and all and will make it into a wonderful coat for you, Simon. Then you will be able to enter the Holy City in a bear skin, just like a king."

Little Simon could not help but laugh through his tears. He began gesticulating wildly with his arms.

"Ho, ho, ho, here comes the bear. We will kill you, ugly bear, we will kill you."

"That's it," said Leonardo. "That's just what we'll do."

Simon skipped away, still shouting:

"Ho, ho, ho, I am the bear, the big brown bear. I'm going to eat you." With his child's imagination, he could already see himself entering Jerusalem, dressed in a bear skin, the Saracens fleeing before him.

Frank, together with his group of tanners, worked like they had never done before. Dolf's stainless steel breadknife was proving invaluable for cutting leather. The fishermen, whose feet had softened from being immersed in water so much, were all provided with short boots made of deerskin. They were proud to be able to wear this distinctive mark of their "trade." Dolf's twentieth century shoes with their tough plastic soles were gradually beginning to wear through and it would not be long before he too would have to accustom himself to rabbit-skin slippers. Thirty warm capes had been made from the wool provided by the sheep, one of which Maria was lucky enough to be given.

It was on the eve of their departure for the mountains that Dolf made an error of judgment that provoked yet another outburst of rage on the part of Anselmus and Nicolas.

He proposed to slaughter the two oxen.

"They are beautiful creatures," he said to Nicolas, "but they will not be able to make the journey through the mountains. Tonight we could smoke their meat, which would be a useful addition to our supplies for later."

"The oxen!" cried Nicolas. "You are not going to lay a hand on my oxen."

Anselmus added with mounting anger:

"Rudolf, you have no right to make a decision about something which was a gift from the Archbishop of Cologne."

"No, you're right," Dolf replied calmly. "But I wasn't making a decision, only a suggestion. I know that they belong to Nicolas, but even he must realize that they can hardly be called mountain goats and will be more trouble than use."

A number of children had noticed that another quarrel was brewing between the leaders and Rudolf of Amsterdam. They left their work and gathered around eagerly. Dolf pointed at the entrance to the gorge which loomed dark and threatening above the children.

"How do you think you can take them through there, Nicolas?" he asked.

Nicolas lost his temper.

"Rudolf of Amsterdam, you are nothing but a trouble-maker and forever challenging me. Why? Who is the leader here, you or I? You say you want to help the children reach

Jerusalem as soon as possible, but all you do is cause delays and spread mistrust."

"Exactly," continued Anselmus. "One day, you suddenly appear as if from nowhere, a complete stranger who has tried to usurp our leadership. Go back where you came from. We don't need you!"

Dolf looked about him and discovered a large crowd of children quietly watching the proceedings.

He straightened his back, knowing that they were impressed by his height. On that afternoon, he wore nothing but his ragged jeans. The sun had tanned his skin and the heavy work had toughened his muscles. His once smooth boyish face had acquired new, grim lines. Dolf did not realize that he presented a picture of a strong, young athlete.

"No, you don't need me, that is obvious," he said sarcastically, but with pride. "What have you done to prepare for the trip over mountains tomorrow? Have you laid in provisions? Have you encouraged the children to take any precautions? The answer to all these questions is simple ... no. Praying, yes, you have done plenty of that. But spare one thought for the road ahead, just one precautionary measure in case of trouble? No, not once. Only I have done that."

The crowd around them was growing ever larger and newcomers were informed in whispers of what was happening. Some walked away fearfully, but the majority pressed closer, hanging on every word. They were predominantly the smaller children, for the older ones were down at the lake and or out hunting. Frank had taken his tanners down to the town to clean skins. The orderlies were chopping wood half a mile away. Everyone had a task and energetically carried it out. In the camp itself, there remained only the cooking teams and the very young, all of whom were now congregating around the argument.

"The children have never had need of you, Rudolf of Amsterdam," said Nicolas with a superior tone. "God is watching over us. He will feed us and give us the strength to overcome all our trials."

The children gathered around, nodded their hands in pious agreement. Dolf raised his head and in a clear, but cold voice said:

"But God also expects us to help and think for ourselves."

"You talk like a heretic," growled Anselmus.

At last the word, which had been on the tips of so many tongues for weeks, had been spoken.

Recklessly, Dolf responded:

"Don't try to threaten me, Dom Anselmus. It will get you nowhere. There is only one task for me to do—to rectify the mistakes which you make and which cause the children so much suffering. God is well aware how much time and energy I am giving to that."

Nicolas uttered a half-stifled cry of protest; he found Rudolf's attitude unbearable. Anselmus raised his hand in an authoritative and forbidding gesture.

"Rudolf of Amsterdam, you are an emissary from Hell. Clearly you are intent on leading us by false paths and preventing us from fulfilling God's holy will."

The children drew back in horror and Dolf thought he could see a terrifying question written in their expressions; is Dolf a servant of the Devil?

It was then that he realized that he was in danger. One word from Nicolas or Anselmus and these little children would probably tear him to pieces. Where was Leonardo and his reassuring cudgel? Where was Carolus? Where were all his friends and assistants?

Suddenly he remembered the Madonna which hung around his neck and grasping it, he kissed the primitive image.

"The Holy Mother protects me, you can not insult me without being punished, Dom Anselmus," he said menacingly.

"Do not blaspheme, Rudolf. Can you deny that you set fire to our wagon by means of magic?" the monk went on, with a steely edge in his voice. "And can you deny that you possess a knife which was forged in Hell's own dungeons, so that it does not rust or become blunt?"

Well, well, thought Dolf. I am a devil because I have a good breadknife. What will they think of next?

Apparently unperturbed, he allowed himself to be showered with accusations. He did not allow his stare to wander from Anselmus's face but fear continued to grow in his heart.

"You are a heretic, a devilish heretic, and so long as you are among us we will be pursued by disaster," Dom Anselmus concluded with a shout.

The children were murmuring. Nicolas stood silent and pale, but there was a glint in his eye. At last, this stranger from the north, who had stolen so much of his prestige, was unmasked.

Dolf too remained silent. He realized he could not hope to match the monk in a religious debate, because half the time he did not understand what the man meant. Further, he knew that the longer he said nothing, the better chance there was that Anselmus would say something that Dolf could turn to his advantage.

At that moment a few uncertain voices were raised among the children:

"Rudolf of Amsterdam is no heretic."

"Rudolf saved my little brother."

"Rudolf bears the Holy Virgin on his chest and I have seen him pray."

They were but a few, cautious, defending voices which were soon drowned by the muttering and whispering of the rest. But Dolf had heard them and they had given him courage. Not all the children were against him ... not yet.

Anselmus had heard them too and laughed mockingly. He decided to intensify his accusations.

"You wear clothes the like of which none of us has seen before. When you first appeared, you spoke a language no human ear has ever heard. When others fall ill, you stay healthy. When others are exhausted, you still have energy left. And when everyone is asleep," Anselmus's voice had reached an almost hysterical pitch, "you slink from the camp and go to your trysting place to make sacrifices to your master—Satan! I have followed you, Rudolf of Amsterdam. I have spied on you and seen the most terrible things, which I cannot possibly mention here in front of these innocent children."

Dolf looked quite unconcerned. His opponent had resorted to lies, which was a sure sign of weakness. All right, he thought, it is time to reply to this fine fellow.

"Dom Anselmus, I remember that the High Canon of Rottweil called you an impostor, a fraud, but at the time you did not deny the charge. Why not?"

"Would you expect me to answer such insulting accusations?" retorted Anselmus, though he was clearly a little perturbed.

"No, but then neither should you expect the same of me. I do not wear a habit or white gown and I don't have time to kneel down and pray at the least sign of trouble. But that does not mean that I'm a heretic, even less a servant of Satan. Do you dare deny that it was I who brought the children bread, when the pitiless people of Rottweil were prepared to let them starve? Do you dare deny that it was I who arranged for their injured feet to be covered with rabbit skin? Can one of these children, whom you are so cunningly seeking to impress with your fine words, accuse me of heartlessness, cruelty or selfishness?" He turned round to face the crowd. "Children, did I ever beat you or kick you or curse you?"

"Never," some of them called back. "Rudolf of Amsterdam has always cared for us like a true and good master."

A little boy emerged from the crowd and went to stand by Dolf's side, grasping his hand.

"Rudolf is a hero," he said in a clear voice. It was Simon. The thought of the bears in the Karwendel may have scared him, but he was quite undaunted by the monk and the holy shepherd boy.

Simon's intrusion into the affair at once swung the general feeling behind Dolf.

Eagerly they awaited Dom Anselmus's next assault, but it did not come. Instead Nicolas's shrill voice cried out:

"So long as Rudolf of Amsterdam remains among us, we will never reach the sea!"

This remark was instantaneously greeted by a grumbling discontent among the children and the situation was once again looking serious for Dolf.

"If we tolerate this child of the Devil, God will desert us," Nicolas went on, raising his voice.

"God has already sent us a warning—the Scarlet Death. He has also sent us bad weather and numerous other problems. And He will continue to send us calamities, so long as Rudolf of Amsterdam and his evil ways are trying to prevent us from reaching the Holy Land."

The murmuring grew in intensity and the throng pressed forward threateningly.

I must gain time, thought Dolf desperately. If it goes on like this, Nicolas will talk the children into lynching me ...

"Wait," he called aloud, raising his arms high above his head. With a look of stern authority he stared at the irate children. "These are serious accusations. Nicolas and Dom Anselmus have a right to charge me with heresy and devilish practices, but they do not have a right to sentence me without a proper trial. It is not enough simply to accuse someone. There must be proofs. Therefore, I demand a fair trial at which all the children are present. I promise to subject myself to the final sentence, whatever that may be. I will not try to escape. But I demand that I be tried fairly and this very evening. I am not frightened, because an innocent person has nothing to fear. God will protect him—and I am innocent. That is all that I have to say."

With these words Dolf turned his back on Nicolas and stepped straight toward the circle of children, who immediately drew back to let him pass. Without looking back, he stalked to his own fireplace and sat down by the cold ashes.

"Guard him!" he heard the shrill voice of Nicolas call out. "He will have his trial tonight."

"Good," thought Dolf with relief, "that means I have several hours in which to prepare myself."

The children scattered their separate ways and about twenty of them, armed with clubs, formed a circle around Dolf and his fire. He did his best to ignore them. Neither did he betray the fear that was mounting inside him.

How important was a charge of heresy to these people? To what extent would he be able to count on his friends or the gratitude of the children? It was beginning to seem to him more than likely that they would reject him and sentence him to be burned to death.

Poor Dolf. If only he had understood a little more about the medieval mentality, he would not have been quite so worried. He would have known that he could completely rely on the unshakable loyalty of his friends, a loyalty that they would not desert, either out of superstition or fear or even under a threat to their own lives. But Dolf was a child of the twentieth century, an age when opportunism and betrayal were rife. A time when the word of honor or a sworn oath meant nothing, when friendship or solidarity had little value.

Behind him, the sheer rock-faces and jagged peaks of the Alps towered up, a wall of menacing blackness, concealing yawning chasms and roaring waterfalls. In the morning the children would begin their ascent of the mountain range, but this very evening it would be decided whether or not Rudolf of Amsterdam would be their leader. Dolf sat with bowed head, conscious of a strange unknown feeling, which irresistibly forced words to his lips: "Help me, Saviour of the weak and oppressed, help me ..."

Dom Thaddeus stood by the little lake watching the children fishing. It was one of his favorite pastimes. He enjoyed the sight of their youthful and vigorous bodies dragging the nets through the water. He smiled at their jubilant cries when the nets came up laden with fish. He even laughed at their groans of disappointment when a net snapped, allowing the silvery catch to escape. To him, everything he experienced was further evidence of the boundless love of God.

Dom Thaddeus had a great love for children, which was why he travelled with them, determined to help whenever he could. Shortly after joining them in the Black Forest, he had noticed a boy whose height and commanding manner indicated that he must be of noble blood—a born leader. Initially, Thaddeus had thought that this must be Nicolas, the shepherd boy, and he felt his heart go out to him. It was some time before he discovered his error.

Nicolas was easily recognizable from a distance by his pure white gown, his fanatical stare and an air of importance which was rather studied and did not suit him. Thaddeus was very disappointed. Who then was that other striking boy? During the three days it took them to reach the town of Rottweil, the monk noticed many contradictions. Young Rudolf, who was clearly the son of a nobleman, did not sleep in the tent with the other high-born children. He seldom spoke to Nicolas or the two priests and when he did, there was an argument. Thaddeus learned that this mysterious lad came from the north and had joined the children's crusade along the way, immediately making his presence felt. He spoke hardly any Latin, but seemed, nevertheless, to be some kind of scholar; a much travelled and courageous miracle doctor, yet one who never went hunting or fishing, who did not participate in baking or tanning or weaving blankets. Still, he was always active. Wherever children needed advice or help, he could be found. He was the organizer and the one who made decisions and the children obeyed him unhesitatingly. Dom Thaddeus had never seen such an air of authority in one so young before. But how old was Rudolf? He had the face of a boy, the body of an adult and the wisdom of a hermit ...

It was only when he found him crying by the wagon outside Rottweil that Dom Thaddeus realized that he was a child after all. But was he crying for himself? No, he was crying because of the threat of the Scarlet Death to the children and because he could foresee the great misery they would have to suffer. He had been amazed by the energy with which Rudolf had fought the epidemic and when the other two monks refused to have the contagious wagon burned, Dom Thaddeus realized there was only one thing for him to do: to insure that the boy's wish was granted. Only then could the children continue their journey happy and healthy.

But from where had Rudolf of Amsterdam acquired his knowledge of medicine? How could he know what no one else did—the cause of the Scarlet Death?

Deep in thought, Dom Thaddeus stared at the children fishing. Indeed he loved them all with their innocent faces, high-pitched voices and dancing feet, immensely. But this was as nothing compared to the deep affection he felt for that one, mysterious boy: Rudolf of Amsterdam. And that troubled him, for he feared that he might be committing a sin. It was his duty to love all children equally and not one more than the others. Thaddeus, an intelligent but humble man, asked God to forgive him for his preference.

He was also troubled by Rudolf himself. The boy was so ill-informed on matters of religion. With his innocent face he could say things which made Thaddeus blanch. Was he a heretic?

Secretly, Dom Thaddeus had little respect for Nicolas and the two monks who had set out from Cologne with the children's army. But he never thought to question their holy mission, as did Rudolf ... and in public. Thaddeus knew that he ought to love both Anselmus and Augustus like brothers. It was due to Rudolf and his insinuations that he felt unable to do this. And it bothered him. Moreover, Thaddeus could see that the conflict between Rudolf and Anselmus would one day reach a crisis and he was unsure whose side he should take. It was his duty to support the Church and therefore Anselmus. But on the other hand, there was his great affection for the boy ...

The children loaded the day's catch onto the mule and moved off singing in the direction of the camp. Leonardo waved cheerfully to Dom Thaddeus as he passed, but the monk did not notice. With bowed head, he followed the band of fishermen; an honest man, torn by doubts.

The Children's Tribunal

When Carolus returned from his hunting expedition, he found an uneasy calm in the camp. Some silently stirred the cooking-pots, while others stacked the dried and smoked fish and tied them into bundles with string made of hemp. Even the little ones were quiet. They were playing with their usual toys—dolls made from fir-cones, sticks and twigs—but they were not shouting or romping around.

"What's going on?" he asked with concern. "Anyone would think you were going to a funeral."

The children looked at him timidly, but said nothing. This annoyed him. Normally the whole camp would excitedly greet the return of the hunters. Angrily he threw down the rewards of his day's effort and stomped off to find Rudolf. He would know the cause of this depression. But Carolus did not see the tall figure of his friend anywhere, nor did he hear the familiar voice issuing orders. He did notice a crowd of children gathered together and he strode toward it.

"What's happened? An accident? Does anyone need help?" The children stepped aside and there was Dolf, sitting on the ground by himself. He appeared to be praying. He was bent over and did not look up, not even when Carolus planted himself squarely in front of him and shouted:

"Rudolf of Amsterdam, look at your king when he addresses you. What has happened?" Then, forgetting all his dignity, he knelt down, took Dolf's hands in his own and whispered anxiously:

"You're not ill, are you? Oh Rudolf, don't leave us."
Dolf lifted his head.

"Carolus ..."

"What is it? Has there been an attack on the camp? Are you hurt? Say something, please."

"Carolus, I have been accused. Tonight Dom Anselmus intends to prove that I am a heretic and a servant of the Devil."

"You! My most loyal servant! My best friend!" yelled Carolus. He gesticulated frantically and was leaping around with fury. "I will not permit it. I, king of Jerusalem, will forbid it. It's ridiculous! Who accused you? I will have him quartered and thrown into the dungeons. He will beg for mercy. Tell me, who dared to accuse you?"

"Nicolas."

Flabbergasted, Carolus came to a halt in the middle of his dance, perched on one leg. Slowly, he closed his gaping mouth, lowered his leg and tried to digest the information. Then he shook his head in disbelief.

"It must be a misunderstanding. Perhaps the nitwit who accused you happens to be called Nicolas. But never mind, I will soon have it straightened out, Rudolf."

Dolf shook his head.

"There is only one Nicolas here who would dare to challenge me."

"Not the Nicolas?"

"Who else?"

"But that's impossible! It's sheer madness! I have never heard anything so ridiculous! The minute I turn my back to other affairs, trouble is stirred up amongst my knights ... I won't allow it."

With the speed of an arrow from his own bow, Carolus raced off to get more information. Dolf watched him with a smile. If there was anyone in the camp whom he loved more than Maria, it was Carolus, the clown with the heart of gold. But Dolf was well aware that if it came to a serious conflict the little hunter would be powerless. He was remarkably adept at playing the king; quick, clever, inventive and everyone admired him. But he was too much of a comedian to be taken seriously—a joker in fine clothes whom Anselmus would brush away like a troublesome fly.

Leonardo and Dom Thaddeus returned with the fishermen. There was now more life in the camp, because the tanners had arrived back also. The news of the impending trial had caused great excitement. Frank made a fiery speech to his group, brandishing the breadknife which he had borrowed from Dolf. Peter urged the fishermen to immediately lodge a protest against the accusation.

A short while later Maria, accompanied by the henchmen and a group of girls, their baskets laden with berries, turnips and herbs, learned of the incident. She wanted to run straight to Dolf, but Dom Thaddeus prevented her.

"Wait," he said commandingly.

"Why?" she cried frantically. "How can they dare to accuse Rudolf of Amsterdam? May God punish them."

"God punish Nicolas?" he asked reprovingly.

Maria paled and stared at the monk.

"Nicolas!" she said shrilly.

"Nicolas and Dom Anselmus have voiced the accusations and a trial will be held tonight."

Maria sniffed contemptuously.

"They won't be able to prove anything. Rudolf is no heretic."

"But Maria … you know that he is."

"I don't care," she screamed, stamping her feet, "And if they sentence him to the stake, I will die with him."

"Let us pray for him," suggested Dom Thaddeus, trembling slightly.

"I don't want to pray! I want to go to Rudolf," she cried and ran away.

She took some food to Dolf and for the next two hours sat beside him in silence, while Leonardo wandered the camp, trying to assess the climate of opinion. Many of the children were completely bewildered by the happenings. Others said that they had always thought that Rudolf was "strange" and not very pious, but they also agreed with Leonardo when he encouraged them to remain loyal to their master—their new master, Rudolf of Amsterdam. Nevertheless, they secretly shook with fear at the mention of the word heretic, wondering what it meant to be a servant of the Devil.

More than anyone else, Dom Thaddeus was greatly distressed. The thought of Rudolf being in danger made his heart quail. But at the same time he knew that the accusation was justified. In the middle of his doubts he came to the realization that the clash between Rudolf and Anselmus was inevitable, but he had not expected it to happen just now. It was as if the conflict had occurred at the wrong time.

Dom Thaddeus was right. Anselmus had indeed made a mistake, which he was now bitterly regretting. He realized that the children's army still needed the boy. Behind the camp the Alps glowered threateningly, and if anyone could lead the children over the mountain pass safely, it was Rudolf of Amsterdam. As far as Anselmus was concerned the greater the number of children reaching Genoa in good health, the better. But in a moment of anger the accusation of heresy and blasphemy had escaped his lips in the presence of a crowd of the children. There could now be no going back. It was imperative for Anselmus to bring about Rudolf's downfall. Angrily he strode around the camp, followed by countless pairs of terrified eyes.

Dom Anselmus took great care in choosing the site

where the trial would take place. A short distance from the camp was a field which sloped gently down toward the lake. It would provide enough room for the spectators and there was a large boulder near one end.

On this stone sat Nicolas dressed in his shining white robe. Next to him was Carolus, dangling his legs. He was wearing all his finery—the beautiful red cloak, his silver-studded belt with the magnificent dagger and his beret bedecked with feathers. Dom Augustus sat beside him, looking miserable, and Dom Anselmus was on the other side of Nicolas. The other aristocratic children were seated at the foot of the rock. Behind this court a hundred orderlies were arranged in a semicircle, each one holding a flaming torch, for dusk had already settled. The boys were standing at attention, their eyes fixed in front of them.

Directly in front of the boulder was an open space where Dolf now stood all alone. Behind his back row upon row of children filled the field. The smallest were at the front and the tallest toward the back, but since the ground sloped everyone had a clear view of the proceedings.

People in the Middle Ages were very fond of grand occasions and displays of power and even though the life of Rudolf of Amsterdam, whom they admired, was at stake, the children were greatly enjoying their part in the occasion. Anselmus was aware of this and intended to put on such a performance that they would be left in no doubt as to who was the real leader.

The trial opened with Nicolas standing on the stone announcing the accusations against Dolf. His clear voice carried far out over the assembly.

"It has been proved that Rudolf Hefting of Amsterdam is an emissary of Hell. He makes sacrifices to devils and demons. He has tried to destroy our holy crusade with diseases and pestilences. He ..."

Quickly Dolf raised a hand and shouted:

"None of these things have been proved, Nicolas. You must provide evidence."

A loud grumbling arose behind him. A defendant was supposed to keep quiet and speak only when he was asked a question.

Dom Anselmus jumped to his feet and bellowed:

"Is it true, Rudolf, that you come from the province of Holland, far away in the north?"

"Yes," Dolf replied calmly. Suddenly he was no longer frightened. This trial was so bizarre he felt that it could not be real. It was as if he were taking part in an exciting television program and, as everyone knows, the hero always wins in the end in such adventures. This idea gave him some confidence.

"Is it also true that you joined the crusade in Spiers and not at the outset in Cologne?" Anselmus continued his cross examination.

"Yes."

"How did you get to Spiers?"

"I was travelling," said Dolf.

"Alone?" asked Anselmus disbelievingly.

"I was on my way to Bologna with my good friend Leonardo Fibonacci."

"Can Leonardo, son of the merchant Bonacci, second that statement?"

Silently the student stepped forward into the circle of light and calmly looked at the accusers.

"I am here."

"Where did you meet Rudolf of Amsterdam?"

"I was travelling from Paris to the southeast when I was attacked by robbers. Rudolf of Amsterdam saved my life. It is thanks to his courage that I can stand here now and bear witness to his honesty, devoutness and intelligence."

The children murmured with approval. They were very fond of Leonardo and especially his mule.

"Tell me, why did you two join the children's crusade?" asked Anselmus.

"Just before we reached Spiers we came across the children and took care of some that were lagging behind. Then we were refused entry into the town and, since the children were following the same route as we were, we decided to join them."

"I cannot see why you should have decided that," sneered the monk.

"But I can," Leonardo answered calmly. "The children were suffering unspeakably. They were poorly dressed and stumbled forward on bleeding feet. We saw some collapse and die by the side of the road and no one bothered to bury them. It seemed to us that the leadership was failing and that we could be of use. We were certainly right. But then we were only doing our duty as Christians."

With this speech Anselmus was in danger of becoming the accused rather than the accuser. Sensing this, he ordered Leonardo to return to his place.

"It has now been proved that both Rudolf of Amsterdam and Leonardo of Pisa joined us along the way and like everyone else they were made welcome. But, Rudolf, who gave you the right to assume the leadership of our crusade? Who gave you the right to give orders to the children?"

Dolf threw back his head.

"No one," he said clearly. "I took it upon myself. But I did not force any child to do anything he did not wish. I have allowed them all to choose their own tasks and for this I have eight thousand witnesses."

The children cheered happily and applauded. They were enjoying every minute of the trial. Anselmus, however, would not be easily defeated and Dolf knew it.

"Rudolf of Amsterdam, do you dare deny that you possess superhuman powers?"

"Of course I dare deny it," cried Dolf. "I am the same

as everyone else. I would lose any fight to Bertho. In a tournament I would be no match for Carolus. Peter and at least twenty others can swim faster. And if you were clever enough to examine us, you would discover that Leonardo has a far greater knowledge than I. I simply possess common sense and a strong body. Since when has that been a crime?"

The children were roaring with laughter but Dolf raised his hand and asked for silence.

"I am strong and do not often get ill, is that a sin? Health, good sense and strength are gifts from God for which we cannot be too grateful. I thank God for them every day."

That at least should convince them of my piety, he thought. But Anselmus sneered at him.

"You thank God? When? You have been with us for more than four weeks and few have ever seen you pray. I myself have seen you pass by the houses of God and not once did you make the sign of the cross. Rudolf of Amsterdam, there are eight thousand children here who can testify that you are a heathen."

Dolf did not feel like defending himself against facts that were essentially true.

He responded in a loud voice:

"I do not serve God with a superficial show, but with my heart."

"Well spoken, my son," said Dom Augustus, nodding at him in a friendly manner.

But the children were no longer cheering Dolf and it made him feel uneasy.

"So, you did not have time to pray, I suppose?" said Anselmus sarcastically. "Perhaps you were too busy playing the big lord?"

Dolf was furious.

"You're talking nonsense," he fumed. "But it is no business of yours, or anyone here, where I come from or how many times a day I cross myself. What is important is whether I have helped or harmed these children and I tell you that I have done them no harm whatsoever!" He turned to face the assembly, spreading out his arms. "Children, have I ever whipped you? Did I ever beat you or kick you or curse you?"

"No! No! No!" they yelled enthusiastically. For the moment Dolf was the champion, once again the children's hero.

"Did I give you food?"

"Yes! Yes! Yes!" the chorus replied.

"Who has nursed the sick? Who dispelled The Scarlet Death? Who has protected the small and the weak?"

"Rudolf of Amsterdam!" hysterically they cheered. "Long live Rudolf!"

With a flood of relief he thought, "I have won." But he was wrong.

"Silence!" roared Dom Anselmus and at once the children fell quiet, because they were pleased that the fight was not yet over.

The monk drew a deep breath and with all the venom he could muster, began speaking:

"My dear children, let me reveal to you the true intentions of Rudolf of Amsterdam, which he has hidden behind the cloak of pretending to help you. With the cunning of the devil he has tried to lead you away from the right path. Time and again he has caused delays, because he does not want you to reach Jerusalem. He has spread his malicious rumors and has aroused his friends against Nicolas. He has openly denied that Nicolas is the chosen messenger of God. He has proclaimed that the sea will not divide before him, but that the crusade will be engulfed by the waves. Listen to me, children, for I am your ordained adviser. Do you want to go to Jerusalem? Do you wish to save the White

City which is being ravaged by the evil Saracens?"

"Yes," shouted the children. "To Jerusalem!"

"So how should we punish those who try to prevent us from carrying out our holy mission?"

"Beat him to death! Stone him! Hurl him into the lake with his hands tied! Burn him at the stake! ..."

The suggestions of torture and methods of execution were inexhaustible. "Being broken on a wheel, hanging, being thrown over a precipice, being torn apart by the oxen." Dolf could not understand. They were so imaginative. How could they suddenly wish to destroy a friend, whom, only a minute before, they had been ecstatically cheering? He had broken out in a sweat and his legs were trembling. Wildly he waved his arms:

"Prove it! Prove that I was trying to prevent the children from reaching Jerusalem." But his voice was drowned in the noise.

In fact, the children's outburst did not mean much. They were simply answering the question and were voicing their opinion of anyone who might try to thwart their desires to reach Jerusalem. Their fury was not directly aimed at Rudolf but he did not know that. To him it seemed to be the greatest show of ingratitude he had ever experienced. He was no longer fighting for their welfare, but for his own skin.

"Prove it!" he shouted above all the other voices. "Statements are not sufficient. Accusing someone is easy but it must be supported with proofs."

"Rudolf of Amsterdam, answer me honestly," said Anselmus. "Did you not bake hundreds of loaves of bread in one night with Satan's help?"

"Those loaves were baked by Gardulf of Rottweil. He was helped by his assistants, my friends and myself. I paid for the bread with all the money I possessed."

"Where did you get enough money to pay for eight hundred loaves?"

Dolf shrugged his shoulders in an off-hand manner.

"What student from a good family would set out to travel from Holland to Bologna without enough money? My father is a rich man ..."

This created among the children just the impression that Dolf had hoped.

"In Rottweil Gardulf the baker is known to be a heathen," shouted Anselmus. "He even has a heathen name."

"Nonsense," responded Dolf. "Gardulf is no more a heathen than you, Dom Anselmus. He is of Irish descent and you should know that Ireland is a stronghold of the Christian religion. It was the Irish who spread Christianity through Europe. You, as a monk, should also know that it was they who founded many of the finest abbeys. It was from these that the word of God began its triumphal march. And if you did not know these things, you are more of a fool than I thought."

"Rudolf of Amsterdam is right," said a voice from the crowd of children. It belonged to Dom Thaddeus. "The church is greatly indebted to the Irish missionaries. It is an honor to be of Irish descent."

Dolf grinned broadly.

"How did you know that Gardulf the baker is of Irish origin?" Anselmus continued, even though he had been taken aback.

"He told me during the night while we were doing the baking."

The miracle of the bread was still fresh in the minds of the children. Few had asked themselves, that morning outside Rottweil, how such a delicious breakfast had suddenly materialized, but now they knew. Rudolf of Amsterdam had provided it. Such things could be left to him, for he seemed to have an answer for all troubles, even hunger. They murmured and whispered to each other, pleased that they should have such a powerful protector.

"Those loaves were poisoned," shouted Dom Anselmus suddenly. "It was from that moment that we were afflicted by the Scarlet Death."

"That is a lie," Dolf shouted back furiously. "All the children ate it and so did you, Dom Anselmus, and myself, and Leonardo and Dom Thaddeus. It tasted excellent. You know very well, Dom Anselmus, that I did not bring the disease into the camp, but that, on the contrary, it was I who fought to rid us of it. But because you hate me, you are intentionally twisting the facts. This is not a trial, it's sheer deceit."

His last remark was a mistake and Dolf realized it at once. He knew he should be careful with his replies, but he could not find the energy. His twentieth century sense of freedom was rebelling against this mockery of justice and even though his life was at stake, he was determined that the truth would be known.

"You Devil! How dare you call an ordained priest a liar?" Nicolas suddenly cried.

"There is a lot more that I dare do," Dolf shouted back at him, having now completely lost his control. "I dare to proclaim that all your statements and accusations are empty shells. Every one is a lie and the children know it well. I am not trying to prevent them from going to Genoa. Why should I? I want to see the miracle just as much as they do. I want to be there when Nicolas stretches out his arms and the sea divides. Who wouldn't want to see that?"

"Then why are you continually trying to delay us?" Anselmus persisted.

"Because my honor forbids me to leave the sick and the weak behind without any help; because I cannot let children die from hunger and misery on the way. That is why. If that is a sin to show kindness to my companions, then I am prepared to do penance. But I am not prepared to allow myself to be insulted by people entrusted with the leadership of a crusade of children, but who have proved themselves to have absolutely no sense of responsibility for those in their charge."

From behind him there came a murmur of assent. The tide was turning in his favor again.

"You insult me, Rudolf of Amsterdam. And you insult God."

"That is not true. How can I insult God by looking after His children?"

All at once, Dolf pointed toward the frightened-looking Nicolas.

"Nicolas the shepherd, he is a saint. He has heard the voices of the angels. Let him say whether the evidence that Dom Anselmus has presented is sufficient for me to be sentenced. I will subject myself to Nicolas's decision."

Dolf had had enough and was trying to force a decision. He was relying on Nicolas's hesitancy, though he realized it was a dangerous tactic. If Nicolas decided to support Anselmus, then Dolf would be finished. But would the shepherd boy dare? Dolf had assessed from the noise behind him that the majority of the children were on his side. Nicolas was not so stupid not to have noticed it also. Would he dare to make an unpopular decision?

Nicolas sat down in bewilderment. Dolf stared straight into his eyes, unaware that behind him Frank and a large group of boys had edged toward the front. In his hand the little tanner was holding the celebrated breadknife, its blade glinting in the light of the torches. The other boys were holding razor-sharp stones and the pieces of iron with which they worked the leather. To one side, another large group of boys and girls carrying short spears, rusty needles and lengths of tough rope knotted at the end, had also stepped forward. At their head stood Leonardo, Peter and Maria. Fredo, who was standing by the torch-bearers, had raised one hand, as if on the point of issuing an order.

Nevertheless, there was absolute silence. Everyone awaited Nicolas's judgment. The shepherd boy could sense the menace in the crowd. The two monks had also noticed the hint of mutiny; Anselmus was pale, but Augustus sat smiling, his hands piously folded in his lap as if he were asking God to give Nicolas the strength to make a just decision. The tension mounted.

It was at this moment, however, that someone else chose to intervene—Carolus. While Nicolas weighed in his mind the "proof" which Anselmus had presented, the little heir to the throne of Jerusalem leaped to his feet. His red cloak glowed in the torchlight and his silver belt glittered.

"I protest at the way this trial is being conducted," he said in a loud voice. "It is not the task of Nicolas or the priests or anyone to sit in judgment here. That is the king's duty. I am your future king and I will not permit an innocent subject of mine to be sentenced, or one of my most valuable servants to be put to death. Children of Jerusalem, listen to me! I declare Rudolf of Amsterdam not guilty of heresy, blasphemy or any heathen practice, because he is a great leader, an honest boy and my most loyal servant. I do proclaim him guilty of a lack of respect and arrogance. But these are not serious crimes. They are small failings of which we are all occasionally guilty. Therefore, Rudolf of Amsterdam, I order you to kneel before this tribunal and ask Dom Anselmus to forgive you for insulting him this evening."

This, was, in effect, an astute move by Carolus and could well have brought a swift and happy conclusion to the affair, for the children's sense of justice would have been satisfied. Dolf gazed at Carolus in wonder and then nodded. He too thought that the little king was right and that the conflict would now be quickly terminated. He began to step forward ...

But Carolus's speech made Nicolas very angry. The dignity which had been bestowed upon him, the sudden change in his status from that of a simple shepherd to that of the leader of a crusade, the fact that he owned his own oxen, that he shared a tent with children of noble blood— all these things had encouraged in him the belief that he was the most important person in the entire army; the one whose word must be obeyed without further question. He felt Carolus was trying to take away all this.

"Be silent!" he cried, jumping up. His white robe billowed around him and in the flickering light it appeared bloodstained. "Your time has not yet come, Carolus. You will become king only after I have led you to Jerusalem. Until that moment this is my crusade! And I say that Rudolf of Amsterdam is guilty. He has signed a pact with the Devil and makes secret sacrifices to his abominable master. He has assumed the dress of a child in order to be one of us and he pretends to want to help us. But in fact, he has done nothing but cause us hindrance. He is guilty, guilty, guilty! Three times guilty! And I, Nicolas, missionary of the angels, sentence Rudolf of Amsterdam, the heretic, to death!"

As the roar rose behind him Dolf swivelled around expecting the children to hurl themselves upon him at any moment. But instead he saw his friends, menacingly brandishing their weapons. Beyond them he noticed that some of the children were pressing forward, eager to carry out the sentence without delay. Others hesitated uncertainly and many more were loudly protesting. A great commotion broke out, as the children started punching and yelling at each other. Above all others Fredo's voice could be heard shouting:

"Protect him!"

Leonardo, with fire in his eyes, brandished his cudgel and cried:

"Death to the traitors! Defend Rudolf!"

At that moment Dolf realized that the affair was on the point of developing into a bloodbath.

"Tear him to pieces!" screamed Dom Anselmus, stomping up and down on the rock.

"Don't touch him! Children, rescue your protector!" cried another voice.

The children had already begun fighting each other and although Dolf shouted at them to stop, there was nothing he could do. With angry snarls they leaped at each other's throats. Leonardo, wielding his great club, led a charge toward a group of children who were trying to get at Dolf.

"No!" screamed Dolf.

Then suddenly, in the midst of all, appeared Dom Thaddeus, his arms raised aloft. He called out in a loud voice:

"Stop! Silence! Silence! Don't touch him, don't touch him. Rudolf is innocent and I will prove it."

Repeating these words over and again, he shouted above the commotion until, curious to know what he had to say, the children gradually calmed down. The orderlies pulled apart those who were still fighting and picked up those who had fallen over.

"Be quiet! Dom Thaddeus is going to speak."

The Benedictine monk remained standing, not too far from Dolf in the mysteriously lit circle, his arms held high. He told Leonardo, Frank and Peter to move back a little, which they did, but slowly and not without protest. Then Dom Thaddeus took Dolf by the hand and led him forward up to the stone. Anselmus, who was standing above them, snapped at him:

"Didn't you hear the judgment of Nicolas, Dom Thaddeus? The sentence has been pronounced and the execution should be carried out forthwith. So why are you still interfering?"

Dom Thaddeus threw back his hood, so that the light glistened on his shaven head.

"You poor, misguided people," he said deliberately and loudly. "You are all fools! Utter fools! Do you not recognize an emissary of God when you see one? For that is just what Rudolf of Amsterdam is. He has been sent by Heaven to make sure that the children's army reaches the Holy Land safely. When God saw that Nicolas was incapable of fulfilling the task of feeding and protecting so many children, He sent another leader, Rudolf, with sole responsibility for the welfare of His children. Has not Rudolf of Amsterdam performed his duty diligently and with a heart full of love? When the Devil, angered by the children's innocence, sent his dark agents to inflict us with the Scarlet Death, it was Rudolf who repulsed them. It was Rudolf who brought us bread. And he brought us health, courage and strength. But now you, Anselmus, and you, Nicolas, dare to accuse this chosen one of heresy. Where is your shame? You have incited the very children who owe their lives to him to be his murderers. Is that how one shows gratitude to God for His mercy? I fear for the fate of your soul, Anselmus, and yours too, Nicolas."

Dom Anselmus was quivering with uncontrolled rage.

"Dom Thaddeus, your words are daggers to our hearts. Do not be misled. How can a heretic be an emissary of God?"

"God performs His will in many mysterious ways, Brother Anselmus."

"That is a mere excuse, Brother Thaddeus. You have accused us of failing to recognize Rudolf of Amsterdam as a missionary from Heaven. But how could we? By his piety? He does not have any. By his beauty? That is a temptation of the Devil."

The children, who were now quite still, pressed forward. They had forgotten their fight and were completely captivated by the spell of seeing the two priests locked in a duel.

"Dom Thaddeus," interrupted Nicolas vehemently, "you say this because you wish to protect Rudolf of Amsterdam, but you have no proofs."

"Oh yes I have," exclaimed Dom Thaddeus with equal determination. "You were able only to accuse, but I have proof, distinctly visible proof."

"Show us!" shouted Dom Anselmus hoarsely, staring anxiously at Dom Thaddeus's empty hands, as if he were about to produce a sealed parchment signed by God.

"Here is the proof," said the monk in a grave voice. He took Dolf's left hand and, rolling up the sleeve of his sweater, revealed … a scar.

When he had been little, Dolf had been bitten by a dog. The dog's teeth had pierced his forearm at three points and although the wounds had healed quickly, Dolf still bore the scars—three uneven dots on the underside of his arm. It was the kind of thing one hardly ever thought about and Dolf was astonished that the scar from a dog bite could prove his innocence. He stared blankly at his arm.

"There is the mark that God gave him—the sign of the Holy Trinity. Which of you fools will still dare to doubt? Can you not recognize the mark of God?"

The effect of Dom Thaddeus's revelation on the children was remarkable. They crowded forward to get a look and Dolf's arm was almost pulled off his body. They knelt down and kissed his feet; the tattered hem of his jeans and his hands; but most of all, they kissed the scar. He was almost squashed flat by the enthusiastic crowd. Those who, a few moments before, had called loudest for his death, were now among the most eager to touch him just once. Even Nicolas came down from the stone and, pushing the children aside (which at least gave Dolf some breathing space), said:

"Show me." Utterly bemused by all that was happening Dolf showed him the scar. It seemed quite absurd to him that three little white spots could make such an impression but he did understand that he was saved. He also realized that Dom Thaddeus's presence of mind had prevented a slaughter.

"Make way!" ordered Nicolas. The children moved back a little, but were still curious to know what would happen. The two "emissaries" were now standing face to face.

Nicolas grasped Dolf by the wrist and stared for a long time at the three white dots. He had seen such scars before on people who had miraculously survived an attack by a wolf. Had Rudolf battled with a wolf in the wintry forests of the north, before he became a crusader, and killed it? Was he that strong? Then Nicolas remembered all the threats his rival had uttered in the tent. There was the time when he cursed the two monks and almost immediately they both fell ill. And then, the very night on which he cursed the wagon, it went up in flames. Rudolf of Amsterdam seemed to have a power far greater than his own. He could not afford to have such an enemy and since it seemed impossible to destroy the boy (for who now would dare to harm Rudolf?), it would be best to have him as a friend. These were the thoughts that flashed through the mind of Nicolas. His peasant intelligence told him what he must do and silently he released Dolf's arm and knelt down.

A great cry of jubilation went up from the children. Anselmus looked down from his vantage point, nervously chewing on his lip. The fact that Nicolas was literally on his knees before Rudolf was such an immense signal of defeat for the monk that he would gladly have stormed off in a rage, never to be involved with the children again. Only the thought of Genoa stopped him.

Dolf considered Nicolas's behavior quite unnecessary. He did not like the shepherd boy, but neither did he wish to see him humiliated. Quickly he pulled the boy to his feet.

"Stand up, Nicolas," he said in a clear voice. "You don't have to kneel before me. Be my friend." And with that the two boys clasped each other.

The children were joyous. They laughed, danced and kissed each other. Those who had been fighting only a few minutes earlier were now the best of friends, their quarrels forgotten. A group of the stronger children raised Dolf onto their shoulders and carried him to the camp in triumph, followed by a relieved Maria.

It was very late before the camp became quiet again. The moon rose and the stars glittered. On the sleeping faces there was a contented smile. Tomorrow they would face the mountains but, with Rudolf of Amsterdam to lead them and with packs of food on their backs, what obstacle could stand in their way? Tired though he was Dolf could not sleep, for he was overexcited by the events of the evening. He felt Leonardo touching his arm. Would the student also now regard him as an emissary of Heaven? He dearly hoped not and then he heard a soft laugh.

"What was it? A large dog or a wolf?" Leonardo whispered. "A dog," replied Dolf quietly. "I was only four at the time ..."

"I bet you bawled your head off," Leonardo said mockingly in a hushed voice.

"I expect so. I can hardly remember, it was so long ago."

There was a short silence and then Dolf felt Leonardo whispering close to his ear:

"Nicolas is no fool. He used to be a shepherd boy and recognized those scars as easily as I did."

"Do you think so?" Dolf asked with surprise.

"And Anselmus ..."

"What do you mean by that?"

"That they saw through Dom Thaddeus's trick. You must continue to be on the watch, Rudolf, though for the time being you are safe. You have many friends and we will allow no harm to come to you, but..."

"Leonardo," said Dolf earnestly, "I don't have the slightest wish for there to be any disagreement among the children. I was delighted with Dom Thaddeus's ruse because we are all now united again."

"In that case you are going to be disappointed," whispered Leonardo. "Just wait until tomorrow ..."

"What's going to happen then?"

"Wait and see. But I promise you that Anselmus is in for a surprise."

For a little while Dolf puzzled unsuccessfully over what this hint might mean. But his thoughts kept straying to the mountains, whose dark shadows were now cast over the camp. Somewhere on the other side of the high ridges a thunderstorm rumbled.

To Dolf the Alps were a huge army which must be attacked and conquered and which he feared greatly.

"Tomorrow," he thought, "may Heaven protect us."

The Karwendel

It did not take long to break the camp the next morning, for it was now a matter of routine. In less than half an hour the children were divided into large groups, and, with the exception of the smallest, all the children carried packs of food as well as their clothing and rolled-up straw blankets. Dolf put on his coat. The jacket no longer closed properly, but it was waterproof and lined with wool; it could still give him good service in the mountains.

The sound of a commotion broke out on the edge of the camp and Leonardo, pursued by Dolf and Maria, ran toward it.

They discovered Fredo surrounded by a large group of children of all ages. Dolf recognized many of the orderlies, some of the hunters and fishermen and even a few tanners.

Anselmus stood in front of Fredo gesticulating with his arms. "Fredo, you are mad. You can't do it. There is nothing but wilderness up there in the north."

"I don't care," said Fredo obstinately. "We are not going a step farther. The wilderness cannot be as bad as the mountains."

"What's the matter?" asked Dolf

Fredo turned toward him.

"We no longer believe in this mission and haven't for some time. I have heard the farmers hereabouts saying that the sea does not lie behind these mountains at all. The original crusaders never came this way. This isn't the road to Jerusalem."

Of course this was not the first time that someone had

lost hope and turned back. But this was not an isolated case—there were hundreds in this group! Quite simply it was a mutiny.

As far as Dolf was concerned he would have been quite contented if all the children had gone home. He decided not to interfere; he was really happy to see that these children were able to make up their own minds and then stand by their decision.

"Where do you want to go then?" bellowed the monk with exasperation. "In the wilds you will come to a miserable end."

"Oh, I don't think so," replied Fredo confidently. "We are quite capable of looking after ourselves."

Dolf nodded in assent. "To the north lies the forest of Bavaria," he said, "and beyond that is Bohemia. The mountains there are of average size and heavily wooded. There cannot be many people living there and if you were to establish a settlement it would be possible to stay alive."

"That's right, go ahead and encourage them," Anselmus hissed and then in a more persuasive tone he said:

"Fredo, how can you desert your orderlies?"

"They can choose another leader," Fredo replied.

"But you will be torn to pieces by the wild animals in the woods," persisted Anselmus.

"We have weapons." Without another word Fredo turned around and beckoned to his followers. Dolf waved happily to the long file as it moved off in the opposite direction. He had confidence in Fredo, the son of an impoverished knight, for he was strong, courageous and cautious. Anselmus grunted and seemed on the point of saying something to Dolf, but instead he just stormed away.

When they had returned to their own campfire, Dolf asked Leonardo:

"Was that what you were referring to last night?"

The student nodded.

"Something like this has been brewing for a long time. Confidence in Nicolas and Anselmus has been shaken."

Dolf suggested to Leonardo that he take over Fredo's position, but the student was not too enthusiastic.

"I am on my way to Bologna; not to Genoa or Jerusalem," he said. The truth was that he did not particularly want a specific duty, for fear that it would impinge upon the freedom he enjoyed.

But Dolf, as obstinate as ever, insisted and eventually Leonardo agreed. He gathered the orderlies together and informed them of Fredo's decision not to continue and that henceforward they would be under his command. The announcement was greeted with a big cheer, because the children were fond of the student and even more so of his cudgel.

Nicolas gave the order for the journey to begin and more than seven thousand children marched in a long column past the stream and straight for the mountain barrier.

Leonardo and some of the orderlies were in the vanguard, while Dolf, Frank and Maria were in the rear. The road they were following was no more than a mule track and at most they could walk two or three abreast. The higher the winding path climbed the more Dolf wished the children to keep close to each other, with the taller ones helping the weaker to clamber over fallen rocks. It was also important to keep to the mountainside, for on the other there was only the drop down to the roaring stream.

Meanwhile the rain that had started as a drizzle that morning had become a downpour. The rain and the narrow path made the journey even more arduous for the animals. Only two hours after they entered the gorge one of the oxen broke a leg and had to be slaughtered. Dolf's heart was pierced with pity by the lowing of the helpless animal which, in spite of its plight, resisted the crude knives and axes with which the children tried to kill it. At last its cries of pain dwindled to nothing and they began to skin it. Once the skinning was completed, the animal was cut into pieces and the food-packs became even heavier.

Nicolas watched in silence, too proud to admit that he had been wrong when it had been suggested that the oxen be slaughtered.

After this delay, they set off again. At this point the gorge became still narrower and the stream thrashed against the rocks, sending fountains of foam cascading over the bushes and moss; the path was often blocked by large boulders which had rolled down from the upper slopes. Frequently those at the front were able to push these rocks over the precipice. But sometimes they could not be moved and the children had to climb over them. Many of the children had begun to shiver under the endless rain. But, more than anything, it was the continuous climb which sapped their energy. Every few minutes the entire file came to a halt while those at the front cleared some obstacle from the path. Then those at the rear would grow impatient and push forward, inquisitive to know what was happening. Children were forever losing their footing and injuring themselves on jagged stones, thorny bushes or sharp, pointed branches. Their arms and legs and sometimes even their faces were a patchwork of gashes and scratches.

The column was many miles long and it was impossible for the leaders to be everywhere at once. Leonardo, at the front, was totally unaware of what was happening behind him. His cudgel often came into use as a lever for toppling rocks over the edge. He was helped by a strong boy, called Wilhelm, who owned an axe with which he hacked off overhanging branches.

Behind the vanguard came children, more children and yet more children; the brave and the timid, the strong and the weak; boys and girls, some laughing some crying. But they all helped each other, giving encouragement or pointing out the cascades on the other side of the gorge, or giving warnings of loose stones, protuberances and roots hidden among the rocks.

Nicolas, Anselmus and Augustus were somewhere in the middle and never ceased urging the children to greater speed.

"We must be through the gorge before nightfall," Anselmus was continually shouting. "Hurry up children, we cannot spend the night here."

The children understood that quite well without him having to tell them. What they did not know was the length of the gorge. For the time being the end could not be seen.

The farther they went, the higher the mountains around them seemed to grow and ever the path climbed upward.

By mid-afternoon a large gap had appeared in the middle of the procession, where Nicolas was leading the remaining ox. But the animal was having great difficulty in managing the treacherous path. Some of the children were trying to urge it on with sticks. It was lowing with fear and for long periods refused to move at all. The sheep were less trouble but, driven by hunger, they frequently stopped to nibble the leaves of bushes.

Dolf was oppressed by the gorge. In his century there was a fine road that ran right through the mountain. But in this era there was only this laborious goat-track which wound around every protruding rock and sometimes disappeared completely.

The mountains were terrifyingly steep. On the lower slopes they were covered by tangled bushes and an occasional tree. But on the upper slopes there was nothing but naked rock, crags, jagged clefts and cascading waterfalls. Of course they did not see any other people. Sometimes Dolf noticed animals—chamois—moving among the ridges high above. There were also birds of prey, circling in the sky above the narrow gorge, larger than any he had ever seen before. Remembering pictures he had seen in old books, he wondered whether they might not be golden eagles. In the twentieth century they had almost become extinct, but here in the thirteenth, they were the lords of the Alps.

Carolus could not restrain himself from loosing an arrow at the birds, but it barely reached halfway, plumping aimlessly down into the stream.

"Save your arrows," said Dolf. "They will be needed."

The pack on his back was burdensome and he was hoping that his shoes would survive the journey. Maria walked lightly by his side. Her pack, which was mainly filled with cakes, was lighter. Dolf had made sure that she had a good pair of deer-skin boots and she looked very fetching in the coat of rough sheepswool. She seemed hardly bothered at all by the rain or the cold wind that howled about them. She leaped lightly over the stones and deftly climbed over the boulders. For her the journey was an exciting adventure. It occurred to Dolf that most of the children were looking a lot healthier than when he had first met them. They had grown tougher from the protein rich food, and the discomforts had steeled their muscles and the longing for Jerusalem had maintained their morale. Nevertheless, for many the journey through the gorge was a torture. Brought up in the plains or in lands of gently rolling hills, they were unprepared for the steepness of the mountain walls. Fearfully they pointed at the birds of prey circling above their heads and screamed whenever a boulder was toppled over the precipice to thunder down to the stream below.

The gorge was only about six miles long, but it took the whole day for the entire procession to traverse it. Then to the great relief of all they came into a wide valley, where, exhausted and downhearted, they immediately set up camp.

At this point there was quite enough room for them all, for the mountains, although still immensely high and growing even higher toward the south, retreated a little.

The slopes were more gentle and covered with forests. When Dolf finally emerged from the gorge with the rear guard, the fires were already blazing in the field. Nicolas's tent had also been put up.

Dolf immediately gave orders for the cooking teams to make large pots of soup from the fresh meat of the slaughtered ox, because he was worried that it would spoil. But this time he found it almost impossible to get the children moving. All their energy had been drained by the frightful journey through the gorge. Without caring about food or anything, many had fallen to the ground and were trying to sleep. Dolf and Leonardo, although they themselves were tired from the day's toil, attempted to create some order. Anyone who could still stand was pulled to his feet and set to work and they forced as many children as possible to eat.

"They must eat, whether they like it or not!" Dolf shouted to his helpers. Little children were roughly shaken awake to have soup poured down their throats and lumps of half-cooked meat pushed into their mouths. They did not even have the energy to resist. Hilda and her nurses toured the campfires bandaging injured arms and legs and distributing herb tea to any child who was coughing. By then it was already night.

Torch in hand, Dolf went off to inspect the orderlies and was deeply concerned by what he found. Many of those on the first watch of the night had fallen asleep, leaving the fires untended. To leave seven thousand children without protection was to tempt fate. Dolf hurried about pulling at arms and legs, hauling children onto their feet and reprimanding them severely.

"Who is on first sentry duty? Why are you sleeping?"

During the weeks of outdoor life his instinct had been sharpened and he sensed that the valley was dangerous. Every sound could be heard in the forest-covered flanks of the mountain. Wolves gathering for their nightly hunt were howling in the distance. The woods were full of the screams of wildcats, lynxes or birds frightened from their sleep by weasels. Dolf was suddenly struck by the ruthlessness of nature and realized that only the strong, clever and watchful could survive in this world. And did not that apply equally to the innocent little children under his care? For indeed, he now felt completely responsible for the children's crusade. For every accident, for every death, he blamed himself.

And today that burden had proved heavy. Through the tortuous miles of the gorge he had walked with but the one thought that he must get them all through safely. But he had failed. Right in front of his eyes he had seen a child fall into the stream and be carried away by the torrent. For two hours he had been frantically digging into the rock-slide with nothing but a stick and his bare hands—only to find one dead child. He had carried on his back children who had fallen down and when they were rested set them on their feet and picked up another. Had they all reached the end of the gorge safely? He could not tell.

Dolf knew that Leonardo, like himself, was not sleeping. He came across Peter, Frank, Wilhelm and Bertho, quivers on their backs and burning brands in their hands.

And where was Nicolas? Sleeping safely in his tent, of course, surrounded by the priests and little nobles. Nicolas put his trust entirely in God and with that his mind was at ease. But Dolf could not do that; his skepticism went too deep. He was a realist who had been brought up on words of warning:

"Take care when crossing the road ..."

"Never go with strange people, whatever they promise you ..."

"Keep clear of electric wires ..."

"Don't play with matches ..." and so on. A thousand warnings of danger had been burned into his mind and now kept him awake.

The camp was littered with half-chewed bones and uneaten meat. The packs of food were spilled everywhere. Could not these silly children realize that the food was precious, that their lives would depend on it? With a sigh, Dolf gathered the luggage into a pile and set a yawning boy to watch over it. No doubt he too would fall asleep as soon as Dolf turned his back. It was impossible to fight such fatigue.

The wolves had disappeared, apparently discouraged by the arrows and flaming torches. Nevertheless, Dolf could not rid himself of the feeling of great danger. He could not imagine what it might be, but he clearly sensed that something was going to happen; something quite unexpected and against which there was no protection.

"Go to sleep, my son, God is watching over us."

The voice was that of Dom Thaddeus, naturally, for he too never slept in the tent and felt the weight of responsibility as much as Dolf. But the monk had a greater faith in Providence and was therefore easier in his mind. How could the man be so calm? He too must have seen the children falling helplessly into the stream during the day.

That stupid monk and his beliefs—Dolf cursed the devoutness. He realized that this was unreasonable, but who does not become unreasonable when exhausted? Without noticing he had gone full circle and arrived back at his own campfire, where Maria stretched out a hand to him.

"Rudolf ..."

He dropped to the ground, resting his head in her lap. A tiny brown hand stroked his forehead and he fell into a deep and dreamless sleep.

The Kidnapping

The next day, awaking to shouts, Dolf jumped up in time to see about ten or fifteen mounted knights charging into the camp. They were dressed in coats of armor and tight-fitting trousers and they were armed with lances and swords. Dolf looked quickly for Leonardo and spied him with a group of a dozen boys or more, armed with cudgels. But he was unable to halt the riders' onslaught and could only run after them toward the tent.

"Hide in a bush," Dolf shouted Maria, who was beside him. "This is a raid. Don't show yourself to anyone."

He sprinted to the tent, where the riders had reined in their steeds.

Directly in front of the tent they were confronted by Nicolas, the three priests, Leonardo, his helpers and the children of noble blood. Carolus had already drawn his bow, though the arrow still pointed downward. His eyes were flashing with anger. Nicolas, hiding his terror, stood tall and straight in his white robe, facing the riders.

The leader of the band was speaking.

"Fifty," Dolf heard him say. "Thirty boys and twenty girls."

"God will punish you for this," Nicolas responded shrilly.

Dolf elbowed his way to the front until he was standing next to the shepherd boy and said:

"What's going on here?"

"That's a good one. We'll take him for a start!" shouted one of the riders. A horse was advanced right up to him and strong fingers felt the muscles of his arm. Dolf shook off the hand and retreated a step.

"What is all this about? What do these riders want?"

Leonardo's face looked gray as he answered:

"These are the men of Count Romhild of Scharnitz. He is demanding a toll from us to cross the valley."

"And a very high one," Dom Anselmus interrupted angrily.

"Pay him," said Dolf contemptuously.

"What with?" asked Leonardo.

"What is the toll your master is demanding?" Dolf inquired of the captain. He was thinking they could redeem themselves with the ox. The rider laughed, but there was nothing cheerful in the sound.

"Fifty of the strongest and tallest children."

The man had recognized Dolf to be one of the leaders, even though he wore no white gown or other finery.

"Fifty ..." The words stuck in Dolf's throat. He could not believe it. This man surely could not think that the priests would allow fifty children to be taken captive.

"That is quite out of the question," he said vehemently. "You must name a different price. You can have an ox and three sheep ..."

Nicolas pushed Dolf aside and shouted at him:

"Be quiet, Rudolf of Amsterdam. It is not for you to make decisions. This is my crusade."

He turned to face the riders.

"God will not forgive this insult to His children's army. We are on our way to Jerusalem to liberate the Holy City from the Saracens and God will not permit anyone to hinder us."

The rider responded with a laugh that was mocking and cold.

"If you refuse to yield us the fifty children, we will take them anyway and in the process give you a slaughter you will remember. You and your brightly polished following will be our first victims!"

Involuntarily Nicolas took a step back, but Carolus cried out:

"You just try." He raised his bow, but Dolf, realizing the danger of the situation, quickly restrained him.

"These are free children, Captain," he said desperately. "You cannot carry them off into slavery. It would be contrary to all the laws."

The riders were now laughing and jeering. They knew that in the valley of Scharnitz the only law was that of Count Romhild.

"This is our law!" yelled the captain, thrusting his spear at Dolf. The weapon would undoubtedly have transfixed the boy, had not Dom Thaddeus suddenly pushed him backwards. The sharp lance missed him by a fraction.

"Stop!" cried Dom Anselmus. "You can have your fifty children, but keep your hands off these, for they are of noble blood."

Dolf was trying to struggle to his feet, but found it quite impossible since Dom Thaddeus was sitting on him, holding him down.

"Quiet," he whispered. "We cannot afford to lose you." The boy was almost completely covered by the monk's habit.

"We do not want the children of nobles," Dolf heard the captain say. "Count Romhild is not asking for trouble. He wants strong, hard-working laborers, but we will do the choosing. Come on men, grab them!"

Dolf's protest was stifled. He could not see anything and was almost suffocating. He heard the riders gallop away and once again the children began screaming. He could also hear Leonardo's warning voice telling the children to hide. But where could so many children hide in an open field? For the next half minute or so, however, he heard nothing at all, for Dom Thaddeus had expertly knocked him unconscious. Hastily the monk pulled him into the tent and covered him with a pile of skins. Then he sat down on the heap and began to pray for the poor children who would fall into the hands of the Count of Scharnitz.

Panic reigned throughout the camp. At first the children hardly understood what was happening, while the riders galloped around, grabbing the most suitable boys and girls. Those who were taken struck out furiously with arms and legs, while the others ran off screaming. Some of the orderlies tried to attack the riders but their crude and blunt weapons were of no avail against the armor. Finally, fifty were brought together and tied up with thick, coarse ropes. Among them were Peter and Frank.

Within an hour the riders departed, taking their miserable prisoners with them. Dolf, his head throbbing with pain, crept from the tent and watched the group disappear into the distance. He burst into tears.

"You should be happy we were able to save you," said Dom Anselmus tersely.

"Don't pretend that you wouldn't have liked them to have taken me too," Dolf retorted. But the monk shook his dark head.

"No, Rudolf of Amsterdam, your time has not yet come. A different fate awaits you."

Dolf did not stop to ponder on the meaning of these mysterious words. He raced off and, together with Leonardo, tried to restore some order to the disarrayed camp. Many children were still crying and quaking with fear. After a while they gathered their possessions together, strapped the food-packs to their backs and prepared to continue the journey. But Dolf was still at his wit's end, running around trying to discover the extent of the tragedy. He was looking for Maria.

"Hey, steady down," Leonardo shouted at him, grasping Dolf's arm.

"Where's Maria?"

"She's safe. You don't think we would have allowed her to be kidnapped?"

"Where is she?"

Trembling, Maria crept out from under a bush and embraced Dolf.

"I thought they'd taken you too, because they were taking the strongest," she sobbed. Now that he knew she was safe Dolf had no time for her tears.

"Yes, yes. I'm all right. Dom Thaddeus saved me again." He looked around.

"Where's Peter?"

Carolus came running up and he too had tears streaming down his face.

"Rudolf, Rudolf! They've taken Bertho!"

Gradually the full extent of the disaster became clear: Bertho, Frank and Peter had all been taken. So had Wilhelm, Carl, Ludwig, and Frieda. The only compensation was that one of the riders had been killed by the children.

Dolf watched silently while, on the orders of Anselmus, the dead knight was stripped of his coat of mail which Nicolas at once claimed as his. With his white robe over it, he was beginning to look like a genuine crusader. Both he and Anselmus were again worried about time and together they urged the children to hurry. On this occasion few protested.

Dolf, however, showed not the least sign of continuing the journey. He stood motionless by the ashes of his fire, trying to digest the loss. The riders had made their choice well. They had done much more than rid the army of fifty extra mouths to feed, he realized—they had broken its backbone.

There was Peter, who for a few weeks had learned what it was to be a free human being. In that time he had shown courage, insight and strength. He was a friend for whom

Dolf had a great respect. Now he would be a serf once more.

And what about Bertho? On at least three occasions he had saved the life of the careless Carolus and still carried the scars he received from the boar. And Frieda, the lovely, sweet Frieda with her extensive knowledge of medicinal herbs.

"We must save them," Dolf said slowly. Leonardo gave him a mocking laugh.

"You can forget that. All we can do is travel and pray that Count Romhild will leave us in peace from now on."

"We must save them," Dolf repeated mechanically, as if in a dream. "Where do you think they'll have been taken?"

Leonardo waved his arm vaguely in the direction of the valley.

"To the castle, of course, somewhere over there. Like many others, it will be built on a high rock, inaccessible and impossible to take. You must accept the situation, Rudolf. You cannot free them. It would not be possible even with a whole army of experienced warriors. Count Romhild knows what he is doing."

"Who is he? Do you know?"

"No, but I can imagine. He lives in this wide valley which lies across the narrow road to Innsbruck and word must have reached him last night from one of his spies that we had entered his domain. He is probably a robber baron who shows little mercy to those who refuse to pay his toll. Rudolf, in about four years time Peter and Frank too will be knights in his service, attacking peaceful travellers and relieving them of their money. What other use could Count Romhild have for them?"

"To put them to work," whispered Maria.

"Yes, that too, of course. A baron of that type never has enough serfs or soldiers. Strong young boys with little conscience and heathen by nature, like Peter ..."

"No," said Dolf. "Peter would never be a robber; it would be against his nature. And Frank even less."

"But they have no choice. If they resist, the Count will change their minds with red-hot irons. If they still refuse, he will simply execute them."

"That is exactly why we must free all of them," Dolf persisted.

"But how? Surely not with force! You cannot be thinking of marching the entire children's army against Romhild's castle. I thought you had more sense than that, Rudolf."

Dolf, who was already very upset, was irritated by Leonardo's mocking tone.

"Why shouldn't we march against the castle? The children intend to attack the Saracens, don't they?"

"Yes, but that's different. The Turks are supposed to flee in terror at the first sight of the children. Far from fleeing, Romhild will shower them with arrows and boiling lead."

"But eventually his castle will have to surrender against such numbers," Dolf said obstinately.

"Oh yes, but do you wish to sacrifice two thousand to rescue fifty?"

Carolus stood beside them growing more and more agitated. "I'm not scared," he yelled.

"That's not the question," said Leonardo calmly. "It is a question of whether it is possible and you know as well as I do that it isn't."

Dolf straightened his back and stuck out his chin. "Nevertheless we have got to rescue them—Frank, Bertho, Peter, Frieda and all the rest. We've got to save them," insisted Dolf.

"Rudolf's right," interrupted Carolus heatedly. "Bertho, Frieda and Peter want to see Jerusalem as much as anyone. They were promised like the rest of us! They must not be left behind."

"For goodness' sake, use your brains," cried Leonardo

disgustedly. "If the army moves against the castle there'll be seven thousand children who won't see Jerusalem."

"Not seven thousand," murmured Dolf, "but seventeen."

"What?"

"Seventeen, an indivisible, devilish number; a prime number. Surely Romhild and his men will be able to count to seventeen."

"What do you mean by a prime number?"

"Oh, be quiet," said Dolf, "and leave me alone. I must think this out carefully. In my age, I mean, in my country we have a saying: the weak must use their wits. We are weak and I detest war and shedding of blood, but I have a plan. It is an outrageous and dangerous plan, which is why I need time to think about it."

"You can rely on me," shouted Carolus without hesitation. "How are you going to get them out of the castle, Rudolf?"

"I'm not quite sure yet, but let's go. As soon as I have worked out the plan, I'll let you know."

Trudging along in the rear guard, they followed the children's army as it hastened silently through the valley. Though the sky was overcast, it was no longer cold. Dolf looked up and prayed for sun—in the plan that was forming in his mind there was no room for rain.

Several hours later the castle of Romhild of Scharnitz came into sight. As Leonardo had predicted, it was an impregnable fortress, built on a steep cliff and only accessible from the rear, where the swiftly ascending slopes were covered by a forest. The children gazed fearfully at the castle and quickened their pace, even though it was far away on the other side of the valley.

"It doesn't look very inviting, does it?" said Leonardo airily. The endless column of children, many yards wide and several miles long, was certain to be visible from the towers. The children would be helpless, utterly helpless if more knights came charging down to attack them. The sooner they were through the valley the better and many of them started running in fear. Anselmus could not have been happier.

Dolf studied the stronghold in the distance and wished he had some binoculars. What would be the layout of a castle like that? How could one break into a medieval fortress which had been built to resist months of siege and which had been sited so that it could not be stormed or taken by force? Carolus! He would know. He probably knew all there was to know about castles.

Dolf found him walking hand in hand with Hilda. The bow and quiver on his back seemed ridiculously small and he looked sad. He was missing his companion, Bertho.

"Carolus, I must talk to you."

"Have you thought of something?" Carolus asked, brightening up. He immediately released Hilda's hand. "What is it? What are we going to do? If there is any fighting to be done, I want to be there too."

"We are not going to fight, you little hothead," laughed Dolf. "We are going to plot something and it must be done with the utmost secrecy.

"A plot!" Carolus's eyes were gleaming with excitement. "Against the Count?"

"Sssshh."

Dolf pulled him by the sleeve and together they sat down by the side of the road. As the procession continued to file past, Dolf said:

"Listen, I know a way to rescue the prisoners from the castle tonight, or rather very early tomorrow morning."

"How?"

"Ssshh, no one must know. I'm going to use a trick."

Carolus nodded with enthusiasm. "I'm going to take part. What is your plan?"

It took Dolf at least half an hour to tell him and as he did so, Carolus grew even more agitated.

"It's a wonderful idea!" he exclaimed when Dolf had finished. "I suppose you want me to get the materials?"

"Yes, but repeat them to me first."

Counting on his fingers Carolus said:

"Seventeen horns, seventeen hairbands and grass skirts, feathers, grease and charcoal, oh yes, and seventeen pairs of shoes with the fur on the outside. We already have the horns, because when they are scooped out they make very good drinking mugs."

"Arrange for a group to make the other things, but don't tell them what they are for. Just say you are inventing something again," said Dolf.

"But why must there be exactly seventeen of us?" Carolus asked.

Dolf hesitated. One could explain something like that to Leonardo, but not to this little king to whom arithmetic progressions were a total mystery.

"It will make the most impression—if they bother to count us, that is. Seventeen is a magic number."

"The Devil's number is thirteen," said Carolus.

"Yes, but it would be too dangerous with so few. Seventeen is just as mysterious as thirteen. Please believe me."

"But do they know that in the castle of Scharnitz?"

"Their resident priest is sure to know."

"Good."

While talking, something else had occurred to Dolf. He put his hand into his pocket and felt for the precious box of matches which he had guarded so carefully during all the past weeks.

"Bird-droppings," he said to himself.

"What?"

"The dry, white bird-droppings which one sees on every stone ... I'll collect some of it this afternoon. And dry charcoal. You, Carolus, must arrange the rest of the disguise and also select fifteen strong lads who are not easily scared. You must ask them whether they are prepared to rescue their friends from the castle and they must have the right to refuse, for we cannot conceal from them that they will be risking their lives. But regardless of whether they volunteer or not, they must not breathe a word about it."

"I know of at least thirty who would jump at the chance to take part."

"Yes, but fifteen is enough; with the two of us that makes seventeen, not one more nor less."

"It's almost like Shrove Tuesday," giggled Carolus.

"My dear friend, this is no joke. It is absolutely serious and we may all die."

"Do you take me for a coward?" cried Carolus furiously.

"Of course not. You are the most courageous king I have ever met. However, we have to discover the layout of the castle. Even looking from here it is quite obvious that the cliff is too steep to climb. What do you think is at the back, where the forest reaches down the mountain side?"

"A cleft," replied Carolus at once.

"With a drawbridge across it?"

"Yes, I've seen it."

Carolus's eyes were very sharp. Moreover, he knew how to study the strengths and weaknesses of a castle from the outside.

"If the drawbridge is at the back," Dolf muttered to himself thoughtfully, "it means we can attack only when the bridge is down. How early in the morning do you think that will be?"

"Very early, shortly after dawn. But there will be at least two guards."

"Yes. What is behind the bridge?"

"The gate, of course. A large, heavy gate which we cannot hope to storm."

"That won't be necessary. The gate will open for us, you can be sure of that." Dolf promised this with much more self-confidence than he felt. "What is behind the gate? A passageway?"

"I don't know. It might be a vaulted passage with a second gate at the other end, or an iron portcullis. But they will raise that when they open the outer gate, provided that they don't suspect anything."

"That is another reason why no one other than the seventeen must know anything about the plan. What is beyond the gates?"

"The courtyard. Say Rudolf, have you never seen the inside of a castle?"

"Oh yes, but in my country there are no cliffs hundreds of feet high on which to build them. It is all flat plains and marshland. When they build a fortress in our part of the world, they dig a moat around it and make the walls very thick."

"Romhild has no need of thick walls, since the cliff gives him enough protection."

"So, a courtyard," Dolf muttered to himself. "Quite a large one, I hope, surrounded by buildings. Are the living quarters opposite the gate?"

Shading his eyes with his hand, Carolus peered at the distant castle. "Yes, I can see fourteen windows looking out on the valley. Those must be the living quarters. There are outbuildings to the left and right and there is the chapel, you can see the tower quite clearly. So, if you were standing with your back to the forest at the entrance to the castle, the stables and storerooms would be to the left and the chapel and armory to the right."

"Where do you think they will have put our friends?"

"In one of the outhouses. But certainly not with the horses. Robber barons are usually very fond of their steeds and won't risk putting prisoners with them."

"How many children were kidnapped this morning?"

"Hans says there must have been more than fifty."

"That's what I thought. Ask Hans to take part tonight."

"Oh yes."

Dolf gazed about him.

"Why do you think Romhild wanted the children? The entire valley seems to belong to him. Do you think he is rich?"

Carolus nodded knowledgeably.

"Yes, if he makes all the travellers pay a toll he must be quite rich. But his land is not very fertile and in winter he probably starves."

"How do you know that?"

Carolus pointed to the valley and the towering mountains which surrounded them.

"Much of the land is not being cultivated. And did you take a good look at the riders this morning, Rudolf? Some of them were badly pockmarked."

"Badly what?"

"Pockmarked; they must have had a smallpox epidemic in the valley not so long ago."

"What has a smallpox epidemic got to do with kidnapping the children?"

"Surely that's obvious enough. The fields are uncultivated, the road is in a bad state of disrepair and those dwellings over there look uninhabited—all a result of the disease. I would say Romhild probably lost at least half of his serfs and desperately needs a new labor force."

By now the last children had passed them by and Dom Thaddeus, who was right at the back, came up and looked down at them with surprise.

"Have you hurt yourselves?"

The two boys jumped up.

"No, it's nothing. We were just resting and talking," explained Dolf.

Dom Thaddeus thought it suspicious that the two most vigorous children in the entire crusade were in need of rest during the daytime.

"I hope you are not ill?"

"Dom Thaddeus, may we have your blessing please?" asked Carolus suddenly. "We are going to need it."

The priest gave them his blessing, but before he could ask them anything else, they were off. He followed them with his eyes, shaking his head.

In order to put as great a distance as possible between the castle and the crusaders, the leaders had decided to omit the noon-time rest. But by four o'clock many of the children were complaining of fatigue. Finally they could go no farther and a camping place had to be found. For once, Dolf did not involve himself, but instead went in search of Carolus.

"Is everything ready?"

"Yes, the horns, the skirts and the shoes. I have rolled them all in my cloak and hidden them under some bushes over there."

"Good. What about the volunteers?"

"They are prepared. Fifteen of them, all well armed and capable of anything."

"Make sure you are not seen leaving the camp and wait for me in the bushes. There is still something I have to do, but there will be at least three more hours of daylight and we can make good use of it. Remember, no one must see us leave. Do the boys know what is expected of them? They're not too exhausted, are they?"

"I haven't chosen little ones," retorted Carolus angrily.

Dolf went in search of Leonardo, who was busy tending to his mule.

"Listen, my friend, I have some urgent business tonight. I am leaving Maria in your charge. Please look after her well and make sure she does not follow me. And ... er ... if I don't return, will you look after her, Leonardo?"

"What are you going to do, Rudolf?"

"I cannot tell you, but please promise me ..."

The student laughed in his mocking fashion.

"Perhaps we are going to see you return soon with fifty stolen children?" he suggested in a hushed, but knowing voice. Dolf felt awkward.

"Sssshh ... where did you get that idea?"

"You don't have to worry; I don't know anything. I imagine that you want to keep the plan a secret and I can hold my tongue. But I know you, Rudolf. Once you have an idea in your head it is bound to happen, even if all the odds are stacked against you."

Dolf sighed and looked sheepishly at his friend, who nodded at him with a friendly expression.

"Go in peace, Rudolf, and do what you feel you must. I will not ask to accompany you."

"No, please don't," whispered Dolf, moved by Leonardo's understanding. "Someone must stay behind to guard the children."

"Tonight I will pray for you," Leonardo promised with a sudden intensity. They embraced each other. Dolf dared not say goodbye to Maria.

It was while the evening meal was being prepared that Dolf stole away. He was carrying two sacks; one contained hard cakes and the other various things which he thought might be useful in the raid on Scharnitz castle.

In the undergrowth he discovered Carolus and the fifteen stout-hearted and well-armed volunteers. He addressed them in a whisper:

"I am sorry to say that even this evening you are going to have to make a long march, with barely any time for rest. We must be seen by absolutely no one, but fortunately it will be dark in three hours. When we reach the fortress, we must make our way to the far side and approach it from the forest. We will wait in hiding in the trees until morning, by which time we must be all set for the attack. It is going to be a dangerous venture and anyone who is afraid may withdraw now and we will find a replacement. The details we will discuss as we march. Are you all willing?"

"Yes, all of us," one of them replied. "Some of our best friends are prisoners in that castle and we cannot desert them."

Dolf was deeply moved by their loyalty. Only a few days ago they had been standing up for him and now, once again, they were showing themselves ready to brave extreme danger because of the plight of their friends.

"Right then. We'll be off."

In silence they followed Dolf back to the place where he and Carolus had been talking during the afternoon. None of them showed signs of fear. They had been on the road for weeks, sleeping under the stars, fighting wild animals, wading through raging rivers and often risking their lives. They had been toughened by the wind, rain, freezing nights, scorching sun and the smell of freedom. Carolus had chosen them with care: every one of them was a stalwart.

The little king now led the way—a general at the head of his army. Dolf brought up the rear, frequently looking around to be sure that they were not followed.

Ever since he had first heard that they would be making the journey through the Alps he had dreaded it as an impossible task. His sleep had been troubled by dreams of wolf-packs, bears, treacherous chasms, snow-capped mountains, avalanches and other calamities ... But never had he imagined that he would need to rescue his kidnapped friends from an impenetrable stronghold.

THE DEMONS' ASSAULT

The fortress of Scharnitz rose tall and black above the dreary valley. Dolf's wish had come true; it was not raining. Indeed the sky even seemed to be brightening a little.

There was no movement in the poverty-stricken huts of the serfs, which dotted the hillside below the cliff on which the stronghold was built. Sentries could be seen patrolling the battlements and the lights in the windows suggested that Count Romhild and his family might be feasting in the great hall.

In single file the group of boys crept closer and closer. They made use of every possible cover—bushes, loose rocks and hillocks. They had to search for some time before they found a narrow wooden bridge by which they could cross a little river which barred their way. They hurried to the other side in crouched positions. There they found a wide path, deeply rutted by wheels, which led up the slope into the forest. Carolus thought it wiser not to follow it, since it was likely that it would eventually lead to the castle. They could not take the risk of meeting someone. Spread far apart and hoping to remain unseen, they crossed the rolling fields, climbing all the time. Eventually they came to the edge of the forest, where the utter blackness and the strange nighttime noises caused them to hesitate a moment. Far above their heads to the right loomed the massive shadow of the castle. There was nothing but silence, a black, stifling silence, until somewhere in the forest they heard an owl hoot.

The boys gathered around Dolf.

"We must all stay very close together now," he whispered. "Hold onto your neighbor's hand so that nobody gets lost. It is about half-past ten and tomorrow morning at five we will make our attack, so we have plenty of time to climb up, have some rest and prepare ourselves. Come on."

After a while the clouds began to break and the moon shone down into the wood, casting some light on their path. This made their climb a little easier, for they dared not risk any kind of torch.

"What happens if we meet a bear?" Matthew whispered into Dolf's ear.

"Bears don't hunt at night, only wolves. But they are not likely to attack a large group since they are sensible creatures and usually scared of human beings."

Much of the time Dolf did not know whether what he said was true or not, but often he said things as much to reassure himself as the others.

Eventually they reached the height which was on a level with the castle and again they discovered a track which appeared to be much used. Skirting around it they took the most direct route straight up to a plateau, from where they could look down on the dark mass of the castle.

"I think we will rest here," Dolf decided. "Toward dawn we must go down to the drawbridge."

They stowed their luggage in the bushes, crawled away in the long grass, ferns and flowers, lay down and closed their eyes; they were exhausted. Three of them were posted to guard duty and would be relieved after an hour. Dolf allotted himself the final watch, when he would make his last preparations. Until then he slept deeply, having put all cares aside. He had gone over the plan a hundred times during the afternoon, looking at it from all possible angles. It simply had to succeed; if not, they would die. There was no other alternative, so there was no need to worry about it anymore.

Carolus was shaking him.

"It's time," he whispered with a yawn. The moon had set, it was pitch dark. Straining his eyes Dolf could just distinguish the figures of the sentries rousing their reliefs. Slowly and cautiously he crept to a place from where he could observe the castle unnoticed. The forest around him was alive with rustling sounds, but these no longer frightened him. He waited for what seemed an eternity until the sky in the east showed the first faint tinges of dawn.

Then he went to work. He took from his pack two wooden bowls, a length of string which had been well greased, a few chunks of charcoal and two handfuls of dried bird-droppings.

He pulled the bird-droppings and the charcoal in one bowl until he had made a fine powder. Then he took from his pocket the precious box of matches. It was still almost full.

He did not really know the formula for gunpowder and certainly not the correct proportions. All he had ever known was that it could be made from saltpeter, charcoal and sulfur. The bird-droppings were sure to contain a fair amount of saltpeter; the matchheads would provide the sulfur; and the children never had any lack of charcoal. It might just succeed ...

Even if the bomb failed to explode, it would quite probably stink and smoke a good deal. He worked for half an hour or more, while all about him the light was brightening. He ground up the matchheads and mixed it with the powder. Then he covered all with the second bowl and tied the two halves together, leaving a piece of the greased string protruding through the gap. He concealed the result of his handiwork in the bushes, wondering whether it really was a bomb. He had kept aside the matchbox and two matches.

"Up you get, chaps, it's time to go."

If they were stiff and tired, the thought that their great exploit was about to begin soon set their blood flowing again.

Out from their packs came the equipment for the raid. There were seventeen headbands, each with a pointed horn sewn to the middle. Quickly they undressed and hid their clothes in the bushes. Then they put on the grass skirts. They shivered in the cold morning air and their teeth chattered, but they did not much mind since they would soon be quite hot enough! They tied the bands around their heads with the horns pointing threateningly upward. They blackened their faces with charcoal and grease and, finally, ruffled their hair and stuck in some feathers.

With a critical eye Dolf surveyed these seventeen creatures. All they now had to do was grime their bodies. Dolf had originally decided that they should paint each other completely black, but he now had a better idea, one that would look even more alarming. Taking the homemade black paint he drew long lines over their chests and backs and then over their naked arms and legs. The light was now strong enough for them to regard each other and the sight was indeed frightening: seventeen striped devils with horns, hairy feet and gleaming teeth.

Dolf nodded with satisfaction, picked up his "bomb" and gestured the boys to follow. They climbed down until they were on a level with the fortress and had a good view of the cleft which separated the stronghold from the mountain. The bridge had not yet been lowered. Between the steep forest and the cleft there was a level open field, nearly a hundred yards wide. The castle could not be surprised from that direction. At the edge of the forest they stopped, keeping out of sight behind the bushes. Flat on his stomach Dolf slowly edged himself forward a little way, praying that he would not be spied from the towers. He placed the bomb on the ground in front of him and slid back to the cover of the foliage, unwinding the fuse as he went.

"Listen," he hissed. "Shortly I will light the fuse and a little afterward you should hear a loud bang. There is no need to be afraid. There will also be some foul-smelling smoke, but you need not be frightened by that either. You can walk right through it; it is quite harmless. Do you understand?"

All the boys nodded, though in fact they understood very little. Tense and trembling they gazed at the still-closed bridge and the heavily barred gate. They were anxious to begin and Dolf hoped that they would not have to wait too long.

It was indeed within a short while that they heard horses neighing, the tramping of their hoofs and orders being shouted. With a loud rattling and clanking of chains the bridge was lowered and fell into position with a clang. Two armed men appeared through the half-open gates and looked around for a while. Then they shouted something to those inside and stepped back as the gates swung wide and seven mounted soldiers galloped from the courtyard, sped over the bridge and disappeared down the path leading to the valley.

The bridge remained in position and the gate was left slightly open so that people on foot could pass in and out. A few women came out to talk with the guards for a short while and then disappeared. The two soldiers stationed themselves on either side of the gate—in the castle of Scharnitz the day had begun.

To wait any longer would only raise the tension and possibly spoil the effect of the seventeen devils. Dolf heard the boys muttering their prayers. A match flared and the fuse was lit.

"Get ready," he whispered. "The bang will follow any moment and we must rush forward immediately. Don't be surprised. It will look like magic, but that is what it is intended to look like."

He watched the tiny spark crawling slowly over the rocky ground toward the gunpowder. Pressing the back of his hand against his mouth he began to make a ghastly scream.

The two guards jumped with fright and peered toward the edge of the forest. The boys held their breaths. The flame was beginning to climb up the fuse into the bomb.

"Whoowhoowhoowhoo," the sinister noise arose from the undergrowth. The guards looked at each other perplexed, then stared back at the forest and ...

Boooommm!

It had worked! A filthy, dark, foul-smelling cloud of smoke rose into the air. For an instant the boys stood rooted to the spot, but Dolf yelled at them:

"Come on!"

They all leaped up and raced forward through the smoke. To the startled guards it was a terrifying vision: blood-curdling noises followed by a thunderous roar, clouds of black smoke billowing across the open space, a devil appearing, then another and another, more and more. Each one was small, striped and horned. They ground their teeth, howled and appeared to be moving very fast. The soldiers were so paralyzed with fear that the devils were onto the bridge and coming straight for them before they reacted. Demons were coming to drag them away to Hell. Yelling, they spun around, thrust open the gate and fled into the courtyard.

"Save us! Holy Mother of God, save us!"

Seventeen terrifying devils surged in behind them, howling and screeching. The tallest one at the front, whose horn was a ghastly white, brandished a cruel-looking blade. The men, women and children in the courtyard ran in terror. Buckets, plates, saddles and belts clattered to the ground as they fled in every direction, pursued by the demons. One woman stumbled to her knees and was trampled over by three devils. A bearded warrior, being chased by the largest devil, suddenly turned around, clutching at his sword. But the demon leaped straight at him, piercing his hand with the flashing knife. The man tumbled backward with a scream and the devil jumped on his chest.

"Mercy! Mercy! Save me!"

He felt a hairy foot against his ear and almost died with horror.

"Where are the prisoners?" the devil snarled in his face. "We want the fifty holy children; we want their innocent blood."

The demon leaped off and tugged at the soldier's coat of mail.

"Get up and take me to the holy children. Quick, or you will be thrown into the deepest pits of Hell, you accursed sinner!"

Groveling, the man tried to escape his tormentor, while all around the courtyard was in chaos. Small black hands pinched, pushed and clawed at screaming people; they hardly thought to defend themselves. Some of the windows around the court-yard were thrown open and pale, frightened faces peered out only to be hurriedly withdrawn. The Count of Scharnitz appeared on the wooden balcony.

"The children, we want the holy children," Dolf yelled and the cry was taken up by the other devils, who were still madly chasing people around the courtyard.

"Give them the children," roared the Count, fearing that his castle would be lost to the legions of Satan. He could quite easily imagine that the devils were more interested in the souls of innocent children than of sinners like himself.

"Give them the children! Hurry up!" came the voice from the balcony.

A double door was thrown open to reveal the captive children—fifty-two of them. The instant they saw the devils coming to fetch them they panicked and yelled just as much as their captors. But quickly Dolf stepped forward and whispered into Frank's ear:

"Don't worry, it's only me, Dolf. Get the others to calm down." Only then did the tanner recognize his friend.

Carolus was tugging at Bertho's arm.

"Come on! This is only a trick."

Nevertheless it was quite some time before all the children believed that the demons were not real and ceased their resistance.

Now that they had what they wanted, the devils herded the prisoners together and drove them before them through the gate, across the bridge and into the forest. Still trembling uncontrollably, but greatly relieved, the occupants of the castle watched them go. Their paved courtyard was in a state of utter chaos: a broken knife, bloodstains, pheasant feathers and all the things the servants had dropped in their panic.

The fifty-two prisoners were quickly led into the forest as far away from the castle as possible. They stopped only for the devils to collect their hidden clothes. Some of the liberated children, who still had not understood that their release was a magnificent piece of duplicity, walked in front of the demons crying and praying. Frank went from one to the other, trying to put them at their ease, but the horned devils still looked so terrifying that they could hardly believe that these were their friends.

Carolus, quite overcome with delight by the success of the venture, walked happily beside Bertho, his great friend.

"Rudolf and I devised the plan and I arranged the disguise. Aren't you pleased, Bertho?"

Naturally, all the fifty-two rescued children were delighted.

They embraced their dirt-stained saviors and were eager to return to the crusade without delay. But Dolf objected.

"We can rejoin them tonight, but for the time being we

must hide in the forest and no one must see us. Romhild and his friends will think that we have taken the children straight to Hell. If they see us crossing the valley, however, they will realize they have been fooled."

So they remained hidden in the wood, appeasing their hunger with berries and cakes which the rescue-party had brought. After dusk they began to descend the mountain and it was almost dawn before they were back where the camp had been. Once again they concealed themselves in the undergrowth for a few hours of sleep.

They were now some six miles from the castle and decided to risk continuing their journey during the afternoon, hoping to overtake the crusade before nightfall and before it reached the mouth of the valley.

The devils had dressed themselves in their own clothes again, but it was difficult to clean off the black grease from their bodies. They rubbed themselves with handfuls of dry grass, but still looked little cleaner than chimney sweeps. They had finished all the cakes and they were hungry.

It was late at night before they finally saw the campfires in the distance. Tottering with exhaustion and blackened with dirt and dust, they arrived in the camp.

Carolus, who could barely stand, stumbled straight into the tent, snatched a piece of meat from the astonished Dom Anselmus's hand and fell asleep while eating. He had not said a word. Hilda, who had been searching for him for two days burst into tears of relief. She wiped his face with a damp cloth, but he did not stir. Frieda, who was also weeping, embraced her friends and asked for food. Bertho, Wilhelm and Carl had stumbled to the ground by the first campfire, their hands stretched out toward the spit, begging for food.

Despite the great wave of excitement which swept through the camp with the return of the kidnapped children, all the questions remained unanswered. Neither saviors nor saved could utter a word. They wanted only to eat and then sleep ... just sleep!

Dolf, Peter and Frank, hearing the braying of the mule, found Leonardo and Maria. They threw themselves to the ground and demanded water. Overcome with joy, Maria grasped Dolf's black hand and kissed it. Leonardo said nothing. He embraced Peter and Frank and then looked at Rudolf of Amsterdam, his eyes brimming with emotion. Dolf had pulled the rabbit-fur shoes from his aching feet before the student at last found his voice.

"So you did manage it ..." he said with admiration.

Dolf had no energy left with which to describe what had happened. Dirty as he was, he went straight to sleep. Somewhere far away he heard Leonardo saying:

"We had already given you up for lost ..." after which he knew nothing more. He dreamed of his mother, and then of the bathroom at home. The shower had never worked properly and no matter how much one turned the hot tap, it always sprayed cold water; fine jets of very cold water ...

At the southern end of a valley in the Karwendel mountains rain was falling in sheets.

THE ALPS

The army trekked through the Karwendel mountains in a long, snaking file. They travelled by narrow paths and roads hardly worthy of the name; beside churning streams, across rockfalls and down into gulleys; through thick forests and thorny bushes and over slippery slopes and jagged rocks. As they climbed it became colder and the rain was ceaseless.

It seemed that the mountains were weeping and all about them was the sound of water murmuring and gurgling. Along the level sections of the road they sank into the mud up to their ankles. The packs on their backs seemed to drink the water, making them twice as heavy, and the children's shoes rubbed their swollen feet. Their hands, clothes and hair were caked with mud. During the day, the only means of satisfying hunger was to munch hard cakes while walking, for it was almost impossible to find dry wood for fires. Making a campfire and keeping it going became a task requiring a great deal of inventiveness and even more luck. At night, when it was essential for them to have some fire, they cut down large trees. Even then it was only the center, rich in resin, that would burn satisfactorily. The dead wood was saturated and there was no dry grass with which to kindle the flames; the sparks from their flints died in the downpour. Shivering, cold and exhausted they climbed on ever higher. Their resolution to continue was only maintained by the hope that on the other side the climate would improve. Dolf had no idea how many children perished during the three interminable days they needed to reach the summit. He had risked his life to rescue fifty-two children from the dungeons of Count Romhild of Scharnitz but he could do nothing to save these unfortunate ones. Pneumonia, wild beasts, snakes and landslides were their constant enemies. Above their heads hovered birds of prey. A small child lagging behind was attacked by an eagle. Bertho, who was with the orderlies in the rear guard, killed the bird, but the child had been so badly injured that it died during the night. Bertho had yet another scar. On the same gray day soon after dusk Leonardo spied a more or less level field, a little higher up, which would provide a suitable camp site. Wilhelm went off to explore the caves and hollows of the surrounding mountain walls, to see if they could be used for housing the sick during the night. As he walked in to one he came face to face with a huge, brown bear. The animal, much taller than Wilhelm, was standing on its hind legs, pawing the air and growling. Those who had followed Wilhelm screamed at the sight of the bear which, frightened and confused by so many different scents, panicked, dropped to all fours and charged.

Suddenly there was Leonardo, panting. He had heard the cries and had raced up the hill. The animal stood growling and swaying over Wilhelm who had been knocked down. Leonardo knew what was expected of him. With all his might he swung the cudgel and brought it down on the bear's head. The bear retreated, howling with pain. Then, almost blind with rage and agony, it turned and careened straight toward a small group of children who scattered out of its way. Bertho and Carolus shot their arrows at him but failed to penetrate the tough hide. Leonardo pursued the bear, though keeping at a safe distance, and the tormented beast scrambled up a slope, groaning and protesting and starting a small landslide of mud, twigs and loose stones. Then the bear disappeared from sight behind some rocks.

When Leonardo returned he found Wilhelm dead, felled by a blow from the frightened animal. Three other children had also been slightly injured. The news of Leonardo's heroic deed—how, all alone, and armed with nothing but a piece of wood, he had chased a wild bear, as large as a house—passed from mouth to mouth. He had become a hero.

The rest of the night was peaceful. The bear did not return and the wolves were kept at a distance by fires and attentive guards. Leonardo, however, got no sleep. He continued to patrol the camp, waking up dozing guards and generally keeping an eye on things.

At daybreak they moved on. They drank from mountain streams and waterfalls which were brown with soil and tasted of earth, dead animals and rotting plants. The smoked fish was going moldy, the cakes had become soggy and crumbly and the dried meat smelled. The continuous rain, the piercing wind and exhaustion from a long climb had numbed the children's senses, so that they walked in a kind of daze.

They prayed fervently for sunshine and warmth, but were given yet more rain. They pleaded with the Holy Virgin for protection, but witnessed a hunter fall to his death in a fissure. The ground was too stony and hard for graves so instead they covered the body under a pile of the loose stones. They realized that their labor would be in vain. It would not be long after they had gone that the wild animals had moved the stones and eaten their full of the dead hunter.

And still they climbed up. Toward the afternoon of the third day the driving rain subsided into a dreary drizzle, which nevertheless drenched and chilled them. And now they had to contend with mist; the higher they went, the thicker it became, rising from the wooded slopes below. Sometimes it was impossible to discern the person walking in front and the little ones became an easy prey for missed footing, sudden torrents, gaping chasms, or losing contact and getting lost.

But the worst of their miseries was influenza. Their chests were racked with coughing; they sneezed, sniffed and cleared their painfully sore throats. They peered through feverish, watery eyes at the stone masses around them, which seemed to loom up mysteriously through the mist and disappear behind them just as strangely. Despite everything they moved inexorably forward and upward, driven by their determination to reach Jerusalem. Just before they reached the summit they had lost the second of the oxen, when it stumbled into a treacherous fissure. The chasm was too deep and dangerous for them to reach the stranded animal and it had to be left, helpless and severely injured, lowing pitifully. Bertho vainly sent down a few arrows, hoping to kill the animal. Dolf hoped that the wild beasts of the mountains would quickly put an end to its suffering.

It was late in the afternoon of the third day when they finally reached the pass. It was still foggy and the valley below them was covered with a thick layer of cloud, so that they hardly realized that they were at the summit. The wind had ceased and the rain had stopped. From the simple fact that they were now descending, they surmised that half the barrier had been conquered.

The descent too, however, demanded its toll. The slippery path zigzagged across the face of the mountain. They could see barely an arm's distance in front of them and the corners were always unexpected. Often a child would trip, roll down a few yards and bump against a tree trunk, where he would remain bruised and crying until one of the stronger ones found him and brought him back. Many of the taller boys and girls were carrying injured, sick or sobbing children. The singing and praying crusaders had been transformed into beasts of burden.

Evening seemed to come earlier and they were forced to camp in the steep forest, for that was all that this side of the Karwendel had to offer. The fires which they managed to light after much difficulty gave off a great deal of smoke and little warmth. Dolf, who had lent his jacket to another child, lay soaked and shivering by his fire and thinking with resentment of Nicolas, the noble children and the two monks, who were now inside the dry tent. It was an effort to restrain himself from rushing immediately to the tent and dragging out each of these privileged ones by the roots of his hair. But what right had he to complain of this self-ishness? The tent was their status symbol. It would never occur to the other children, who were just as cold, wet and short of sleep, to complain about this inequality, since it was a natural part of their view of the world.

Dolf felt he would never cease to be amazed by the strength and endurance displayed by these children. Cold and tired as he was, Dolf felt a warm glow growing inside him, as the full significance of the children's crusade became clear to him. For the first time in their miserable existences, these children had been able to do something for them-selves. This alone had been sufficient to create an army of neglected orphans and neglected serfs with a collective determination so strong that it would permit nothing and no one to deter them from their objective. He felt proud of them—proud of their courage and proud of their ability to overcome suffering. Now he understood why he felt such a great compulsion to help them. They were worth it.

They reached the foot of the mountain the following evening and pitched camp in the broad valley. The first high stepping-stone of the Alps had been conquered.

The mood in the camp was cheerful, despite the recent suffering. The two heroic deeds—the expedition to Schar-nitz castle and Leonardo's fight with the bear—had been heard of by all and were almost the only topics of conversation. The children told each other the stories as if they had heard them all their lives.

Dolf's deception of Count Romhild was a wonderful joke, but the cudgel of Leonardo, which had delivered such a mighty blow to the tough skull of a huge bear and sent it packing, had become the weapon of a giant.

The valley was wide, fairly flat and extremely fertile. But behind this peaceful land rose another horror—the towering mountain barring the way into Lombardy. One day's journey after leaving the Karwendel, the children reached the old town of Innsbruck. The people brought the first vegetables and fresh milk that they had had in many days. At long last the sun had raised its cheerful face and the valley was bathed in a golden glow.

They spread out their soaking clothes to dry and kneaded the hardened leather of their shoes in order to make it supple again. Broken limbs were put in splints and treated, albeit rather roughly, by the town surgeon. The Bishop left his palace and visited the children's army to give it his blessing. The three sheep, which had miraculously survived the journey, were sold to a butcher in exchange for smoked ham and sausages. Everyone felt better. The Karwendel had been a severe test of their endurance, but it had not broken them and they now looked toward their trip through the Brenner Pass with confidence.

Ambling around the camp, Dolf came upon Carolus.

"Are things going well with you?" he asked cheerfully.

The king smiled brightly at him and Dolf suddenly remembered a question he had long been wishing to ask.

"Carolus, how did you come to be designated the future king of Jerusalem? Did the children elect you?"

"The children? Of course not." Carolus drew up his small, elegant figure. "I was appointed by the Count of Marburg to whom I was page. It was quite an honor, you know. He had four pages and I was the youngest. The others were green with envy."

Dolf sat down pulling the little king down beside him.

"So you didn't run away from home, like Fredo?"

"You know I couldn't do a thing like that. I had sworn loyalty to my master. The Count of Marburg sent me along to look after his daughter, Hilda. And since Hilda would become queen of Jerusalem ..."

"Hey, just a minute," Dolf interrupted, suddenly remembering something. "So you were sent by the Count of Marburg, who also permitted his daughter to come ... with the Archbishop's consent if I remember rightly?"

"Yes, the Archbishop gave us his blessing and put us under Nicolas's care."

"But isn't there a king of Jerusalem already? I don't mean a Saracen, but some Christian nobleman who claims the title for himself?"

"Oh, of course, but it doesn't mean anything while the city is in the hands of the Turks. In any case, it is nothing more than an inherited title. I will become the real king."

"Who is the nominal king of Jerusalem?" he asked.

"I am not quite sure, there have been so many. Some French nobleman, I think."

What completely astounded Dolf when he heard this was that not only did powerful adults such as the Count of Marburg, the Archbishop of Cologne, and goodness knows what other conspirators, really believe that the children's crusade would succeed but also that they would exploit children who were close to them. It seemed that the Archbishop had been the prime organizer and had been helped by Anselmus and Augustus. He had been the one who gave Nicolas a wagon, two oxen and a tent. And the Count of Marburg had been quite happy to send his little daughter and one of his pages ... Had they no sense at all?

"It's not very nice in the tent, these days," said Carolus

suddenly. "Anselmus and Augustus are always quarreling, because Anselmus wants us to speed up. He's always in a hurry. But Augustus thinks the children are in need of rest."

Dolf was surprised by this piece of information, but Carolus continued heatedly:

"Nicolas pleaded with them to maintain unity, since it would be a bad example to the children if the two monks were seen to be quarreling. Augustus seems quite friendly, doesn't he? I think he is a good man."

"Oh?"

"Of course, Anselmus is too," Carolus added hastily, as if he did not wish Dolf to see his bias. "He is very pious and strict, but that is necessary, since there are so many children here who won't listen to anybody. On the other hand, they listen to Dom Augustus and even more to Dom Thaddeus, and they aren't severe at all."

"What are they arguing about?" asked Dolf.

"I'm not quite sure ... about some Boglio or other. Augustus kept saying that Boglio will wait. But Anselmus seems concerned that whoever he is won't wait very long. Can you make anything of it?"

"No," replied Dolf, "but I am going to find out more."

It was the first time he had heard the name Boglio and it sounded decidedly Italian. Dolf wondered what plan the monks had for Genoa.

Once again they set off into the mountains and struggled up the twisting pathway. The bright sun had transformed the dried mud into dust, which billowed up under the thousands of feet, clogging the marchers' noses, torturing their throats and stinging their eyes. Higher and higher they climbed, pestered all the while by insects, and stumbling over sharp-edged stones; one moment in scorching sunlight, the next in chilling shadow. With every step they ascended, but they were slow, short steps which required a lot of energy.

Once they were twelve to fifteen hundred feet above the valley they were able to look down on the wooded lower slopes and beyond to the friendly town of Innsbruck.

After a short while, however, they turned a bend in the road and the town was hidden from view. They were now hedged around by the grim mountains: towering rocks, forest abounding with wildlife, cascading torrents of water, fir trees of immense age, thorny bushes, downy moss and flowers; there were flowers everywhere. They spied eagles and foxes, buzzards and chamois, trout in the rivers and guinea pigs between the rocks. The scenery was overpowering in its beauty. They passed by thundering waterfalls and motionless lakes. Once they met a shepherd with his flock of sheep and the following day six robbers fled in fright on seeing the size of the children's army. They also encountered some mountain-dwellers who, alarmed by the procession, threw stones at the children. The hunters retaliated with arrows to show that the children were quite capable of defending themselves and the people left them alone.

They passed by ravines, gorges and sheer cliff-faces and over fields of flowers. They scrambled across rock-falls, stumbled over tree-roots, cut out snake-bites, tore their clothes and lost their shoes. They ate mildewed cakes, smelly fish and fresh meat from the chamois and mountain goats. They drank ice cold water which gave them stomach aches. Carolus and the hunters and Peter and the fishermen did all they could to get food. Dolf marveled at the number of birds he saw. They circled above the ravines in great clouds. The forests teemed with them; and not just in the trees. Many could be found pecking around on the ground and the children caught, shot and slaughtered all that they could lay their hands on. It pained Dolf to see Carolus wringing the neck of a pigeon, grinning as he did so, but it meant that one more child would have a meal that evening.

Once they had breasted the summit, thousands of feet up, they dropped down again to the next valley and another frothing river. Often crossing the rivers took many hours, since the stronger children had to form a chain by which the younger ones could help themselves to the other side. While the water was never deep, it still hurled itself against their legs with an unbelievable force so it was hard for them to get their footing on the slippery rocks of the riverbed. Once or twice the chains broke and some of the children were carried away.

Despite hardships in crossing the Brenner Pass, the army lost few children. Almost every child, however, had some kind of injury, and their clothing was ragged and soiled. Augustus's habit hung about him in rags and Nicolas's right eye had been closed by a bee-sting (he was very fond of honey). The weak and defenseless children had been fodder to the mountains, which in return had provided the others with fresh meat, strength and a heart full of freedom and happiness. At long last they came down the Alps to follow the broad river Isarco. When they finally arrived in the brilliant sunshine at the gates of the town of Bolzano they were tough, tanned and half-wild human beings—dressed in rags. Seven thousand children who had been through Hell, but who had returned happy and singing, bubbling over with joy and resolve.

The Bolzanese marveled at the sight!

THE BATTLE OF THE PO VALLEY

To the children, Bolzano was simply another place to rest. As was customary by now, the citizens offered homes to those who were sick or exhausted. The camp was outside the town, and there they luxuriated in the sunshine, the warm nights and the abundance of food—especially fruit. Anselmus could be heard complaining about the distance still to be covered to Genoa, but the children refused to be hurried. The journey to the Holy Land had already taken so much longer than they had expected that another short delay hardly mattered. The highest of the mountains had been left behind and they had entered a new world, full of sunshine and flowers, where people went about their business at a leisurely pace.

Furthermore, these children were only just beginning to learn about distances. Heretofore they simply believed that once they were over the mountains they would find the sea and, in turn, the sea would be divided in front of them. They had always lived entirely in the present and barely gave a second thought to the difficulties that lay ahead. Such matters they allowed others to decide for them. It was a mental attitude that they had inherited from their parents: do what you are told and you will be safe. They were just like sheep; uneducated and incapable of thinking about their own existence, it made no difference to them whether they were travelling through mountains, wandering homeless through dirty streets or were forced to do heavy manual labor on the land.

But by no means all were like this. There were many

who were able to recognize the advantages of being free and to whom the trip had been a revelation. These children had begun to develop into capable and inventive human beings. Despite the hardships, dangers and discomforts, they loved the crusade. They had started to take an interest in the organization and to feel some sort of sense of responsibility for their own groups. Children who had formerly been illiterate beggars began studying plant and animal life on their own initiative. Others filled their spare time with wood-carving, basket-weaving and making utensils for which the army always had a great demand. They fabricated primitive looms, wove a cloth of plant fibers and made new shirts.

It was not until the following day that Dolf discovered the reason why the Bolzanese were so helpful. The answer came from Leonardo.

"There are the most extraordinary rumors going around the town and yet the people really believe them. They are saying that when the children's army left Cologne it was thirty thousand strong. Thirty thousand! Where could they have got that crazy figure from?"

"How much is thirty thousand?" asked Maria.

"An unbelievably large number, my dear. There aren't that many children in the whole of Cologne. The people of Bolzano believe that we have lost at least twenty thousand on the way and that we have left a trail of dead children behind us. That's why they are being so welcoming to us, the survivors."

"Who on earth started talking about thirty thousand children?" asked Dolf.

"The devil only knows, but the idea is catching on fast. Soon we will be believing it ourselves."

"The number never was counted," Dolf murmured.

"No, but you don't need to count to see the difference between eight and thirty thousand. When we encountered them at Spiers there couldn't have been many more than eight thousand."

"Nevertheless, our losses have been severe," the boy said sadly.

"They have not been that bad," Leonardo replied. "Out of the eight thousand, seven thousand at least have arrived in Lombardy. And don't forget that Fredo took something like eight hundred with him when he left. And then, not all the others perished along the way. How many have we left behind in towns and villages? I think we can be pleased with our work."

"But we are still a great number, aren't we?" asked Maria with concern. "There is still enough of us to liberate Jerusalem, isn't there?"

"What's all this about liberating? The Saracens are going to run off screaming as soon as they see you," said Leonardo, his voice thick with sarcasm.

"You don't believe in it," Maria said with a hurt tone.

"Do you still?" Dolf asked sharply.

The girl hung her head.

"I don't know," she whispered dejectedly. "Sometimes I think ..."

"Goodness," thought Dolf. "She is beginning to think."

"Yes?" he and Leonardo asked simultaneously.

"Sometimes I think something must be wrong. Why is the sea so far away? Nobody told us that before we left. I don't think even Nicolas knew. And why did so many children die? God was supposed to protect us!"

"God protected you, Maria," Leonardo replied quickly.

She looked up at him reproachfully.

"No, it was you and Rudolf." She was becoming quite a little heretic! "And the Saracens, will they really run away from us? They didn't run away from the proper crusaders. They fought very bravely and were often victorious."

"I think this child is progressing very well. Don't you

agree, Rudolf?" Leonardo laughed. "But you are right, Maria. There is something wrong somewhere."

Dolf was greatly cheered by this conversation. If Maria was beginning to have doubts, it could well be that she was not the only one. What would the children do, he wondered, when the miracle of dividing the sea, in a few weeks' time, didn't happen?

They continued to follow the river Isarco, which led them once more into the mountains. Although the weather was burning hot and the old military road winding its way along the river bank was in bad repair, the mountains were now lower and stood farther apart. They passed by orchards full of ripening apples and wide valleys. They experienced both friendly and dangerous encounters with other travellers: robber-bands, pilgrims, hostile villagers, cheerful farmers and suspicious townspeople. Each day brought new adventures, pain and suffering, hope and happiness. They journeyed through deep ravines and beautiful valleys, over hills and down into yet more valleys, until after about a week's travel, they arrived at a magnificent mountain lake.

Joyfully they rushed to the water and began washing, fishing and swimming. For ten days they had had no rain or mist and the Alps were behind them. The hills which now confronted them were fertile and abounding with wildlife, and the lake provided them with fish and water fowl.

Dolf was amazed by the beauty and joy of a thinly populated region. The Lake Garda he remembered from vacations with his parents was very different. In the twentieth century it was a commercialized area with hotels, camping sites and souvenir shops. But now he could hardly believe what he saw in this virgin countryside: cranes, ibises and spoonbills. There were storks nesting high up on castle walls and wild swans in the reeds by the lakeside. In the afternoon the surface of the water was almost entirely covered by various birds, diving for fish or resting after a long flight. The children devised contraptions, some ingenious and some ridiculous, with which to catch the birds; nets, sticks with barbs, arrows on the end of long pieces of string and pointed spears. They devastated the animals but they had no choice. Otherwise they would have died of hunger. Carolus, in particular, was having the time of his life. The possibilities offered by such a bountiful nature stimulated his imagination more than ever. He even collected large fishbones, out of which the children could make combs, brushes and needles.

Under the burning sun their skin had become coffee-colored and they were no longer concerned about clothing. However, they desperately needed protection for their heads and within a few days nearly all seven thousand were decorated with the most amazing hats, platted from straw or grass and often adorned with flowers. A few days after leaving the lake they came to the town of Brescia, where the frightened citizens barred the gates and asked the children to leave the region as soon as possible. Uncomplaining, the children complied and took the road south toward Genoa ...

"Where is the sea? Will we reach the sea today?" they never stopped asking. But now all they saw was a vast, seemingly endless plain. It was the plain of the Po River.

"All we have to do is cross these lowlands, then over a few hills and there you will see the sea," promised Dom Anselmus. The children stared at him in shocked disbelief.

"How far is it? Is it much farther?"

Dolf knew it was an enormous distance but he kept his knowledge a secret. He had decided that the more dissatisfied the children became, the easier it would be to understand that they were being deceived.

More children died in the Po plain and with each death

the rebelliousness increased. The causes now were sunstroke, a lack of water, and snakebites. They were still a long way from the river Po, which ran across their path from west to east, and water was getting scarce. Most of the land was uncultivated and an area which would later become the food store of Italy was now little more than a barren plain. The inhabitants of this drought-tortured area were not very friendly. The Lombardians, whose farms had so often been destroyed by the German emperors, had good reason to distrust a German-speaking army. For centuries Lombardy had been the battlefield of Europe and less than twenty years had elapsed since Frederick Barbarossa had ravaged the region. Now they were faced by an invasion of German children.

"We are peaceful crusaders," said Nicolas, but the people were not impressed. Crusaders should not be tanned, wild and disobedient. These children were hardly normal, let alone holy. The Saracens were not likely to flee from this undisciplined rabble. Goodness, what innocence! It was a crowd of impertinent ruffians which raided farms and fought like experienced soldiers. They knew no fear and were brazenly disrespectful. The girls were no better than the boys.

They were a marauding band of thieves which respected nothing, swarming over the land like locusts and eating everything they could find. They burst into houses and barns, weapons in hand and demanded food.

All of this was true. The difficult journey through the mountains had hardened the children's attitude, so that they were angered by the cool reception the people gave them. They wanted food and they wanted water and when they did not get it they took it. What need did they have of orderlies now? They had become their own orderlies. What need did they have of hunters, when they all had their own weapons and were skillful in using them? What could fishermen do in a land without water? They too went hunting or stealing ...

In two months the devout children who had left Cologne with clasped hands, singing hymns and praying, had become a large gang of reckless robbers and self-assured soldiers, scared of no one. An increasing sense of doubt and mutiny encouraged them further. Perhaps they would not reach Jerusalem, perhaps God had changed His mind, but that was not going to stop them from eating! Anselmus did nothing to halt this decline in discipline. Augustus was the same as he always had been: a friendly man who loved the children and to whom they could always voice their complaints. He even seemed to find their treatment of the farmers amusing. Nicolas took no interest whatsoever in what was going on around him. He was obsessed with the idea of going to Jerusalem and performing his holy mission; what happened along the way was no concern of his. Dolf, Leonardo and Dom Thaddeus did all they could to keep the children under control, but they were spurned. By this point in their journey the children had realized that, far from God being the one to provide food, they had to do it themselves—which was exactly what they did.

But slowly the anger of the inhabitants of the region was being roused, until it eventually led to a battle between furious farmers and the children's army.

They had been walking for several days through the hot, scorched land, when they came upon the little river Oglio. Screaming with delight, they threw themselves into the water to soothe their parched throats and cool their burning bodies. They drank until their stomachs ached. Although it was still early afternoon, they refused to continue and began to set up camp in the shade of a small wood. Anselmus ranted and raved to no avail. With the shady trees and the cool, clear water close by, this was where they wanted to stay for the rest of the day and the night. Dolf, inwardly grinning at these signs of the children's revolt, helped with the gathering of wood and dry grass for the fires. He had wandered a little way off, when he suddenly heard a sound which made him stiffen. He quickly shinnied up a tree and gazed into the distance, where a church spire, outlined against the horizon, shimmered in the heat. But it was not that which held his attention. There were dozens of people, marching through the long, yellow grass, armed with pitchforks, cudgels, knives and old pieces of iron.

Dolf wasted no time, but slipped from the tree and ran toward the camp.

"Get your weapons! We are being attacked! Get the little ones to the middle of the camp!"

He bumped into Frank.

"My knife! I must find my knife! Call the orderlies and hunters together, quick! We are about to be attacked by an army of peasants."

The alarm sent the whole camp into action. The orderlies ran to take up their positions to ward off the attack. The smallest children and the tottering patients were herded together at the center of the camp, where they were put to work making arrows. The other boys and girls grabbed whatever they could find with which to defend themselves: blunt, rusty knives, cudgels and flaming brands.

They had barely had time to organize themselves when the peasants charged, holding their weapons in front of them and trying to drive the children's army into the river and out of their territory. But the children stood their ground and repulsed the attack, hurling burning wood amongst assailants. To the tough fists and crude weapons they retaliated with their own fists and sticks. Some of the attackers managed to break through the front line of furious defenders, but they were confronted by a second line of defense, which had hurriedly been assembled and which showered them with stinging arrows, expertly thrown stones, cudgel-blows, teeth and nails. The children leaped on the farmers, wrenching the pitchforks out of their hands. Such a weapon in the hands of a quickwitted twelve year old, toughened by weeks of unimaginable suffering, could not be underestimated.

The Lombardians were surprised by the viciousness and determination of the defense. They were greatly outnumbered and it became a battle of ten against one. Even the little ones became wild, rushing forward and thrusting burning pieces of wood into the faces of the attackers, scorching their hair and eyebrows. The screaming peasants turned and fled.

Dolf was at a loss what to do. He was quite prepared to fight for his own life if attacked, but he had no idea how to command a battle. Peter ran up to him and tore the knife out of his grasp. What for? To cut throats of people like himself?

"Hey, give it back," Dolf yelled, but the one-time serf had already disappeared through the trees. He felt uneasy without a weapon and stooped to pick up a stone. Suddenly his body jerked upright.

Staring out from the edge of the wood, he saw that the whole plain was ablaze. The farmers were fleeing before the wall of fire, but already some of the moistureless trees were alight. The whole camp was threatened and back raced Dolf.

"To the other side! Everyone over to the other side!" he yelled. He grabbed a wounded child and dragged him to the bank. The children poured out of the woods, ran down to the river and waded to the other side. Several risked their lives to dismantle Nicolas' tent and carry it with them. Dolf went this way and that, desperately searching for any others who were too badly wounded to escape from the burning wood, but the flames approached so fast that he had to jump between the glowing clumps of grass in order to reach the river. In a matter of minutes, the battlefield had become an ocean of flames. Nothing could be seen of the farmers.

It was impossible to know how many children had been killed, either by drowning or burning. Those who had lost their lives in the battle received a roaring funeral as they were engulfed by flames. All that was left of the wood was a few smoking stumps of trees.

The children set up a new camp on the other side of the river. Dolf discovered Maria and Leonardo with Peter, Frank and Carolus, whose beautiful clothes were scorched and blackened. He noticed Nicolas, the three monks, Frieda and Hilda and heaved a sigh of relief that they had all escaped.

That night Leonardo doubled the guard, but the farmers did not return. They had obviously learned a hard lesson.

The next morning Dolf and some others went and searched the battlefield and scorched surroundings. They dug a deep grave for the dead, all of whom were quite unrecognizable. He counted twenty-six adult corpses and thirty-two smaller ones

Meanwhile, on the other side of the river, the children were forming their groups to continue the journey. Dolf arrived back just as the tent was taken down. Carolus, the little king, was crying uncontrollably.

"Hans has gone. I can't find him anywhere."

Dolf comforted his sobbing friend. Dolf also felt sad over the senseless death of a brave lad, a true friend and a bold hunter.

Battered but untamed, they moved on, trudging through wide, hot plains, grim-faced and bitter. They were stared at by frightened peasants and timid women. They were attacked by swarms of horseflies and wasps. They hunted anything that moved and promised food. It was a bunch of almost seven thousand wild, filthy wanderers—on their way to the Holy Land.

THE WILL OF THE KING

They passed the town of Cremona on the river Po and, after a few more days travelling through flat country, reached the foothills of the Apennines. At the sight of still another mountain range, there was almost a rebellion among the children. It was with great difficulty that Anselmus convinced the children that this really was the last obstacle they would have to overcome before Genoa.

"Children, please believe me," he cried aloud to the grumbling crowd. "The sea is on the other side of these mountains. It is not a wide range and we can be through it in five days. In just five days we will be in Genoa and there you will see the sea divide for Nicolas. By all that is sacred I swear that this is true. We are almost there. Don't lose hope, dear children, your perseverance will be rewarded."

The children, however, remained suspicious.

"We are lost," they retorted. "This isn't the way to Jerusalem. We have walked in a circle and come back to the mountains again."

"No," cried Anselmus desperately. "These are not the Alps. These are the Apennines, a low range of rough hills. They are not nearly as high or as cold as the northern mountains. I know them, I was born here ... I mean, I lived here for many years. Ask Rudolf of Amsterdam, since you have so much confidence in him, he has been here before and knows the geography of the towns and the country hereabouts. It is not my fault nor that of Dom Augustus that the journey has been so long. It was Rudolf of Amsterdam who insisted on our taking a roundabout route.

You have no right to be angry with us. If you have any complaints about the long and dangerous journey, you should make them to Rudolf."

The children hesitated, not wishing to call Rudolf of Amsterdam to account for himself. Augustus stepped forward to speak.

"Have patience; dear children. Rudolf was right to persuade us to take the longer way and, after all, we are in no hurry. In this region the weather is warmer."

Anselmus gave him a shove the children could not see but Augustus was not to be stopped.

"These mountains are not as difficult to climb as they look. But if you don't wish to go on, there is no reason why we shouldn't turn back."

"Have you gone mad?" Anselmus hissed to him, but Augustus took no notice. Raising his voice, he cried:

"Who would like to go home?" and it sounded as if he were hoping to hear seven thousand cries of: "I would!" But he did not. Turn back, when they were so close to Genoa? Turn back, when in just a few days' time they would be standing by the sea to witness the great miracle?

For some time they argued about it among themselves and then someone decided to ask Rudolf whether what Anselmus had said was true. Surely he would know whether this was the last obstacle before the sea. But Rudolf could not be found.

They were searching for him when Frank came running up, out of breath.

"Quick," he shouted. "Something terrible has happened," and he had gone again. Several hundred children snatched up their weapons and ran after him. Perhaps the rear guard was being attacked.

Frank led them to a shady thicket about half a mile up the road, where the children were confronted by the cause for concern.

On the ground in front of them, lying on his beautiful red cloak and groaning with pain, lay Carolus. A small group, including Dolf, sat around him looking worried.

"Carolus is ill," the word was passed from mouth to mouth and the rebellious mood was at once transformed into one of concern.

Dom Thaddeus elbowed his way through the crowd and bent over the boy, who was doubled up in pain. The little king was suffering agony. The pulse which Dom Thaddeus felt was beating much too fast.

Dolf desperately tried to think what might be the matter with him. He had already thought of poisonous berries or rotten food, but in his few conscious moments Carolus had murmured that he had not eaten for two days.

There could now be no question of moving on; the mountains would have to wait. The children began to set up camp and Carolus was taken to the tent. Dolf allowed no one to come near, except Hilda, Leonardo and, of course, Dom Thaddeus. After a short while, however, he sent for Maria, because Hilda was powerless. She had no trouble in tending the most hideous wounds or cleaning up the little ones, but the suffering of her future bridegroom was so upsetting to her that she could do nothing but cry.

Naturally everyone else expected Rudolf of Amsterdam to perform another of his miracle cures for Carolus. But Dolf himself was completely at a loss. He had no idea what was making him so sick. Ordinary indigestion could not cause such pain. Gently he felt Carolus's stomach, until he had localized the center of the pain. Then, slowly, the incredible truth dawned on him. It was appendicitis!

In Dolf's age appendicitis was nothing more than a troublesome minor ailment, which could be quickly cured by a short operation. In a few days a patient could be well and walking around again. But here an operation would be quite impossible. How advanced was the inflammation, he wondered. Was there still a chance? No! In the Middle Ages appendicitis was fatal. To Dolf it seemed the ultimate irony that Carolus, of all people, should be afflicted. He did not want to believe it, it was just too terrible.

"Maria," he whispered. "I need dressings, soaked in icy water. Quick."

A short way from the camp was the little river Trebbia and Maria soon returned with clean cloths and a pitcher of water. Dolf soaked the cloths and placed them on Carolus's stomach, changing them every few minutes. He had some lukewarm herb tea prepared and tried to speak to the delirious Carolus.

"How long have you had these pains, Carolus?" he persistently asked, praying that it might not yet be too late.

Carolus made no response, but Hilda replied: "He hasn't eaten anything since we left Cremona. Sometimes I have heard him groaning and he said that he was suffering from the heat ..."

Dolf now realized the inevitable. For the past forty-eight hours Carolus had been walking around with acute appendicitis. It was part of a king's duty to suffer pain and hardship and Carolus had not told anyone. Barely an hour ago he had collapsed and he was now beyond help. Rest and cooling water could do nothing and he probably would not live to see the morning. Sobbing, Dolf covered his face with his hands. Leonardo and Maria exchanged an anxious glance, seeing the sentence in Dolf's despair. Maria, with quivering lips, continued to change the towels herself.

Each time the little king regained consciousness, his eyes searched for Dom Thaddeus, who did everything he could to comfort the child, promising him Heaven. On one occasion Carolus muttered:

"Bertho, chief hunter." A moment later he opened his eyes and said:

"Rudolf of Amsterdam, my heir, I order you ..." and

once again he lapsed into delirium.

Dolf paled. He realized that the others must have heard and when he looked up, his eyes met those of Nicolas, who was standing in the entrance to the tent. The shepherd boy said nothing, but the expression on his face betrayed his envy.

All that night they sat and watched over the dying boy. At daybreak, the little king of Jerusalem said farewell to his subjects. Dolf stood like a statue while he watched Dom Thaddeus close the lids over the broken eyes and fold the cramped hands across his chest. He saw the cloak pulled over the little corpse and he noticed Maria silently clearing away the towels and the bowls, large teardrops rolling down her cheeks. He heard Hilda pray and Augustus cry. But of none of these things was he really conscious. He was still unable to believe the truth. He had never experienced such an utter sense of loss. Together they had all conquered the Scarlet Death, kept hunger at bay while they crossed the Alps, rescued the kidnapped children from the castle of Scharnitz and defeated the farmers on the Po plain. On each occasion children had died, but Dolf had still considered all these things to have been victories over a cruel and unrelenting world. This time, however, he had lost. He had been unable to save the life of the child he loved the most. Dolf was crushed with sorrow. He left the tent and went off to be alone.

Dom Thaddeus left the tent with head bowed. Outside stood hundreds of children who had waited up all night, keeping guard and praying. The monk told them that God had called His servant Carolus and that the burial would take place that evening. He also mentioned Carolus's last wish—that Rudolf of Amsterdam should be his heir. The news spread through the camp like a forest fire. Carolus, clothed in all his finery, was placed on a bier in front of the tent. In a long line the children filed past to pay their last respects. They laid flowers at his head and feet, crossed themselves and, crying, moved on to make room for the next group. It was a sorrowful procession which lasted almost all day. There was no thought of eating, bathing, hunting or fishing. A king, in every sense of the word, had died and the children wished to display their love, honor and deep sadness.

The little king was buried at sunset. Because they had no coffin, Carolus was wrapped in his red cloak, covered with flowers and carried to a grave which had been dug in the shade of an ancient tree. As the body was lowered into the grave on ropes, the whole army sang a hymn. Dolf, the new king, was allowed to throw the first handful of earth into the grave. It was all he could do to bring himself to do it. With dull thuds redbrown earth was shoveled over the corpse. On the mound over the grave they planted flowers, dug up, roots and all, from the vicinity. Under Bertho's guidance, some of the children had made a cross of a beautiful, smooth wood. Leonardo carved a Latin motto onto it, using Dolf's knife. Dom Thaddeus conducted the service. It was indeed a funeral worthy of a king. Night descended on the camp and the mourning children went to bed. Many were still crying and others prayed. Timidly they looked toward Rudolf of Amsterdam, but he steadfastly refused to take his place in the tent of the elite. Even when Dom Thaddeus reminded him of Carolus's last wish, he shook his head emphatically.

"King or no king, my place is with the children."

He had not the least inclination to play monarch to seven thousand cheated children.

"Let them elect a king for themselves. I can't do it."

But the children could not understand Dolf's refusal to carry out Carolus's last wish and they understood even less about elections. Eventually, to alleviate their obvious concern, Dolf promised:

"All right, I will be your king, but not yet. For the time

being I am just an ordinary crusader like the rest of you. You can honor me later, after we have liberated Jerusalem, but not before."

With that they were content.

The impact of the death of Carolus was so great that discipline returned to the army. Dom Anselmus, who had been keeping some kind of diary during the journey, estimated that they would reach Genoa around the middle of August. That would be about three weeks later than he had hoped, but it might still be in time. Once again he began urging the children to greater speed and now, since they yearned for the end of the journey, they listened to him. They all had the same objective in mind as they moved off into the mountains. Few people lived in this barren and dry region and they managed to keep their supplies at an adequate level by fishing, hunting and picking berries. Bertho proved to be as good a leader of the hunters as Carolus and considerably more careful. The few mountain-dwellers that there were lived chiefly from robbery, exacting tolls and poaching. But the children were left in peace. Their large number, their songs and their inexorable movement soon dissuaded any who might have thought of robbing them. Furthermore, under Leonardo's leadership the defense was better organized. He was forever insuring that the orderlies were performing their duties properly and, at times, it seemed as if he was in just as great a hurry to reach the coast as Dom Anselmus and Nicolas. It was at this time that Dom Augustus began to behave very oddly. He refused to sleep in the tent any longer and shuffled along in the rear guard, shaking his head as if broken with sorrow.

"Rudolf," he whispered one evening, "be on your guard in Genoa." But, no matter how much Dolf pressed him, Augustus would say no more. It was not just that he was very sad about the death of Carolus, he also seemed frightened. Dolf did not know what had brought on this change.

SEA AT LAST!

"Tomorrow we will see Genoa! Tomorrow we will reach the sea!" The words flew from child to child and the pace of the army quickened. Nicolas, who was as impatient as any, went to the front. As usual, he was wearing his white robe, but around it was a bejeweled belt from which hung a precious dagger in a silver-studded sheath. It was Carolus's belt. Dolf had thought that all of Carolus's possessions had been buried with him, but Nicolas apparently had been unable to resist the temptation to claim this item for his own. Dolf thought it a rather childish act, but did not let it bother him. No matter how impressive Nicolas looked he would never be a real leader. Even if he were showered with jewels and gold he would never be anything more than the puppet of Anselmus, without a mind of his own and without any real dignity.

Dolf did not realize that in the Middle Ages appearance meant everything and that he himself had lost some respect in the eyes of the children by allowing Nicolas the opportunity to wear the insignia of royalty.

"Genoa! Tomorrow we will be in Genoa!" The atmosphere was electric. They all believed that they would be able to see Jerusalem from the beach at Genoa. They were almost there. They had only to wait for the sea to divide and, cheering with joy, they would storm toward the Holy City. How the Saracens would run! Little Simon talked incessantly. He felt as strong as a bear and told everyone that he could handle at least ten of the heathens all by himself.

All of a sudden the children's army came to a halt. They had reached the first sentry-post of the town and had come face to face with a menacing stone tower, manned by bowmen. A blockade had been raised across the road, guarded by knights and pikemen. On its seaward side, Genoa was open, but the town needed to be well protected from robbers and vagabonds on the mountainous side. In those days Genoa was the richest, most powerful and best-fortified city on the Mediterranean. It was impossible to approach it unnoticed. Unaware that the vanguard had been halted, the impatient children behind pressed forward and Leonardo had great difficulty controlling them.

Together with Dolf he pushed his way to the front, where Dom Anselmus and Nicolas were negotiating with the officers. Dolf was surprised to discover that Anselmus spoke fluent Tuscanese. Leonardo had given him Italian lessons along the way but his knowledge was not great enough to follow this conversation. Leonardo acted as interpreter.

"The city already knows of our approach. The Duke will not allow the children inside the walls, but will allow them free access to the sea by a different route which will bring us to the beach south of the town."

The children were quite happy with this because all they wanted was to reach the sea. But Anselmus was angry and showed it.

"Genoa will live to regret this … ," he said, and much more besides. He threatened them with the wrath of Heaven and cajoled them like a travelling salesman trying to sell an unwanted article. But the soldiers remained unmoved. No one would hinder the children's path to the sea, but they could not go through the town. Genoa did not want them.

Dom Augustus, who had also come forward, was still acting strangely. Weeping, he embraced the officer.

"God will reward you for this, my good man. I will pray

for your soul every day." For this performance he received another blow in the ribs from Anselmus, but he took no notice.

"We don't need the city," he exclaimed, turning to the children. "We will go to the beach and be happy." Dolf was confounded by this show of joy, and he could see that Nicolas was puzzled too.

When all was said and done the cordon of soldiers in front of them meant another detour. A few knights were detailed to accompany them and show them the way. It was shortly after noon, at the hottest time of day, that they breasted the hill and saw below them ... the sea! Away to their right, in a wide valley, lay Genoa, glinting in the sun. From above, the city seemed like some jewel which a giant had hacked from the rocks and let slip through his fingers. Its many towers shone in the sunlight like the facets of a diamond. Between them shimmered a sea of rooftops and towering above all else was the dome of the cathedral, still half-hidden by scaffolding.

Surrounded by thousands of children, Dolf gazed down on this mighty stronghold, the richest and most powerful port of Europe in 1212. It was a city of contradictions: magnificent churches and filthy inns, palaces and slums, warehouses and dumps. On the one hand it was a town of secrecy, intrigue and attempted assassinations, while on the other it was a gathering place of art treasures from all over the world. A stupendously rich city where poverty was rampant.

Beyond the city was the sea, a sea which seemed to have no farther shore. It was the Mediterranean, which in Dolf's century was an irresistible attraction for vacationers from the north, but in this era it was an enemy to the people.

The children stood in silence, so captivated by the sight of the sea, that beautiful blue, unending sea, that they barely noticed the mighty town. So very few among them had ever seen the sea that they had not known what to expect. They were overwhelmed by the reality. Open-mouthed they gazed out over this immense mass of water. Shortly they would go down to the beach, Nicolas would stretch out his arms and the waters would divide. But now that they were actually confronted by the sea and could see how it seemed to stretch until the end of the world, they began to experience a vague feeling of doubt. How could so much water divide?

Many of the young ones believed that the town below them must be Jerusalem. They had been travelling for so long that they could not believe that the world was any larger. Cries of joy escaped their mouths and they pressed forward in their desire to descend and watch the Saracens flee. The elder ones managed to restrain them, although they themselves were growing impatient. They too wanted to witness the promised miracle and watch so great a mass of water separate for the shepherd boy. Shouting and yelling in their enthusiasm, the entire army suddenly lurched forward and streamed down the hill toward the beach.

The rocks scattered along the rough coastline were submerged under waves of children, who streamed along the beach until they found a level patch, in the shade of fir trees, on which they set up camp. Many tried to reach the town but were stopped by the soldiers and sent back. Clearly Genoa wanted nothing to do with the children's army, but this in no way discouraged the little ones. Long-ingly they stared to the far-off horizon, beyond which they childishly imagined must be Jerusalem, the gleaming city of their dreams. Hungrily they watched the fishing boats sailing along the coast and then they turned their eyes plead-ingly toward Nicolas, Leonardo and Rudolf. There was nothing left to eat.

"Tomorrow," cried Anselmus in a loud voice, "Nicolas will perform the miracle. But he must first fast and pray for twenty-four hours, so erect his tent, children, quickly."

Despite their impatience, they could understand this. Miracles could not be conjured up just like that, one had to prepare oneself beforehand. Under the spreading branches of a few fir trees the tent was pitched and Nicolas silently withdrew. No one was allowed to enter, not even the children of noble blood. Dolf almost felt pity for the poor shepherd boy, because he obviously believed that the miracle would happen. Belief can console people when they are suffering greatly, but it cannot change the design of nature—and that includes dividing the Mediterranean. Nicolas was doomed to failure and Dolf felt sorry for him for that reason. But what Dolf feared was the reaction of the children when the miracle did not occur. They were his greatest concern.

Dom Augustus stalked about the camp like a chicken unable to lay an egg. Dolf noticed how nervous he was and also that Augustus continued to cry. He cried unceasingly, embracing the children and stroking their hair and repeating all the time:

"God will protect you, my dear children." Dolf was convinced that he had gone quite mad.

Vainly Anselmus tried to calm his anxious companion.

"Keep calm, brother, or the children might think that some disaster is about to befall them."

"And is not that so … ?" Augustus began to tremble, but Anselmus shouted at him:

"Oh, be quiet! Get those children working. It is still quite early and I must go to the town."

"No, no!" cried Augustus, suddenly dropping to his knees on the stony ground. He raised his hands pleadingly to the other monk.

"Don't do it, Anselmus, don't do it. I pray you!"

By chance, Dolf had approached without their noticing him and he stopped in surprise at this strange sight.

Angrily Anselmus kicked out at the groveling monk so that the fat Augustus nearly fell over.

"Get up, you fool. Have you forgotten how much silver awaits us?"

Suddenly noticing Dolf, he stopped in alarm.

"What are you doing here? Get away! The affairs of holy men are nothing to do with you. You should be providing food for the children."

Dolf said nothing, turned around and walked off. His mind was racing, for he had just realized that he might be able to discover Anselmus's intention, providing he approached Augustus in the right manner. Evidently Augustus no longer wished to participate in ...

In what? What was he trying to prevent Anselmus from doing? Why was he so anxious and so full of concern for the children? Augustus knew why Anselmus was going to Genoa and he was pleading with his swarthy companion not to do it ... but not to do what?

"You should be providing food for the children ..."

Yes, that was his task and he had reacted to Anselmus's words automatically. However, he knew by now that the children could easily look after themselves. Already the hundreds of boys and girls were wading out into the water, armed with nets and spears. They were surprised to find the water so warm. The sea seemed welcoming to them after the ice-cold streams and rivers that they had fished during the journey. They drank, but quickly spat out the salty water with disgust. How could fish live in such warm, salt water? But they certainly could! There were large shoals of them and varieties which they had never seen before, both large and small.

They scrambled over the rocks and fished all the pools empty. They caught lobsters, crabs and other shellfish, but did not know what to do with them. Dolf showed them how to clean and prepare their catch and convinced them that, if done properly, the sardines, transparent shrimp and small octopuses would be very tasty. Enthusiastically, they turned their attention to cooking the food, though they sometimes recoiled at the sight of the sharp claws, the sucking pads and strange eyes of the slimy sea creatures.

"Salty fish soup tonight," thought Dolf eagerly. "Something tasty at last."

Many of the fishermen were bitten and pinched on their hands and feet by the lobsters and crabs and the nurses had to work overtime. But one learns quickly enough with experience and children faster than most. They became more wary and soon discovered how to pick up shellfish safely and which rock-pools were likely to yield the best catch. Peter was enjoying himself immensely.

The hunters too had been busy and the wooded hills surrounding Genoa were ransacked. The forests here were less rich in wild animals than some they had seen and poaching was forbidden as it was in the north. But their hunger made them heedless of danger. Moreover, they discovered a supply of fresh water half a mile from the tent.

The Genoese left the children to their own devices. Apart from preventing them from entering the city, they allowed them to do as they wished and even the poachers were left unhindered. If they encroached too near the town, a few soldiers would appear with crossed lances so that the children turned around and went to try their luck farther to the south. Dolf was perplexed by all this. Clearly the Genoese were not hostile, but just as obviously they did not intend giving the children any help. It would seem that the citizens could not understand why the children had come to their town.

And I don't understand either, thought Dolf. Why Genoa? It's a long way off the route.

Dolf decided to look for Augustus and found him praying in a thicket of bushes a short way from the camp.

Dolf sat down beside him and gently shook his arm.

"Dom Augustus …"

"Leave me alone," the monk answered with a sob. He pulled the hood of his habit down and hid his head in his hands.

"Dom Augustus, are you ill?"

"I am afraid."

"What of?"

"Of the sea …"

Dolf thought that he was beginning to understand Augustus's anxiety. If Nicolas failed to control the sea there was no knowing what might happen and the leaders of the crusade would have to admit that they had deceived the children.

"I am afraid too, Dom Augustus," Dolf admitted with concern. "I am a doubter like you. I don't believe the miracle will happen."

The monk raised his head and looked at the boy in amazement.

"That's not it at all," he mumbled.

"So you do believe in the miracle?"

Augustus shook his head.

"The ships," he whispered almost inaudibly. "I cannot stop thinking about those poor children who were taken aboard those boats in Marseilles."

Dolf was now completely lost.

"Which children?"

"The French children, five weeks ago."

Dolf was still no nearer understanding.

"When the sea failed to dry up in front of them, they were taken on board five ships," whispered the monk. "Of those five, three were wrecked in a storm. The other two are said to have survived and reached the coast of Tunisia, where the children …" He fell silent, overcome with sadness.

"Dom Augustus, I don't understand this at all. Who were these children and what were they doing in the ships?"

"The ships were waiting for them in Marseilles."

"Yes, but why? And ..."

Suddenly Dolf recalled that Leonardo had mentioned another children's crusade in France. It had been similar to this one and had left about the same time.

"Dom Augustus, can't you be more explicit? What happened to these children and why did they go to Marseilles?"

"It was a plot. They were led there by two men and a shepherd boy. The children believed they were going to the Holy Land and that Stephan, the shepherd boy, would command the sea to separate for them. But, of course, it didn't and the children were desperately disappointed. The five ships had already been waiting a week and the leaders told the children not to despair, because the ships would take them to the Holy Land."

"Then what were they doing in Tunisia?"

"Don't you understand, Rudolf? The children were taken straight to the slavemarkets of North Africa. That had been the intention right from the start."

"What!" It was several moments before Dolf completely understood, but slowly the magnitude of the treachery came to him.

"So the children ... were destined for ... but that is terrible! Are you trying to say, Dom Augustus, that these children also ... that there are ships waiting in Genoa harbor to take us to Africa to be sold as slaves, is that what you mean?"

The man nodded, his eyes downcast with shame.

"So that is ... that's why we had to come to Genoa ... good God that's ..."

Dom Augustus sat silently, his head bowed with shame. "You are trying to tell me," Dolf whispered in horror, "that there are ships here, too, in Genoa, waiting to take the children to Africa, while they think they are on their way to Palestine?"

The man nodded.

"And you ... you are going to let it happen?"

"No!" cried the monk. "I can't, not now. I pleaded with Anselmus but he would not listen. He is determined not to lose his bags of silver."

"So it was all planned." Dolf almost spat the words between his teeth with anger. "I have been convinced all the time that the children were being duped with this wonderful fairy tale and I knew there must be some mysterious treachery behind it. Dom Augustus, how long have you known about it?"

The man made no reply.

"You have known all the time, haven't you? Even in Cologne?" Dolf asked incredulously.

Still the monk sat unanswering.

"You ... you planned it yourself?"

"No, it wasn't me! Nor Anselmus, though we carried it out."

"Who did then? Who devised this foul plan to herd together thousands of children with empty promises, only to lead them in slavery? Who?"

Augustus shrugged his shoulders.

"Was it Anselmus perhaps?"

Still no reply.

"Oh please, Dom Augustus, you must tell me what's going to happen."

"I don't know," whispered the man desperately. "We have arrived late and I am praying to God that it is too late and that the ships will already have left."

"Too late?"

"It is now well into harvest time and we should have been here a month ago."

"Yes, it's halfway through August ... so that's why

Anselmus was always in such a hurry. That's why he was always urging for greater speed and got so annoyed with every delay."

Augustus nodded.

Dolf was still unable to grasp the enormity of it all. It seemed so incredible that anyone could want to sell thousands of innocent children as slaves in North Africa.

"Jerusalem is not in North Africa," he said slowly.

"I know that, so does Anselmus and so do you. But the children don't suspect anything."

"But why? Why should you want to do such a thing?" Dolf asked despairingly.

"We were promised a lot of money. When we reached Genoa we were to receive one denarius for every strong and healthy child."

"Hm, not bad," Dolf said before he could stop himself. By now he had a good appreciation of the value of silver in the thirteenth century. "Seven thousand denarii, that is a fortune!"

Augustus nodded and then shivered.

"But I don't want it anymore," he whispered. "I can't do it. All those children are so innocent. They suspect nothing and are longing to see Jerusalem. Rudolf, I have really grown to love them."

Dolf nodded, but his revulsion increased. He tried to imagine Maria in the slavemarkets of Tunisia; and the beautiful, strong-willed Hilda; or the blond Frieda with her knowledge of herbs; or the tough Bertho, Peter, Frank and Carl ... It was unthinkable.

"It must be stopped, Dom Augustus."

The man cowered.

"Don't call me Dom. I am unworthy of the title."

"Aren't you a real monk?"

"No, not now ... Ah Rudolf, once I had a good heart, once I wanted to be a holy man. But I was unworthy and they expelled me from the monastery ... It was a terrible time. I had no future and no occupation. I became a wanderer and had to steal to keep myself alive. In Genoa I met Anselmus, who was in just as bad a state as I. But he was much more clever ... and more unscrupulous. He kept company with some of the worst villains, pirates and smugglers ... A man that he knew called Boglio asked us for help. I don't know who originally devised the plan, but Boglio told us that in Tunisia, strong, blond children from the north fetch a lot of money. The Arabs like them."

Dolf shivered with disgust and tried to fight down his rising anger. He wanted to leap on Augustus, grab him by the throat and ... It was all he could do to keep calm.

"And you agreed to it?"

"What else could I do in my position? I had no choice and, at the time, there did not seem much harm in it."

"You saw no harm in cheating children and sending them into slavery?" asked Dolf in complete disbelief.

Once again Augustus hung his head.

"The Arabs are supposed to be humane masters and their slaves have quite good lives, providing they accept their position. And what sort of children would we find? Orphans and outcasts, unruly little serfs who had run away. Vagabonds who lived by lying, begging and robbery, who would all die young, either on the gallows or during the hardships of winter. It seemed to me almost to be a Christian act to round them up and sell them, because they would go to a warm country where people were rich and civilized and where their standard of living would be far higher than anything they could have hoped for ..."

"But as slaves!" Dolf exclaimed.

"Yes."

"... and of the heathens, moreover."

Augustus nodded pathetically.

"But why did they have to come from the north?"

"Because the heathens like them blond and pale-skinned. In addition, here in the south the knights of Lombardy and Tuscany were never greatly attracted by the crusades. The Italians were quite happy to make money out of the crusaders, but not to join them. In the north, however, it has become almost a tradition to go on crusade and the desire to free Jerusalem is still very much alive, especially among the simpler people. The nobles are no longer so enthusiastic, but the children are easily seduced by the idea. Both Anselmus and I come from Lombardy, but we speak German fluently. So we journeyed to the German states to see how many children we could muster. The number was far greater than we had expected; too many for the six ships that would be awaiting us."

"How despicable!" whispered Dolf. "You abused their trust, their devotion. You tricked them with the myth of the gleaming White City, while all the time you knew … How could you do it, Augustus? These wonderful children, who have so courageously overcome all difficulties, who … who have at last discovered the meaning of freedom … you wanted to sell them—as slaves!"

"I can't do it now," the man mumbled wretchedly. "I love them so much. Oh Rudolf, don't you understand. I feel they are my own. I have watched them defending themselves against wild animals, against robbers, against the cruel weather … I have watched how they helped each other. Rudolf, help me. They must not become slaves. These are not useless creatures, they are wonderful people, each and every one of them, and they must be saved."

"You are right, but how?"

Dolf lapsed into deep thought. He could see that Augustus's regret was genuine and he wanted to feel happy that the man had been unable to go through with the monstrous plan, but his anger was too great.

"We must stop them," whispered Augustus who,

relieved that he had been able to unburden his sorrow, had regained some hope. "We must stop them from being lured onto the ships."

"The ships are still here? They've waited for us after all?" asked Dolf brusquely.

"I'm not sure. Augustus went to the town this afternoon to try to find Boglio. I pray that it will be too late, but I'm not sure ..."

A thought suddenly struck Dolf.

"Nicolas," he cried. "Does Nicolas know why the children were brought here?"

"No. He believes in the crusade."

"How did you trick Nicolas into believing that he was a saint who could perform miracles?"

"Oh, that was no problem. At the end of the winter, Anselmus and I crossed the mountains and went north. We searched until we found a strong-looking shepherd boy and then confounded him with 'miracles.' One night we made a wooden cross, set it on fire and raised it in the air above a hill, in such a way that he could not see us, but we could watch him. He dropped to his knees and raised his hands to Heaven. We quickly lowered the cross and extinguished it. Then Anselmus cupped his hands to his mouth and said in a deep, hollow voice:

"God is calling you, my son. We did not yet know his name. We performed many other tricks. Later that night, while he was asleep—he slept outside, because he had no home—we crept toward him and Anselmus began whispering all sorts of things into his ear. He told him he was hearing the voice of an angel, who was calling on him to lead an army of children to the Holy Land and things of that sort. He half woke but continued to listen, rigid with terror and amazement. But whether you believe it or not, from the very first moment he never doubted his holy mission. We had at last found the person."

"At last?"

"Yes, we had tried the same ploy twice before. The first time, the boy ran off screaming into the marshes and drowned. The second one too ran away, but he went straight to his village priest and told him all about it, so he was of no use. Nicolas, however, immediately believed that he had been chosen by God. He must have a very high opinion of himself."

"He certainly has," agreed Dolf. "What happened next?"

"We continued to confuse him with magical fire and unseen voices for three nights, until we noticed that, believing himself to be an emissary of God, he began to neglect his flock. Then we approached him openly in the middle of the road, wearing our habits, of course. We knelt down in front of him, honoring him, and told him that it had been revealed to us in a vision that he had been chosen to lead an army of innocents to the Holy Land and that we had been chosen to help him."

"And he fell for it?"

"What?"

"He believed you immediately?"

"Yes. The three of us left the region and went to Cologne. As we travelled, Nicolas spent all the time preaching and we soon acquired quite a large following. By the time we arrived in Cologne, we already had hundreds of children and Nicolas then became even more diligent. Every day he preached in the square in front of the large cathedral and the children simply flocked to join us. Two weeks before Whitsuntide we set out from Cologne and still they were coming from the surrounding region. While we had been in Cologne, Anselmus and Nicolas were summoned by the Archbishop and I am glad that I was not present at that interview. I still don't know how they managed to convince the Archbishop of their holy mission.

But Anselmus is cunning. The result was that the Archbishop gave us a wagon, two white oxen and a tent. As you know, he even sent his niece, Hilda, with us—and Carolus, to be her protector. Because of this more children of noble birth joined us at our departure. Anselmus was rather concerned at this. He knew that nobody would worry if outcasts and orphans were never heard of again, but if it was ever discovered that children of the nobility had been sold as slaves, there could be a lot of trouble."

"Revenge by their fathers, I suppose?"

"Yes, but fortunately there were not many and they have been treated with great respect."

"I noticed that," said Dolf bitterly.

"That's why I was pleased that Fredo left us before the mountains. The other thing was that we never expected so many children to follow Nicolas; it made our progress slow and presented us with the problem of starvation. And then you and Leonardo arrived. That changed everything. At first we thought you were the son of a nobleman, because of your self-assurance. You blamed us for neglecting our responsibilities toward the children and you were right. I felt ashamed and had already begun to tire of the whole undertaking. It seemed to me that you had been sent by Heaven, for you showed us how to organize ourselves better, so that fewer children would die. But still, I didn't trust you completely."

"What do you mean?"

"You were working so hard for their welfare that I suspected that you and Anselmus were of the same mind."

"You mean you took me for a slave merchant?" Dolf asked, livid with rage.

"Sometimes I did, but I was never sure. When I asked Anselmus, he evaded my questions but I noticed how he hated you and that he was trying to use you, like he did Nicolas."

Dolf was trying hard to understand the twisted mind of Augustus, but it wasn't easy.

"I thought you were a servant of the Devil," Augustus said in a hushed voice, "because the whole hateful plan could only have been the Devil's work and you were actually helping Anselmus by keeping the children alive ... every time there was a delay, I was delighted, because the longer it took us to reach Genoa, the more chance the children would have of escaping their fate. But then I discovered that you didn't want us to hurry either and I wasn't sure again. The Scarlet Death I thought must be a sign from Heaven that God didn't want us to reach Genoa. But what did you do? You drove it away! I just couldn't understand."

"You should have told me all this a long time ago, Augustus."

"Yes, I realize that now, but I didn't dare. I was frightened of Anselmus. If he had discovered that I had lost faith in the operation and didn't want the children to go into slavery, he would have thrown me over a mountain. But neither did I completely trust you ... Throughout the journey I was praying for a miracle, something which would force us to turn back. Every calamity was a joy to me. But the children never gave up hope. They were determined to see the sea and the miracle which Nicolas had promised them. Oh Rudolf, what can we do now?"

"Warn the children and prevent Anselmus from contacting the privateers."

"I pleaded with him."

"You shouldn't plead with a man like Anselmus. The only way to stop such a villain is to kill him," Dolf said grimly.

"You are right, Rudolf. Anselmus is merciless."

"It is about time he got some of his own medicine," said Dolf angrily.

"But what can you do? If you try to tell the children

what Anselmus plans to do, they won't believe you. And if Anselmus discovers that you are aware of his plans, he will murder you."

"And you," said Dolf. Augustus started trembling.

"But it is already too late," the boy suddenly whispered. "Anselmus has gone to the town ..."

"You know," interrupted Augustus, "he was looking forward to the moment when you were taken on board one of those ships. The thought of you, with all your strength and cleverness, being sold in a Tunisian slavemarket, filled him with a sadistic joy."

Dolf's mouth opened and closed, but he was speechless. Augustus was right. Motivated by his concern for Maria and all the others, and suspecting nothing, he would simply have gone with them!

"By Heavens," he grunted, "I am going to make that wretched Anselmus pay for this."

"Yes, you do that, Rudolf. You are so strong and clever—and you are not afraid."

"Are you still?"

Augustus turned his head away in shame.

"Yes," he murmured. "I am scared. I am a sinner and don't want to die; not yet, because I'll be damned."

"Augustus, why are you suddenly trusting me?"

"Not suddenly ... I have trusted you for a long time now. I saw how Anselmus hated you and how he tried to destroy you during the children's tribunal. Then I knew that you were not his accomplice, but his greatest enemy."

"But why didn't you tell me what Anselmus intended doing?"

"I didn't dare and I thought, I hoped ... that God would intervene. He will never let us reach Genoa, I thought. But..."

"But we did!"

The man stopped unhappily.

"Oh, why didn't you tell me all this before? If you had,

Carolus might still be alive," said Dolf irrationally, and he was suddenly crying.

"Yes," the man whispered miserably. "But still I couldn't do it, I was scared ... I am a coward, Rudolf. You, though, you have courage. You must take the burden from me, because I am too weak. Stop the children! On no account must they board the ships. It will be their ruin, Rudolf ..."

"Of course I'll stop them," exclaimed Dolf.

"What are you going to do?"

In truth, Dolf had no idea. To tell the children would be simple enough, but would they believe him? They had been so indoctrinated with the dream of the White City. He tried to think, but could not control his whirling thoughts. Augustus's confession had been too much of a shock for him. However, he realized that there was no time to lose. Anselmus was probably already in conference with his conspirators, organizing the shipment of the children.

But how does one set about shipping thousands of children who are expecting a miracle and who would probably be raging with fury when the promised miracle did not materialize tomorrow?

"Augustus, what does Anselmus intend to do tomorrow? Will he be there when Nicolas tries to perform his miracle?"

"No. He will wait until the miracle fails and the children are staring out over the water in disappointment, their dream of seeing Jerusalem shattered. Then he will suddenly appear with the news that God has performed a different miracle and provided them with ships."

"Exactly. And without hesitating, the children will storm onto the ships, shouting for joy. That's it, isn't it?"

"Yes, something like that."

Dolf heaved a great sigh. How could he, on his own, dissuade seven thousand hysterical children?

But he was not on his own. Augustus would have to help and he would need the help of all his friends.

"Augustus, can I rely on your help? Can you overcome your fear of Anselmus to help me stop the children, if only to save your own soul?"

"Rudolf, I ... yes."

"Right, then first you must go and talk to Dom Thaddeus and tell him everything; everything, mind you. He is a good man and wise. He doesn't have the least suspicion of this murderous plot and he has a great deal of influence with the children. Maybe he will know a way of stopping them."

Augustus was trembling and it surprised Dolf to realize that the man was more scared of the friendly Dom Thaddeus than he was of the furious Dolf of Amsterdam.

"Don't wait, Augustus." The boy jumped to his feet. "There is no time to lose. We must act immediately."

"Dom Thaddeus will curse me," the man, white with fear, whispered.

"No he won't. He will forgive you with all his heart," promised Dolf and he dragged the repentant sinner after him.

They found Dom Thaddeus in a corner of the camp, where Hilda was treating the patients. Dolf left the two monks together and went in search of Leonardo. Evening was coming on and the campfires were ablaze. Dolf discovered his friends eating their evening meal.

Dolf grabbed a handful of boiled shrimps and beckoned to Leonardo. "Quick, I must speak to you."

Breathlessly, Dolf related Augustus's tale. Leonardo listened in grave silence.

"We must do something," concluded Dolf desperately. "How can we make the children understand that they have been cheated?"

Leonardo considered. He was outraged, but did not lose his control.

"What exactly do you want to do?" he asked quietly.

"Prevent the children from boarding the ships."

"Yes, that at the very least."

"But how?" Dolf asked in despair.

"Oh, that's quite simple. No ship can leave Genoa harbor if the Duke has forbidden it."

"The … the Duke?"

"Yes, the Duke of Genoa. He is a very powerful man, I can promise you," replied Leonardo. "Listen, you stay here. The crucial time will come tomorrow and you will have to prepare the orderlies. I'm going to the town and I'm taking Hilda of Marburg with me."

"What do you want to do in town? And why Hilda?"

"Just for one moment, Rudolf, try to use your head, please. I am Leonardo Fibonacci of Pisa, the son of a rich merchant. My father has influential business contacts in Genoa. I will get letters of introduction from them, which will gain me admittance to the Duke's palace and I will tell the Duke everything. He will not be too concerned about the future of homeless German children, but he certainly won't allow the children of Christian nobility to be sold as slaves. That is why Hilda must come with me, to prove that this is not just an army of outcasts."

"Do you think you will manage to see the Duke?"

"One way or another I must. But there is also something else. We must inform the Bishop of Genoa immediately. All the children are Christians and he will certainly be outraged by the thought of their being sold to heathens. Has Dom Thaddeus been told yet?"

"I took Augustus to him to confess."

"Good, then the best thing would be for Hilda and me to go to the Duke and for Dom Thaddeus to inform the Bishop."

"But surely it is too late to go to the city. You won't be admitted."

"No one is going to stop me," said Leonardo quietly.

Dolf took his hand in gratitude.

"What would I do without you, my friend," he said with feeling.

"Yes, I sometimes wonder that myself," the student answered casually. He strode away toward the campfire and bent down over the sleepy Maria.

"I have to leave you for a few days, my dear. Take good care of Rudolf and if I don't return, think of me a few times."

"Leonardo, what are you going to do?" the girl asked with surprise.

"Rescue you, my dear child."

He kissed her, quickly untied his mule and disappeared into the dusk. Maria ran to Dolf.

"What's happening? Why is Leonardo leaving us? Is he going to Bologna after all?"

"No, not yet, Maria. He will be back soon," Dolf said to comfort her, though he wasn't so sure himself.

Dolf looked around at the peaceful camp. The children were eating, laughing and talking about the future. Dolf knew it was up to him to warn them but he still didn't know how he would do it.

"Don't you want to eat?" asked Maria with concern. Abstractedly Dolf took a few mouthfuls and sighed. He had now been travelling for weeks and suddenly everything hung on a few hours! Where could he start? How could he break the news to the children?

"Can't you tell me what is wrong?" urged Maria. Dolf looked at her and then at Peter, Frank, Bertho and Carl. He thought of Frieda in the sick-camp and all the other small, but courageous leaders and suddenly he knew the answer!

"Yes," he said. "We will have a council."

The Council on the Beach

Dolf dispatched Peter and Frank to summon the section leaders of the orderlies. In a short while, Dolf found himself at the center of a circle of a hundred strong boys and girls.

"Listen, my friends," he said. "We must have a council, but not here where we can be overheard. Let's go to the beach."

"Has something happened?" Bertho's question was what they were all curious to know.

"No, but something is going to happen and we must be prepared."

Dolf led the group to a little creek which ran between the rocks. It was some time since the sunset, but it was not completely dark. The moon, rising above the umbrella-shaped firs, set the water sparkling with tiny silver rays so that the sea itself seemed to be a source of light. Inquisitive as monkeys, the children gathered around Dolf and Maria and looked up at their leader expectantly.

"You know that Nicolas is now inside the tent fasting and praying. He is preparing himself for the miracle," began Dolf, who still did not know how he would get his message across to the children. They nodded enthusiastically.

"Because Nicolas thinks," he went on haltingly, feeling as if he were giving a lecture at school, "that the sea will divide for him as soon as … as soon as he orders it to …"

Again they all nodded.

"Do you believe that it will happen?"

"That is what we were promised," Frank replied softly.

"Yes, I know. But, you see, there is a problem."

They looked up at him with concern.

"Jerusalem," he continued, beginning to sweat, "is not on the other side of this sea. It is more than a thousand miles away to the east, that way." He gestured vaguely in the direction.

"I don't understand," said Frieda anxiously.

"You soon will," promised Dolf. "My friends, please believe me. A long time ago a wise, old man taught me how the world is laid out, where the countries and the cities are. On the other side of the sea from here is Africa, where all the people are heathens."

"Africa?"

It seemed that they were acquainted with the name.

"Where the lions come from?" Peter asked in disbelief.

"Yes. Africa. The country of wild animals. It is also a country where Christians would not be very welcome."

"We aren't afraid of heathens. We will chase them away," shouted Carl.

"Maybe, but we were going to attack the Turks in the Holy Land, not the Mohammedans in Tunisia, on the north coast of Africa. They are of no concern to us."

"Aren't they the same people then?" asked Frieda.

"No, not at all. You know that the world is enormous, don't you? It has taken you many weeks to walk to Genoa and yet you are not even halfway to Jerusalem."

"Jerusalem is on the other side of the sea," Peter said obstinately.

"No Peter. It is true that you have to cross a sea to reach Jerusalem, but it is not this one. Beyond this sea is Africa and until now I have been amazed that Nicolas and Anselmus were leading us here. I simply could not understand why, but now I know the reason."

"They told us that the sea would divide in Genoa," said a strong-looking orderly, whose name Dolf did not know.

"Because that is what God promised them. How can you deny that?"

Dolf braced himself in readiness for their reaction to the revelation he was about to give them.

"Don Anselmus was lying."

A general consternation broke out and there was a growl of indignant muttering.

"Because," Dolf went on quickly, "Anselmus is not a real priest. He is not even a monk. He is an adventurer, a robber, a pirate."

"He can read!" shouted Frieda.

"Yes, he has had a good education and at one time he went to school to be a priest. But his heart was rotten and he was expelled."

"Rudolf of Amsterdam, are you trying to tell us that Nicolas is not holy?" a voice called out threateningly from the back.

"Nicolas has heard angels' voices and has seen the flaming cross!" shouted another.

"Yes, I know and Nicolas did not lie. He has been perfectly honest, but he was deceived just like the rest of us."

"God does not deceive anyone!" exclaimed Frank.

"Listen, children, I will tell you how it happened. The flaming cross that Nicolas saw was no more than an ordinary wooden cross, made and set alight on a hill top by Anselmus. Nicolas believed that it was a vision. He had no way of knowing that a villain was tricking him."

The children were speechless with shock.

"And the angels' voices," Dolf continued, "were also a trick. Anselmus needed Nicolas to play the part of a visionary and it was essential that Nicolas really believed he had been chosen. So at night, when he was asleep, Anselmus whispered into his ear all kinds of magical things and Nicolas thought that the angels were speaking to him."

"How do you know all this?" someone asked suspiciously.

"I will tell you that later, but I haven't finished my story yet."

"I don't understand any of this," Maria suddenly spoke up. "You say that Anselmus deceived Nicolas. I don't like Anselmus at all and I am quite prepared to believe that he is a villain; but why? He must have had a reason for doing it."

"Look, Anselmus is actually a Lombardian and you know that they cannot be trusted."

Dolf was inwardly ashamed of giving such a nonsensical reason, but he was desperate to get the children to believe him and, therefore, had to appeal to their emotions. The battle by the river Oglio, where more than thirty brave children had died, was still clear in their memories. He saw the children nodding fervently in agreement.

"They are the dregs," he heard a voice say.

"Now listen carefully. Anselmus had a cunning plan. He went to the German states to find children for the slave-markets of North Africa. Obviously, no child would willingly allow itself to be taken to Genoa, transported to Africa and sold to the heathens. So Anselmus thought of all these lies. If the children were under the impression that they were going to Jerusalem, there would be no difficulty in getting them to follow him. And the whole plot would seem more genuine if he had a boy who believed he had been chosen by God to lead a holy mission. Now do you understand?"

The group needed time to digest it all. Dolf raised his hands and spoke:

"Listen! Anselmus wanted to bring the children to Genoa because he had friends waiting for him here—six pirate captains with empty ships. That is not nearly enough to transport seven thousand children, not even if they are all tightly packed together. But that does not worry Anselmus. He intends to select the healthiest and best-looking children to go on board the ships. He doesn't care what happens to the rest, the small and the weak. As far as he is concerned, they can stay behind on the beach and die."

"But if the sea divides, we won't need any ships," said Carl.

"No, but will the sea divide? Nicolas believes it will but Anselmus knows otherwise. He knows that it won't happen and that you are going to be deeply disappointed tomorrow. Because it wasn't God who made the promises to Nicolas; it was two counterfeit monks, two villains who wanted to lead thousands of children into slavery. Do you think God is going to let the sea divide so that you can walk to the slavemarkets? For that is all you will find on the other side. There is no Holy Land over there, no Jerusalem with fright-ened Saracens. There is only a barren, hot coastline, with towns full of Arabs who are willing to pay a lot of silver for slaves from the north."

"But we haven't seen any ships," Frank voiced a doubt.

"No, but I think they are in the harbor. Listen, we were often delayed along the way and it has taken us longer to reach Genoa than Anselmus had reckoned. Don't you remember how concerned he was that we were moving too slowly? He was worried that the ships might not wait. Believe me, my friends, I know his plans. Tomorrow, when the sea remains unchanged at the feet of Nicolas, Anselmus will come to you and say: 'My dear children, God has heeded the prayers of the people of Genoa, to whom the sea is their livelihood and has not allowed the sea to dry up. But, in His great mercy He has performed another miracle and sent ships to take you to the Holy Land. They are waiting for you now, follow me!' And what will you do? You will run, shouting for joy onto the ships and sail away.

Happily, my friends, we are not too late. There is still time for us to prevent the holy army from boarding the ships!"

"Rudolf of Amsterdam, you are lying," a tall boy cried out. "Tomorrow the sea will fall dry. Nicolas promised us and he spoke the truth."

"My dear friend, I wish it were true," Dolf replied. "I too would love to see that miracle, but I swear to you by all that is holy that it will not happen—because Nicolas has been fooled by Anselmus."

To enhance the force of his words, he took the pendant of the Holy Virgin from under his sweater and kissed it. A murmur of approval greeted the gesture.

"But Rudolf, how did you find out about all this?" asked Maria indignantly.

"And how long have you known about it?" Peter added quickly.

"I have known only for a few hours and, as to the first question, you are forgetting that Anselmus was not alone when he deceived Nicolas with fake miracles and visions; there was another, his partner in crime."

"Dom Augustus!" exclaimed Frank in sudden comprehension.

"Precisely. But Augustus is not so much of a snake as Anselmus, though at first he played an equal role in the wicked plot. Later he began to regret it and when Carolus died he was heartbroken. This afternoon, he confessed everything. He can no longer bear the thought of the children becoming slaves of heathens and that is why he told me. Then he went to repeat his confession to Dom Thaddeus."

"Is Dom Thaddeus a liar too?" Frank asked doubtfully.

"No. Dom Thaddeus has known as little about this sordid affair as any of us."

"Where are they?" screamed a girl, hysterical with anger. "I want to cut their throats."

"Be quiet, Martha. They are no longer here," said Dolf. "As soon as Dom Thaddeus heard about the monstrous conspiracy, he left to inform the Bishop of Genoa. Leonardo has also gone to the town, with Hilda of Marburg, and they are seeking to get an audience with the Duke. And do you know where Anselmus is now? I will tell you: He is down at the harbor. Without doubt you will see him reappear tomorrow afternoon, followed by a group of pirates and telling you not to despair ... because he believes his disgusting plan is still secret. He does not know that Augustus has confessed and that his intentions have been betrayed to us."

"Where is Augustus?" cried Frieda angrily.

"Yes, let him tell the story to us," agreed Frank.

Peter also jumped to his feet.

"Where is he?"

"You'll have to find him, he is somewhere in the camp," said Dolf. "But don't harm him. Remember that by making his confession he is trying to save you. He really loves you very much."

"Maybe, but it's because of him that we have come all this way to Genoa for nothing," Peter retorted bitterly. "And what did he do when hundreds died on the way? He just let us go on walking, farther and farther across the mountains and hot plains. And all the time he knew what was awaiting us in Genoa and he said nothing."

"But now he has spoken, Peter, and just in time."

The children were muttering and discussing the matter among themselves. Some still could not believe that they had been so greatly deceived. Frieda, Frank and Peter went searching for Augustus and, in the meantime, the children fired their questions at Dolf, who patiently tried to answer them. Using shells from the beach, he made a kind of map on a rock, to prove to them that only Africa was opposite Genoa and that Jerusalem was farther east. Half an hour later, the other three returned, tugging Augustus by his hand. At the sight of over a hundred children, with threatening, angry faces, he drew back in fear.

"Don't be afraid, Augustus," said Dolf, "they are prepared to listen to you. Tell them what you told me this afternoon. They have respect for a repentant sinner."

In halting words he told his story; his dark past, his despair and his longing for wealth. He described how they had duped Nicolas. He told how his love for the children had grown and with it his feeling of guilt. The children were fascinated and although they now knew that this man whom they had trusted so much was a villain, they still could not hate him. He had always been so good to them, consoling them when they were sad and helping them when they were in need. Moreover, a genuine, deep repentance always encourages a feeling of forgiveness. It was important to them that he had been unable to go through with his deception. In this man, love had conquered evil, and that made an impression on these children from the thirteenth century.

By the time Augustus had finished his stammered confession, they were finally convinced. Instinctively they turned to Dolf again.

"So now you believe it," Dolf said with relief. "Then listen carefully. Tomorrow is the day of decision. Nicolas knows nothing about all this, because the tent is guarded and no one can enter. In any case, he would not believe us if we told him he had been cheated by Anselmus, but tomorrow he will find out for himself. The sea will not divide. But what will happen then? The children are going to be desperately disappointed at first and then furious. They may try to murder Nicolas, but we must stop them, because it is not his fault. They may become rebellious, but we must try to keep them under control. Above all, however, we must prevent them from being lured onto the ships by Anselmus. Here is what we must do: we must try to prepare the children for the failure of the miracle; we must protect Nicolas when the miracle fails; and when Anselmus appears with his story of the waiting ships, we must silence him immediately."

The discussions went on until almost midnight and when the moon had finally disappeared, the meeting broke up. The children looked apprehensively at the white tent where Nicolas was locked away, and then, full of sadness, they curled up beside their fires and went to sleep.

Dolf felt afraid and began to sharpen his knife, wishing that Leonardo was there. He wondered whether he would be able to control the fierce orderlies without Leonardo's help. He had no way of knowing. He was not even sure whether the children completely trusted him.

"And I would not be surprised," the thought suddenly occurred to him, "if tomorrow, when the miracle fails, Nicolas tried to blame me for the entire disaster."

Exhausted with fear and concern, he fell asleep.

The Settling of the Account

The morning sun climbed above the hills behind the town, cast its golden rays out over the sea, and kissed the sleepy children, who stretched themselves happily. They all remembered that this was the great day, the day of the miracle, and they jumped up joyfully. Only a few went off to their daily fishing duties. The little ones, in particular, walked around impatiently, repeatedly asking: "Isn't it noon yet?" They looked longingly toward the lifeless tent, wondering what Nicolas could be doing. Praying? Sleeping? They did not know. Five boys with cudgels stood guard at the entrance and no one was admitted. Only at noon would the shepherd boy emerge and they had to be patient until then.

Meanwhile, Dolf and his team started their work of preparing the hopeful children for the disappointment that was to come. Naturally, they were not believed. Time and again one of the orderlies would take a group of children to one side and begin to whisper his story. Every child was being subjected to this treatment, but the only reaction was one of complete disbelief. The story was so incredible to them that they went straight to Rudolf of Amsterdam, tearfully complaining that they were being bullied by the big boys again. But Dolf could not comfort them and sent them to Augustus, who was sitting by the entrance to the sick-camp, looking sad. To him, the children's continuous stream of questions was complete torture, but he too was unable to console them.

As the morning wore on, the tension approached a

climax. The well-armed orderlies had stationed themselves on the beach. Their faces were grim and the children who had already gathered averted their eyes timidly. Some imagined that they could hear the sky groaning and indeed somewhere inland a heavy thunderstorm was raging, but above them was nothing but a serene blue sky without a hint of rain. Dolf looked at his watch—half-past eleven. Long ago he had ceased to know whether the watch was right or not, for often the bells he heard tolling the hour did not agree with it. But the measuring of time in the Middle Ages was still primitive and was done by monks who did not have the use of sensitive instruments and who sometimes could only guess themselves. Normally it did not matter that the watch gave only an approximate time, but at a moment like this, with the tension mounting every minute, he missed the reliable precision of the twentieth century.

Together with Maria he went down to the beach and climbed an overhanging rock, from which they could survey the whole scene. He had no wish to be in the middle of the children when Nicolas made his vain attempt to command the sea. Moreover, he had now learned to keep out of sight when the need for a scapegoat was being felt.

Anselmus was nowhere to be seen. Dolf was not sure whether that pleased him or not. If the monk were here, he would be sure to realize that his evil plan had been discovered. But if he stayed away and did not come at all, then how could Dolf prove that he was a villain? It would be difficult to fight an unseen foe.

Meanwhile, on the beach, excitement was mounting. The children could see from the sun that it was almost noon and any moment the bells of Genoa would begin to toll. Unconsciously the children had left a wide-open path leading from the tent to the beach. At the sea's edge they jostled each other for position. Many had climbed to the top of the higher slopes, from where they would hear little, but see everything. The camp under the trees was almost empty.

Dolf intently studied the thousands of children who were waiting, closely packed together, for the moment of truth. He noticed how stern-faced the orderlies were and admired their calm. His attention was also taken by the excitement of the little ones, standing ankle deep in the water. The exuberant little Simon outshouted everyone else:

"The Saracens are going to run! Oh how they are going to run."

Nothing would shake his belief. Indeed, he would believe anything, providing it promised enough excitement.

"There they are," said Maria suddenly.

Dolf looked in the direction she had indicated and, some distance from the deserted camp, spied the dark habit of Anselmus. He was accompanied by three bearded characters, who stood close behind him on the slope. Dolf's heart began to pound. The villain had come! Obviously he had had no word of the betrayal. The three men were probably pirates. Their presence made him very uneasy.

Perhaps Leonardo had failed to get an audience with the Duke. Maybe Dom Thaddeus had been unable to convince the Bishop. What had happened to his friends? He needed them now.

Time alone could provide the answers and what time was it? Dolf's watch indicated ten past twelve. With every minute the children's impatience increased. Some of the little ones, unable to resist the pushing and barging of the crowd, had fallen headlong into the water and were crying. Two orderlies roughly put them on their feet again. The murmuring of the thousands of voices was like the drone of a furious swarm of bees humming over the beach. All of a sudden, in the distance, the bells began to toll. At once a deep silence descended over the children. No one stirred, no one pressed forward and all shouting ceased. Every single head was turned in the same direction—toward the tent under the trees.

The tent flap was thrown back and there stood Nicolas, looking magnificent. He was wearing the captured coat of mail covered by his white cloak and tied around with Carolus's belt. His carefully combed, long, blond hair glistened in the sunlight.

"The Archangel Gabriel," Maria whispered. And that was indeed how the shepherd boy appeared.

He seemed to have grown thinner in the last twenty-four hours. His face pale and tense, his eyes staring straight ahead, he began walking toward the beach between the living walls of children. The five boys who had been guarding the tent followed him in silence. Behind them the silent ranks of children closed in. Dolf felt that it was not simply a silence of expectation, but also of doubt.

Dolf watched Nicolas striding toward the sea, seemingly unaware of all about him. His hands were clasped together and his head bent. The bells had stopped their tolling and the only sound was the lapping of waves against the rock. When he reached the water's edge, Nicolas did not stop, but continued a few more paces until his bare feet were submerged and the hem of his cloak floated on the crests of the little waves. Then he stopped.

"What can be going through his mind," Dolf wondered. With his inquisitive brain, he was trying to imagine himself in the place of the shepherd boy. He felt as if it were he himself standing there all alone, facing the sea.

Then …

Nicolas raised his arms.

"Oh mighty sea, I command you to retreat for the children of God."

There was silence as seven thousand children held their breath. They were spellbound by the simplicity of the words and the utter conviction of the tone with which they were uttered. It was a powerful experience to see the boy standing there, his voice resounding over the waves.

But the sea, stretching into the distance over the horizon, remained unchanged. It was a great ocean full of fish, crabs and hidden secrets.

"My Lord and Protector, I beg you to make the sea divide for your holy children who have come to liberate Jerusalem."

The deep silence was broken only by the lashing waves, the water retreating over the pebbles and the soft hissing of the children releasing the air from their lungs.

But again there was nothing; just the large, wide, shimmering ocean.

The shepherd boy remained standing in the sea, his eyes firmly fixed on the surface of the water, motionless, his arms still raised aloft. The highly polished coat of mail glinted and a breath of wind scuttled across the water and billowed his cloak. This breeze rekindled the hope in the hearts of all the children. Now it would happen!

Nicolas stood up even taller, as if he was trying to touch the azure sky with his fingertips. "Retreat, oh mighty sea! Retreat for the children of God. Let us pass. It is God's will!"

So blue, so deep and so seemingly unending the water stretched into the distance. Far out from the shore the sun glistened on the white, foam-flecked crests of the waves.

A large ship sailed out of Genoa harbor. Seagulls swooped low, diving for fish and crying out to the blue sky ...

Suddenly Nicolas spun round and screamed: "Pray, go on, pray!"

Some of the children tried to kneel, but there was barely enough room. The majority, however, remained standing. They did not clasp their hands together, nor did they look upward. Tense, silent and motionless they stared at Nicolas.

"Pray!" he begged them desperately.

Again Nicolas turned to the sea and ordered the waves to make a path for the children's crusade. He screamed aloud, his voice cracking with despair. He hitched up his cloak and began to advance farther, raising his legs high in the air, as if he were trying to walk on the water. It was already up to his waist, when his bare foot suddenly trod on a sea urchin.

The whole coast was littered with these terrible creatures. If you trod on them their sharp needles broke off and remained stuck in your foot. Frieda had spent much of the previous day working them out of the tortured feet of dozens of children. After that, most of the children had worn their shoes when they went bathing. But Nicolas had walked in barefoot and now the sea, which he had tried to control, had given him its painful answer: no!

He stumbled and lurched back to the beach and was confronted by the angry faces of the children. He looked into their eyes and saw the menace. Quickly and desperately he turned back toward the sea. There was a cruel pain in his foot and the sea would not obey him. The boy, who a few minutes earlier had appeared like an incarnation of the Archangel Gabriel, was now revealed to them for what he was—a fake, an over-dressed serf without dignity.

Once again he raised his arms and shouted his orders to the sea; a general, trying to induce the enemy to flee; a magician, ordering evil spirits back to the realm of darkness; a poor, deluded shepherd boy, who believed he was a saint with the power to change the laws of nature.

The sea ignored him. It lapped unremittingly against his feet. It was laughing at him.

Then the children erupted. Rudolf of Amsterdam had been proved right. The miracle had failed. They had been fooled into walking a thousand miles through deadly dangers, the cold, the heat, hunger and disasters—and all for nothing! They did not stop to think that Nicolas had been cheated as much as they.

Like a frightened animal at bay he looked about for a way of escape. Howling and screaming with fury they threw themselves at him. Unquestionably they would have torn him to pieces had not the orderlies immediately stepped in and begun dragging the hysterical children away.

"They are killing him!" screamed Maria. But Dolf had already moved into action, leaping down from the rock and hurling himself into the children. With all the strength he could muster, he forced a path through the enraged crowd. The orderlies fought their way toward the center of the seething children, trying to get at Nicolas. Only the captured coat of mail saved his life.

He lay on his back on the stony beach, his clothes torn and his head bleeding from several wounds. As Dolf knelt down beside the boy, he was suddenly aware of Maria next to him. She gently raised Nicolas's head and cradled it in her lap. Tears were streaming down her cheeks. She looked up and shouted at the children:

"You should be ashamed of yourselves!"

She washed the bleeding face with salty water. The stinging pain made him open his eyes.

"God has deserted me," he whispered with an immeasurable sadness.

"God has not deserted us," thundered a deep voice in response and there was Anselmus. Behind him stood the three evil-looking men.

"My dear children, God has not divided the sea," he said in a honeyed tone, but loud enough for almost all to hear, "but He has not deserted you and has sent a fleet of ships to bear you over the water to the Holy Land."

Dolf leaped up, his eyes blazing.

"You are lying," he screamed. A grumbling arose among the children.

"I tell you, Rudolf of Amsterdam, that you will not be found worthy to set foot in one of those ships; the ships which God, in His mercy, has sent us ..."

"Slave ships, you mean!" Dolf spat the words into his amazed face. "And never fear, not one of these children will set foot on them. Rudolf of Amsterdam is not for sale in the slavemarkets of Tunisia, nor is anyone else here!"

The color had drained from Anselmus's face. He turned around and spoke in Tuscanese to the three men behind him, who at once leaped into action. A knife flashed. Maria screamed and Dolf dived at Anselmus's legs. Unprepared for this sudden assault, the man lost his balance and fell forward on top of the boy.

Over all else, Peter's voice roared out:

"Destroy them! Destroy the villains!"

With that, pandemonium broke out. Anselmus was wrenched off Dolf and overpowered by hundreds of children. Dolf found himself gasping for breath as little feet trampled over him. The beach seemed to be whirling around. The air was filled with yells and screams and the sound of pounding blows. There was a sharp cry from someone in the agony of death. Dolf tried to sit up, but was again bowled over. The next he knew he was lying in about two inches of lukewarm water.

Around him the chaos was still raging. He finally managed to stagger to his feet and could hardly believe the sight which met his eyes.

Most of the children were running back toward the camp. Some of the boys had picked up Nicolas and were carrying him to the tent. Maria was tugging at Dolf's arm and shouting something, but he could not hear what she was saying, because a little way away a howling mass of bodies was moving slowly along the emptying beach. Cries of terror arose from the mountain of fighting children, but they were growing fewer and suddenly they ceased altogether. In another direction, Dolf saw the three sailors desperately scrambling up a hill, pursued by hundreds of baying children …

The heap on the beach fell apart and he saw Peter emerge with blood on his hands. Bertho appeared and ran into the sea to bathe his swelling eye with the salt water. The children began to withdraw and limp back to the camp, their clothing ragged. Whatever had they done, thought Dolf— and then he saw.

Amidst the strips of torn clothing lay what remained of Anselmus. His face was unrecognizable. His body was twisted into a strange shape, as if not one bone had been left unbroken. The hairs had been torn from his skull. Dolf felt his stomach heaving. He quickly turned his gaze away and vomited over the pebbles, while tears gushed from his eyes. He had hated Anselmus, but his fate filled him with revulsion.

His legs trembling, he staggered back to the camp. One of the frightened noble children came and beckoned him to the tent.

Inside he found Frieda busy washing and bandaging Nicolas's wounds.

"How is he?" he asked.

"Not too bad," replied Frieda, "scratches and grazes mainly. What happened down there on the beach? Why did they try to murder Nicolas? He had not hurt anyone."

The boy was moved by her simple logic, but with horror he thought of the broken body of Anselmus.

"No, not Nicolas," he said with difficulty. "Take good care of him, Frieda."

Then he hurried from the tent and gathered some orderlies together.

"Anselmus must be buried at once. We cannot just leave him lying there on the beach."

He found that he was unable to look Peter in the eyes.

Never in his wildest imagination had he thought that the children's army, once aroused, could be so dangerous. Secretly, he hoped that the pirates had escaped.

The camp was in a ferment and Dolf, himself bruised all over, felt deeply unhappy. In an attempt to calm the children's excitement, he began to give orders at random. He ordered the fishermen down to the water. He called to Bertho and said:

"There is nothing left to eat. Get your followers together and go hunting."

He told Frank to put the tanners and shoemakers to work. He sent some groups of boys and girls to fetch water and others he commanded to scrub the cooking pots. Still others he sent to make beds out of dried seaweed. Everyone had to be employed with something, it did not much matter what. The majority obeyed his wishes, but the disorganized atmosphere persisted.

What had become of the devoted army of children which had left Cologne more than two months ago, with prayers, hymns and hope? The seven thousand survivors had become more of an army than ever, but they seemed to have lost all their piety and innocence.

"They are going to be even more difficult to control now," Dolf thought worriedly. "With their dream of the White City gone, nothing is going to keep them in check. So far from home and with no trade to follow, what else can they do but rob and fight to keep themselves alive? Nothing will be allowed to stand in their way; not mountains, nor plains, nor people."

He would have liked to call another conference of the orderlies, to decide what they should do now. Return to Germany? Across the Po plain and over the Alps again? He realized, however, that it was now out of the question to call a conference without Nicolas. He lay wounded in the tent and probably would not dare put in an appearance for the time being. The tent, the home of Nicolas and the children of noble birth, was a kind of sanctuary. The shepherd boy was safe in there, but if he stepped outside ...

It was almost an hour later when a triumphant group returned to the camp. They were brandishing a trophy—a large, curved knife which they had taken from the only captain they had managed to catch. Dolf had no need to ask what had happened to the man—he could guess.

Is the Dream Still Alive?

To Dolf's great relief, Leonardo and Dom Thaddeus returned the next day, bringing with them a dozen soldiers and a group of distinguished gentlemen from the city of Genoa.

Leonardo told Dolf that he had eventually managed to gain access to the town council, who had listened to his story. Once he had convinced them that his story was a true one, the council gave orders for all ships to be searched before leaving the harbor. Then, realizing that Genoa was surrounded by thousands of deserted little crusaders, the Mayor consulted with the Bishop (who had already been informed by Dom Thaddeus). The Bishop, too, had wasted no time. He had ordered the priests to make a massive collection of clothes, food and shoes from among the religious of Genoa—and who was not religious in this century? The gifts would arrive by wagon in the children's camp that afternoon.

Nor was that all. The city council had decided to be rid of the children as soon as possible, which could only mean they must be sent home. They had agreed to take in twenty or thirty children, and the others they agreed to send home, with an armed escort as far as Milan.

Dolf heaved a great sigh of relief. They could return home after all. Augustus suddenly stepped forward.

"I will take charge of the journey home," he promised.

But one of the noblemen on horseback looked down on him with a scowling face.

"Aren't you one of those fraudulent monks who

wickedly enticed the children to Genoa?" he asked menacingly. "I have orders to arrest you. Guards, seize him!"

Dolf, who had only half understood what had been said, suddenly realized what was happening when he saw two soldiers step forward. Pleadingly, he turned to Leonardo.

"Tell them to leave Augustus alone. The children need him."

Leonardo began rapidly talking to the gentlemen and eventually seemed to have his way, but the outcome was that Augustus would be exiled, never to be allowed onto Genoese territory again on pain of death.

"Where is Anselmus? Or do you wish to save him too?" asked Leonardo in his usual mocking tone.

Dolf remained silent and tense, but Peter replied for him:

"We tore him into little shreds." His voice was so thick with hatred that it made Dolf shiver, but Leonardo seemed to find it amusing.

"That's just what the scoundrel deserved." He turned to the noblemen and explained that the other slave dealer had already received the punishment that he deserved. They nodded with satisfaction, turned their horses about and rode off. They seemed a little unnerved at the sight of so many wild children. Leonardo and Dom Thaddeus remained in the camp.

"Where is Hilda?" asked Dolf, suddenly realizing that she had not been with them.

"The Duke of Genoa has taken her under his care and offered her a position in his household," the student answered brightly. "Next spring, he will send a message to the Count of Marburg, her father, and then her fate will be decided."

"Poor Hilda, what did she have to say about it?"

Leonardo looked at his friend in surprise.

"What could she say? I expect she is pleased. She won't have to wash any more smelly wounds or sleep on straw.

They will probably find a rich man for her to marry, either here or in her father's state. There is no need to worry about Hilda."

"Hilda was happy with us," Dolf said softly.

"What! Among this wild bunch of ruffians? Oh, no ..."

Maybe Leonardo was right, thought Dolf. Maybe it would be the best thing for her, but he was not so sure.

"Didn't the Duke offer anything for the other noble children?" he asked.

"No. He asked me who they were, but when he heard that they were only children of insignificant knights, he lost interest."

Dolf shook his head. He would never understand the wide differences of rank in this century.

Dolf was now under the impression that the children's crusade was at an end. But he was wrong. In his own age, children who had been so cruelly treated would at once have lost hope and eagerly grasped the chance to return. But not so these children from the thirteenth century; at least, not the majority of them.

What was the attraction in returning to the German states where the rain lashed the fields, where the winters were long and cold and where their lives would be nothing but misery?

In mid-afternoon, a long caravan of wagons arrived from Genoa. They were laden with bread, vegetables and fruit; old clothes and worn shoes; thin blankets and images of the cross. Much of it was useless rubbish and cast-offs, but to the children it was a treasure.

After the wagons had left and everyone had eaten to his heart's content, Dolf, Augustus, Leonardo, Frank and Peter set about the task of organizing the return journey and immediately met resistance.

The section leaders were particularly vociferous in opposing the idea and a large majority were in favor of moving on to Jerusalem. Did they still not realize that the dream of the White City was nothing more than a myth, a fantasy which could never become reality?

"Of course we don't want to go home," protested Peter, who had decided to join the rebels. "What's the use of that? There is nothing there for us."

"We don't have a home," said Carl stubbornly.

"I'm not going back to beg in the streets of Cologne again," shouted Maria.

Dolf could only blink and turn to Leonardo for help. But the student only laughed and clapped Peter on the shoulder.

Just at that moment Nicolas emerged from the tent. Clearly he had assessed the mood in the camp correctly, for the children seemed already to have forgotten their anger with him. These children had very short memories; as soon as he appeared in his white robe, which had been mended, they treated him with as much respect as ever.

He was still wearing Carolus's belt and in his hand held a silver crucifix. It had taken all the courage he could muster to face the children again. He tried to conceal the fear in his heart behind an air of pride and he held his head high. Dolf stepped quickly forward and took his hand and there they stood, surrounded by children, many of whom were still nibbling a piece of bread, an apple or a handful of nuts. Maria offered Nicolas half a loaf of bread, which he accepted with a nod. It grew quiet around them.

"Children," said Nicolas. "I was completely dumbfounded by what happened. I thought that God had deserted me. But now I realize that He simply refused to perform a miracle for an army of children amongst which were numbered rogues, slave dealers and liars. I have heard that Anselmus is dead and I have heard that Augustus intends to return to the German states with those who are yearning for home. You have all heard the words of the aldermen of Genoa and those who wish to return may do so. I have heard also about the trickery of Anselmus, by which we have been led astray from the correct path. Jerusalem is not to be found on the other side of this sea, but on the shores of another, east of here. That is why—and pay good attention to this—those who wish to go no farther may stay here in Genoa or travel north with Augustus. But those who still wish to see Jerusalem can follow me. I am going to travel east to the sea, for that is where God will perform His miracle!"

Dolf was thunderstruck and even more so when thousands of children, hysterical with joy, cried in response:

"Nicolas, we will follow you!"

Surely they had not all taken leave of their senses? Surely they could not still believe in the myth? No indeed, very few were that foolish. It was simply a question of not wanting to go back. The pleasure and hardship of living rough under the open sky had come to have a special meaning for them. They had seen something of the world and it was larger, wider and more wonderful than they had ever imagined. For weeks their lives had consisted of marching toward a dream and that was what they wished to continue doing, until they either reached the end of the world or of their lives.

It was in this way that the children's army came to be divided. Some of the very young really did wish to return home and in the following days they gathered together outside the gates of the city, under the leadership of Augustus and three children of noble birth. A few elected to stay in Genoa. To Dolf's surprise those who chose to return home were mainly the sheep, the little ones and the foolish. But that did not include little Simon, who still wished to hunt the Saracens; nor Frank, Peter, Frieda, Bertho, Carl ... In vain, Dolf bombarded his friends with every reason he could think of for turning back.

"But Maria," he protested, "what has Italy to offer us? The sea in the east won't divide any more than this one did."

"Does that mean I must go back to Cologne then?" asked Maria sadly. "What's the good of that?"

Dolf sighed. Maria had nothing to which she could return. "Then why don't you stay in Genoa? You could become a servant to Hilda, a chambermaid or something. Hilda is your friend, she would protect you."

Maria shook her head. She had no wish to stay in this large town, because it reminded her too much of her birthplace. There were the same narrow streets, church squares and disinterested people.

"If Nicolas is going on, then so am I," Maria insisted.

"And what about me," sighed Dolf. "What am I going to do?"

"I thought you were going to Bologna with Leonardo."

"Leonardo wants to visit his parents in Pisa first. He is not going to Bologna until next year."

Dolf had been surprised when he first heard of the student's decision to remain with the children's army for the time being.

Leonardo was very casual when he mentioned it:

"It's years since I saw my family and since I am now so close anyway, I would just like to see my mother."

Was that true? Dolf still had difficulty in understanding the young man. He had learned by now that the medieval people often said one thing, while meaning something quite the opposite and this was more true of the Italians than most. Leonardo had never given any indication of being homesick until now. Perhaps it was because of Maria that he did not wish to leave the children?

"Stay with us then, Rudolf," pleaded Maria, and Dolf nodded. He did not seem to have an alternative.

The army of children which set off into the Apennines

once more was almost five thousand strong. It was still quite large enough to frighten away the mountain-dwellers and, in fact, since those who had returned north had primarily been the little ones or children who had lost courage, their depleted ranks seemed stronger than ever. It was an army of fearless little desperadoes who journeyed slowly (for there was no longer anyone urging them to hurry) through the land under the hot sun; poaching, fishing and singing.

Dom Thaddeus went with them as did the two remaining noble children. There was Mathilda, a conceited girl who hoped to be the queen of Jerusalem, since Hilda had stayed behind with the Duke of Genoa. The other was called Rufus, the son of an impoverished baron, by nature a very timid child who was too frightened to go home. He had originally run away from his father's castle for fear of his elder brothers and he now continued with the journey, silent, shy and discouraged.

Eventually they entered Tuscany, Nicolas at their head, still recognized as the official leader. He was followed by columns of disorganized children, who ran wild with their looting and begging. So long as they were in thinly populated regions, they did as they pleased. They stole goats, chickens and pigs; they picked the grain from the fields and the apples from the trees. They laughed at the furious farmers, irate knights, indignant merchants and admonishing priests. All of them were armed and they believed themselves to be invincible. They had developed one tactic in particular, which made Dom Thaddeus tremble but which Dolf found rather amusing. As soon as they approached a city or a heavily populated area, they forgot their tricks and games and transformed themselves into holy children once more, journeying to Jerusalem. They clasped their hands together, raised their eyes to the sky and marched along singing hymns. It was then that they presented the impressive image of the children's crusade which would later be described in history books. They wore expressions of suffering on their faces and indicated to the horrified populace that their clothes were in rags and their stomachs empty. The inhabitants of the beautiful Tuscany were deeply impressed. They readily gave the children bread and cakes and brought barrels of fresh water and smoked ham to the camp. They were simply unable to believe the rumors they had heard about the plundering horde of vagabonds. The children indeed appeared to them as the chosen ones of God in whom His light had been kindled. Dolf wondered who might have devised this tactic, for they could not all have had the same idea. He suspected Peter, since he was sufficiently clever and unscrupulous.

The children were hardly out of sight of a town before they had returned to their former ways. This was really living! They tasted the sweet freedom of warm winds blowing around the hills. Brazen and exuberant they moved on and on. Sometimes they came across a spot, the beauty of which even these indifferent children of the Middle Ages could appreciate; a little lake with flower-covered banks, or a small river which meandered through the open fields. With such peacefulness, flowers, birds and timid animals, how could one ever leave such a place? Why go to Jerusalem when one was surrounded by paradise?

At such times, maybe one or two hundred children would stay behind and build themselves huts, hunt, catch and tame wild goats and begin a new existence. Dolf had no idea if these new settlements would survive. Sometimes he doubted it and sometimes he felt like staying behind himself. But those who stayed behind no longer needed him. During the long months of travelling, they had learned the art of self-reliance. Although in this country it seemed as though summer would never end, they had brought with them memories of long, cold winters, of famines and fuel-shortages. They began to make preparations against the possibility of winter coming to Tuscany too. They built huts, stables and granaries and erected walls around the new settlements. If they had ever been idle in the past, they had long since forgotten it. They worked hard and enjoyed it, because they were working for themselves.

Their numbers dwindled daily, but Nicolas hardly seemed to notice. He was obsessed with the dream of the shining White City in the east and he did not realize that the myth no longer had meaning for the vast majority of his followers.

They travelled along the old military roads which crisscrossed the country and sometimes got lost; but what did that matter? Dolf was hoping that it would be a long time before they reached Pisa, for then they would have to say goodbye to Leonardo. It did indeed take a long time, but eventually they arrived.

The previous year Dolf had been to Pisa with his parents and had been rather disappointed by the famous town. It was such an insignificant place. The hundreds of thousands of tourists who visited it came only for the day, mainly to see the famous tower and walk through the Square of Miracles. Then they would move on again, because Pisa had nothing else to offer.

But now, what a difference! At the beginning of the thirteenth century Pisa was a thriving city, mightier than Florence, larger than Rome and busier than Genoa. The cathedral had already been built, complete with the leaning tower. The fortresses and walls stood, not as the sleepy ruins of a famous past, as in Dolf's age, but in their full magnificence and glory. Dolf was delightedly astonished. Leonardo urged him to stay in the city as the guest of the Bonacci family. It was an attractive proposal ...

"But what about Maria?"

"She can stay with us as well, of course."

"I am not sure that I should leave the children's army ..."

But finally that was not the only reason for Dolf's refusal. He was simply unable to abandon this wild and free life, even for the temptations of Pisa. Thus it was that the friends bid each other a sorrowful farewell. Maria could not hold back her tears.

"Oh Leonardo, how we will miss you!"

Peter and Frank silently took the student's hand and Bertho clasped him, saying:

"Try to think of Carolus from time to time."

Then the children moved relentlessly onward, through the magnificent hills, through the marshes and forests in a southeasterly direction.

No more than two thousand children still remained by this time. Many had stayed in Pisa and others had moved off in large groups toward Florence, two days' journey away, since it was rumored that Florence was in need of laborers and was preparing for war.

Within a short while pockets of German children could be found scattered throughout central Italy, stammering broken Tuscanese and searching for work, food and shelter. They were soon accepted and absorbed into the local population. It was a small army of perhaps fifteen hundred children who finally arrived in the province of Umbria at the beginning of September. They were wild, hungry and reckless.

In a Trap

Things were growing more difficult for this army of little professional wanderers.

The summer was drawing to a close, the harvest had been gathered and the farmers and knights were defending their granaries with pitchfork and sword. The lords and barons were organizing grand hunting parties and woe to the child who was caught poaching in the forests or hills! Once again hunger was threatening the children.

Nevertheless, they were still stunned by the beauty of the country through which they were trekking. Umbria in late summer was a paradise. Dolf's eyes were forever popping out of his head, as each bend in the dusty road revealed a new view of unbelievable beauty. It helped him forget his empty stomach.

The lake of Trasimeno nestled between the hills like a shining jewel. The children had heard it mentioned by the people of the region and had understood it to be full of fish and easy to find. After some aimless wandering around the vicinity, they eventually arrived.

Fifteen hundred children, particularly if they are hungry, represent a formidable army. The same thought had occurred to the Count of Trasimeno, Ludovico, who was both at war with the city of Perugia and threatened by the rebellion of his peasants. Angered at being attacked from two sides, he had dispatched an expedition to punish the rebellious farmers. Smoldering farms, ruined granaries and herds of dead cattle would teach the rebels not to challenge the authority of the master of Trasimeno! But the rebellion had not been halted. With winter coming on, the farmers realized that unless they received help from elsewhere they would be in for a hard time—so they had allied themselves to the city of Perugia. The inhabitants and Mayor of Perugia were delighted with the opportunity to destroy Count Ludovico. Not only had the master of Trasimeno forbidden them to fish in the large lake, but he also demanded heavy tolls from the trade caravans which passed back and forth between Florence and Perugia.

Some hours before the unsuspecting children's army reached the banks of the lake, Ludovico had been informed by his spies that a large force had left Perugia and was marching toward the castle. At the same time and from the other direction, several hundred peasants approached who were prepared to fight to their last breath. The castle of Trasimeno was exceedingly strong. It had been built on a peninsula which jutted into the lake and was, therefore, protected on three sides by water. But would it be strong enough to resist three armies?

In the Count's eyes, the children arrived in the nick of time, though the news of their approach had at first caused him to panic. Another army? Were they trying to attack him from three sides? But then, realizing that the children were unaware of their position, he decided to make use of them. He hurriedly dispatched a few soldiers and his chaplain to greet them.

It was a friendly invitation that they brought them. The Count was offering the children the hospitality of his peninsula. The children could establish their camp around the castle and were permitted to catch as many fish as they wanted. Moreover, Count Ludovico would consider it a great honor if the leaders of the crusade would come to the castle to be feasted.

Nicolas was surprised and delighted by the message. It was the first time he had been treated so respectfully and by so powerful a personage. The simple shepherd boy accepted the invitation as an honor. Swelling with pride, he drew himself up to his full height, adjusted his belt and said:

"I am the leader and these are my officers." He indicated Mathilda in her beautiful dress and the timid Rufus who was blushing with embarrassment. Rufus would have preferred to stay in the camp, but he dared not refuse. Counts and castles put the fear of death into him. He had not run away from home for nothing! But he had never been able to say no in his whole life and, moreover, he was a leader, even if a bad one ...

When Leonardo had left the children's army at Pisa, a new commander had to be found for the orderlies. Dolf had had no wish to take on the task, for he was no fighter. Bertho was the tallest and strongest, but he was precluded since he was not one of the nobility. Fredo had been the son of a knight. Leonardo was the son of a rich merchant and also an educated person. But it would be quite wrong for the son of an ordinary serf, thought the children, to be a general. In that way Rufus, the only boy of noble birth, was given the task of commanding the few orderlies who remained. Inevitably, he was not up to the job. Shy and fearful he turned scarlet every time he gave an order. He was tyrannized by the conceited Mathilda and when all was said and done, it was Bertho, his second in command, and Dolf who organized the children's protection, though in name they remained section leaders. Officially, Nicolas and Rufus were the generals of this army.

When Dolf heard of the Count's invitation, he considered going with Nicolas and the other two, but Peter pulled him by the arm:

"Don't, Rudolf, you would do better to stay with us."

"Why? I would very much like to see the inside of one of these Umbrian castles and I don't suppose I'll ever have another opportunity."

Peter shook his head.

"If a Count becomes friendly, you can be sure that he has a good reason for it," he said sinisterly.

"Don't be stupid," replied Dolf. "The Count is a religious man, who wishes to help our holy mission."

Peter looked contemptuous.

"An Italian? Oh no ..."

"But I have seen how pious the people of this area are," persisted Dolf "They live in wretched little huts and houses, but the churches they build are magnificent."

"They are cunning," said Peter obstinately. When it came to stubbornness, he was every bit a match for Rudolf of Amsterdam. "They are not overfond of crusaders, unless they see a way to making profit out of them. Before anything else, just ask yourself what this Count might want from us."

Dolf could not understand it at all and went to see Dom Thaddeus.

"Dom Thaddeus, Peter says that he does not trust the Count's hospitality, what do you think?"

"I really don't know," the monk said honestly. "I hardly understand any of the local language, but today I have seen things that trouble me—ruined farms, burned-out villages, weeping women, very few cattle and even fewer men. I would say there is a war raging in this region and it troubles me."

"Exactly," interrupted Peter. "When you have passed through deserted and ravaged areas, you have to be on your guard."

Dolf nodded. Peter often struck him as being unnecessarily cruel, but sometimes he revealed a very keen intelligence and Dolf had complete confidence in him. If Peter said something was wrong, then it was sure to be so. As a result of his warning he stayed behind in the camp and organized the fishing with Peter. The children set themselves to their daily routine tasks and everything seemed peaceful.

Meanwhile, to the sound of clarion calls and the beating of drums, the drawbridge had been lowered for Nicolas, Rufus and Mathilda. Inside the castle, the three children were treated as royalty. A magnificent banquet had been prepared for them in the great hall, while in the light of the setting sun outside, the other children were lighting fires, grilling fish and nibbling the fresh bread which had been sent from the castle bakery. Once again they were on holiday.

In the early morning, the serenity was shattered. At the edge of the forest, to the west of the peninsula, appeared more than a hundred farmers. They were grim, determined and armed to their teeth with pikes, pitchforks, knives, axes and clubs. They emerged from the shadows of the trees and stood there as if waiting for something, or as though they did not wish to come within range of the castle walls at the other end of the peninsula. The children rubbed their eyes with surprise and began to mill about nervously. What did these armed people want? Were they going to attack them?

They were then suddenly aware that they were also threatened from the south and this time it was no small band of desperate men. There were mounted knights, armed with swords and lances and dressed in coats of mail. They were followed by foot soldiers, pike-bearers and bowmen. There were siege weapons carried on heavy wagons, drawn by oxen. This new army quickly blockaded the southern side of the peninsula and the children were trapped.

This, of course, was exactly what Ludovico had expected. Smiling grimly to himself, the Count ascended the ramparts of the tower and looked out over the besieging army. The peninsula had been completely sealed off and escape was impossible, but how could his enemies storm the castle when it was surrounded by fifteen hundred well-armed children! Ludovico laughed aloud. His walls were manned with soldiers and in the courtyard below, women were boiling cauldrons of pitch and water. The three guests, who had been feted the previous night, were now in the dungeons. Ludovico had laid his plans well.

An officer appeared on the battlements and called down to the frightened children:

"Who are your commanders?"

"Bertho!" some shouted.

"Rudolf!" yelled others.

The officer had spoken German and they had had no trouble understanding him. Dolf, Bertho and Frank came up within hearing distance.

"Are you the leaders?"

"No," Dolf shouted back. "Nicolas is the leader."

"Nicolas and the other two are temporarily our prisoners. We are holding them as hostages and they will be released only when you have driven off those who are attacking us."

At first Dolf could not believe his ears. It seemed that Ludovico intended using the army of children to protect himself. What a miserable trick! We must gain time, he thought. He cupped his hands to his mouth and shouted up to the man on the wall:

"I don't understand you!"

This was ridiculous! He could not allow the children to sacrifice themselves, even in an attempt to break through the besieging armies and escape. Perhaps they were strong enough, but it would certainly result in a terrible slaughter, and even then they had no guarantee that the three hostages would be saved.

The officer above repeated his message, but this time the message was heard not only by Dolf and his friends, but also by hundreds of the others. A howl of rage went up from the children.

"Nicolas is a captive!"

They were not particularly concerned with the fate of the

other two, but Nicolas was one of them and they loved him. Despite his failure in Genoa, the thought that this simple serf had been chosen by God to lead a crusade of children, was of great importance to them. Nicolas was more than a leader, he was a symbol of the outcasts of the world, who in God's eyes were of equal worth to the children of kings and knights.

"We will discuss your proposal," Dolf called back and then he turned away. Peter, Frank, Bertho and many others were gathered around, looking at him expectantly. How he now missed the inventiveness of Carolus and the calm of Leonardo!

"What can we do?" he asked desperately.

"Fight," said Peter decisively. "But not against the army behind. We must storm the castle and free Nicolas."

Dolf shook his head. He had no wish to allow the children to throw themselves to death against the castle walls.

"Why don't we negotiate with the people who want to attack the castle?" suggested Frank. Bertho looked over his shoulder nervously.

"They are already making preparations. The attack may start any minute now.

"Then there's no time to lose," Dolf said decisively. "I need a stick and a white flag. Maria and Frieda, you two must come with me."

"No, don't go," Maria cried with alarm. "They will kill you."

"They will kill us all if I don't try to stop them," Dolf said with an undeniable logic.

Since a negotiator should not be armed, he hid his knife in the lining of his jacket. Frieda carried the white flag. Holding his empty hands out in front of him and followed by Maria, Dolf went off to meet the army, which had amassed at the end of the peninsula. His heart was beating faster with fear.

They had covered half the distance when they were met by a Perugian officer who had galloped out from the waiting ranks. He looked down on them sternly.

"Have you come from the castle?" he asked in Tuscanese. "If you are bringing a message from Count Ludovico, I hereby inform you that we have no intention of negotiating and the castle must surrender to us immediately and unconditionally."

Despite the lessons from Leonardo, in which Maria had participated too, Dolf did not understand half of what he said. Beseechingly, he raised his arms to the officer and in broken Tuscanese, liberally sprinkled with Latin and German expressions, he managed to stammer:

"Your business with the Count is no concern of ours. This is a crusade of children, on its way to Jerusalem. We were lured into this trap by Ludovico and he is now demanding that we raise your siege for him. We have no wish to do that. We do not make war on Christian knights."

Had the officer understood him? Would he have been flattered by the title "Christian knight"? It was clear that the man was no more than a junior officer.

He continued to stare down at the children suspiciously.

"All we wish to ask," said Dolf respectfully and pleading, "is for the children to be allowed to depart unmolested."

"Who are you?" asked the man, seeming to ignore all that Dolf had said.

"My name is Rudolf Hefting of Amsterdam in the state of Holland. And this is my sister, Maria. This is Frieda, our nurse.

"You don't look like the son of a nobleman to me," the officer grunted insultingly. But it was true enough; Dolf, in his torn trousers and tattered jacket, looked no more than a beggar.

"I am a poor pilgrim, sir, like all these children."

Maria folded her hands and turned the gaze of her large,

gray eyes on the man. For a moment, the expression of this battle-hardened soldier softened. Perhaps he himself had a daughter of Maria's age.

He was now visibly unsure of himself. He gazed out over their heads toward the children waiting at the foot of the castle. They stood, closely packed together and praying for the success of Dolf's mission. But with their clubs, bows and arrows and axes they did not present much of an image of peace-loving children.

"How do I know you have nothing to do with Count Ludovico?" the officer growled.

Dolf took a deep breath.

"Why don't you let us through in groups," he pleaded. "I cannot believe that you set out with the intention of fighting children. Count Ludovico is your enemy, but he is also ours. He has deceived us with friendly words and feigned hospitality. He is trying to hide behind us. But we are peaceful crusaders and pilgrims and have no wish to meddle in politics."

The conversation reminded him of his first meeting with Leonardo, when he was still having so much trouble with German. It was with great difficulty that the twisted medieval Italian words came from his lips. He was continually searching his mind for the expressions he wanted and sometimes he feared that he said something quite the opposite of what he had intended. No doubt his pronunciation was all wrong too, but the officer seemed to have understood him, because he laughed jeeringly.

"I don't believe in your protestations of peacefulness. From the rumors I have heard your army is anything but peaceful. Mean, little plunderers would be more like it. And, if all I have heard is true, you can fight too!"

"We have encountered great dangers along the road, General," Dolf said earnestly. The officer seemed quite pleased with his new rank.

At this point, a tough-looking man approached him from among the waiting farmers.

"My followers are eager to know when they must attack," he said, peering suspiciously at the children. Dolf understood even less of this man's dialect, but he had caught the word "attack" and the man had pointed toward the restless farmers and the castle. He looked up at the mounted soldier questioningly.

"You just wait!" the commander rebuffed him. "I will give the order when the time is ripe."

"Negotiating won't get us anywhere. We want Ludovico's blood," said the farmer, shaking his head.

"So do I, but you keep quiet. Surely you would not have me attack children?"

"Bambini!" the farmer sniffed contemptuously. "Children indeed! They came down on our land like a plague of wild locusts and the little brutes stole everything that Ludovico had not destroyed. My men have no more love for these children than they do for Ludovico."

Dolf had managed to understand enough of what was said to realize that their position had once again become precarious. He hastily folded his hands.

"I beg you, sir, give us the chance to leave and God will reward you."

"Scoundrels, that's what they are," shouted the farmer. "Vagabonds from the north who have been dumped on us by the emperor. We will kill the vermin with pleasure."

Dolf pulled himself up and, casting aside his pose of respectfulness, shouted:

"All right then, draw your swords against innocent children. But, I promise you, their blood will be on your souls! I will not mention the shame which will fall on the army which made war against defenseless little children. Go ahead and make your pact with the Devil. Murder the children and the priest who is accompanying them. Murder us and hear the cry of horror that will shake the whole of Umbria."

Maria had caught her breath with fear. The white flag trembled in Frieda's hand. Foaming at the mouth, the farmer was about to leap at Dolf but the officer quickly spurred his horse between the two.

"You are a bold boy, Rudolf of Amsterdam," he said, but like all medieval people, he had a great respect for courage, even if it did border on impudence.

"Swear!" he said, raising his voice at the trembling boy. "Swear by all that is sacred to you that your request for a safe passage for the children is not some ruse of Ludovico's."

Fortunately, Dolf had understood. He drew the image of the Holy Virgin from under his jacket, kissed it and held it aloft.

"Mary, Mother of God, is my witness that I am speaking the truth. We have nothing to do with Ludovico at all. We hate him as much as you do. We have been enticed into a trap, from which we now wish to escape.

"Amen," said Frieda, holding her voice steady. "Amen," Maria whispered. Once again, she turned her large, pleading eyes on the face of the officer and in broken Tuscanese stuttered:

"Will you allow us to pass now? Please, I beg you ..."

"You can have one hour," he said curtly. "I will give orders to my soldiers to let you through in groups. But remember, just one wrong move, one hurled stone and we will spare absolutely no one. Is that understood?"

Dolf dropped to his knees out of gratitude.

"You have a noble heart, General. We will offer our prayers to God that you may have victory. But there is one last thing I would ask."

"You want more?" the man grunted with impatience. "Please sir, three of our number are imprisoned in the castle; Nicolas the shepherd boy, and two children of noble birth.

Will you, please, spare their lives when you have taken the castle?"

The officer's mouth fell open.

"They are holding some of you hostage in the castle? And you are heartless enough to abandon them?"

He looked closely at the boy with an expression of disapproval. Dolf replied:

"The children have the confidence that you will free our three innocent companions, General."

"Yes, yes, all right." The man now seemed to be at the end of his patience. "Now get a move on! We will be attacking in an hour's time!"

Dolf did not hesitate any longer. He got up, bowed awkwardly, and then ran back to the camp with Frieda and Maria.

"Quickly! Arrange yourselves in groups of twenty and hide all your weapons under your clothes. Bows and arrows must be left behind, since it must appear that we are unarmed. Hurry up!" He was greatly relieved to be able to talk German again.

At once the orderlies began organizing the evacuation. The groups marched toward the besieging soldiers who stepped aside to let them through. Dolf could have cried with joy. They were saved! Ludovico's ploy had failed.

But fifteen hundred children, in groups of twenty, form a very long column and, in the meantime, behind the castle walls, Ludovico had realized that the children were departing. The living wall of defense, which the Count had erected around his castle, was crumbling. The Perugians were allowing them to escape.

Incensed with anger, the Count began to bark his orders. A rain of arrows fell upon the children, followed by branches with burning pitch. The children screamed, broke their formation and, in panic, stormed toward the rows of soldiers and farmers, who parted even more to let them through, leaving their battle formation in disarray. The castle drawbridge was quickly lowered and more than fifty mounted knights came thundering over to take advantage of the confusion. Perceiving the danger, the voice of the Perugian officer resounded over the peninsula. His soldiers speedily closed their ranks, forming an immovable blockade. Something like five hundred children, including Maria, Dolf and Peter in the rear guard, were caught between the two armies and were in danger of being trampled.

Roughly knocking aside any children who obstructed their path, the soldiers from the castle stormed forward, howling savagely. Dolf spun round to see that the foremost rider was almost upon him. Oblivious of everything around him, he ripped out his knife and lunged at the horse galloping toward him. The sharp blade penetrated deep into the animal's breast. It whinnied with pain and reared up on its hind legs. It would undoubtedly have crushed the boy, had he not been thrown aside by an advancing farmer, just at that moment. Immediately, four peasants leaped on the rider and dragged him from his saddle.

The clash between Ludovico's soldiers, the rebelling farmers and the Perugian soldiers was frightening in its ferocity. The children trapped in the middle grabbed whatever weapons they could find—pieces of splintered swords, their own knives, rocks, branches and clubs—and turned against Ludovico s men. Groups of them clung to the riders' legs, dragging them from their horses. They were in everyone's way, but they fought like tigers, because they had seen Rudolf of Amsterdam fall and they were determined to avenge him.

But Dolf was not dead, nor even slightly wounded. The very peasants who hated him so much, had actually saved him. He had lain on the ground in danger of being trammeled under the hooves of the horses. But no one took any heed of him and he eventually managed to scramble to his feet, under the cover of a fallen horse. He looked around desperately for Maria, but could not see her. Holding his knife, dripping with blood, in his right hand and a rock in his left, he fiercely drove a path for himself toward the forest. There under the protection of the trees all the children who had managed to escape had congregated. Many had already begun to cut new bows and arrows, as if at any moment they were expecting to have to fight for their lives again. Down on the peninsula, the battle continued to rage unabated, though it was gradually moving in the direction of the castle.

Battered, bruised and bleeding from a hundred small wounds, Dolf gained the edge of the forest where he was greeted by Frieda.

"Where is Maria?" he cried, but no one knew. He turned around and saw more and more children stumbling up from the peninsula. They too had had to fight their way through and bore the scars. Maria was not with them.

Ludovico's soldiers found themselves outnumbered by the alliance of their enemies. Moreover, they were severely hampered in their movements by the children who had turned on them like enraged bees. They fell into retreat, trying to regain the drawbridge—only seven succeeded. All the others were caught and beaten to the ground. When the seven were safely within the gates, the bolts were thrown and the bridge drawn up.

Ludovico must have realized that he could not hope to hold the fortress against three armies, with nothing but a handful of men, women and children. But he did not surrender. He ordered everyone in the castle who could stand, walk, fight or shoot onto the ramparts and with boiling water, burning pitch, flaming arrows and large rocks they tried to beat off the assault. Some of the children, who had gone completely berserk, swam across the moat and hacked at the chains of the bridge. A shower of deadly arrows and stones rained down on them from above, but the peasants, forgetting their previous hatred of the children, went to their aid and before long the wooden bridge had fallen into position with a resounding crash. Shouting with joy, the Perugians pounded the gates until they finally gave way. The farmers, children and soldiers stormed into the castle courtyard, slaughtering anyone who still dared to resist.

Realizing that all was lost, Ludovico tried to escape. He left the castle by a secret exit and climbed into a boat. But he had been seen by the children and twenty little fishermen dived into the lake and capsized the boat. Weighed down by his heavy coat of mail, the Count was drowned—so were ten of the children, but the castle of Count Ludovico di Trasimeno had succumbed.

The victors soon discovered the prisoners, the three children and seven peasants in the dungeons. All of them had been murdered.

Back in the forest, the children who remained alive had already set up a new camp. For the time being, moving on was out of the question. Many had been wounded and Frieda and her helpers spent all their time bandaging, positioning splints and cooling swellings. Frieda had impudently taken the seriously wounded victims to the captured castle where they were admitted directly.

The Perugian commander was grateful to the children who had turned on their enemies so fiercely, making the quick, easy victory possible.

Meanwhile, Dolf was unable to do anything. Distractedly, he walked around asking everyone:

"Have you seen Maria? Where is Peter?"

In truth, he was not too troubled by the death of Nicolas and the two noble children. He had never loved Nicolas as he had Carolus, or Maria or Peter. But where were they now? Fearfully, he went down to the peninsula and began searching through the piles of dead bodies. The soldiers were busy digging large graves and some of them came up to the battered boy and asked:

"Are you looking for someone?"

"My sister ..."

Three deep graves were dug; one for the dead Perugians, one for the children and one for their enemies. Laid out on the ground were three rows of corpses, between which walked Dom Thaddeus, praying. Neither Maria nor Peter was among them. Where were they? What could have happened to them? Perhaps they had been pushed into the lake and drowned among the plants, or maybe they were here, so badly trampled that they were unrecognizable?

He searched for hours, helping the soldiers bury the dead, but frightened all the time that at any moment he would discover his friends, dead after all. Seeing his fear and anxiety, Dom Thaddeus spoke his usual words of comfort:

"Have confidence, my son. God watches over our loved ones."

Oh forget it, thought Dolf angrily.

"When the fight began, I thought only of myself," he mumbled to himself with shame. "I fought only to save my own life, while Maria ..."

It was late that night before he returned to the camp and was welcomed by Frank, who came running toward him, his arm bandaged but otherwise unhurt.

"Where have you been? Peter has been looking everywhere for you. He wants to see you."

"Peter! Where is he?"

"By the campfire, of course, with Maria."

To Frank's complete surprise, Dolf dropped down on the carpet of pine needles and began to cry.

THE TOMB OF ST. NICHOLAS

And so they began their journey again. What else could they do, go back? That was just as senseless as going on, except that going back would have been an admission of defeat. The majority continued simply out of habit, but there were still some children who retained the belief in the myth of the gleaming White City.

"If God does not make the sea divide because Nicolas is dead, will He send ships to take us to the Holy Land?" little Simon asked Dom Thaddeus. The monk could only reply:

"Whatever God may decide, you can be sure it will be good." Frieda, a few of the nurses and the seriously wounded had remained behind in Trasimeno castle. Later, the survivors would go to Perugia. The commander believed he had much for which to thank the children, and he had been so impressed by the blond, decisive Frieda that he offered her a place in his own household.

After many weeks of travelling, the children finally reached the Adriatic coast. Nobody tried to perform miracles with the water and they simply turned south, journeying over the sandy beaches, marshes and hills. Here, they were afflicted by another plague—malaria. The marshes were swarming with thousands and thousands of mosquitoes, though only Dolf knew that they were the source of the illness. The little ones thought that the fever they contracted came from the poisonous smells of the marshes. Every evening, Dolf ordered them to build large, smoky fires to keep the insects away. In addition, he had them wash in the sea as often as possible and forbade them to dry themselves.

"Let the sun dry you. That way you will have a thin layer of salt on your skin and it will keep off the mosquitoes."

He was not sure if this were really true, but they were bitten less after that and the number of malaria cases decreased.

One day they experienced a very happy surprise. They were camping by the side of a large lagoon on the shore, enjoying an evening meal of crabs, when their supper was suddenly interrupted by a call of alarm from one of the sentries.

"Rider approaching!"

"Just one?" thought Dolf with surprise. Only a well-armed and very courageous man would dare to travel the roads alone. His curiosity aroused, he ran to the roadside and stared at the approaching cloud of dust. He could soon see that it was indeed only a single rider, who was waving an arm and shouting something as he galloped toward them. Dusk was already falling. Automatically Dolf drew out his knife.

Not until he was almost upon them and was reining in his horse did Dolf recognize the rider as Leonardo. The animal was sweating and there were tiny beads of moisture on its breast. Leonardo slid exhausted from the saddle and was caught by Dolf.

"My word," the student let out a deep sigh. "That was some journey …!"

Dolf was speechless with joy. Maria came running up and threw her arms around Leonardo's neck, Frank stood quietly smiling, while the other children gathered around cheering.

"It's Leonardo! Leonardo has returned!"

"I am hungry," the student from Pisa said simply.

That could soon be put to rights and, while Bertho tended to the tired horse, Maria quickly fetched a bowl of cooked mussels, a mug of shellfish-soup and two boiled crabs.

"Judging by this, your menu is improving," mumbled Leonardo with his mouth full. "But I notice that your numbers are somewhat depleted. What happened to them all?"

The tone of his voice was casual, but his eyes wandered restlessly over the camp.

"They have been lost along the way," explained Dolf. "Whenever we pass through a town some stay behind. This is no longer a crusade. We have become professional wanderers, in search of a future."

Leonardo nodded.

"Why did you follow us?" Peter voiced the question they all wished to ask.

"Oh, no particular reason," the student replied evasively. "I soon got tired of Pisa and my father had found a wife for me whom I didn't like. Moreover, Pisa is on the point of another war, against Florence this time and, as you know, all the young men are pressed into service and I would have had no time for study. I didn't fancy getting married and even less becoming a soldier. I thought I would go to the imperial court at Palermo this winter. The Emperor Frederick is an educated man and I have something important for him—Arabic numerals."

He turned to Maria and smiled.

"You are still as beautiful and as healthy as ever, my dear, but when I kissed you, you tasted of salt."

"It is a precaution against the fever," explained Dolf. "With salt on your skin there is less chance of being bitten by mosquitoes and it is the mosquito-bites that cause the fever."

"How do you know that?"

"I just happen to know."

"But mosquito-bites aren't poisonous."

"These are," said Dolf abruptly. "The poison gets into your blood and that makes you ill. Many have died from the illness already and I won't be happy until we have left this unhealthy region behind."

"You should come to Palermo too," said Leonardo with a mocking laugh. "Emperor Frederick is apparently appreciative of courtiers with common sense."

Once again he looked about him.

"I don't see Frieda anywhere."

"She stayed behind in Perugia."

"Oh yes, I heard about the battle at Trasimeno," nodded Leonardo, seemingly unconcerned. "A friend of my father's, a merchant from Perugia, visited us and related the whole, miserable story. He also said that the leader of the crusade had been murdered."

"Yes, poor Nicolas," sighed Frank. "His soul is now in Heaven."

Leonardo said nothing, took another mouthful and stared over the fire at Dolf.

The thought suddenly occurred to Dolf: He thought I was killed. Is that why he followed us? For … for … Maria?

"It was horrible," said Maria. "I saw Rudolf fall under the hooves of the horses and I thought he was dead. But when I tried to get to him, Peter picked me up and carried me away from the battle. I was furious with him for not letting me go to Rudolf's aid and I scratched his cheek, but he continued to pull me along until we reached the forest."

Peter was silently staring into the fire.

"You shouldn't be angry with Peter, Maria," said Dolf quickly. "He saved your life and I, for one, am extremely thankful."

"I didn't want to be saved," Maria turned on him sharply. "I saw you fall and I wanted to help you."

"That didn't mean anything," interrupted Peter in a husky voice. "Rudolf is invulnerable. He stumbled, that was all."

"But I am most decidedly vulnerable," laughed Dolf. "I still have the scars to prove it and for three days I was as stiff as a log of wood. I ached all over. But I will never forget, Peter, that you saved Maria."

"You rescued me from Scharnitz castle," said Peter softly. "Now the score is even."

"Anyway, I am pleased to find you all in good health," said Leonardo earnestly.

"Apart from Nicolas, that is," sighed Maria sadly. "Rufus and Mathilda were murdered also."

"What about little Simon?"

"Oh, glowing with health and as enthusiastic as ever. He talks of nothing else except for chasing the Saracens out of Jerusalem."

Dolf still could not understand why Leonardo had followed the children's army. Although he was naturally delighted to have his friend with him again, he could hardly imagine that Leonardo preferred the hardships of the road to the pleasures of life in Pisa. Was it really because he had believed Rudolf of Amsterdam to be dead and that Maria needed help?

They journeyed on through Umbria until they reached the kingdom of Sicily, which made up almost half of Italy. Their skin was ravaged by swarms of mosquitoes and fleas and they were hungry. To judge from their appearance, the inhabitants of this low-lying coastal area fared little better. They looked like thin dwarves and were distrustful and hostile. On several occasions the children were forced to skirmish with them and all the time the health of the army was deteriorating seriously. Their clothes hung from their tough bodies in rags. Whereas before they had eaten too little salt, now they were getting too much. Malaria continued to reduce their numbers and it was now Leonardo who was urging them on to the hills in the south.

Finally they arrived at the old city of Bari, which was a source of great wonder to Dolf.

Even with his parents he had never been so far south and, therefore, had no knowledge of Bari in the twentieth century. He had expected to find an ordinary little port like the many others they had passed through. Another of those towns where the stench of the rotting remains of fish dominated all else and where the lives of the people were at the mercy of the sea; where even the incense in the churches could not quite overcome the smell of fish. But Bari was quite different.

It was a thriving seaport with a busy trade with the Orient. This was where one first tasted the East. Just as in Genoa, one could meet all nationalities in the streets: Arabs in long, white gowns, and Turks in turbans; Greek sailors who tried to cheat everyone and Persians dealing in carpets and silk. Towering above all else was the mighty castle—a strong, invincible, Roman fortress.

Leonardo, who knew that Dolf always went to visit the cathedrals and basilicas whenever they entered a different Italian town (since, at such times, he assumed once again the habits of the twentieth century tourist), told him that he would have the time of his life in Bari.

"Now you will be able to prove your piety again, Rudolf. You will find the tomb of St. Nicholas here."

"St. Nicholas?" stammered Dolf, suddenly thinking of the murdered shepherd boy.

"Yes, the Bishop of Myra. And patron saint of sailors, travellers and children. Over a hundred years ago, twenty-four sailors stole his remains from Myra and brought them to Bari. The town is proud of the relics and has built a church in which his bones have been placed upon a bier. They say that a pilgrimage to Bari will give you health, protection in times of danger and a brave heart. All things that we can do with."

"Health," murmured Frank who was feeling poorly.

"Courage too?" said Maria. "I could use a little of that."

"And we need protection," said Peter.

They were right. The children were slowly beginning to lose hope. Gradually the autumn was overtaking them and although they had now reached the hills, which were dry and beautiful, they were faced with the problem: what next? Where could they go?

Dolf, however, was very excited. St. Nicholas, or Santa Claus to give him his other name, was buried here! St. Nicholas, the patron saint of Amsterdam and protector of children, sailors and toy manufacturers. But what did people say in the twentieth century? They said Santa Claus is a legend. He never existed.

Bari was surprisingly kind to the children and maybe it had something to do with the influence of the saint. They were not prohibited from entering the town, although the citizens did ask them to camp outside the inhabited area, since the streets were already overcrowded. Those who wished to work, or become a crew member on one of the ships, or who wished to visit the houses of God to regain their strength and courage, were welcome. The German children, almost all of whom now spoke Italian fairly well, wandered around the streets in small groups, staring wide-eyed at the bustle around them. Many decided to stay to seek their fortune here.

Dom Thaddeus, Maria, Dolf, Leonardo, Peter and Frank all went together to visit the holy basilica of St. Nicholas. All except Dolf wanted to pray for the soul of the murdered shepherd boy. The boy from the twentieth century, however, was gazing around with the eyes of a vacationer who is fascinated by anything ancient and strange.

The church was magnificent; one of the most beautiful Roman buildings he had ever seen. They went down into the crypt, where the bones of St. Nicholas were lying in a carved, wooden coffin, strewn with the flowers and treasures brought by pilgrims. Dolf was not a sentimental person and he still had a good measure of his twentieth century skepticism, but now he was deeply moved.

Once there had been a bishop named Nicholas, who had taken care of the poor and helpless children, of travellers and sailors in difficulty. He had brought happiness and joy into the lives of many and had stretched out his protecting hand to assist children of all kinds: homeless boys and impoverished girls, like Maria, who had no future. Was such a man a myth? No, for here was the proof. It was impossible to know to whom these bones, which had half crumbled into dust, had belonged. But Dolf was in no doubt. He was suddenly able to believe in this holy man and, like his friends, he knelt down and prayed. The modern scientists could say what they liked, but Dolf believed in the existence of Santa Claus. From the bottom of his heart Dolf thanked him: for his health, his strength, for the sweet Maria, for the trust and friendship of Leonardo, for the goodness of Dom Thaddeus, and for delivering them out of all the dangers they had encountered over the past few months. But most of all, he thanked the holy saint for the simple fact that a hopelessly stranded traveller in time might still have a future, somewhere in this thirteenth century.

In the square outside the basilica, a small, polished box was glittering in the sun. As yet, no one had noticed it.

MESSAGE FROM THE FUTURE

The next town they travelled to was Brindisi, a two-day journey southeast of Bari.

Bishop Adrianus, one of the most pious and kind-hearted men who ever served the church, resided in Brindisi. He had already been informed of the approach of the children's army and by the time they arrived outside the gates, dispirited and numbering barely a thousand, his heart was bleeding for them. He knew they had walked an immense distance, but the hardships they had suffered were beyond his imagination. Thirty thousand had set out, one thousand had reached Brindisi: it was unbelievable!

The fabled figure of thirty thousand, which had originated in Bolzano, had spread to the other Italian cities. It was never to be denied and the history books of a later age would all contain this exaggerated figure.

The Bishop, overflowing with pity, pleaded with the people of Brindisi to be merciful to the children. The citizens, however, refused to take these unruly children into their houses. The children were unconcerned at being kept outside the town, since it had happened many times before and it made no difference to them whether they were camping outside Brindisi or some other city, provided they had something to eat. Their feeling changed, however, when autumn finally caught up with them. After a very dry, hot summer the autumn began early and with it came rain every day. The enormous olive groves on the hillsides looked sad and drooping. The sun, which had been their loyal travelling companion for so many weeks, was now hidden behind clouds swollen with moisture. The wind lashed the waves along the coast, making fishing a hazardous occupation. Shivering with cold, the children scurried along the beach, collecting the shellfish which had been washed up and decorating themselves with necklaces made from the shells. They tried to build sandcastles under the scant protection offered by the trees, only to see them washed away by another shower. Their enthusiasm was drowned in all this water.

Bishop Adrianus came to visit them and, seeing their misery, offered them a home in the ruins of an old abbey. There they could camp until the weather improved.

Those children who were suffering from influenza, bronchitis and tuberculosis were taken into the monasteries around the city. The others moved to the dilapidated abbey and made themselves as comfortable as possible. In between the showers, they went out and gathered wood from which they made crude tables and benches. They were also given straw for bedding. They were living like a band of gypsies, since there could be no question of moving on for the time being.

It seemed to them as if they had reached the end of the world. What came after Brindisi? Nothing. There was only a barren stretch of land, which was almost devoid of people. The old military road went no farther than this city and only a few ill-kept and muddy paths led south to the farthest point of the immense peninsula. If they were unable to cross to the Holy Land from Brindisi, then that would be the end of the crusade, for there was nowhere else.

But Bishop Adrianus shook his head deliberately and said:

"My dear children, on no account must you believe the promises of the captains. Almost every one is a pirate and it would be best for you to keep well away from them." Of course, many of the children took no heed of this warning and boarded the ships.

At long last the rain stopped and the sun appeared. At

once the children streamed out of the abbey into the court-yard to dry their clothes and to warm themselves. Dolf and Leonardo sat down together on a moss-covered stone bench, facing the ruined chapel.

"I've found something rather strange," said Leonardo suddenly.

"Oh yes?"

Dolf was not really listening. He was worried about the future—he could not see how the children could ever get away from Brindisi and, on the other hand, staying there was equally out of the question.

"Look," said Leonardo. Out of his pocket he took a small metal box.

"Do you know what it is?"

Dolf stared at the object, his eyes bulging from his head in amazement.

"That is...that is...," he stammered, "that is aluminum!"

"What did you say it was?"

"Aluminum, a very light metal. How did you get hold of it?"

"I told you, I found it."

"Where?"

"In Bari, outside the basilica of St. Nicholas. It was just lying there in the street and looked so odd that I kept it. I'd forgotten all about it till now. What was it you called this metal again?"

"Aluminum. May I have another look at it?"

Dolf's heart was pounding. Had they discovered this light metal in the thirteenth century? He did not think so and Leonardo certainly had not heard of it.

With great caution, as if he was scared of burning his fingers, Dolf took the little box and studied it. The lid had been fastened tightly and he had to tinker with it with his knife before it opened.

"Don't break it!" said Leonardo with concern.

"There is something in it!"

"You are right. It's a message!" cried the student with surprise. "But what thin parchment!"

"It's paper," whispered Dolf. All the color had drained from his face.

"I can make neither head nor tail of it. Are those letters? I can't read them, can you?"

Dolf was speechless. The shock was so great that there was a mist in front of his eyes and he could not decipher the symbols. One thing, above all was clear to him—it was a message from the future. Finally he read:

> *Dear Dolf,*
> *If you find this, write a message on this same piece of paper, replace it in the box, and put it back exactly on the spot where you found it. Do not alter any of the code at the bottom! Twenty-four hours after the box has arrived, we will retrieve it. We are trying to locate your exact position.*
>
> *Dr. Simiak*

At the bottom of the piece of paper was a row of figures and symbols. The reverse side had been left blank for Dolf to write his note.

"Are you ill?" Leonardo asked with sudden concern.

"Yes ... no ... Where did you find this box?" Dolf could feel that his whole body was trembling.

"In Bari, when we came out of the tomb of St. Nicholas. It was lying in the street, near to the entrance."

"But that ... that was more than a week ago," Dolf mumbled in dismay.

So when Dr. Simiak had tried to retrieve the box, it had not returned. Dolf hung his head, his mind swimming with conflicting emotions: regret, disappointment but also a kind of relief. It was too late; once again, it was too late.

But how had Dr. Simiak known that Dolf was in Bari precisely on that day? His head reeling, he closed his eyes and leaned back against the wall.

"What does it say?" urged Leonardo, shaking his arm. "Rudolf, wake up! What does all this mean?"

"Oh please, don't ask so many questions!" snapped Dolf, tears in his eyes. "I ..."

He jumped up and ran to the abbey. He had to be alone. He crept into a dark corner of the dormitory and tried to think. One thing was obvious: they were searching for him. Dr. Simiak was trying to find him in the jungle of the past and, for one moment, he had almost succeeded. Dolf shivered as if he had a fever.

"Why couldn't I have found the box in time? Why did it have to be Leonardo, who had no idea what it meant? And if I had found it," he thought in confusion, "would it have pleased me?"

Strangely enough, he was not sure. Of course, he was longing to be home with his parents, but still ... Did he really want to go back? Back to Amsterdam, back to the modern age, back to school?

He looked about him. A few rays of sunlight slanted through the ruined roof, lighting up the impoverished surroundings. Bedding of straw and dry grass was scattered over the dirty floor. Two children, recovering from an attack of malaria, were asleep in a corner. Outside he could hear the others at work and play.

They had finally realized that Brindisi was the end of the line. There was nowhere else for them to go and returning was out of the question. Moreover, winter was coming.

If Dolf had the opportunity to leave them, could he do so? He still felt responsible for them. Where could they go, these little beggars and outcasts? What kind of future could Maria, Frank, Peter or Bertho hope to have? Unhappily, he fingered Dr. Simiak's letter.

"I didn't protect Maria all the way to Brindisi to desert her in the end," he muttered to himself miserably. For no apparent reason he suddenly thought of Carolus and it made him sad. The little king of Jerusalem would never have deserted his subjects, he thought, not even if he had been offered all the treasures in the world.

"Oh Carolus, help me," he whispered in despair. "What should I do if another box arrives?"

He had no doubt that Dr. Simiak would continue searching for him.

He read the message over again and the warning not to change any of the code set him thinking. Suddenly he realized that the symbols at the bottom were of vital importance to the scientist, since he must have sent several boxes to different places. But what system could the man be using? Leonardo had found the box outside the church of St. Nicholas and Dolf presumed that the church must still be there in the twentieth century. Was the physicist showering all the church squares with the boxes? How could he have known that Dolf had joined the children's crusade?

It suddenly came to him. The peasant boy who was transported to the twentieth century in his place. They obviously managed to communicate with him and he must have told them about the children going to Jerusalem. He wondered if they knew anything about this crazy undertaking in the twentieth century? He had never heard of it before. But maybe Dr. Simiak knew about Brindisi.

Maria came in and walked over to him. Anxiously, she knelt down by his side.

"Leonardo says that you are ill," she said softly. She placed her hand on his forehead. "Yes, you have a fevered brow."

Dolf hurriedly hid the note and the box in his trouser pocket.

"No, I'm not ill."

"There is news," Maria went on excitedly. "Bishop Adrianus has sent a message to Dom Thaddeus inviting the leaders of the crusade to an audience tomorrow. I'm worried, Rudolf. Perhaps the people of Brindisi want to get rid of us."

"It wouldn't surprise me," said Dolf dispiritedly.

"Where can we go then? Is there anywhere else?"

"I don't know."

"And I have noticed that Leonardo is getting restless too. He does not know what we can do either and I think he wants to return home."

Dolf sighed.

"... but he won't leave us just like that," Maria chattered on. "He told me that himself. He wants Frank and Peter and Bertho to stay with him, as his servants and then he could send them to school."

"That would be wonderful."

"Yes, I think so too, but why have you hidden yourself in here in the dark? The weather is gorgeous outside."

Dolf suddenly pulled the girl to him and stared at the clouds of dust dancing in the sharp beams of sunlight. He thought:

"Dear, dear Maria, what will become of you? I cannot take you with me to my century."

"Rudolf, why are you crying?"

"I'm not." But he was. It was all so difficult, a problem he couldn't solve. However, that very evening Dolf made his decision. When all the children were gathered together for the evening meal, he took out Leonardo's discovery and showed it to them.

"My dear friends, take a good look at this. In the next few days, if any of you finds a little box like this, no matter where it is, pick it up and mark the place where you found it. And then would you please bring it to me immediately."

No one really understood and they wanted first to

examine the miracle box. They handed it from one to the other, amazed at how light it was.

"What is it? Why do you want it? Why must we mark the spot?" Questions, questions and more questions but he could not answer them.

"Is it witchcraft?"

"No, no! Someone from my country has lost them, that's all."

"Lost them?" asked Leonardo sharply. The intelligent student was not prepared to accept all kinds of illogical answers. "Who would lose something like that? After all, it must be something very precious."

"The boxes are precious only to those who understand their meaning," Dolf answered. "But Leonardo, you are right, they have not really been lost. They simply mean that my father is searching for me. He doesn't know where I am, so he leaves the boxes in a conspicuous place, because I am the only one who would recognize them. In that way he is trying to find me. Do you understand?"

"Your father?"

"Oh children, help me," pleaded Dolf. "For months I have helped you and now I am asking for your help in return. Anyone who finds a box like this, please bring it to me immediately and tell me exactly where you found it. Remember, the exact spot is very important to me."

The children, who had no reason whatever to distrust Rudolf of Amsterdam, nodded their assent. Only Leonardo looked doubtful. Obviously, he considered the scattering of mysterious boxes a very strange way of trying to trace someone. And so it was, except when you had nothing but a material-transmitter with which to find someone.

The following morning Dom Thaddeus, Dolf, Leonardo, Frank and Bertho went to the town for the audience with the Bishop. Peter took a large group to the beach for fishing.

Frank and Bertho waited outside the gate of the stone

building that was the Bishop's palace. Only the priest, the student and Dolf were admitted. Present in the Bishop's study were his secretary and a few merchants and sea captains.

Bishop Adrianus came directly to the point. He spoke Latin, which the priest and the student understood perfectly well, but which had to be translated for Dolf.

"It is evident that the children housed in the ruined abbey can journey no farther," said the Bishop. "There is no road beyond Brindisi. Furthermore, no one in his right mind can believe that children can cross the sea and liberate Jerusalem. There is, therefore, only one alternative. They must return home."

Dom Thaddeus spoke:

"Monsignore, your words show wisdom and understanding, but the problem is that these children have no home to which they can return. They are orphans and outcasts."

"I know that," replied the Bishop quietly. "Moreover, returning would be difficult, because winter is approaching. Long before the children reach the mountains in the north, they would be snowed under. But they cannot stay in Brindisi. We have done what we could for them, but we cannot support all these children throughout the winter."

Leonardo nodded. His usually cynical expression was now serious. Dom Thaddeus clasped his hands in despair.

"Nevertheless," continued the Bishop, "it is my duty as a Christian to help the children to the best of my ability." He waved his hand toward the merchants and sea captains, who were looking on silently. "These men are rich merchants and trustworthy captains who are prepared to undertake transporting the children by sea to the Republic of Venice. During the journey, the children will be expected to work for their passage. The captains will carry letters from me to the Bishop and aldermen of Venice.

"In those letters, I will ask that the children be looked after, that they be housed in the town and, so far as is possible, that they be helped on their way after winter is over. If any children wish to stay in Venice, I am sure that can be arranged. I know that they are strong and prepared to work hard, even if they have become a little undisciplined during their ordeal ..." He stopped for a moment to draw breath and Leonardo quickly translated the essential points for Dolf.

"I know of no other solution," concluded the Bishop.

Dom Thaddeus knelt down and kissed the Bishop's ring.

"I thank you, Monsignore," he murmured. "May God reward you for this."

"Get up, Dom Thaddeus. It is not me you should thank, but the Almighty, who provided me with the solution to so difficult a problem. In three days' time the ships will sail and the children must be ready. You can discuss the details with these gentlemen. Goodbye and may God bless you."

The audience was at an end and Dolf was overjoyed. Now that the children's army would be taken care of, he was free to return to the twentieth century, providing ...

Frank and Bertho, who had been patiently waiting outside, were at once informed of the good news.

"But I will not be going to Venice," added Leonardo quickly. "I am going to Palermo to the court of the Emperor Frederick."

Together with the merchants and the captains, they went to the harbor to inspect the ships. They looked very small to Dolf, but Dom Thaddeus was delighted with them, for, in his eyes, they were seaworthy vessels. They agreed on a time to sail and then hurried back to the abbey to tell the children.

Dolf was not sure what he should do. Should he say goodbye to Leonardo and go to Venice? Or wait here in the hope of finding one of Dr. Simiak's little boxes?

Leonardo noticed his confusion.

"Venice doesn't seem to appeal to you much. Why don't you come with me then?"

"I don't know," sighed Dolf. "My father is looking for me and if I leave here, he will never be able to find me."

"Do you want to be found?" the student asked quickly.

"Yes, I do now."

"Well, wait here for your father."

"Yes ... but what about Maria?"

"What about her?"

"If my father finds me, he will take me home. Maria wouldn't be able to come with me. There is nothing I would like more, but it would be impossible."

"You don't have to worry about that," said Leonardo calmly. "Maria will come with me."

"Are you sure? Oh, my friend, that is wonderful of you."

Nevertheless, Dolf was a little surprised, but Leonardo went on, averting his gaze:

"Have you ever taken a good look at her, Rudolf? She is the sweetest girl in the world. I will take her to Pisa, to my parents and she will be brought up there. Then I will go to Palermo with Frank and Peter and, if I manage to find employment with the Emperor, I will send for Maria and marry her."

"But what if she doesn't want to?"

"Of course she will want to, unless you are there."

Dolf could not really understand it all. For a brief moment, he was extremely jealous, but then he realized that it was the best thing for the girl. She would grow up into a wonderful woman: beautiful, intelligent and tender. She loved Leonardo almost as much as she did Dolf.

"She is still so young ... " he whispered.

"About eleven and in three years' time she will be old enough to marry."

Dolf knew that in this age it was common for girls to be

married at the age of thirteen or fourteen, especially among the aristocracy.

"Won't your family object? Maria is as poor as a church mouse."

Leonardo chuckled.

"She has a heart of gold and that is all the dowry I could wish."

Dolf nodded. He could feel a hurt growing inside him, with the realization that, in a few days time, he would have to say goodbye to them all. Silently he turned away.

It was at that moment that Frank approached him.

"Rudolf."

"Not just now, Frank," mumbled Dolf sorrowfully. "I don't feel much like talking."

"But ..."

Dolf continued walking away. They had reached the entrance to the abbey and he wanted to find Maria.

Frank grabbed him by the arm.

"Yesterday you said it was very important."

"What?"

"The box."

Dolf stopped dead in his tracks.

"The box!" he cried.

The little tanner took out a light metal object.

"This is what you meant, isn't it?"

Dolf grabbed it from him so abruptly that Frank was startled.

"How did you get it?"

"I found it, this morning."

"Where? Can you remember where?"

"In the city. I suddenly saw it lying at my feet, while Bertho and I were waiting for you outside the palace."

"What time?"

"I'm not quite sure. It was while you were with the Bishop."

"That was around ten o'clock," thought Dolf. With trembling fingers he opened the box. Inside was an identical message to the one found by Leonardo in Bari. But the ciphers on the bottom were different.

"I know I should have shown it to you at once," said Frank apologetically, "but I forgot all about it when you came out with the good news."

"That doesn't matter. Do you think that you could find again the exact spot from which you picked it up?"

"Probably."

"Let's go then."

"What are we going to do?"

"Go back to the town. I must know where you found it."

Half an hour later, they were back in the cathedral-square of Brindisi. Frank indicated the narrow alley which led to the Bishop's palace.

"Bertho and I were standing here, leaning against the wall. Then suddenly I saw something glistening, right by my feet. I picked it up and ..."

"The important thing is the exact spot. Are you sure it was here? It wasn't a yard one way or the other?" Dolf urged him.

He examined the bumpy cobblestones, but saw nothing but dry mud, dust and dirt. There was not a single identifying mark.

"I'm sure I was standing here," murmured Frank. "Yes, because that bump in the wall was sticking between my shoulder blades. My feet were positioned like this, that's right. Then suddenly, there it was, right by my left foot. Just here, on that red stone."

He was pointing down at the dust and Dolf knelt down, swept aside some mud and nodded.

"I must mark that place clearly, so that I can find it again tomorrow."

He looked around desperately and the small gate of the

office to the Bishop's palace gave him an idea.

"Frank, stay by this spot and wait for me. I'll be back shortly."

Dolf pushed open the gate and walked into the office. He asked for the secretary and, after some argument, was admitted to him.

"Signore," he said in his broken Italian, "I have come to ask you a favor. May I borrow your writing equipment for a moment? I must send a message to my father."

"You can write?" asked the man in amazement, looking at Dolf's rags.

He handed Dolf a goose-quill pen and a pot of ink and watched in astonishment as the ragged boy took something white from his pocket, dipped the quill into the ink and carefully began drawing strange letters.

"Could you tell me what the date is, the day after tomorrow?"

"The day after tomorrow? St. Matthew, of course!"

"Oh yes."

In fact, it did not tell Dolf anything, but he assumed that they would be able to find out back in the twentieth century. On the reverse side of Dr. Simiak's message he then wrote:

I'm in Brindisi. You can use the same coordinates as are on the other side. Twenty-four hours after you read this, I will be on that spot. I don't know the date, but they call it St. Matthew's day here. Take me back.
Dolf

He was just able to fit it all onto the piece of paper, since he made a lot of blotches with the ink. Also, the paper was much thinner than the parchment on which the medieval people wrote with their thick ink. He had to blow on it for a long time before the letters dried.

"Is this a letter for the Bishop?" asked the secretary.

"What kind of parchment is this? It is so soft and thin …"

"We call it paper," replied Dolf evasively. "Signore, may I borrow your pot of ink for a moment?"

"Borrow it?"

It was a beautiful little alabaster bowl and Dolf realized that the man must be suspicious. He clasped his hands beseechingly.

"I will be very quick. I only want a little ink and I will return the little bowl immediately."

"What do you want the ink for?"

"I must make a cross, outside."

"In the street?"

"Come with me and you will see that I'm doing no harm. In my country this is a very pious act."

"All right, I will come."

The little bowl of ink in his hand, his heart full of hope and accompanied by the secretary, Dolf went outside to Frank.

"Look," he said.

He bent down and cleaned the spot on the bumpy pavement with his hand. Then he took the bowl and carefully poured some of the permanent ink over the stone. Using his finger, he painted a cross, knowing how much respect medieval people had for it. Then he stood up and gave the little bowl back to the puzzled churchman.

"Do they really perform such religious ceremonies in the street, where you come from?" he asked.

It was impossible for Dolf to explain his strange actions to him, so he just smiled warmly until the secretary finally returned to his office. When he had left Dolf turned to Frank and said:

"We must wait for the ink to dry."

"But what does it all mean?" mumbled his friend. "You're behaving so strangely." Dolf was staring at the black cross and said nothing. Tomorrow morning he would place the box containing his message on the spot and wait for it to disappear. The day after that, he would stand there himself and wait for … perhaps …

He stood over the mark to prevent people walking on it. After a quarter of an hour or so, he tested it to make sure it was dry. He rubbed it with his dry hands, then with some spittle and finally he scraped at it with his feet.

"Well, that's all right. Now we can go back to the abbey. Thank you, Frank, you have no idea what a service you have done for me today."

"Are you a conjuror, Rudolf?"

"No, of course not, but I want to go home. The people who are looking for me will see the cross and know where I am, you see."

"Yes," said Frank, "our crusade is over."

"Still, it was a wonderful adventure, don't you think?" said Dolf. "It is true we have had many hard times, but it has always been exciting. I am glad that I have taken part in it."

"And survived it," added Frank.

"Yes, that more than anything." Dolf put his arm around his friend's shoulder. "Frank, wherever I go, I will always remember you. I could always rely on you and Peter. Is it true that you are going to stay with Leonardo?"

"No," answered Frank. "Peter, Bertho and I have decided to go to Venice with Dom Thaddeus. We want to stay until the very end."

Dolf nodded. He had come to have a deep respect for the loyalty of these fine medieval people.

Back at the abbey, there was a great bustle. The children, excited by the thought of going to the wonderful city of Venice, had already begun to gather their things together. Leonardo and Maria were not there, for they had gone to the city to try to find a ship which would take them to Pisa.

Early the next morning Dolf was on the street corner outside the Bishop's palace. He placed the aluminum box on the cross and sat down beside it, determined to prevent anyone from kicking it away or picking it up. The secretary came past and looked at Dolf in surprise. Then he shrugged his shoulders and walked on. Dolf sat waiting, glancing at his watch every few seconds. At precisely a quarter to ten, the little box disappeared.

Silently and with a heart which sometimes raced and sometimes missed a beat, Dolf continued to stare at the black cross. The box had gone. The transmitter had retrieved it. It had worked! At this very moment Dr. Simiak would read the message, shout for joy and run to the telephone ... "We've found him! We've found Dolf and will be bringing him back in twenty-four hours from now! Dr. Frederics, charge the transmitter to full capacity!" or something like that ...

It began to rain again. Muddy water flowed down the gutter and over the cross, but that didn't matter. Dolf could not bring himself to stand up and go back to the abbey. Tomorrow! Tomorrow he would see his parents again. Tomorrow ...

His head sank on his knees and crying with relief, he allowed himself to be soaked by the rain.

"Rudolf of Amsterdam, what is the trouble?" asked a warm voice. A consoling hand was laid on his shoulder. It was Dom Thaddeus, of course, who had just returned from the harbor, where he had been making the final preparations for the children's journey to Venice.

Dolf jumped to his feet.

"I am going home," he whispered. "My father has found me at last."

He clasped the monk's hand.

"Can you imagine? I'm going to see my mother again!"

"So you won't be coming to Venice with us, will you?"

"There is no need now, I can go home. And what about you, father? Will you stay with the children?"

"I will not leave them until the very last has been found a place or has arrived home safely."

"What great people you are in this century," exclaimed Dolf.

"I don't understand you, my son."

"I mean," said Dolf, searching for the words to express what he felt, "I mean that I am almost sorry to be leaving all this." He waved his hand in an expansive gesture to indicate the tightly packed houses, almost all of which were made of wood, the square in front of the church and the narrow streets and alleyways.

"This whole world ... it will all change, that's what I mean. I think it is a shame. I had always thought that this was a magnificent age, because of the knights in armor on magnificent chargers, the beautiful ladies, the minstrels. I had expected to see beautiful churches being built and guild processions, but it was all so different. I have barely seen the inside of a single castle, I haven't been to a tournament and I have tried to avoid meeting armed knights. But I have seen the countryside, the peasants, the beggars and deserted children. It is the ordinary people I have come to know, not the famous men one reads about in books. And the people I have met—sometimes they were cruel and stupid, sometimes they were so kind and good ... and from you too, Dom Thaddeus, I have learned so much."

"From me? What have you learned from me?"

"Goodness ... love for one's fellow man ... loyalty."

"That is our duty as Christians, my son."

"Your actions were not the result of duty, but love." And in later centuries we have forgotten that love, thought the boy. Perhaps not entirely; for we now have social laws which insure that the sick, the poor and the invalids do not starve, like they do here, in the thirteenth century. But what did we do with love? With that simple, almost secretive love displayed by Dom Thaddeus. We have lost it and replaced it with forms in triplicate.

That night Dolf slept little. Wild thoughts were tumbling around his mind. Sometimes he would doze for a short while, but the fear that he might oversleep made him grow increasingly restless. Dawn had hardly broken when he got up: In the faint light, he looked at Maria on her bed of straw. He had already said goodbye to her on the previous evening and it had been very upsetting. He noticed that her face was stained with tears. Poor Maria …

Then he looked at the sleeping figure of Leonardo, who was curled up like a shrimp; Frank and Peter and, beyond them, little Simon. He picked up his jacket and spread it carefully over Frank. He kissed Maria softly on her forehead, but she did not stir. For a long time, he looked down on Leonardo and listened to the snoring of Dom Thaddeus. His heart was full of emotion.

"Goodbye," he whispered and stole out of the dormitory. The chill of the early dawn made him shiver. The four sentries at the entrance to the abbey were awake and watchful. As soon as they recognized Dolf of Amsterdam, he put his fingers to his lips.

"Don't tell anyone that you have seen me leave. Goodbye and have a good trip to Venice."

Then, all alone, he turned down the road to Brindisi.

WILL IT WORK?

Dolf arrived too early, much too early. The old ladies on their way to first mass had to walk around him in a wide semicircle, as he sat motionless, his chin resting on his knees. He was sitting directly on top of the black cross and looking over the cathedral square. He was entranced by the sight of the city coming to life. Merchants were erecting their stalls and magicians were calling out to the passersby. Many people were festively dressed, as if it were a Sunday. Was no one going to work today?

He waited. The square and the streets began to fill with men, women and children. There were peddlers, acrobats and pickpockets milling around. He saw sailors, inquisitive Arabs, soldiers and beggars. Would it never be quarter to ten?

He glanced at his watch. To his surprise, it told him that it was a quarter to five. But that was impossible. Angrily, he shook his wrist, listened and heard nothing. For months it had served him faithfully. But now, on the very morning when exact timing was most vital, it had stopped.

Anyone who wanders around in the Middle Ages for months on end can easily become superstitious without realizing it. Dolf suddenly felt certain that something would go wrong: the transmitter would fail; or it would put him in the wrong place; or something unexpected would happen as it had in Spiers, or ...

All the confidence drained out of him. The sun had risen above the houses and was bathing the square in a golden light. Dolf felt hot. He took off his sweater and threw it in the dust beside him. He stood up, wearing nothing but his faded and worn shirt and his frayed jeans. People bumped into him, cursing under their breath because he hadn't stepped aside. Where were they all going? It seemed as if the entire population was gathering outside the cathedral.

Surely they had not all come to see a stranger being spirited away. Someone thrust a coin into his hand. They thought he was a beggar! He put it into his pocket nevertheless. The air above the town was filled with the sound of tolling bells. Whatever was happening? Perhaps there was to be an important funeral? Or maybe a nobleman was getting married?

No, of course, it must have something to do with St. Matthew's day! Perhaps it was an important religious festival with processions and a fair ...

Dolf looked about him with concern. He was standing with his feet exactly on the black cross, grimly determined not to be pushed aside. The narrow lane was already crammed with people who were all looking in the direction of the cathedral, as if they were waiting for something.

Dolf began to grow irritated by the continued tolling of the bells. He braced himself and looked at his feet to make sure he was standing in the right place. When he looked up again he saw a procession emerging from the cathedral. It was led by Bishop Adrianus, in his full ceremonial dress, who was walking beneath a canopy, held above him by boys dressed in white. Behind him came a column of priests, acolytes and girls in white dresses. They were bearing reliquaries. Above their heads swayed a wooden image of the Holy Virgin, on a sort of bier. The statue was decorated with jewels and reminded Dolf of Hilda.

The people in the square and streets had knelt down in the dust.

"Goodness, I hope they are not coming this way," thought Dolf. "They would want me to step aside and I daren't do that. I must stay here. It must be almost time."

The procession was approaching slowly and the crowd began to press against him. His whole body was trembling, but he held his ground.

"There is Rudolf!" cried a familiar voice. "He is head and shoulders above everyone else."

Pretending he had not heard, he folded his hands behind his back and looked up at the bright blue sky. It was a beautiful day.

"Oh hurry up," he begged silently. "I mustn't let them push me aside."

"Rudolf!" he heard someone shout above the singing concourse. He recognized the voice to be that of Peter. Probably many of his friends were in the crowd, but he did not want to see them.

"Rudolf!" It was Leonardo's voice and it was right behind him.

"Go away!" hissed Dolf. He prayed that Maria wasn't there too.

The procession was now less than five yards away. Of course, of all the streets in Brindisi, it was sure to pass along this one, where the Bishop's palace was situated. Now he was standing almost eye to eye with Bishop Adrianus, who was holding out his hands over the people in the crowd, blessing them. Everyone was kneeling except for Dolf, who felt as if his heart would jump right out of his chest.

"Stand aside!" a voice yelled at him in the Brindisi dialect. Someone carrying a halberd pushed forward and thrust a hand at him.

"Make way for ..."

"No! Leave me alone!" Dolf screamed frantically. Suddenly everything in front of his eyes went black. He felt a hand grab his arm and pull him. He resisted with all his strength, struggling and shouting.

"Let me go! Get your hands off me!"

But the strong hands did not let go. There was a roaring sound in his ears, which drowned the bells.

"No!" he screamed. "I must remain on the cross!"

"Dolf ..."

Who was calling him Dolf? He was Rudolf Hefting of Amsterdam. He blinked. He tugged at the hands that held him fast and flailed his arms in the air, roaring at the top of his voice:

"I damn you to Hell! Help me! Leonardo!"

Desperately he felt for his knife and bared his teeth ...

A shrill voice pierced his brain:

"Oh no, it's another peasant!"

Suddenly he realized that the voice and the language in which the words were spoken were strangely familiar to him. The mist cleared, the hands released him and he staggered. Quickly he looked down at the cross. It had gone!

Beneath his feet was a smooth, green patch. His brain was assaulted by heat and numerous voices.

"But it is him. Dolf ..."

He could no longer hear the bells tolling. He slowly opened his eyes and looked into the face of a woman, an unusually tall woman with gray eyes, who peered at him anxiously. He was conscious of others, curiously dressed, who were also staring at him. Weren't those Maria's eyes? No but he knew them all the same. The strange language whirled about him and he understood every word. He shook his head to stop it spinning.

"Give him some time to collect himself."

"My God. He looks dreadful!"

"That's the shock ..."

"Dolf ... my own darling Dolf ..."

He was suddenly aware that he was standing there with his knife raised threateningly. The sobbing woman approached him wearily and lightly touched his arm. Then, slowly, but unmistakably, he realized the truth. He was standing in Dr. Simiak's laboratory. The woman with the beautiful gray eyes was his mother. The stench he could smell came from the half molten material-transmitter and the man who carefully led him to a chair was his very own father. The knife fell from his powerless grip and stuck in the floor, vibrating.

Rudolf of Amsterdam was home.

About The Author

THEA BECKMAN was was born in Rotterdam. She began writing in 1947, but it was not until her children (she has three) were grown, that she devoted herself to writing full time. She wrote *Crusade in Jeans* in 1973. It became an overnight success, making her one of the most popular authors of juvenile books in the Netherlands. Ms. Beckman is fascinated by history. She has written books about many historical periods — from the Middle Ages to the future.

In 1974 *Crusade in Jeans* was awarded The Golden Pen (the most prestigious Dutch national award for children's books). In 1976 the Province of Trento, Italy, named it the Best European Historical Juvenile Book. In 1984 Ms. Beckman was awarded the Huib de Ruyter Prijs (a prize from Dutch teachers for all her historical novels). In 1975 she fulfilled a lifelong dream and began studying social psychology; she graduated in 1981.